JOHN FARRIS

Bad Blood

GOLLANCZ HORROR

Originally published as *All Heads Turn
When the Hunt Goes By*

First published in Gollancz paperbacks 1989
by Victor Gollancz Ltd
14 Henrietta Street, London WC2E 8QJ

Copyright © 1977 by John Farris

British Library Cataloguing in Publication Data
Farris, John
  Bad Blood.
  I. Title
823'.914[F]

ISBN 0-575-04648-1

Printed and bound in Great Britain
by Cox & Wyman Ltd, Reading

ACKNOWLEDGMENTS

The quotation on page 93 is from *Fabulous Beasts and Demons*, by Heinz Mode, originally published in 1973 as *Fabeltiere und Damonen*, translated from the German by Edition Leipzig. English edition published by Phaidon Press Ltd., London.

The italicized quote on page 115 is the last line from *Peter and Wendy*, by Sir James M. Barrie.

AN APPRECIATION

A prodigious amount of research preceded the writing of *Bad Blood*, and I'd like to thank my sister, Su Mead, of Memphis, Tennessee, for making necessary contacts, arranging interviews, providing arcane source material, and lending invaluable support and encouragement during the months the novel was in progress.

FOR MARYANN

In your eye
was the sea,
in the sea
a fish,
in the fish
a dream,
in the dream
a stone,
in the stone
the seed
of the flower
that breaks

the stone.

January 4, 1978

"Take what you want,"
God said. "And pay for it."

—SPANISH PROVERB

I

BLUE RIDGE
MILITARY INSTITUTE

Gaston, Virginia
May 23-25, 1942

The honor of your presence is requested
at the marriage of
MISS CORINDA LAMONT BILLINGS
to
SECOND LIEUTENANT WILLIAM JEBEDIAH BRADWIN
Saturday, the twenty-third of May,
at two o'clock in the afternoon
Cadet Chapel
Blue Ridge Military Institute
Gaston, Virginia

FROM the Journal of Captain C. R. Bradwin,
Fifth Regiment, First Cavalry Division,
U.S. Army

Saturday night, May 23

The horrors have ended; or at least I have them at a distance. For now.

I've always wondered about my ultimate capacity for good sour mash sipping whiskey, and now I see that I've nearly finished the bottle which the indispensable Hackaliah brought to my room about eight this evening. It is now shortly before midnight. And I am cold staring sober. True, there is numbness along one edge of my tongue that might be attributable to drinking. But my hand is steady, and I easily read that which I have been setting down in these pages; read without the faintest blur, or those appalling moments of frozen blankness that troubled me earlier. (Curious that I can write at all. Another discipline well learned, what Boss calls the "taxing art of self-revelation.") I suppose, rather than drinking myself into a stupor, I've achieved a state of dreamlike consciousness in which I can function creditably, as a professional soldier should, touched but not paralyzed by the tragic circumstances that

by the dreadful tragedy we have

Almost lost control. I am not as remote as I thought. I felt drastically unbalanced on a narrow ledge of the mind, about to go crashing—not into the aisle below, that aisle

15

already packed with hysterically shoving men and women, but into a dirty dark drowning oblivion . . . another drink wouldn't hurt. And the pain in my ankle has reasserted itself. Fortunately it isn't broken. Soaking has already reduced the swelling by half.

Is there a taint of smoke in the room? The wind must have freshened from the mountains. An hour ago soft rain fell, but not enough rain to dampen the inferno still raging in the George Washington National Forest a few miles away. Fires are burning from Georgia to New England this spring, the most destructive outbreak in memory, with millions of acres of prime timber in peril. It's sabotage, of course, the work of what the president has called a "sixth column" operating in this country. Those cadets who have not yet taken leave for the summer have been in the mountains all day, supplementing the weary fire-fighting crews of the park service. This lovely old town is in no danger, but I have only to walk (to hobble) across the room to the balcony doors to observe that the eastern sky is a billowing blood-red

    bloody

    blood everywhere spurting

    soaking into the

The mind balks. But, quite apart from the conscious mind, the pen writes on as I sit and watch it, writes scarcely faltering, clean legible words words words waiting. Waiting for me to. And I must. If I am to have my sanity, then before memory is sealed like a grave I must account for it—all that I instinctively reject as inexplicable.

God grant there *is* an explanation: not to be found in poor Clipper's face; oh, my dear brother, nothing there but the harrowing madness . . . I need to look elsewhere to begin, to understand.

Boss could have used his considerable influence with our chief of staff to arrange a week's furlough for me, which would have meant precious additional days with Nancy. Despite the stunning naval victories in the Coral

Sea and the jubilant talk one hears now of total victory in the Pacific by year's end, I doubt it will all be over so quickly. Who knows how many months, or years, we will be separated? Of course only in wartime is it possible to win promotion as quickly as I hope to. Just two years ago Eisenhower was a Lt. Colonel with the 15th Infantry and, it must be said, not particularly well thought of; Patton, in my estimation a great soldier, advanced only from captain to colonel in the twenty years between the wars.

Weighing every consideration, I felt that 72 hours was as much time as I could spare. My troop is combat-ready and the entire "Hell-for-leather" is long overdue for assignment.. Marking time on border patrol is hard on the men, and there can be no more boring place to wait than the dry, brutally hot plains of west Texas. After months of crack training, morale is our chief problem: Men who are spoiling for a fight and who feel they are being ignored by the high command (we are dismounted cavalry, to be sure, but still looked upon as quaintly out of fashion) soon lose heart. I have confidence in Lt. Neal (Blue Ridge '39 and a K.A. brother) and his ability to command; perhaps he does have an unfortunate tendency to ingratiate himself with his superiors. No matter, I would have felt derelict enjoying so long an absence from duty at this critical time.

With only 72 hours at my disposal it was not possible to attend both the graduation exercises at Blue Ridge and the wedding two days later. I chose to arrive the night before the wedding. Nancy and I would then have nearly all of Sunday to ourselves. (I thought her decision not to join me at Ft. Bliss was a wise one. The old post is wretchedly overcrowded; because of her allergies she would find the heat and the punctual, twice-a-day sandstorms all but unbearable. Also, without a family to care for there is not very much at the fort to keep her occupied. I was afraid of another spell of deep brooding, heartbreaking lament for the lost child. For the duration I felt she was better off at Dasharoons, with Boss to look after her—and she did seem to get along very well with Nhora.)

My transportation was arranged by the Air Service

17

Command. I would fly from Ft. Bliss to Kelly Field to Ft. Bragg in North Carolina. Boss would have a car waiting in Fayetteville.

Unfortunately an engine of our transport overheated, resulting in a delay of three hours in San Antonio. The flight was subsequently diverted to New Orleans to take on high-priority cargo, which turned out to be the household effects of an air corps brigadier reassigned from the Canal Zone. By the time the plane was loaded, heavy weather prevented our taking off. Assigned to an uncomfortable billet at the airport, I was sleepless throughout the night, always hoping that the next hour would see an end to the fog and drizzling rain. The roof leaked, and the Louisiana mosquitoes made me yearn for the comparatively mild nuisance of the flies at Bliss.

By daybreak Saturday (only this morning? How could so much of my life be destroyed in a single day?) the weather was still dismal. Fortunately I was able to complete another long-distance call to Boss. I regretfully told him that I couldn't make it. Then I tried to talk to, and console, Nancy, but we were abruptly cut off. I spent an angry ten minutes in a futile attempt to re-place the call.

"Are you Captain Bradwin?"

What a small world it can be! The speaker was Lt. Colonel Milo Cotsworth of Malvern, Arkansas, Air Corps Ferrying Command. Col. Cotsworth's father, a state supreme court justice, was a friend of Boss's (but nearly everyone of consequence in the state has been to Dasharoons at one time or another). As luck would have it, Col. Cotsworth was returning East, having flown a number of distinguished British visitors, among them Field Marshal Sir John Dill, to observe mechanized maneuvers at nearby Camp Polk. He'd heard of my predicament and offered a solution on the spot.

"Captain, I'm flyin' to Washington when it clears up enough so I can see to get off the runway. Now, I believe that new landing strip at Camp Pickett, Virginia, is long enough to accommodate my airplane. How far's that from where you want to be?"

"Camp Pickett? A two-hour drive, at the most. But—"

"Don't worry about the weather, wind's northwest at 23 knots now, should blow most of this crud out to sea in another hour or so. I'll talk it over with the limey brass I'm haulin' around, but I don't think they'll raise a fuss about havin' you aboard." He looked thoughtfully at me. "I could drop a name or two, I suppose."

"Only if necessary, colonel. And thank you, sir. This means a great deal to me."

"Okeydoke then, look to be takin' off at about 0730."

Col. Cotsworth's estimated time of departure was on target. Minutes after seven-thirty we rose skyward to meet the rays of the sun above a low-hanging cloud bank. Soon we were winging north in a sky of purest cerulean. The aircraft was a new four-engine Boeing Stratoliner, so recently requisitioned from Pan American Airlines it had not yet been repainted. A hearty breakfast was served by stewards. Our guests from Great Britain, all of eminent rank, were flatteringly courteous to a junior officer. Many of them were scholars as well as soldiers, and even Field Marshal Sir John Dill appeared to be well acquainted with Boss's six-volume history of the Civil War. Following a stimulating discussion of Longstreet's tragic flaw, I withdrew to nap for almost two hours, until we touched down at Camp Pickett.

Another pleasant surprise awaited me at the field. As I stepped from the plane a staff car flying the insignia of the camp's commanding officer drove up.

"Sir," the driver said, throwing open the door for me, "General Blaisdell's compliments, and he hopes you enjoy your stay in Virginia."

I looked up just as the starboard engines of the Stratoliner restarted and saw Col. Cotsworth signaling thumbs-up from the cockpit. I smiled my thanks and saluted as he taxied down the landing strip. All of the frustration I had earlier suffered was now forgotten. Relaxed after my rapid journey to the Old Dominion, I eagerly anticipated my reunion with those whom I love most dearly on this earth.

My driver, Sgt. Lew Chittum of Roanoke, made excellent time despite the fires burning along the Blue Ridge.

A pall of smoke and ash across the southern approach to Gaston brought us to a standstill at times, but I reached the institute shortly before two o'clock.

It was my first visit since my own graduation in 1937; even so I wasn't prepared for the pleasant wave of nostalgia that rose in my breast, lifting my heart well into my throat. If there is a more beautiful campus in the world, I have yet to be informed of it. Designed by Thomas Jefferson, the famous Hilltop Parade is lined with notable examples of classic revival architecture. There are six temple-form structures of dark red brick with extensive porticos and whitewashed columns thirty feet in height. The fourteen-acre Parade is surrounded by towering ash and elm trees. To the right as one enters upon the Parade are the cadet barracks. Against a panorama of the mountains the cadet chapel rises in isolated splendor across the field, overlooking the campus. Today, however, as we drove along the Parade the mountains were not visible and the sky was queerly burnished by an indistinct sun. The air was unusually sultry for spring.

As the car approached the chapel I heard what sounded like the 50-voice boys' choir from nearby McKinley School. Horse-drawn carriages waited on the wedding party. The line of limousines along the chapel drive could not have been less than a hundred yards long. Undoubtedly half of official Washington had driven down for the wedding of Secretary Lawton's granddaughter, and Boss's own party had required the use of a ten-car private train. There would be few seats remaining in the chapel.

Two of Clipper's classmates, wearing full-dress uniforms, saluted as I went double-time up the steps to the ivy-framed doors. One of them recognized me.

"Sir, didn't think you were going to get here."

"It seems like a miracle to me," I replied, and went in.

The choir had concluded their prenuptial anthem and already bridesmaids were starting down the right-side aisle. Six of the girls, all dressed in pale orange chiffon, fidgeted next to sashed and sabered ushers as they awaited their turns.

Corrie Billings turned slowly on her father's arm and

stared nearsightedly at me through the fine net of her veil. I pay scant attention to what women wear to be married in, but her gown struck me as being something very special—I'm sure it was an heirloom. The gown was cream satin embroidered with tiny pearls; it had a full skirt and a long train. Instead of a bouquet, Corrie held a small prayer book in her gloved hands. All around her, the children: spit-combed or meticulously braided, pale with the excitement and prestige of the moment, in their velvet and ruffles richly overdressed, like scaled-down royalty. Two boys to carry the train, two girls with baskets of tiny wild-flowers.

With her charming quirk of a smile, Corrie pulled her veil aside, showing not a trace of nerves.

"Champ, come here," she said softly, but with a sense of command few officers of my acquaintance could equal. "We sure are happy you could make it."

I lightly kissed her cheek and shook hands with her father, who stood half a head shorter than Corrie and smelled of bay rum and sharp sweat. It was stuffy in the small vestibule, but Corrie was oblivious.

"You look wonderful," I told her.

"Thank you, sir. I let mama and all the cousins and aunts do the worryin' for me. It's the only way to get married. Well, now everybody's here, almost. Nhora's back at the train with her navel packed in ice, poor thing. Might be appendicitis, the doctor says. Or maybe it's something she ate didn't agree with her."

"Damn shame. Nancy?"

"Sittin' down front beside Boss. She's been all smiles these last couple of days, havin' herself a *good* time. Guess you're glad to hear that. Sure sorry about the baby, Champ. Don't you go givin' up, hear? There's gotta be a Champ junior in the family."

"There will be. And how's Clipper?"

"He's been just a little strange lately—that's normal I guess. I peeked around the corner at him just a minute ago. Oh, Lord, he looks s'handsome in that uniform! I know I'll do somethin' *dumb* at the last minute. Cry. Reckon nobody will see me blubber because of this veil.

Isn't it lovely though? Belonged to my great-grandmother, Sally Armitage Billings—What's the matter with you, honeybuss, you got to go pee?"

One of the trainbearers nodded woefully.

"Can you hold on a couple extra minutes? Then when you get up there on the altar—like at rehearsal, remember?—just ease on out the chancel door to your left, there's a toilet there you can use."

The organist was already well into "Here Comes the Bride." "Corrie," her father said hoarsely, "for God's sake, you're gettin' *married*."

"Reckon I better go before Clipper thinks I changed m'mind," Corrie said. She readjusted her veil. "Big brother Champ, be seein' you."

"Save the next to the last dance for me, Corrie."

"I surely will." And off she went with her father, and into the chapel; I could hear a wave of rustlings and the murmur of voices as heads turned to the tardy bride.

I went upstairs to the gallery, and was not pleased to note that the steps sagged and the cracks in the stucco walls had widened since my days as a "midge"—a lowly Fourth Classman. The chapel was built in 1834. During the Civil War it was shelled and severely damaged in the battle of Rickett's Mill, fought in the nearby woods. Rebuilt after the war, the chapel now stood sadly in need of restoration. I resolved to bring this to Boss's attention; as the senior member of the board of regents, he was in a position to get something done.

I passed the ranks of the boys' choir and moved toward a vacant spot in the front-row pew at the end of the gallery, which overlooked the altar below.

There were roses, stephanotis and gardenias everywhere—in hanging baskets, woven into the white latticework that transformed the altar into a pleasing bower. Droplets from an alabaster fountain were ignited by the light focused through an octagonal window in the back wall of the chapel. I saw a mild rainbow, and unexpected halos appeared in the greenery. The air in the chapel was sweet, very nearly oppressive. Hand-held paper fans waved everywhere, to little effect. It might have been my imagination, so recently had I come from the burning hills to the east, but I was certain that I smelled woodsmoke even here.

Corrie was now approaching the altar with her father. There may have been tears behind the veil. From a distance I couldn't tell, but as she moved regally those last few yards to join her betrothed she acknowledged a non-agenarian auntie seated in a position of honor on the aisle. She paused ever so briefly, spoke, and fetched a smile from the frail old lady. Yes, Corrie was totally self-possessed even during these tense moments. Which was more than could be said for Clipper, who stood far more rigidly than military demeanor required, very nearly trans-fixed, his china-blue eyes wide as he stared at Corrie.

I sighed for him, recalling my own unreasonable terror just before I was married to Nancy. I had walked out on the altar with my attendants in a mood of quiet antici-pation, perhaps just a trifle impatient to have it over with. But my first glimpse of Nancy in her wedding gown did me in; my throat filled, my heart stuttered pathetically, I was afraid of fainting. I cannot imagine that even my first experience in combat will so completely separate me from my wits. I married Nancy two years ago, and even now I have only the dimmest memory of our exchange of vows. Nancy has said that when I placed the wedding band on her finger I was so cold to the touch she almost cried out. Boss raised us, trained us, to be afraid of nothing, but somewhere along the line he forgot to mention what an ordeal it could be to stand with someone you love desper-ately and say a few simple words before a minister. Boss has married three times himself, the last time to a woman a year younger than I, so I suppose the idea of marriage has never fazed him. But my father is an unusual man in every respect.

Perhaps it was the depressing heat, or it may be that the tension of the unexpectedly long journey, filled with detours and delays, caught up to me just then. Thinking of my own wedding while watching another cast me into a mood of rueful lethargy. Suspended in a vale of fascina-tion between past and present, I felt overwhelmed by shadows, an apprehension of events within events I couldn't hope to articulate.

While the wedding proceeded as pageantry, at a cadence peculiar to dreams, my inner vision was sharpest for oddities, fragments, notions: the slight indentation of Corrie's slippers in the plush blue carpeting of the altar steps; the sibilance of water in the fountain, drops indelible in light and air like Lachryma Christi; the vaulted, soaring organ; a nod, a smile, a yawn—all seemed too vivid, unbearable as reality. I looked at my Nancy, but was shut out by the floppy brim of the hat she wore, denied even the fleeting comfort of imagining that she would turn and find me (her long look, her astonished, blissful smile), for she sat next to my father, that powerful, coarse and goaty gentleman with one galled eye and a Viking's bent for ravishment.

My qualms—childlike, rankly sexual—were of dispossession, though of course he had a young wife of his own, bolder and gayer than Nancy, and he would not be a predator within the limits of his own family. Nancy spoke to him. He dipped his head below the brim of her hat to listen. His hair was longer than ever, inches below his collar, coarse white and peppery gray and yellow-streaked, the precise yellow of nicotined fingers. He squeezed her slim hand with his own. The organ ceased, the silence thundered, I was sexually aroused as I often am in church, I looked elsewhere.

On the altar Corrie's father had stepped back; the beads of sweat on the back of his balding head caught the light and glistered. The trainbearer with the overburdened bladder did his vanishing act; two photographers tried to be inconspicuous as they snapped pictures. And Clipper had moved stiffly to Corrie's side. I noted the single gold star on the collar of his tunic, an honor for which only a handful of graduates of Blue Ridge have qualified: For four consecutive years Clipper had stood first in his class.

I expected him to be wearing the sword presented by the company to their First Captain on graduation day, the usual ornate affair, gold-encrusted, perhaps capped by an eagle about to take wing. I have such a sword, and I am always thrilled by the sight of it. But Clipper had chosen to wear another saber, straight instead of curved, a practical fighting man's weapon which I recognized. The blade was thirty-seven inches long, one and one-eighth inches wide at the hilt. It had been given to Boss in 1911 by the famed "Monsieur l'Adjutant," Cléry, master of arms and instructor of fencing at the French Cavalry School in Saumur—a rare appreciation of an outstanding pupil by the professional champion of Europe in the foil, dueling sword and saber. Now the saber belonged to Clipper, and it was no surprise that he had chosen to wear it in preference to the First Captain's saber. Honors do not come easily at Blue Ridge, but Boss bestows his blessings even more sparingly.

It was a moment of conflicting emotion for me: There is no doubt that I was envious, yet a lump came to my throat that resisted swallowing. I was so proud of Clipper I wanted to shout—perhaps also I wanted to break the languorous, melancholy spell that had enfolded me, to give Clipper respite, bring a smile to his strained face.

"Dearly beloved, we are gathered together here in the sight of God . . ."

The pastor, wearing the scarlet hood of his Oxford University degree over a black academic gown, had begun the ceremony. In a few minutes then, with a burst of Mendelssohn and the traditional arch of sabers, it would be over. My mind wandered. The reception, I recalled, was to be at the historic Stonewall Jackson residence situated just off campus, a landmark now administered by the state of Virginia. It had been secured for the reception through much arm-twisting, I was sure, plus a heavy outlay of cash, but the usual site of cadet wedding receptions, the Officer's Club, would not have been large enough or grand enough for this affair.

". . . an honorable estate, not to be entered into unadvisedly, but reverently, discreetly, and in the fear of God."

Out of the corner of my eye I noticed Hackaliah standing at the rear of the gallery near the steeply pitched choir stall, a long way for his dimming eyes to perceive the exchange of vows taking place a hundred feet away. But I'm sure that just being there was enough for Hackaliah, our other "boss," a part of the family from my earliest memory. He was already well into his thirties when he became Boss's "striker" just before the turn of the century, which made him at least 75 years old. Even Hackaliah couldn't reckon his true age. He remained broad-shouldered and imposing despite the years, but now as he stood there in his wrinkled linen suit he also looked haggard and ill to me, off-color, and his hands wrung a Charleston planter's straw as if he intended tearing it apart.

"If there be any present who can show just cause that these parties should not be legally joined together . . ."

When I returned my attention to Clipper and Corrie I felt it for the first time: a faint shuddering movement, as if the entire chapel had been jolted noiselessly to its foundations. A large tree falling nearby would have produced an identical sensation, and I recalled walking on Park Avenue in New York, feeling the street quake in a similar manner from the vibrations of the many trains in the tunnels of Grand Central Station. I thought nothing of the chapel tremor, and apparently no one else did either.

"Who giveth this woman to be married to this man?"

But there was a second tremor, perhaps three seconds after the first. *Earthquake?* Possibly, yet I doubted there had been a noticeable quake in this part of Virginia for hundreds of years. Again it happened! Truly shaken this time, a few of the more apprehensive wedding guests began to look around and whisper.

"What was that, daddy?" a child asked.

Her voice was not loud but it carried. On the altar the minister hesitated and rubbed his cheek, staring at Clipper as if he'd forgotten his name. This time I noted the interval: exactly three seconds between tremors. So it could not be an earthquake, as I understood the mechanics of earthquakes: They rumbled and roared and shook the earth continuously. Here in the chapel there was a definite pause between episodes, almost as if—

"Jebediah Wil—uhhumm, excuse me. *William* Jebediah Bradwin, wilt thou have this woman to be thy wedded wife—"

The venerable chapel shook for the eighth time; it was obvious to all that the shaking had become more pronounced, as if the walls and beams could scarcely withstand these mysterious tremors. There was a fine cloud of dust in the air; it could be seen sifting down near the back of the gallery. The boys in the choir were staring at the ceiling above their heads. The stout organist inadvertently pressed a key and the organ pealed dismally. Nine—ten—Now voices were louder throughout the sanctuary, the wedding seemed all but forgotten. There was no panic, only a restless dismay.

"Ladies and gentlemen," said the pastor, "if you please—"

His mouth clamped shut as we all were jolted. This time a general outcry resulted which grated on the nerves. Wedding guests were everywhere on their feet. I was astonished to see Clipper step away from Corrie, clasping his head as if in pain.

Hackaliah's callused hand pressed my right shoulder. I looked up into his eyes. He stank of fear.

"It's the bell, God help us, the bell!"

Yes, the bell! It had been in the back of my mind but I had dismissed the notion as incredible because no sound accompanied its destructive, forbidden tolling. Nonetheless only the 9000-pound bell in the tower above the choir stall and organ loft could cause such stress as it swung back and forth. Because of the deteriorating condition of the chapel, the bell had not been used for twenty years, and I wondered angrily whose idea of a joke this was. Undoubtedly the clapper had been muffled so that its stroke would go unheard while losing none of its force.

"I'll put a stop to this," I said, rising, but Hackaliah held me in place.

"No way you can stop it," he said. "Nobody there! You just get Clipper out of this place. Quick, 'fore he—"

Hackaliah's eyes left my face; startled, he reared back, still clutching my shoulder so hard that pains shot up my neck. Then he released me, turned me in the direction of the altar.

Clipper had drawn his saber. He stood looking into the

air, disoriented, demoralized, the narrow blade half-raised, flashing like a mirror as he turned and the chapel shook and the sound of the cracking roof threw the wedding guests into an uproar.

From seats all around me a scramble ensued. I was jostled but could not look away from Clipper, although there remained a moment during which I might have acted, taken command to quell the frenzy. On the altar no one moved. The pastor, clutching Scripture, was staring at the ceiling, tongue between his teeth. Opposite me the gallery wall cracked and a window shattered in a dislocated frame. This provoked fresh screams, renewed clawing and shoving as the few doorways became clogged with people trying to get out before what now seemed the inevitable collapse of the chapel.

On the altar Clipper whirled full circle, reckless with the saber, which he held in both hands; his best man was forced to dive to the carpet to escape injury. I could not believe what I was seeing. I was brave enough—my courage cultivated, enforced by will and an ingrained sense of obligation not to fail, not to let anyone down—but Clipper had been born fearless, he would take any risk, accept any dare, and emerge laughing from a self-imposed ordeal.

What had happened to my brother?

The floor of the gallery was moving. I felt as if I were trying to maintain my balance on a barrel rolling lumpily downhill. I grabbed the railing to keep from falling. Hackaliah was yelling at me, but I couldn't distinguish words. A bridesmaid had run for her life; two more of the girls clung to each other, stood sobbing in a litter of flowers and fallen trellis. Clipper's attendants were rooted, their own eyes reflecting his manic distress.

Only Corrie Billings seemed not to have surrendered to pandemonium. Reaching out, she attempted to calm Clipper, bring him to his senses, by holding the blade of the saber immobile in a gloved hand. I caught my breath, pulse knocking like death at my temples, because I was aware of the extraordinary keenness of that blade.

No one will ever know what she said to him, or if she

spoke at all. But I'm sure there must have been love in Corrie's eyes even as Clipper's eyes congealed with loathing and he drew the blade from her fist. It was an easy, unforced, practiced withdrawal, as if they'd done it many times before in a ceremonial way. Corrie opened her hand and the palm was already red with her blood. And I think it must have been the sight of blood as the silent bell continued to pound the chapel to pieces and the screams of the trapped guests assaulted the senses, the inescapable fact of first blood, that sent Clipper into his paroxysm of destruction.

Oh, and he was good with the saber, as Boss had patiently taught.

A flick of his wrist and slight thrust and the level blade went right through Corrie's veil and the column of her throat inches beneath her raised chin. Then the veil behind her head filled as if inflated by a gust of air, a backward breath, and I saw the elegant tip of the wetted blade holding the veil away from her nape for an instant before Clipper retracted it, stood stiffly presenting his saber level and red at the razor edge for her inspection. Corrie nodded, weakly, hands going to her throat; then she turned and, head high, eyes deeply dreaming behind the veil, both hands clasping the wound so that nothing showed, started down the altar steps as if to return to her father, who was already packed and panting in the middle aisle, unaware like almost everyone else of what had been done to Corrie.

On the last step she suddenly and awkwardly lost her motor control and fell to one side into Boss's arms. Her hands came away from her throat and blood began pumping everywhere, as if from a burst hose.

I screamed—unheard—and vaulted over the railing, not caring who or what was below me. I landed feet first on the seat of a nearly abandoned pew, teetered, almost had my balance, then lost it and twisted my left ankle as I stepped off the bench. The pain brought tears to my eyes but didn't stop me for long.

While Nancy shouted for help and Corrie lay bleeding to death in Boss's arms, her limbs jerking so ecstatically she was difficult to hold, two of Clipper's attendants seized him. But they were unable to contain him. Clipper ducked, shrugging one boy off, holding his saber in a firm two-handed grip. With an artful swipe he flicked away an offending hand; it fell somewhere among the green plants on a trellis and stuck there, climbing disembodied toward heaven. The second boy received a blow on the head but with the flat of the saber, and so his life was spared.

I heard more sounds of shattering windows and glimpsed men throwing themselves through the jagged panes to safety outside. Plaster fell in chunks from the ceiling. I clambered over the rows of pews toward Boss, ignoring the hot irons in my ankles. A woman had fainted in her seat. A little boy, perhaps her son, was down between pews, clinging to her hand, shivering. He pleaded for help as I crawled over them. But I instinctively felt that Boss most needed my help.

On the altar Clipper had whirled again, his saber above his head. Overheated by the act of murder, his face was awry with a crazed passion. Boss was pushed off balance by a woman who stepped over the doomed Corrie without a glance. Boss saw me coming and was momentarily stalled by surprise; then he reacted to my frantic, panto-mimed warning.

He turned, but Clipper was already on him. The long arc of the saber sheared Boss at the neckline and his expression was still puzzled, the blighted eye squinted almost shut, as his head bounded onto a pew seat (a horror so extreme I refused to acknowledge that it could have happened). Nancy, chalk-faced, backed away from Clipper, only to be shoved forward almost to the saber's edge by someone in the aisle behind her. I realized that Clipper intended to kill her too. And there was no way I could reach them in time.

But Clipper was distracted as a large piece of the ceiling fell close to him. He dropped his saber, then groped for it. One of the bridesmaids had completely lost her wits and was sitting with her back to a side pillar of the altar, brow knitted in concentration as she tried to brush the white streaks of plaster from her delicate chiffon dress.

30

The boy whose hand had been cut off was receiving emergency treatment from brother officers. The pastor had led two hysterical girls to a chancel door half-hidden by greenery and was doing his best to persuade them to leave. For some reason they balked at going through the doorway, although from there it was just a short flight of steps to safety.

I propelled myself over the last pew and seized Nancy's arm.

She looked at me as if she'd never seen me before. "See what happens? See what happens?" she cried, her eyes curiously without life. "I think—"

I shook her and screamed in her ear. "Nancy! Follow the pastor! He'll get you out of here!"

"Can't leave. Boss—oh—ahh—and Corrie—don't you see Corrie?" Her eyes widened, her voice squealed. "You're *standing* on her!"

I was, but poor Corrie would never know. I pushed Nancy toward the nearby steps. "Run!" I begged her. I knew Clipper had retrieved his saber. I turned, protectionless, one arm raised against the attack I was expecting.

Clipper was poised to hack me to pieces, but when he saw my face he froze. I don't know why.

"Clipper," I said, "don't do it anymore! Don't do it." I was babbling, but I didn't care. Anything to keep him motionless, to stay the saber and give Nancy precious seconds to escape. I was conscious of her moving away, stumbling up the altar steps. I knew she was watching Clipper too. But his eyes were on me as the silent tolling bell continued its slow demolition of the chapel. By then the chapel may have been half-emptied; there was no one else around us and I was barely receptive to the morbid wail, the voices of the trapped and threatened. My lack of awareness undoubtedly was due to shock, that plus the strain of continued eye contact with my demented brother as I summoned the will to control him.

His shoulders were bunched, his head lowered, from my viewpoint precisely divided by the erect line of the saber. I tried to divine the intimate processes of his mind and felt myself reeling into a complementary madness. More of the ceiling fell. Clipper spoke, but it was nonsense.

"Da—Da—Dom—Danbhalah Ai-Da Wédo. Gen-loa! Mawu!"

On the altar Nancy lost her footing and fell. Clipper turned, his saber dipping away from me. I tottered on my bad ankle, hit him twice with my fists—a clumsy one-two. The blows had little effect. He ducked a third punch and jumped to the altar. It seemed to shake under his weight. Altar lights flickered. Rolling pots spilled flowers, and candles smoked on the carpet. Clipper arose moaning loudly and went after Nancy's head with his saber.

One of Clipper's attendants had drawn his own saber, a parade piece not intended for warfare. He lunged at the blade in Clipper's hand. As the sabers clashed and Clipper's killing stroke was deflected, Nancy crawled from between them and got to her feet. Clutching the front of her dress in one hand, she ran to the chancel door.

I threw myself on Clipper's back. We fell together. The other boy, his sword cut in two, backed away. Clipper got up. I couldn't get up, not so quickly, and then all of the ceiling above the altar seemed to be falling on me. For the most part it was harmless ornamental plaster, but the lime was acrid and blinding. I cried out and felt something sharp against a collarbone. Clipper stood over me, the point of his saber inches from my jugular vein.

"Not you," he said. "Not here." Gaunt deliverer of sleep, his eyes half-closed. *Where do you think you're going to do it, if not here?* I thought. He cast around the altar, but Nancy was nowhere in sight. At least she was safe for now.

"Finished," Clipper said unexpectedly.

Instead of cutting my throat, he walked away through the mist from the fountain to the octagonal window at the rear of the altar. The glass was still intact. He looked out the window. I wept. He braced by the window, military-fashion, and tilted his head back until the tip of his chin was almost on a line with his long throat. He raised the saber. A drop of water from the tip fell into his open mouth. With a swift downward motion, Clipper sheathed the blade in his gullet.

For a few moments he stood on his toes; his hands fell away and I saw the gleam of steel between his teeth. Blood began to stain the crotch of his high white trousers. Still balanced in agony on his toes, he fell against the window and went through it in a sparkle of exploding glass.

I don't know how long my attention was focused on that window but it was like the crystal of a dropped watch and time is motionless in hell. Then Hackaliah fumbled in ruins and stood me on my feet. The air seethed with dust, but the chapel stood still.

"It stopped," I said.

There was a lump on Hackaliah's forehead; his eyes were dazed, the whites speckled with old bloodknots. "Come on," he insisted, "might fall down anyhow."

"Boss?" I said, attempting to turn back, but Hackaliah wouldn't let me go.

"Leave him," Hackaliah groaned. "You don't want to see him."

"But I saw him already. His head just fell off." Like a fantasy with ogres, a wicked cartoon, his bad eye closing in a spontaneous giggle as it sometimes did when he was peevishly drunk, putting on a bragging show: *Look at me, bet you can't do this!* Lost his head. But then what Clipper did—The dust in my throat gagged me and I vomited.

Next I was mindful of clean air, my face pillowed on grass. My midsection was knotting with spasms. I stood and, without Hackaliah to support me, fell right down, an electric shock traveling up my leg and spine to the base of my skull. Next I tried sitting, my back against a low wall.

The sloping lawn was filled with wedding guests, some as helpless as I. Women in rag finery were having hysterics under the trees. The compressed violence from within the chapel had flowed outdoors and was dissipating, but slowly, beneath a low sky. The sun was absent; yet the day burned almost invisibly, like a gas flame, its light turning the leaves to a shade of weathered bronze, turning faces soup-bone gray. Open wounds had the glitter of

33

cheap spangles. Bodies were lifted out of the chapel while men watched for the collapse of a severely bowed brick wall on which vines dangled, mooringless. Despite the many men in uniform, no one seemed to have taken firm command. Doors slammed as limousines were loaded and raced each other madly across the pristine Parade, behaving like beetles in a tipped-over cracker box. I knew that some of the limousines would not stop until they had returned to Washington.

Tyrone, Hackaliah's youngest son, vaulted the wall I was sitting against and kneeled beside me, his priestly face nearly ultraviolet from exertion, his eyes nervous but inquisitive as he surveyed the grim scene. Distantly I heard the wail of the community's fire siren, calling together those volunteers who were not already occupied with the forest fire along the Blue Ridge.

"Captain," Ty said, "come with me." He put an arm around me. He was a tall thin man two years younger than I, and wiry-tough.

"Where's Hackaliah?"

"Gone to the hospital with Miss Nancy. Where you need to be."

"I'm not hurt that badly," I protested. "Someone will have the good sense to set up emergency facilities in the cadet barracks. Help me over there."

"You need a doctor," Tyrone said, lifting me.

"What about Clipper? I can't just leave my own——"

Tyrone had white man's eyes the color of spit on a sidewalk, keen enough to light up a woods on a dark night; and those eyes, which at times seemed to express an undisguised resentment, had caused him a good deal of misery until he'd learned to veil or never show them at all, like the sort of downcast, turd-kicking nigger he could never be. He looked steadily at me and said without attempting to spare my feelings, "What's the use? Clipper is done for, captain. He rolled and rolled with that sword stuck inside him."

"At least we can cover him up, for God's——"

"Did that first thing. Now, you don't know what's best

34

for you. Your mind is confused, captain. You just come along with me and I'll look after you."

A truck from the institute's motor pool came blaring up to the chapel, and more than a dozen cadets in grimy fatigues, their faces blackened after hours on the burning mountaintop, jumped off the tailgate and formed rank, waiting weary and bewildered to be told what to do. Timbers groaned in the chapel; part of the roof settled ominously. The tipped bell tolled once, a mournful sound. Tyrone turned and stared at the bell tower as if hypnotized. Men were spilling out of the chapel, but the roof didn't cave in. One of the men was Lt. General Jack T. ("Erie Jack") Bucknam, the school's superintendent and a long-time friend of the family. Undoubtedly Erie Jack was considered too old for active duty in the new war, but he looked alert and fit as he dusted himself off and surveyed the cadets available for the emergency.

"General Bucknam!" I called, rudely pushing Tyrone away.

Erie Jack changed direction and trotted up to me. "Well, Champ. Didn't know you were here. This is a hell of a thing. An appalling tragedy! I don't know what happened yet. We have to get organized. Thank God, I believe we have everyone out of there. You don't look good."

"I'll be all right."

The white-haired old soldier turned and called two cadets over. "Lieutenant Jenner, there's a scout car parked at my gate. Fetch it for the captain. See that he's comfortable in my house and has everything he needs."

"General Bucknam, I can't leave—"

Bucknam's eyes were smarting, from dust or grief. He seemed to be looking beyond me, at the wreckage of a long and satisfying career. In the last analysis, no matter what explanations were forthcoming, he would be held responsible. "What can you do now, Champ? What can any of us do but pick up the pieces? Chapel should've been repaired years ago. No one listened. Never enough money. Time to clear this area. Sort out the injured from

35

the ambulatory. Go with these cadets, that's an order, captain."

"Yes, sir." I looked at Tyrone, who had backed slowly away from the military pecking order. He stood, long hands jammed into his jacket pockets, studying me with a frown.

"Ty," I said, pointing the way through the woods in the hollow of Rickett's Mill, which separated town and school, "the hospital's six blocks from here. Find out how Nancy is. Then get me a complete list of Boss's traveling party. We'll have people to account for and arrangements to make."

"Yes, captain," he said reluctantly, but he was on his way without urging. While the newly commissioned Jenner raced off for the general's scout car, the other cadet, whose name was Brakestone, gave me a shoulder to lean on and helped me toward the general's house, which dominated the terraced avenue just outside the west gate of the post.

Jenner met us halfway across the Parade and by then I had remembered Nhora, Boss's wife, confined to the train and surely unaware of the tragedy.

"The depot," I said to Jenner, as Brakestone eased me into the scout car. I was sweating coldly, and every move I made intensified the pain in my ankle. My mind flashed with chaotic images of madness; Clipper's tormented face became a black beetle crawling inside a hard white skull.

"Sir—"

"I know what the general said; damn it, I have family business to take care of! It won't wait."

The Southern Railroad's main line and Gaston freight yard were located in a mile-long valley a stone's throw from the playing fields of the institute. To the south the valley was steeply walled by one of the several finger ridges that culminated in the now charred and devastated Blue Ridge just a few miles away. From the widow's peak of Railroad Ridge, a favorite Sunday picnic ground for cadets and their dates, one had a clear view of school and town, on twin hills immediately to the north.

At the eastern end of the valley the Roanoke Highway

crossed the tracks on a sooted iron bridge. The brownstone depot and passenger platforms were beneath this bridge. When we arrived, the famed Washington-New Orleans flyer, the Jean Lafitte, was standing in the station. Smoke lay thickly over the rail yard—a combination of wood and train smoke. Boss's long train had been parked on a southerly siding hard against Railroad Ridge. There was an impressive Missouri Pacific mountain-type engine at the head of the train (the railroad which we owned in Eastern Arkansas, the Delta, St. Francis and Dasharoons, had nothing to compare with this jumbo locomotive) and a total of ten cars, including two flatcars for the convenience of those wedding guests who had brought their own limousines along. Behind the flatcars were a baggage car, a Pullman and a diner for servants, a lounge car, a restaurant car, more deluxe stainless steel Pullmans with the best of drawing room accommodations, and Boss's own 90-foot car.

We crossed the bridge and bumped down a narrow bad road to the private train.

Somehow word of the disaster had already reached those servants who had not taken advantage of free time to have a few drinks and a game of cards in Foxtown, Gaston's colored section. They were milling on the tracks outside the train, their agitation clearly defined even from a distance. One of the maids had been encircled by others; she gestured toward the hilltop institute. I surmised that she had been waiting at the chapel for an elderly mistress, perhaps peeking through a vestibule door at the wedding. When the carnage began, she ran in a panic all the way back to the train.

Bull Pete was there, of course, the only colored man Boss ever trusted with a gun, the only man I knew large enough to carry a .45 automatic in his back pocket and scarcely show a bulge. As long as Bull Pete was in charge, the railroad's property would remain inviolate, and each and every nigra—there must have been fifty aboard, counting the New Orleans jazz band—would be the picture of decorum.

Bull Pete was alongside the scout car as soon as it

stopped. Behind him some of the women were keening and crying, throwing themselves down in the filthy ballast between tracks.

"Lord, Mist' Champ!" Bull Pete said, eyes bulging in distress. "What's happened up there? Dubretta say Clipper went clean out his head! She say—"

"Bull Pete, has Nhora heard about it?"

He was slow to speak again as he struggled with the impact of the news. Murder, destruction, calamity. And Boss dead. The worst news of all. I could see it in his eyes. Day and night he had watched over Boss, for twenty years.

"Suh! Suh!" Tears were rolling down his cheeks. He held on to the scout car, quaking at the knees like a common drunk. I thought he would fall down too. "You gots tell me. It cain't be true. Aowwwww, suh! Not the Boss! Not the Bosssssss!"

"Boss is dead," I said sharply, tasting bile. "Clipper—Corrie Billings too. I can't explain, not yet. For God's sake get control of yourself. Quiet those women down. I have something to do. Bull Pete, will you listen to me?"

He sobbed once more, and was done with it, although I doubted the misery would ever leave his eyes. He hadn't been there. No thought that he was needed, not on Clipper's wedding day. Still, he would blame himself.

I ordered Jenner to back up to the private car. "Find something I can use for a crutch," I said to Jenner.

Brakestone helped me aboard. It was dim and cool in Boss's car. The butler's pantry was empty. I knocked and waited and knocked again, banging the door with my fist. No one answered. I had Brakestone wait and let myself in.

The long railroad car was divided, half parlor, half bedroom. The parlor, Boss's domain, was unoccupied. Fine paintings and books and gaming tables for the serious cardplayers Boss liked to have with him on a trip. The odors of humidors. I made my way from one piece of Victorian furniture to another, my left leg all but useless. The slightest pressure created extravagant pains. And my face hurt from the plaster dust.

I leaned against the bedroom door and pounded. "Nhora," I said, "it's Champ. Please let me in."

Again there was no answer.

Fumbling with the gold knob, I found the door unlocked. I went into the Venetian baroque bedroom. No tobacco allowed here. The air was cool but somewhat stale. Conflicting odors: woodsmoke, Ivory soap, a mild antiseptic, a sachet sweetness, the tantalizing cologne Nhora wore infrequently. In the gray, artificial twilight of this traveling palace, painted cherubs lolled on the ceiling. I saw silk sheets lying in a tangle on the carpet outside the absurd tented bower where Nhora and Boss made their bed, and a set of discarded ice bags. A lax bare leg protruded through the layers of diaphanous curtain. I was startled and felt ill, imagining for the moment some further disaster had occurred. She seemed so lifeless.

Then without warning Nhora sat up in alarm. "What is it? Who is that?"

"Champ," I said, my voice a croak. I cleared my throat. "Nhora, I have to tell you—there's been——" I was trying to move toward her, but I miscalculated the strength of a brocaded armchair and in leaning on it broke its back. I fell. Nhora gasped and scrambled from the bed and kneeled beside me. I put a hand on her and discovered she was completely naked. At my touch I felt a faint velvety tremor, but she didn't shy away.

"Champ, are you hurt?"

"No. Clumsy. I'm all right."

"Champ—I don't have anything on. Wait——"

Nhora left me sitting there and walked quickly to the other end of the bedroom; I glimpsed her putting on her robe. Then she reached up and turned on a hanging crystal lamp. Even barefoot she was a very tall woman, only a fraction under six feet.

She turned and looked at me and was horrified. She clutched her abdomen and I remembered the appendicitis attack, which perhaps had saved her life today. I could well imagine how I appeared to Nhora as I grimly pulled myself to my feet.

"What—what—there's blood—my God, have you had an accident?"

I made her sit down, in a boudoir rocker that was too small for her. Then I told her the full appalling story. There was no way to spare either of us, but for Nhora it was like surgery without anesthetic. I suppose I had expected a different reaction, given her size and proportions—Amazonian stoicism. Possibly I had always underestimated the depth of her feeling for Boss. But she cried like a child. She rocked and groaned and finally screamed for me to stop. But she couldn't stop rocking, although she was nearly doubled over in the chair.

There was a decanter half-full of Irish whiskey on the marble pedestal table I was using for support. I was awkward, I spilled it all over both of us, but I got her to drink some of it. It may not have been the best thing for someone with a problem appendix, but the whiskey that went down soon had a restorative effect. She gulped hard a couple of times, looked vaporous, mumbled an apology and hurried into the cabinet-size bathroom. I noticed then that her feet were very dirty, as if she'd been out walking barefoot just before taking to her bed.

A smoked mirror confirmed the worst about my appearance, and I hadn't brought a complete change of uniform with me. For now I would have to endure the mess.

Nhora came out of the bath, her fine green eyes still wide with shock. "Something more happened," she said accusingly, an edge of panic in her voice. "Something you haven't told me about. People just don't go crazy like that!" Then the expression on my face, and the pressure of my hand on her arm, stopped her. Pain flooded her eyes before I realized how tightly I was holding her. I let her go. She took a step back, her own face softening in sympathy. "Oh—Champ, I don't know what I'm saying, I'm sorry."

People just don't go crazy like that. . . . But my scalp was crawling. I smelled blood all over again. I fought a strong, irrational urge to sink down on the spot and fall fast asleep. Movement, action was what I needed; I had to keep my mind off Clipper for now, I told Nhora that.

"What do we do?" she asked me, lips barely moving.

"You'd better stay here. I have things to do, but I'll send one of the colored women to—"

"No! Don't leave me!" She looked fearfully around the opulent bedroom, as if it now suggested a tomb to her.

"Nhora, I don't think you're in any condition to go."

"I'll be okay," she said, earnestly appealing to me, twisting the heavy shock of her light brown hair behind her head and tying it with a scrap of velvet. "I've had these attacks before, since I was a little girl. Ice always works. There's not much pain now. Honest!"

It was at odd moments like this, when she hurried her speech, stumbled charmingly, that the sibilance of her Gallic background became audible. "Please wait. I'll get dressed. There must be *something* I can do. You said people were hurt. Won't they need help at the hospital? Just don't leave me alone, Sshamp! I need you."

I waited outside while she dressed. Jenner appeared unexpectedly with a crutch, the wood gnawed like a dog's bone, the padded crosspiece stained with age and stinking of dried sweats, but it was exactly what I needed.

"I bought it from that World War vet who hangs around the depot. Five dollars. Probably hasn't seen that much money in years."

I repaid Jenner and called Bull Pete for instructions. It had occurred to me that since we were but a two-hour drive from the capital we would soon be under siege by representatives of the world's press; the privacy of our guests, some of whom were of frail constitution, had to be ensured. I wanted to get the train and as many of the wedding party as possible on the way back to the mid-South, preferably before dark. I knew there was going to be a nasty scandal, the family had to be protected. In the meantime it was Bull Pete's job to round up those servants loose on the town. Second Lt. Jenner, for whom I had developed a great deal of respect on short acquaintance, volunteered to stand armed guard at the train to discourage trespassers.

Brakestone drove Nhora and me to the community hospital, named for Robert E. Lee. The lawns were extensive

41

and lovingly kept; unfortunately the small infirmary was not equipped to handle the survivors of a disaster. A detachment of cadets under the direction of staff officers from the institute had begun to establish order, although the approaches to the hospital were badly crowded with vehicles of all types; even a horse-drawn barouche had been pressed into service as an ambulance. The noise—horns blowing, people shouting for assistance—was maddening. The Civil War itself could not have been more disruptive to the town.

I directed Brakestone to leave us and return to the train in case Jenner needed reinforcement. A soft northerly wind had come up and dogwood petals fluttered in the air as Nhora and I made our way along the brick sidewalk, around makeshift litters and past limping, weeping victims of the silent chapel bell. Tents for emergency first aid were being unloaded from the back of a military transport and hastily erected on the front lawn.

At the hospital gates, guarded by cadets, we were jostled by people congregating in a lump, feeding each other's fears, clamoring for friends or relatives. Nhora, unearthly pale, looked around in bewilderment. I had not prepared her for this scene—my explanation of the chapel's near-collapse had been hurried, incomplete, largely incomprehensible.

"All this," she said. "But *why?*"

"Let us through! Let us through! This boy'll die if you don't let us through!"

The animal terror in the man's voice charged the hairs on the back of my neck. A group of men were lugging a writhing thing in a soiled bedsheet to the hospital. They were all local men, farmers, wearing overalls and cloth caps. As they passed us I had a good look at the boy in the sheet, who carried on unmercifully, like a cat drenched with kerosene and set afire. He was about ten years old, and completely naked. "I'm burning!" he screamed. "Stop it, stop burning me!"

The crowd murmured and gasped and made room by the gates, which were thrown open by the cadets inside. Most of the farmers continued on through with their burden, but one of them, perhaps a brother of the tormented youngster in the sheet, left off and stood staring at me with that peculiar, heart-rending sweetness of someone breaking down emotionally. His face was filmed with perspiration.

"I don't know," he said, as if compelled to explain to both of us. "Found him just the way you see him. No clothes on his body. Running down Railroad Ridge to the home place, falling down, rolling, screaming how he was burning up. Well, you saw him. Not a mark on his skin. That right? He just ain't burnt—nah, ain't burnt no way I can see." Tears rolled down his cheeks. "Can't stand his screaming no more. Tell daddy I'll wait in the truck, please, sir."

"Doctor!" the father called, as his little son flailed and shrieked. "Get me a doctor quick!"

With a look of dread fascination Nhora drifted after them while the gates remained open. I hesitated, then followed. My attention was transferred to Hackaliah, whom I saw striding toward the hospital doors carrying a box of supplies marked with a big red cross. I called to him, but he didn't hear. Nhora had reached the farmers and the frenzied, mysteriously harmed boy. They lowered him to the cool grass. Nhora stared, then bent over the boy and tried to soothe him with her hand. He bucked and kicked and never stopped screaming. Nhora flinched as if she'd been hit. One of the farmers shook his head in dismay and kindly led her aside. She was looking at her clenched fist when she returned to me.

"That boy—"

"I know, it's terrible."

"I only wanted to help. But I think I scratched him." Timidly she opened her fist and showed me colorless neat fingernails. There were a few bloody flecks of skin under one nail. Nhora winced. "I couldn't help it." She looked back suddenly. A doctor had been found for the boy; he came running with his black bag.

"They'll give him morphine," I said. "He'll be all right. I have to find Nancy."

Nhora nodded, preoccupied. "I want to stay with the

boy until they know what's wrong with him. I'll catch up."

There was not the pandemonium I'd expected inside the hospital. Apparently at least five physicians had been guests at the wedding, and those who were able had pitched in to supplement the hospital staff. And there was no shortage of volunteer nurses or nigras, such as Hackaliah, to fetch and carry and clean up. Looking around, I saw familiar faces from home: aunts, uncles and cousins several times removed. They sat huddled in groups, some with bandaged hands and heads, and appraised me tentatively as I went by on my crutch. "Is that you, Charles?" "My, my you've filled out so I didn't hardly know you." "Charles, what do we do now? Do you think we can all go home?" I asked them to be patient while I spoke to Tyrone, who was in the hallway checking names on a list of our wedding guests.

"Your wife is in a ward on the third floor," Tyrone said. "Knocked out, but peaceful. Aunt Clary Gene's with her."

"Aunt Clary Gene? Boss brought her along? She's half-blind herself."

"Nobody I'd rather have by my bed if I took sick," Tyrone said sternly.

Nhora had come in the door; she was crying but calm. A group of kinfolk formed slowly around her. Without commotion they embraced and kissed Nhora. This show of sympathy and affection obviously gave her strength. She stood a head taller than the others and, although I'd never found her particularly beautiful, she seemed stunning in her grief. Tyrone was looking at Nhora too. He could be so quiet at times you'd swear his heart had stopped beating.

"Tyrone—the bodies—" I said.

"Oh," he said, his voice distant, his pale eyes still trained on Nhora, "here already. Come with a military escort." He looked at me. "I wrote down the number of the local funeral home."

"I have a lot of people to see before I—and Nancy comes first."

"Better take it easy, captain. You look about all used up yourself."

I disregarded his advice and found room on the single busy elevator.

The eight-bed ward on the third floor was full, and there were occupied beds in the hall outside. Nancy was at the end of the ward, under a north window so brilliant her body seemed to give off blurred light in return, like a saint wrapped for burial in some Florentine oil masterpiece.

Aunt Clary Gene, who had been nursemaid to the lot of us—Beau, Clipper and me—sat in a straight-back chair wearing the prim black hat with the lace veil she wore for all "gettin' out" occasions, baptism, wedding or funeral. She held her limp Bible in her hand, unopened because she couldn't read it anymore. But the old colored woman had committed long passages of Scripture to memory. She raised her head at my approach; the crutch squeaked like holy hell. Behind the veil the round lenses of her spectacles, catching the light stream from the window, were like milk glass rimmed in fiery red.

"Oh, Champ, you're not killed after all. Praise God!"

Nancy stirred and muttered on the bed. She was wearing a flimsy cotton hospital gown. I took her hand, looked at her small mute face. Her lips had pulled away from her teeth in a bloodless gash. There was a long streak of eye makeup down one cheek. Her hair was dusty. Too many bones seemed visible through her skin. She had never been very strong. A gleam of life in the slit of an eye seemed a light-year beyond apprehension of my presence, my voice. I tried anyway.

"I'm here, Nancy," I said. I told her that she was safe now, and that I loved her. Her hand lay cold and unmoving in mine.

"There is a plague on our house," Aunt Clary Gene said in her light, clear voice. "Beau. Clipper. And Boss. Is it true, about Boss?"

"Aunt Clary, don't."

"I'm praying-*you* will be spared, Champ. May the Lord

be satisfied with His tithe in blood. Let peace descend on our house."

She was just an old woman, thoughts loose as straws in her windy belfry, yet the notion that we Bradwins were formidably cursed struck me like a body blow. Again I was forced to grapple with the matter of the silent bell, the tortured chapel, the merciless slaughter——and again I reeled, shaken, numbed, unable to cope with the demands of reason, a simple yearning for purchase in the difficult flow of life. If it could have happened, then how was I safe from a fate as vile and unreckonable as my brother had suffered? If madness would be common, and all of nature in a fit, why shouldn't this building collapse beneath my feet, a tree fall on me from a windless sky, a tiger tear me from my bed some mild and dreaming night?

"Champ?" I barely heard him the first time he spoke. Then I felt his hand tighten on my free arm and looked around.

"Oh, boy, you damn well look like you've had it."

I shook my head irritably. Everett John Wilkes looked no better than I felt. There was blood in his sandy hair matching the freckles that pattered across his flat nose and cheeks. He was holding himself stiffly, one shoulder higher than the other. His Palm Beach suit was ripped and the remains of a red carnation drooped on his left lapel. A doctor had bound the knuckles of one big hand in tape.

He let go of me and stared at Nancy. "How's your little doll? Sleeping it off? Godalmighty, last thing I remember, boy, Clipper was swingin' that big old swift sword. I could've got there in time, maybe, but I tripped up, and then it felt like a hundred maniacs running over me. Worse than the Alabama game in '26, and buddy after that one they had to take my spleen out down there in Tuscaloosa. I'm one big bruise all over. Don't let me bore you with my troubles. I just came up here to tell you we're gettin' organized. Plenty of good people now to help out. I can sort of take over from here on, Champ. You go get yourself looked at. Save yourself for later, y'know?

We'll talk when you're ready. Legally there are questions to be answered, but plenty time, Champ."

I readily forgave him for running on in a manner one could feel was insensitive; it was his nature to talk when there was nothing much to say. Evvy was middle partner in the law office that looked after the affairs of Dasharoons. He was a Harvard law school graduate, third in his class, I believe. He had a great deal of lazy charm, but his brain never stopped working. Boss had thought he would make a fine governor of Arkansas after a few years of seasoning. He would've been Boss's third governor.

I was suddenly too weary, and too much in pain. There was no need for me to sit the rest of the day by Nancy's side.

"Don't leave Nancy," I said to Aunt Clary Gene. "As soon as she's conscious tell her I'm all right. Keep telling her until you're certain that she understands."

Downstairs a whiff of ammonium carbonate cleared my head, but I refused analgesics, afraid of the lull that was sure to follow. The doctor who examined my ankle was of the opinion there was no fracture, but undoubtedly I had torn ligaments. He recommended soaking in epsom salts and told me to stay off my feet for several days.

Evvy Wilkes reported that Nhora, still badly shaken but in control of herself, had returned to the train, where she felt she would be most useful. Hackaliah drove me back to the superintendent's home. I borrowed a fresh tailored uniform from my old French instructor, Col. Ben Giles, which fit me almost perfectly; it was only a trifle snug across the shoulders. Then Hackaliah accompanied me to the Stonewall Jackson Hotel, where the bride's wedding party was staying.

I sought to express my sorrow to Corrie Billings's immediate family. I don't know what reaction I expected; I think I would have been relieved if they had spit on me. But for the most part they were subdued and as bewildered as I. Clipper's homicidal behavior they described as an "accident." Apparently not one of them had a clear picture of the tragedy. Corrie's father, for the most part quite lucid, could recall nothing of events subsequent to his arrival at the chapel. He rolled an empty shot glass between his hands the entire time I was there, and on several occasions referred to me as "commander." I don't know who he thought I was.

Memory is capricious at the best of times; the panic in which they participated had forced reality into grotesque images best encountered in the safety of our dreams. But to Clipper and me, Boss had always stressed the "quality of our observation." If we were going to be good soldiers, he said

~~~~~~

Returned to General Bucknam's at a quarter to six. Reporters had gathered in front of, indeed they blocked access to, the gate. Their behavior was outrageous. Unfortunate that the house is located outside the post, on a public street. We went in a back way so as not to be photographed. I refused supper. It was now 4 A.M. Almost dawn. Birds are singing. I have half-finched finished a second bottle of whiskey which Hackaliah brought to the room two hours ago. But my hand is steady I am cold staring

~~~~~~

Monday, May 25
6:30 A.M.

We would all do the perfect thing with an angel's indifference, but the primitive animal within each and every one of us demands appeasement for the shocks it is forced to bear, a total sacrifice of dignity, common sense and honor. And so it happened that I took my father's wife to bed little more than a day after his passing.

Sunday noon I awoke standing in the bathtub pissing myself sick from a minus blood potassium. A meal of dried apples is a slow but certain cure for the worst hangover, so by five o'clock I was in a condition that permitted me to attend special services with Nhora at the Episcopal church. Nhora was still experiencing occasional abdominal pain, but the doctor now thought it was a
48

characteristic case of *Mittelschmerz*, or pain of ovulation, which she had suffered as a young girl. Nancy had come around in the hospital but was still too debilitated to leave her bed. Nhora and I managed a visit for a few minutes despite the ever-increasing annoyance of the reporters and photographers who had flocked to Gaston to cover a story that was claiming equal attention with the war news on the front pages of America's newspapers. I didn't know what was being written, and I didn't want to know. I couldn't bear to think about Clipper at all.

We also saw newsreel cameras grinding away as we were driven through a gentle rain from church to hospital and back to General Bucknam's house. Because the train and most of our wedding party had departed for Arkansas while I slept off the effects of my incredible consumption of sour mash whiskey, the press had concentrated its attention on Nhora and me. Everett John Wilkes thought it advisable to speak for us, and so he drafted brief statements which I approved.

But I knew the press would not be satisfied so easily. It was a story of sensational proportions, of lunacy and bloodshed even as sacred vows were recited, and no one yet had explained the mysterious tolling of the chapel bell. The clapper, we knew, was worn but intact. The bell rope had been removed some years ago to prevent mischief. Thus the bell would have had to have been manipulated by hand, by someone in the tower. Someone with the grotesque strength of a Quasimodo, which of course was nonsense. That left the supernatural hand of God— or the devil, considering the results. More nonsense.

It was Evvy Wilkes who proposed a sensible answer as we sat picking at a modest candlelit supper while the rain continued and the reporters huddled doggedly beneath black umbrellas outside the house. Something strange, perhaps unique, had occurred in the atmosphere, a freak of nature caused by colliding air masses—thermal air from the burning Blue Ridge, colder air sliding past us from the North. The collision produced an extremely localized tempest, like a stationary tornado, that whipped the giant bell back and forth while scarcely disturbing the

49

leaves on the trees around the church. And, because this tempest was occurring some fifty feet above the ground, it did not attract the attention of the many chauffeurs and servants loafing along the Parade.

"But there was no sound," I said.

"Because the clapper was muffled, years ago. General Bucknam can't recall, but they probably wrapped the clapper in burlap or something to retard rust. Once the bell tolled a few times the rotten burlap just fell away. That's why you finally heard it toll when the tower started to go and the bell tipped. Look hard enough and you'll find some rusted old sack wrappings up there on the floor of the bell tower. *You* might. I wouldn't go poking around with that tower ready to collapse."

"I just don't believe it," Nhora said quietly.

Evvy had a grin that came and went, often at inappropriate moments, like an affliction of mirth. "Stones and hoptoads and ice cubes have rained down from a clear sky. A little bitty bit of a meteorite, traveling who knows how many billion miles through space, hit a house in Bogalusa, Louisiana, and burned up a fat woman in her bed. So I have heard from my granddaddy, who collected such curiosities."

Nhora drew breath censoriously and it was then I knew, watching the downcast almond eye in the candled side of her face, that she didn't much like Everett John Wilkes. "What causes little boys to die screaming, when there's nothing wrong that anyone can see?" Plainly she was still brooding about the naked ten-year-old boy in the grimy bedsheet who had died before the doctor could be of any use to him, body warped in a back-breaking curve, lips pulled taut in a cur's grimace, coughing blood from his herniated throat.

Evvy shook his head politely. "I wouldn't know, Miss Nhora," he said, his politeness thereby made insulting. but perhaps playfully so, as he invoked an image of old-fashioned darkie servitude. She was, after all, Boss's widow, an inheritor, although ownership of Dasharoons and other businesses had passed on to me.

Nhora drank from her wineglass and turned somberly

to me. "I went to visit the boy's parents this morning, to tell them how sorry I was. Jimmy. His name was Jimmy. And do you remember the other boy, the older brother? That's Custis. We took a long walk together, up along the ridge where it happened—the back side of Railroad Ridge. Saturday Custis was doing some plowing in the field that lies below the ridge on the other side of a little creek. He saw Jimmy before he heard him. When he got to Jimmy, he said, Jimmy was nearly hysterical, but not yet in such terrible pain that he couldn't speak. Jimmy tried to explain. He'd been up there picking wildflowers for his mother, who is bedfast, when something on top of the ridge came out of the woods at him."

"An animal?"

"No. Nothing animal or human. Just light, a brilliant ball of green light, and a wind. The wind was so powerful that it tore off all his clothes and blew him a dozen feet from where he'd been standing. Custis found a few pieces of overall, some brass snaps. Nothing but rags."

"Probably he sampled some mushrooms that gave him such a burning bellyache he thought—"

"No, Sshamp, listen! Custis showed me the place where Jimmy liked to pick flowers for his mother. Everything is dead there, in an area nearly fifty feet across. Dead, ashen, leaves stripped from the trees, bushes withered and shrunken, the grass brown—not spring there but autumn, after cold comes, the killing frost."

"Not unusual to find a small area like that inside a healthy stand of trees," Evvy pointed out. "Lightning does it."

"But lightning causes burns, it blackens where it hits, even the skin of someone struck by lightning will turn black. Jimmy wasn't marked. I believe he was telling the truth about what happened to him. And it was nearly the same time as the wedding—"

Nhora shifted her gaze and bared her teeth, dropping the wineglass. She uttered a yowl that unnerved me. Evvy and I looked at the French doors that opened onto a small terrace. A tall man stood just outside the doors staring boldly in at us. He was wearing a slicker and a

51

dark slouch hat that dripped rain. There was enough light from the glow of candles within to illuminate his deep eyes, cruel but intelligent. He looked at Nhora and looked at me with a crooked smile that ran up one side of his face like an emblem of self-torture.

When Evvy Wilkes's chair crashed backward to the floor, the intruder faded away. I got up more slowly. Evvy reached the doors in a couple of bounds and threw them open as General Bucknam came running from another part of the house. Both men went out into the rain. We heard voices and saw flashlights. Nhora sat very still, white in the face. I put a comforting hand on her arm.

"Just a yokel, I think. A curiosity seeker. Don't worry."

"But he looked as if—"

"What?"

"Sshamp. I know I've seen him before."

"Where?"

"Home. At Dasharoons. Yes. That's where. Just a glimpse."

"Then how can you be so sure?"

"How could I forget that smile?" she said dispiritedly. She looked at the mess on the tablecloth, which a maid was sponging up. "What a disgrace. My nerves—"

"Anyone would have been frightened."

Evvy came back inside with the general. "Damn," he said. "Nothing. I thought maybe it was one of the reporters, but—"

"How could any man have slipped past the sentries?" I asked the general. Cadets from the institute had been posted outside to prevent just this sort of intrusion.

Erie Jack didn't know. He apologized to Nhora. We all chatted for a few minutes longer about the indignities that thoughtless and ghoulish persons seemed intent on visiting upon us, then Nhora excused herself and went upstairs. I followed not long after with a stack of messages, for the most part telegrams of sympathy from some of our venerable national treasures, all of whom had known Boss well. There was an especially poignant note from FDR, hand-delivered. Boss had had a grudging admiration for the

52

president, though in the early days of the New Deal he was fond of describing Roosevelt as "an enema of the people."

I soon found myself unable to concentrate and drifted into a reverie of home that hurt like puppy love. Quail hunting in rimed pastures at dawn, the three of us, gun-bearers, a dog handler or two, setters like barking silk, a weeping density of woods along the St. Francis River: the throat-catching spell of guns.

Boss, not much of a shooter anymore because of his eyesight, was an extraordinary companion—wise man, lit-terateur, cutup and rogue. He was superstitious rather than religious, revering all saints, ancestors of proven worth and gods of the past. He respected shrines, graven images and the power of the crystal ball. Why take chances? Boss said. He was a visionary; a pragmatist; a skeptic ("There are no great men. There are sometimes good men who play over their heads"). He liked loving, and loved war. Through no fault of his own he had missed the Great War, which only intensified his desire to be a hero to himself. He was forced to settle for much less, investing his hopes in his three sons, two of whom had betrayed him. One son had withdrawn his love; an-other, twenty years later, had killed Boss with a swifter stroke. And I—

Nhora startled me by appearing in my doorway, and sudden moves made my head throb unmercifully.

"I'm sorry; I knocked twice. I had to see you tonight."

I said she was welcome. Nhora was barefoot again, but she wore an elegant long robe of green Chinese silk with a tunic collar. There were spots of feverish color on her high cheekbones, but the green next to her face gave her a rather poor complexion. Nhora had brought a pot of coffee with her, and I was grateful for that if not entirely delighted by her presence.

As I sipped the coffee which she poured for me I was surprised to hear the pendulum clock in my sitting room strike ten; more than two hours had slipped by me unno-ticed. The house was very quiet. Outside the rain had set

53

in for the night, a blessing: It would bring an end to the forest fires along the Blue Ridge.

"We don't know each other very well," Nhora said, standing by the balcony windows, tracing an interior pattern of raindrops with one fingertip.

"No."

"I can see you look at me—one moment approving, the next comme ci, comme ça. All right. Did you think like all the rest, that I had no business marrying Boss?"

"No, because I was happy for him. You made him happy."

"And he made *me* happy. If you can believe that."

"It isn't hard to believe. Whatever men thought of him, women were—"

"Mesmerized?" Nhora smiled. She had a slightly prognathous appearance transformed by good humor, and heavier brows than I care for in a woman, but she was never without sensuous appeal. Her cat's eyes, the exact leaf-green shade of the robe she was wearing, had very large pupils; her eyes softened all the strong planes of her face. No, I wasn't starry-eyed as all that. The day after we met, we butted heads. Oh, he liked me in a rage! I was always on my toes anticipating what must come next, and wrong so often, fooled but not made a fool of. Do you know what I mean?"

"I was raised that way. You had a crash course."

"But I was never just a daughter to him. There *was* that part of it, for both of us. Why not? There was everything else besides."

She blurted those words and hid her face briefly. "I don't know where to go now," she groaned. "I don't know what to do."

I heard real terror in her voice. "You're one of us now," I said, and meant it. "Boss's death hasn't changed that."

Nhora looked around at me. "We were only married a year. I don't feel that I belong. Not at Dasharoons."

"A part of Dasharoons is yours. A one-eighth share, I think. If you remarry there'll be a reasonable cash settlement, around three hundred thousand dollars—"

Nhora shrugged, hands dropping to her sides. "But that's meaningless. Thanks to Boss I have money already. Dasharoons is yours now, and Nancy's. As it should be. I'm only trying to tell you—do you know what sort of life I've had? My father was a French civil servant with high ideals who ate his heart out in Equatorial Africa. My mother came from Boston; she was one of your high-flown romantic souls, a little bit beautiful despite her bones but bloodless as a moth, and never an ounce of purpose in her life. We drifted through exotic places, playing to each other, reading poetry aloud on lizard-infested terraces. Oh, God, can you imagine? Mother married again and again until we were cheated of everything except the small legacy my grandparents put away for me. I came of age just in time to save my sanity. I settled in Paris to study architecture; six months later the Nazis arrived. One gloomy miserable night I stepped ashore in New York from a little tramp steamer, everything I owned packed into one suitcase. Boss all but carried me off that pier—I was too terrified to take a step on my own. Bless the man! Dasharoons is the only real home I've known."

"And I need you there," I insisted. "With Nancy."

"Yes—but—what about you, Champ?"

"I'm a soldier, Nhora. All my life I've been prepared to fight a war."

"A war for Boss's sake!" she said, too shrewdly for my liking. "You don't need his approval anymore. Who's going to look after Dasharoons?"

"Our foremen have always run the plantation. We'll suffer from a loss of manpower, but Boss saw the war coming three years ago and began changing over from mules to machines. . . ."

Well, I'd made Nhora's point for her. It was foolish to deny there would be difficulties without Boss, and I knew if I requested it I could be reassigned from cavalry to a post closer to home, such as Camp Joseph T. Robinson, for the duration of the war. No one would think any the less of me, but my career as a military officer would proceed in low gear—no battlefield promotions, no quick

55

rise to the star I coveted. I had always taken comfort in the knowledge that Dasharoons would be there when I wanted it, after I'd had the opportunity to prove myself. I was not ready, as Boss had not been ready when tuberculosis ended his career, to settle down to the life of a gentleman farmer. Boss had applied his restless nature to a considerable literary engine and a capacity for political machination, eventually doing himself proud. I was less inspired to write, not his equal at gamesmanship and disinterested in forums.

Nhora was both right and wrong about my motivations. I needed war because without it I faced a predictable course: reward without struggle, a sameness of days and events to dull the heart, and—much worse—should I allow myself to concede even a part of my ambitions at this time, the slow but consuming rot that would surely proceed from a blemish of self-indulgence. And I needed war because I was convinced that in the fulfillment of battle I would understand at last what part of Boss I really was. I had to prove to myself that I was superior to the brother who had run away in shame—and the brother who, unable to sustain belief in himself and his high promise, had gone berserk on his wedding day.

I tried to explain to Nhora. She proved to be a good listener, an absorbed companion. As the clock ticked and the hour wore down to midnight she encouraged me to reminisce about life at Dasharoons, perhaps taking comfort in the fact that for 121 years, through deaths and all manner of disasters, Dasharoons had grown and prospered. It was literally a sovereign state within a state.

"Boss even fought his own war," Nhora said. "The colored uprising. What do they call it—?"

"Outside the family they call it the Chisca County War. But we've tried to put all that behind us."

"Do you remember anything about—Boss's War?"

"I was only six at the time. I remember the guns firing, the burning, the screams—it went on all night. The tragedy is that so few of our nigras were actually involved. Boss had sixty men armed and riding. Next day he took me to the field where the bodies had been laid out in rows under canvas. Forty-eight dead. Their women were everywhere, weeping, trailing behind cotton wagons loaded with bodies and creaking along the road from Chisca Ridge. It was a pitiful sight, the sore remains of a pointless rebellion."

"Not a rebellion—they weren't slaves."

"Whatever you want to call it."

"And that was the day Beau left Dasharoons."

"After smashing Boss full in the mouth with a rifle butt. You've seen the scars."

"Yes," she said, looking faint. She went to the bathroom for a glass of water. Rain hit the window glass in salvos. Nhora came back and sat on the carpet near my chair, legs tucked beneath her. There was a side slit in the robe through which a good part of her left leg was revealed. Nhora casually masked this openness by the positioning of her arm.

"Would you like some water?" she asked.

I was still dehydrated from the whiskey of the night before. I took the glass from her. The rim tasted faintly of her lips, a natural sort of sweetness. The clock ticked. Tired but unwilling to separate, we stared at each other, gravely curious.

"Do you think Beau's dead?" Nhora asked me.

"Most likely. It's been almost twenty-two years without a word or a sign."

"But Boss believed he was still alive. He said that his flesh and blood couldn't die anywhere in the world without his being aware of it."

"Beau was the firstborn. The favorite. After he left, no one in the family was allowed to mention his name, much less talk about him, in or out of Boss's hearing. I'm surprised Boss told you—"

"He trusted me," Nhora said, a bit harshly. "He would have told me everything about Beau, when the time was right."

We sat a while longer, ignoring time, which collected us regardless, mote by mote. The dead were all collected. Only the meaning of their deaths was missing.

"What was Clipper like when you saw him last?" I asked Nhora.

"At the rehearsal dinner? He was——tense, rather tired, I'd say, overextending himself to be hearty. He seemed to wish he were somewhere else. I think he and Corrie had a cloakroom spat, but it didn't amount to much."

"Less than twenty-four hours later he killed her."

"Champ, it was obvious how much he loved Corrie!"

"It's how he did it that troubles me most. All along I've believed that Clipper just ran amok. But he was much too deliberate in murdering Corrie. With his saber he might have dismembered half a dozen of his attendants. He did cripple one boy who was interfering, but another he struck with the flat of his saber to get him out of the way. Yes, because he intended to kill only certain people. Mad as he was, there was a plan behind it——"

"Dear God, you can't be serious!"

"Nhora, he went directly for Boss, and Nancy. Nancy surely would have died if I hadn't pushed her aside. Here's something else I don't understand: Twice Clipper had the advantage, either time he could have killed me with a stroke. But he acted as if he didn't recognize me. And of course everyone, including Clipper, believed I wouldn't be there in time for the wedding."

"What are you getting at?"

"The second time I was flat on my back on the altar, half-blind from the dust of the plaster that had fallen. The point of his saber was against my collarbone. 'Not you,' Clipper said. 'Not here.' I took him literally, thinking there was some lunatic reason why he didn't want to spill my blood on the altar. The truth is, as far as Clipper was concerned *I wasn't there at all*. I wasn't an entry in his—— bloody cotillion program."

"But——then——it sounds almost as if he were drugged."

"Or in a psychotic seizure similar to hypnotism. Obviously Clipper intended to destroy every member of the family within his ken. If you'd been in your place beside Boss and Nancy——Sheer luck we weren't *all* lined up in that pew waiting for him to come down on us like an angel of death."

58

"*Why?*"

"There's no way we'll ever learn the answer to that."

"I'm not so sure. Did he keep a diary?"

"I don't know. Boss encouraged him to."

"All of Clipper's things are in a bedroom on the third floor," Nhora said.

The small guest room under the eaves was chilly. There was firewood in a brass chest on the hearth. Nhora helped to get a fire going. The sound of rain was loud on the roof. We searched Clipper's belongings for the diary we presumed would be there. I felt sickened by this violation of my brother's privacy, though it couldn't matter anymore. But it was late and I was more frightened than I could say of emanations, the unexplained. I was obscurely conscious of Clipper's haunting displeasure in the room. Despite the fire, Nhora's teeth chattered intermittently, and her hands when I touched them in the course of our search seemed clammy. She tried to smile and hunched her shoulders. I put an arm around her and we paused, not speaking, to catch our breath and take heart.

And we found a diary, under lock and key in a strong-box.

Nhora sat beside me on the bed as I turned pages, each beautifully calligraphic. Clipper's diary was detailed and intensely personal, but in a totally unexpected, shocking way. There was little in these pages of his achievements at school, no thoughts that revealed how he felt about the direction his life was taking. He seldom mentioned Boss, or Dasharoons. Hunting, riding, football were ignored. What he had chosen to write about were his sexual adventures. It was difficult to believe he could have been so active in the two years the diary covered, with such a variety of young girls—ranging from one whom I knew to be just fourteen years old, to mature, for the most part married, women.

As soon as I realized what I would be reading over and over, I tried to close the diary. But Nhora stopped me.

"No," she said. "Keep reading. All of it. Don't you see how important it is?"

I didn't see, but we continued to read together. He

59

spelled the Latin words badly, but most of it was couched in readily understandable English. I couldn't keep track of all his conquests. The girls Clipper's age or younger were named and described with scatological relish. They were from all parts of the country: poor black girls from Dasharoons, socialites from Sweetbriar. From some of his accounts it was plain that girls who had resisted him were raped. The compliant ones, those who appeared many times in his feverish chronicle, had been subjected to gross indignities which Clipper apparently believed they enjoyed.

"This is ninety percent fantasy," I said.

Nhora looked queerly at me. "I don't think so. Let's finish it."

"Girls who are not feebleminded could never allow themselves to be smeared with—"

"It happens, though. Shhh."

After a while I couldn't choke down any more of Clipper's filth and sat gazing at the fire. Nhora calmly took the book from me and continued to turn the pages, mild as a nun at vespers, until she was done. Then she got up to move around the room, sighing, the diary in her hand.

"Throw it on the logs," I said.

"Not yet. The last entry was just four nights ago. Corrie Billings's older sister, Angela."

Clipper had always been precocious. At the age of ten he'd come to me in a high state of excitement and described at length spying on Boss while Boss enjoyed one of the more comely colored women at Dasharoons. "Flopping crazy on her back like a big frog when a dog plays with it," Clipper said with lubricious enthusiasm. So he'd been very much like Boss in one respect, which I pointed out to Nhora.

"No, Sshamp," Nhora said. "Boss loved, he truly cared about, women. Clipper hated them. That's plain from what he wrote. It wasn't the sex he craved, it was their pain and humiliation."

"What does this prove about Clipper? How does it make him a murderer?"

"It doesn't. But there *was* a side to him none of us suspected. Sexually he was perverse, driven. A slave of his particular demon. There's a notable omission in his diary."

"You mean Corrie?"

"Not a single word about Corrie."

"All of the older women were identified by a code letter. He may have done the same for Corrie, because of some, uh, as you suggest, perverse form of gallantry."

"I doubt that he ever did more than kiss Corrie goodnight," Nhora said thoughtfully. "Poor Corrie. No way for her to know just what she'd fallen in love with. Fooled like the rest of us—she was doomed any way you look at it. Oh, and if you were wondering, I'm not in Clipper's diary."

"I didn't think you were," I said, flushing.

"He never so much as looked at me the wrong way."

"We still don't know any more than we knew before. About why he killed." I lay back on the bed, lightheaded, my heartbeat erratic.

"I could make some tea," Nhora said. She was near the hearth. She stooped and threw the opened diary into the flames. Gratefully I closed my eyes.

I must have gone to sleep almost immediately. But I kept rising and falling, as if levitated, from the depths of unconsciousness to a fevered half-awareness of wind, rain, fire and shadow. Awareness of Nhora, coming and going, and watchful beside the bed. Once she had me drink the tea she'd prepared. It was scented lightly with hibiscus, spoiled by a bitter aftertaste.

"Why don't you close your eyes?" Nhora said, a sheltering hand on my forehead. "You're afraid, aren't you? Don't be afraid, Sshamp. I'll take care of you. Close your eyes. Sleep."

But I wasn't comfortable in this room. Instead of sleeping, I dwindled. The ceiling banged up and down like the lid of a box played with by a bored or angry child. Magic threatened. Nhora yawned, revealing perfect back teeth and a moist pink palate. I shuddered. She was too big, and I was too small. Her tongue curled lazily, touched the roof of her mouth. Then, with the yawn fading, Nhora's

61

stealthy, opened eyes caught a gleam of firelight. The green of her eyes slicked to idol gold, dazzling and iridescent. The libidinous diary of my brother smoked in chunks, occasionally flaring as air reached the thickly layered pages.

Nhora stroked me, raising gooseflesh. I dreamed phantasmagorically.

The fire swarmed and was animated. Clipper and his playmate-victims came whooping from the flames that consumed his diary. Antic, nubile, not many of them past childhood, they tricked and flashed like ravenous eels in acts of copulation. I was shamefully aroused by their orgiastic cries.

Other monsters appeared: black men, their bodies calcimined, puckered with meaty bulletholes. They chanted in African tongues. Boss wore Nhora's head like a stopper on his bloodstained shoulders, her pinpoint eyes now hooded, rimmed a dreadful black. Her hair was twisted in strong coils around the still sinewy but aged body of my father; I heard the crunch snap buckle of bones. The demons of the hearth chased Corrie from the flames. She watched, in a brown study, eyes intolerably broken, Clipper's tupping gallop between her knees. I cried out for relief for all of us.

"But nothing's there," Nhora said, bending over me, the green silk robe peeling dryly from her body. She had a smaller bust than I'd imagined, demurely teated.

"Look," she said. Just for a moment there were two of Nhora, one kissing me with a flickering tongue, the other a mirror image standing before the hearth, where the fire had gone to char and ashes, this Nhora undraped to the waist like a marble goddess, looking pensively over one shoulder at our intimate alliance.

My trousers had been opened and my blouse was unbuttoned. Nhora was delicately astride for all her size, somewhat finicky and hesitant about my vigorous protrusion, prigging testily, recoiling, then with a wisp of breath going down and relaxed as if into a soapy bath, saying, "I'll be careful; won't hurt you," as she mistook my own sharp intake of breath for an expression of pain. Instead I was light-headed with desire.

In the palm of my hand I weighed the suspenseful fullness of one breast and then the other. I said, "I thought you were having—"

"It stopped. Don't worry, let me make love to you. Lie back, don't do anything. I'll do it for us."

So I dreamed again but not dementedly, this time from the center of my groin, the pleasure being deep and all the more enjoyed for its casual wickedness. Nhora swayed in the tree house of my manly trunk, eyes like caged deathbirds brightly tuning, her hair let down to drape my thighs, navel coming unraveled as it gave suck, viny limbs arustle and wrapping me to the bed. Cunning nails traced all the long bones, studied the smoky running of my veins, hands cold but neat oval nails colder still and whitening out in my brain like fish gleam in heavy ice, like stopped comets. Splitting then at her demand, first with difficulty like a virgin rosebud then a ripe splashed apricot yielding up all fruit, blood, plasm, marrow to fill the dark and quiver everywhere around us, a dense cold cloud in which our collective breath burned like radium.

Long afterward, stretched full length in a drowse upon me, her breasts flattened on mine, she licked my ears. It felt strange, and tickled. But I liked it. I liked whatever Nhora wanted to do to me.

"Now," she said, laughing, "you'll hear the thoughts of animals. Like Melampus of the legends, you'll always understand their language."

I kissed her humid lips. "Do you?"

"Sometimes," Nhora said, and sighed. Her beating heart made a warm spot on my chest, but the rest of me was moldering cold.

When she slept for a while I returned to my rooms and took a hot bath, hot as I could stand it. But the chill returned as soon as I was dry. I had so little vitality I could barely move about. A shot of whiskey helped, but I think I may never be warm again. Nor in a state of grace. My mind turns to images of sere landscapes, ice-burdened seas. Only Nhora'a heart has warmth. Only her passion matters to me.

She has come naked into the sitting room, a hairbrush in one hand. She smiles faintly without looking at me. She goes to my bed and sits where I may see her through the door, just by lifting my eyes.

Nhora brushes her hair, hazing it down over her breasts.

Her lovely bosom bobs and weaves.

In a moment she will be finished, and wanting me.

And I'll go.

II

HAWKSPURN MARSHES

Yorkshire, England
June 16, 1942

The ancient estate of Hawkspurn, three miles south of Nuncheap village and on a hill overlooking the placid marshlands, boasts an extensive Georgian house with a façade of magnesian limestone, maintained gleaming white by the action of rain and scouring winds from the not-too-distant North Sea. There is a domed roof considered to have architectural significance, and a well-stocked library 100 feet in length on the ground floor. A portion of the estate is lease-farmed, crossed and recrossed by luxurious blackberry and lingonberry hedgerows, some of which are fishnetted during summer to discourage birds from stripping them clean—the 680-acre marsh contains one of England's first bird sanctuaries.

A spring-fed race divides the estate (the spring water has long been valued for its supposed medicinal properties). There is a gristmill down where the race widens and yields its tumbled clarity to the dankly green River Ouse; a ruined friary dating from the fourteenth century; and an ornamental park half-heartedly kept up by the Fullerite Medical Missionary Society, which inherited the estate and uses it as the final home of those honorable men and women gone to seed, some prematurely, after long service in the grueling heat of Africa.

On the morning the bomb exploded in the park at Hawkspurn, killing one old man instantly and causing great fear in the neighborhood—particularly among children boarding at the farm next door who recently had been evacuated from hard-hit sections of London and Manchester—there were a total of eight retired Fullerites and a staff of fourteen, mostly middle-aged women, in residence.

A call was made to the local Civil Defense office shortly before 11 A.M. In turn the Bomb Disposal Unit at Driffield Aerodrome was alerted, and within the hour the BD lorry arrived.

Lieutenant Ronad Kellow, R.E., soon discovered that something unique had transpired. A flash sufficiently brilliant to have been observed for at least a quarter-mile on a gorgeously clear day was not the result of any bomb or parachute mine the experts were familiar with. There was no crater, which signified a rare explosion above ground level, ruling out the possibility that a buried UXB had gone off. Also, no report of an unexploded bomb had ever come from the Hawkspurn area. An explosion above the ground was certainly feasible, but this close to Hawkspurn House any type of explosion involving more than a minimum burster charge would have created a shock wave strong enough to pulverize every window in the place. No one who was in the house at the time reported feeling the slightest bump. Only a couple of panes showed cracks, which examination proved had been there for many weeks.

Testimony of several children who were bathing in a pond 200 yards from the park was, at best, confusing. All had been aware of the pale green flash, and two children facing the park when it occurred suffered painful but superficial corneal burns. It was as if they had tried to stare down the sun. Two children maintained there had been a terrific bang and roar, of the sort they were accustomed to hearing at home. The others vehemently challenged this observation, but said they had noticed a brief, hurricanelike wind.

Lance Sergeant McDougal's sensitive nose detected no odor of TNT lingering anywhere in the park. No shrapnel damage was visible, yet trees, shrubs, the grass itself had been withered and bleached in a circle nearly fifty feet in diameter. And there *was* a victim, the poor man reportedly disfigured, all clothing ripped away by the force of whatever it was.

Lieutenant Kellow didn't know, he only feared there might be more of them around: some novelty Jerry's armorers had concocted, "sapper funnies" the BD lads called them, although there was nothing at all amusing about the devastation caused by the pie-shaped butterfly bombs painted a bright yellow to attract curious children, nor the big ones that rained down and dug in but didn't go bang until some luckless soul set off a trembler switch or a sapper ran afoul of a new type of antihandling fuse.

After making a report to his group captain by telephone, Lieutenant Kellow sealed off Hawkspurn estate and began to conduct a thorough search for examples of small but deadly ordnance—a long-range shell, perhaps—loosed from German planes operating over the North Sea beyond the scan of coastal radar.

In the early afternoon, help arrived—in style: Kellow looked up from a hedgerow he was investigating to see a chauffeur-driven Rolls-Royce Phantom III Sedanca de Ville bearing slowly down on him. His first angry impulse was to order it out of the area; then he noticed the distinctive red mudguards and the blue filter over the near sidelight and guessed correctly that a legend had appeared.

Sir John de Roke Massengill, 14th earl of Luxton, 10th earl of Sattersfield, M.P., a fellow of the Royal Society, was a youngish man of fifty who had voluntarily attached himself to the Department of Scientific Research and had a number of men from the Bomb Disposal Experimental Unit under him. He'd made it his business to investigate the unusual, and he specialized in defusing unexploded bombs under the most urgent and perilous conditions, including, recently, one that had landed within the confines of the National Physical Laboratories, threatening a number of top-secret research projects. The hands of a safecracker, extraordinary patience and intuition and, of course, pure good fortune through the grace of God Almighty had saved him from being atomized on a number of occasions. In an emergency he'd once put a delayed-action fuse out of commission by firing a pistol bullet through the fusehead. Nervy, that.

Lord Luxton didn't appear the least daring: His features were regular enough, but he had vague eyebrows and a pale pencil mustache; a pained, shy smile diverted attention from his eyes, which were intelligent and softly curious. They'd said his lordship despised protocol in the field, but Lieutenant Kellow stood at attention until Lord Luxton was forced to salute. It seemed to embarrass him.

"I'd heard you were in Cardiff, my lord."

"I motored to Ripon yesterday to read a paper at the Engineering School. Word came down about your funny; thought I'd have a look."

"Delighted, my lord." Kellow gestured toward the house and grounds. "But I haven't come up with a thing." He had to make an effort not to stare at Lord Luxton's hands, which were oddly without nails, the end of each finger blunt and pink as a cow's muzzle, of no use for labor. His lordship had the habit of carrying his hands protectively against his body, snuggled beneath the breastbone, as if they'd just been born. They did look exquisitely sensitive, which may have accounted for his success in handling intricate detonating mechanisms.

Luxton looked with interest at the great white house as they descended into the park. On the veranda a man in a wheelchair was placed in the sun by a nurse who wore a severly ecclesiastical pale-blue-and-black uniform.

"Fullerites, aren't they?"

"Yes, my lord. A vanishing sect, but still active among the heathen. They're well endoved with estates such as this one."

"I know. Cousin of mine left them a vast sum many years ago."

"Do stay within the flags, my lord; we haven't ruled out the possibility of something lethal in the ground hereabout."

"Sorry."

Luxton took his time within the devastated circle, fingering leaves and studying browned blades of grass. He stared at the clear blue sky, then summoned Kellow.

"Where was the body found, Mr. Kellow?"

Kellow pointed to an oak tree with a branched trunk

that stood thirty feet away. "Wedged nearly upside down in the crotch of the great oak. All clothing blown away, some bits of it embedded in the flesh. The shoulders and arms were partly flayed, undoubtedly from being driven with such force halfway through the tree."

"Is there a reliable description of what the blast, or flash, looked like?"

"One of the children survived a parachute mine that went off not far from her home in Manchester. She said our blast was similar to that of the mine, but without the terrible growling, the concussion waves and pressure on the eardrums."

Lord Luxton nodded. "A large ball of shimmering light, with, perhaps, concentric rings of color—lavender shading to green—at the heart of the fireball."

"Why, yes, almost word for word. How did you—"

"I've survived a magnetic mine blast myself. But this, obviously, was not a mine. Nor could it have been a bomb filled with flash compound for night aerial photography. Either one would have left at least a trace of its substance behind. Therefore we have something entirely new, an experimental weapon fearsome beyond belief, or else all this"—he swept a hand around the withered circle—"resulted from a spontaneous and perverse act of nature."

"A bolt from the blue?" Kellow said incredulously.

Instead of replying, Lord Luxton walked slowly to the oak tree, after a while venturing to touch the trunk carefully, as if it were a bomb casing.

"Who was the victim?"

"A Dr. Eustace Holley," Kellow said, consulting his notebook.

"No one else in the park at the time? That *is* fortunate."

"Many of the in—the residents, my lord, are too unreliable to be left on their own out of doors."

His lordship looked around. "Inmates? Is that what you were about to say?"

"They're not referred to as such by staff, but some of them are—apparently they often went mad in the bush.

71

The attrition rate, even among our colonial officials in the more hospitable coastal regions of tropical Africa, is quite high."

"Yes, isn't it. Perhaps I should have a look at the body. Would it be inside?"

To Kellow's surprise, their request to view the remains encountered resistance, even resentment. No one seemed to have time for them. There was a great deal of muted but urgent scurrying about in the dim halls, cries and whimpers from befuddled, apprehensive residents. The gentlemen from Bomb Disposal were allowed to cool their heels for an unconscionably long time in the outer office of the administrator. When Kellow began to be vocal about the delay and threatened action in the name of the minister of home security. Lord Luxton smiled more painfully than usual and excused himself.

In the ground-floor hall he encountered two workmen carrying buckets of calcimine and brushes to the stairs.

"Can't scrub it off," one of them complained. "Charcoal on these old walls? It's there for eternity."

"Waste of time painting it over," said the other. "A new course of stucco, that's what's needed."

"Old duffer, scribbling on his walls. Not like him, Thomas. He was always the tidiest one of the lot. Picked up after himself. Never careless about where he moved his bowels."

"Have they decided it was a bomb did him in?"

"What else could have done? There's just no place that's safe anymore, Georgie. Next thing you know we'll be having one through the roof."

Lord Luxton watched the workmen up the oak staircase, then on impulse followed them to a second-floor chamber with a small brick hearth. The room had been fitted out with bookshelves, a comfortable Morris chair and reading lamp, a prie-dieu at the foot of the iron bedstead. Chessmen stood in rows on an octagonal game table. The private library consisted of classics in at least three languages. There were bland Currier and Ives prints on three walls. The unpolished parquetry was overlaid with rag rugs of the type displayed at rural fairs. It seemed almost a typical institutional common room, lacking keepsakes, the flavor or reflections of one man's personality.

Except for one odd thing: An invocation (perhaps) had been starkly scrawled on the wall at the head of the bed, apparently with a piece of wood char from the hearth.

> LADY
> IN THY SERPENT
> PRISON-HOUSE
> SOME PITY SHOW

Luxton noticed iron brackets in the wall, where something had hung for a long time. A large cross? The yellowed calcimine within the brackets confirmed this.

"Who has this room?" Luxton asked.

The workmen turned in surprise. "Shouldn't be up here, guv'nor," Georgie said.

"May I know whose room?" his lordship repeated pleasantly.

"The one that was blowed to smithereens in the park this morning." Thomas said. "Holley. Dr. Holley."

"When did he write that on the wall?"

"Begging your pardon, guv'nor, we're not allowed to natter about the residents. Regulations is strict here."

"Quite all right. Actually I was looking for the loo."

"Right, sir. Just down the hall to your left."

He was washing up when he glanced through the partly opened loo window and saw below a keg of a woman with a black bag trudging across green lawns to her car. His lordship opened the window wider and leaned out.

"Doctor, may I have a word with you? I'll just be a moment."

The doctor's name was Mary Burgess. She maintained her surgery in Nuncheap, and for more than twenty years she'd looked after the health of the residents of Hawkspurn House. She had a rather grizzled, mole-infested face and black eyes like moles that moved. She held her head erect and thrust slightly forward as if she dared

73

anyone to find her homely. Plenty of pepper in her manner, too, but her mouth couldn't hold a firm line for long, and her hands trembled when Lord Luxton respectfully begged a few moments with the late Dr. Holley.

"He's in pitiable condition."

"I'm afraid I must insist," he said.

"Might I ask why, my lord?"

"The condition of the body could be informative. We have virtually nothing else to go on."

"What do you suspect?" the woman said, with the slowest-curdling smile his lordship had ever seen. Still, her hands would not stop trembling. "Some sort of secret weapon? I understand there've been bombs seen entering the ground and burrowing along beneath roadways, humping and bumping the surface as they move toward their targets."

"Of course you don't subscribe to such public fantasies."

"I *never* fantasize. And my common sense tells me you've nothing to gain by poking about Hawkspurn estate. What exploded in the park this morning was a single, stray bomb—"

"Which happened to kill a gentleman of whom you were very fond."

"He suffered enough in his life. The least I can do is spare him the indignity of strangers—"

"This is official business, madam," Lord Luxton said, summoning the nerve to speak with more authority. But his unconscious cuddling of the pink queer hands against his solar plexus somewhat mitigated the effect.

Her eyes were contemptuous, then sad. "If you must put it on that basis—"

"Well, yes."

"Come with me, then."

The woman led him back into the house and down to a cellar. In a rat-tight and dry storage room lit by a bare globe hung from the ceiling the shrouded body of Dr. Eustace Holley lay on a trestle table awaiting removal by morticians. Mary Burgess hesitated only a moment before stripping the sheet from the body. She stepped back, mechanically folding the sheet, her eyes fixed on a blank wall, while his lordship examined the remains.

Eustace Holley had been a gaunt man of sixty-five or so, with a hairless torso and one deformed foot, perhaps the result of a monstrous abscess; the scars of surgical correction were still evident. The face was intact, the eyes closed. Judging from the size of those lidded orbs, like parboiled pigeon's eggs, he'd had large, perhaps soulful eyes under a compelling overhang of brow. The furrows of the forehead were straight—an honest, diligent man—the full mustache neatly cared for. Someone, Mary Burgess most likely, had carefully recombed his hair. The upper torso was, as Kellow had mentioned, severely flayed. There was also a gaping wound in the groin area, now crusted over. The genitals were entirely missing.

His lordship swallowed hard and caught the eye of Mary Burgess.

"Would you turn him for me, doctor?"

That made her angry, but she moved the knobby long body in accordance with Lord Luxton's wishes. Except for a couple of faint old tropical ulcer scars, the skin of his back and legs was clear. His thin buttocks, however, were stippled with minor but distinct lacerations, almost like puncture marks. Four in a row on each cheek, and recently made.

"Thank you," Luxton mumbled, and he got out of there, ungraciously leaving the corpse for Mary Burgess to reshroud.

By the time she reappeared in the open air his color had returned and there was a cold pipe clenched between his teeth, upside down after the fashion of Ronald Colman in some movie or other where it had rained interminably. His lordship greatly admired Ronald Colman.

"I trust you know more now than you knew before," the doctor said coldly, intending to pass him right by.

Lord Luxton smiled disarmingly. "I'm totally baffled." He fell in step beside Mary Burgess, to her great annoyance. "What do you make of his condition? I'm referring specifically to the absence of—"

"Shrapnel wound, of course."

"Doctor, believe me, of one thing I'm entirely certain. There was no bomb in the park. Something else did him in."

"Hah," she said, dispiritedly.

"It rather looked to me as if his genitals had been pulled out by the roots."

Mary Burgess faltered as if kicked, then put her head down resolutely and continued on to her open car, a small vintage De Dion Bouton with a high transom windscreen and solid tires. Not what he'd pictured her driving; was she something of a Francophile?

"Good day, your lordship."

"I was wondering—about that time, isn't it?—perhaps tea."

"I'm much too busy for tea today. I've patients waiting and—"

Lord Luxton put a hand on the opening car door, then snatched it away before she could be further offended. But he succeeded in claiming the woman's full attention for several moments.

"Dr. Burgess, something quite odd occurred here this morning. Bizarre, I should say. If I'm not satisfied with my investigation, then there is every possibility that a more comprehensive investigation will be made, perhaps by Military Intelligence. You stand to lose a great deal of your valuable time to those gentlemen. Although I seem to be a considerable nuisance at the moment, if you'll only give me an hour or two perhaps I can spare you further inconvenience."

"What is it you'd like to know?"

"Everything about Dr. Eustace Holley. I especially want to know what possessed him to scrawl those words on the wall of his chamber, above the bed. I want to know what he meant."

"So you saw that," she said, distressed that he would go snooping around. But she couldn't sustain her indignation; her eyes clouded, and a certain elemental force seemed to leave her body.

"Yes."

76

"Then I'll tell you what I can," Mary Burgess said, her manner for once subdued.

"May I ride with you to Nuncheap? My chauffeur will follow."

"Very well."

Neither of them spoke the first mile and a half as Mary Burgess gave most of her attention to the laboring automobile, which pulled to the left and wheezed disastrously on the most minor grades. The doctor glanced several times at Lord Luxton as he fiddled with his pipe and absently patted his jacket pockets for matches, and finally she grumbled, "Smoke if you must, it doesn't bother me."

"Oh—no. I've given up tobacco. A nasty catarrh this past winter decided me. But I can't seem to wean myself from the battered old briar."

"Purely as a physician I couldn't help speculating about the condition of your fingers. Would it be hereditary?"

"It's the Massengill family affliction. Crops up every third generation, sparing neither male nor female. All that money going on and on forever, must pay for it in some wise, I reckon."

"Another man would wear gloves day and night."

"I'm long since past feeling any sense of shame about my lack of nails. Quite trivial, really, although my fingers can be easily damaged. Of course it was hell growing up, the hazing, the gratuitous cruelties, but school's out now."

After a few moments Mary Burgess completed the exchange of confidences by saying, "I was thought somewhat odd myself. Cutting open frogs to see what made them tick was not a ladylike thing to do. But I was never on an equal footing with girls my age. I couldn't interest myself in their airs and silly conceits. I began my medical training in 1904—after five years and many attempts to be enrolled."

"A singularly lonely enterprise, I should imagine."

"Yes. But I was determined to have a useful life. Whether or no anyone wanted me."

She made a turn into a crooked lane just off the High Street of Nuncheap and stopped at the second of an unjoined row of two- and three-story houses with overstepping gables that looked down on a cattailed mere. Steam was issuing from under the bonnet of the little roadster.

"Damn! It's the radiator again."

"Why don't you see to your patients, then? My chauffeur and I will have a look. Medwick is marvelous tinkering with engines."

"Thank you—my lord."

A pat of solder from the commodious repair kit which Medwick carried everywhere in the Rolls sealed the trickly radiator of Mary Burgess's car. Twenty minutes later his lordship was admitted to the parlor of the doctor's quarters on the second floor of the house by an ancient Scots housemaid who carried on an incomprehensible dialogue with herself while largely ignoring him.

The parlor had sunny windows and betrayed Mary Burgess's passion for needlepoint and illuminated manuscripts. Lord Luxton whiled away the remaining time by trying to identify vague medicinal vapors rising from the surgery: camphor, iodine, sulfur depuratum. The rose garden just below the half-opened windows was doing famously. Swans coasted on the mere. In this pleasant backwater he felt part of another century; the war that visited England almost on a daily basis was far from his mind. Then the appearance of a flock of Hampden twin-engine bombers in ragged formation on the horizon, heading inland to Driffield, brought him back to the complexities of his chosen service. Luxton, uneasy, rattled the stem of his pipe between his teeth and thought about Dr. Eustace Holley.

Mary Burgess appeared, followed by the muttering housemaid, who was pushing a cart. The doctor said, with a geniality that seemed foreign to her, "I'm afraid I have nothing more savory to offer than tinned biscuit. The shortages, you know."

"You needn't apologize."

She bustled about getting him settled. They faced each other from matching settees that bracketed the hearth. The sun was on the ceiling, turning a deep orange. Mary Burgess had scrubbed her face. It glistened like parchment despite the irritable punctuation of many moles, blobs of ink from a nib pen. Why did she tolerate them, he wondered, or were they inoperable? She'd changed her dress, from dark gray to a medium shade of blue, possibly the gayest article of clothing she owned. Her eyes had a noticeably high, nimbused shine, as if she'd resorted to something powerful as morphia to settle her nerves.

Lord Luxton wondered if her evening tonic might not be habitual, then felt bad about the inference. After all, a close friend had died today, and despite her professional detachment she must have suffered to see him so disfigured.

She had asked if he would mind the wireless, which was now distantly playing "Don't Sit Under the Apple Tree [with anyone else but me]." Luxton smiled as he sipped his tea and jiggled one foot in time to the swing rhythm of the popular song.

"You've recently received the George Cross," Mary Burgess said.

"Well, yes, as a matter of fact."

She nodded. "It was in the *Pictorial*, which a patient of mine happened to have with him today. So I couldn't help noticing, you see—there was rather a large photograph."

"Yes, yes, haven't seen the article myself."

"How long have you been at it? Poking at these unexploded bombs?"

"Two—well, should say a little longer than two years now."

She said with her granite-jawed candor, "You've overstayed then. You'll be killed."

His lordship smiled broadly. "Oh, no. I've no intention of being killed."

"Hmm. Let me make it clear how greatly I admire your courage. You've matched yourself against incalculable odds, and you'll continue, no doubt, until you're no longer needed. It's the only sort of courage that matters. Eustace was a man not unlike yourself. One of a handful of physicians pitted against the immense, hostile, soul-rotting hulk of Africa."

Luxton was grateful that the subject had changed so

abruptly. "How long were you acquainted with Dr. Holley?"

"Nearly twenty-two years."

Now *there* was a surprise. "That's how long he was in residence at Hawkspurn House?"

"Yes."

"Then he was still rather a young man when he—"

"Went mad? He was just shy of his forty-fourth year, and in his prime."

"So Dr. Holley was a lunatic," Lord Luxton said, with a doleful shaking of his head.

Unexpectedly she smiled. "I said he went mad, but he came around with proper rest and treatment. He was perfectly lucid for most of the years I knew him. He had his sinking spells and peculiarities—don't we all? But a more charming knowledgeable, sensitive man I shall never meet." Her cup rattled on the rim of her saucer; an emotion had caught her by surprise. But her voice continued without a tremor.

"It took time and patience on my part to win his confidence. There were things he could not, would not, talk about, including the practice of medicine. It was my misfortune at the time to suffer from shingles. One day while I was making a routine visit to Hawkspurn House he observed that I was in torment and insisted on making a diagnosis. I humored him. He suggested an infusion principally of chaulmoogra oil, a great rarity obtainable only from India, and gave me the name of a supplier in Switzerland. The treatment worked a miracle. From time to time thereafter when I had a patient with a condition difficult to clear up I'd mention the case to Eustace. But," she concluded, smug and pining at the same time, "he made no more recommendations."

"Obviously, though he'd recovered his faculties, he no longer cared to practice medicine."

"Eustace was lame, as you undoubtedly observed, and never very strong again physically, certainly not strong enough to withstand months in the forests of the K'buru. Nor could he support any unusual demands on his emotions."

"No family?"

"He had a son," said Mary Burgess. "When I last saw him he was still very thin from the effects of a serious head injury, complicated by malaria. That was in autumn, 1921."

"Living now?"

"Yes. Jackson writes to me twice a year to inquire after the health of his father."

"Writes? Doesn't visit?"

"That would be much too painful for him," she said, staring at Lord Luxton.

"Painful? How d'you mean?"

"All because of one of Eustace's—peculiarities. He believed his son was dead, and that he was responsible. An attempt was made to reunite them in 1921, after Jackson returned from his long sojourn *en dispensaire* in Kisantu. He was nearly eighteen years of age. But Eustace refused to see him. He kept repeating, 'My son is dead. I killed him. I did it to save us all.' Quite naturally the boy was shattered. In just over a year's time he'd lost his mother and younger sister. Now he was being obsessively rejected by his father, whom he deeply loved."

"Incredible."

"At last we arranged for Eustace to meet Jackson face-to-face—'accidentally,' as it were. We hoped the shock would restore his memory. It had no such effect: not a flicker of recognition. The matter was hopeless. Even Jackson soon realized his father was lost to him as well."

"What was the meaning of Dr. Holley's obsession?"

"It's difficult to say. Not much is known about the tragedy of Tuleborné. Jackson's own memory has always been drastically incomplete. If Eustace knew precisely what happened there, he never said a word to anyone."

"Not even to you."

"That is correct."

"And what was this—tragedy of Tuleborné? I gather it's somewhere in Africa—"

"Tuleborné, I'm told, no longer exists. And no Negro of the forest will venture within a mile of its former location. In 1909, when Eustace was posted to Africa by the Fullerites, Tuleborné was a thriving village on the upper reaches of the K'buru River system of French Equatorial Africa, just north of the equator and some two hundred miles from the sea. In addition to sawmills and timber enterprises, there were a mission station, school and hospital already in existence at Tuleborné. Dr. Holley added greatly to the hospital facilities during his stay of more than a decade in the forest. He had with him his wife and son, who was six years old at the time. Several months later Mrs. Holley went back to England to await the birth of a daughter. When this child was almost a year old, Eustace took his first and only leave of absence, and the family was reunited.

"They all returned to Tuleborné in the spring of 1912, where they remained. They seem to have been reasonably happy despite the hardships and confinement. The children were educated at the mission school. At an early age Jackson demonstrated a talent for medicine, and was of considerable value to his father as he grew older. There was nothing they wanted except to be of service. But, despite the best of motives, they were defeated in the end."

"How?"

"Nowadays the white man can live for rather long periods of time in tropical Africa. He can protect himself from the sun and the damp, from insects and animals and even the power of the primeval forest itself, which when unchecked obliterates the hardiest niche of civilization in a matter of months. But once he is confronted by superstition and its attendant evils, then he must fall back or die. What do you know about Africa, my lord?"

"Virtually nothing. Oh, I devoured Rider Haggard and Sir Richard Burton in my youth."

"Then you've read *She?*"

"Engrossed and palpitating, like any twelve-year-old boy with a lust for romantic adventure."

"Matriarchies are not unknown in primitive societies. The Great Mother of antiquity was both priest and sorcerer. As for the so-called white goddesses of popular novels and movie serials, there is some basis in fact. Haggard, who for a time was in colonial service in the Transvaal, may have heard tales of a white woman who actually ruled a tribe of warriors feared everywhere along the notorious Slave Coast. Captains of slave ships, masters of barracoons claimed to have dealt with her. The warriors were members of a secret society, such as the 'leopard men' of Dahomey and Gabon, but their ruling deities happened to be river spirits—crocodiles, hideous antediluvian shapes, reptilian figures of evil. We know, of course, that natural violence in a world ruled by fetish easily becomes savagery, and then the direst forms of cruelty—human sacrifice; anthropophagy; women and children slaughtered to provide a draft of blood.

"It's said that Gen Loussaint not only survived in a territory noted for the toll it exacts from all races, but that she became quite as powerful as Haggard's fictional Ayesha. As cruelty became her pleasure and one bloodthirsty excess led to another, she grew inhumanly alluring, a fabulous creature not only of this earth but of the dark side of the *anima mundi* in which dwell the gods she propitiated."

"Interesting. And how much of this hearsay is one to accept?"

"I have spent several years investigating. The facts are few. Gen Loussaint was the eldest daughter of the soldier-explorer Trojan Loussaint. She was born in Chartres in 1736. From her earliest years she was a gifted athlete, an adventuress, a soul unfettered by the inhibitions of her sex or the expectations of society. Physically she had a very beautiful complexion which in later years the tropic sun could not wither nor darken, auburn hair and the disturbing, somewhat baleful eyes of a bitch wolf. She possessed odd talents, such as the ability to simultaneously copy a line of poetry with both hands, the right hand producing a mirror image of what the left was writing. As a child she had profound religious experiences. She spoke in tongues. She would not eat where anyone could observe her. She was temperamentally unsuited to master the intellect of a genius. She had a terrifying sense of humor and never forgave a slight. Other children avoided

83

her company. Her father, who could deny her nothing, despairingly called her *la folle petite la plus sympathique*. Their relationship may have been an unnatural one. On the occasion of Trojan Loussaint's search for the headwaters of the K'buru in 1755 Gen accompanied him. She was disguised as a young officer and served as her father's adjutant, going by the name of Jules."

"*What?*"

"It was Gen's first taste of Africa, Trojan Loussaint's last exploration. According to a journal kept by a sublieutenant who was deliberately spared following the massacre of Ajimba Lagoon, where a full company of Loussaint's military expeditionary force was decimated by the reptilian Ajimbas, Gen, in order to be accepted into the company of those whom she soon ruled, partook of her father's flesh. That portion of him which came from the pot clinging to a thighbone, if we are to trust the lieutenant's—"

"Oh, for the love of heaven! None of this can be real."

"I believe it is," Mary Burgess said calmly. "There are numerous accounts of that ill-met expedition in the archives of the French Colonial Service. I have copies of them all, in addition to the pertinent biographical data which I quoted. The documentation required a great deal of my free time during the last decade. Until shortly before the Occupation I visited Paris regularly, all but ruining my eyesight grubbing through forgotten papers. Accounts of Gen Loussaint's reversion to the savagery of her remotest ancestors are, I believe, irrefutable. Of the remainder of her extraordinary career, little that has come to light can be verified."

"But why have you been so obsessed with—"

"Because there is one more vital fact about Gen Loussaint. She was last seen alive in the region of the Ajimba Lagoon by Dr. Eustace Holley, in August of 1920."

"Nineteen twenty? And she was born in 1736? Preposterous."

"Medically speaking. In this modern age not even those remarkable Georgian peasants who father children at the age of ninety, and who enjoy useful years well past their
84

first century of life, can expect to attain an age of one hundred and eighty-four years. What Eustace Holley found on the shores of the Ajimba was a tribal remnant presided over by a living corpse: blind, frail, garishly wigged, rouged and costumed in the fashions of the eighteenth century, able to communicate only in whispers. Nothing like the ravishing creature of legend. Nevertheless it *was* Gen Loussaint, begging the doctor to prolong her miserable life."

"How did this—remarkable meeting come about?"

"By 1920 the hospital at Tuleborné was famous; Negroes rowed the dangerous river for thirty-six, forty-eight hours at a stretch to deliver a diseased or dying relative into the healing hands of Eustace Holley. It would be difficult for you to imagine the impact his reputation had in a district where food has always been scarce and suffering endemic. I have no words to describe the horrors of *cancrum oris,* of children swollen by dropsy and men dying of strangulated hernias. He could cure such things, with medicine or the knife. He was very like a god to the Negroes. Though Gen Loussaint was two hundred miles away, in that place where the K'buru rises from the earth in a boil near the highlands of Cameroon, she had heard of the power of his medicine. She dispatched two dozen of her personal *garde indigène* to bring the doctor to her side."

"They kidnapped him?"

"Yes, and caused havoc after their fashion. They must have been a terrifying sight, as it was customary to go raiding dressed in the shimmering skins of poisonous reptiles, wearing huge lizard or crocodile masks. They perhaps should not have been so flamboyant, nor so murderous in carrying out their mission. The kidnapping excited the attention of the governor-general, who resolved to do away with the Ajimba forever. Throughout the nineteenth century French soldiers skirmished with the Ajimba, driving them from their haunts along the coast, but the military had never penetrated to their ultimate stronghold, the banks of that healthfully sulfurous lagoon where they lived in surprising luxury, attended by many slaves who farmed and built for their masters mud houses which were replicas of Roman villas.

"This time the governor-general placed in charge of the expeditionary force his *chef du cabinet militaire,* Colonel Charles Delafosse, who had under his command veterans of the infamous *Bataillon d' Afrique,* a battle-hardened disciplinary unit that rivaled the voluntary and better-known Foreign Legion. *Les Joyeux,* they were called, rather ironically. The soldiers were well equipped, carrying explosives and automatic weapons in shallow-draft patrol boats capable of penetrating the tall, knife-edged grasses of the lagoon. After Dr. Holley was rescued, airplanes were used to strafe and bomb the Ajimba villages. Virtually nothing remained, to the dismay of anthropologists intrigued by the unique and predatory Ajimba."

"And Gen Loussaint?"

"Possibly she was spirited away by her bodyguard and other survivors into one of the natural tunnels that extended for miles into the rocky highlands. All of the tunnel entrances that could be located were dynamited. Gen Loussaint was never seen again."

"You said Holley was rescued. What was his condition?"

"Colonel Delafosse's report stated that Dr. Holley was gaunt but otherwise in good health. Initially he seemed confused, perhaps drugged. He thought at most three weeks had passed since his abduction. In reality he was rescued on October twenty-ninth. He had spent nearly three months in captivity, ministering to the failing Gen Loussaint. He talked freely about her to the colonel; surprisingly, he was rather taken with that terrifying ghoul, whom he saw as just another sick, helpless old woman. But there's no doubt it was she, and not a descendant. Her memory was unimpaired by her great age; she talked at length to Eustace about her girlhood in France. Her mother dutifully had recorded young Gen's birthmarks and broken bones in various letters, and these descriptions match exactly statements regarding her appearance which Eustace made in 1920."

"So it was not because of the Ajimba, or Gen Loussaint, that he lost his wits. How did that come about?"

"Upon his return to Tuleborné, Eustace was urged to take a leave of absence. Except for brief visits downriver and a short holiday in Tenerife, he had not been away from his beloved hospital for more than eight years—fool-hardy, considering the hours he put in, the working conditions. His wife was unwell; weeks of not knowing if he was alive or dead had drained her strength. Instead of returning to England, Eustace immediately began rebuilding that part of the hospital which was damaged during the raid. Meanwhile he dealt with a full schedule of patients, this time without his two Negro assistants, who had returned to the bush during his absence. For a week or so everyone was deceived by his energy and devotion, but it was a false recrudescence; he was spending all the remaining years of his life in one reckless binge. Despite his insistence that he was treated well by the Ajimba, something profoundly disturbing had happened to him in that remote place. The appearance of the most common water snake caused him to tremble and scream in anguish. He refused to sleep at night, preferring to sit up guardedly by the light of an acetylene lamp, shivering despite the several blankets in which he wrapped himself. Waiting, as if for the devil to appear. He took strong doses of morphia, scopolamine, chloral hydrate, and bromide of potassium."

"For his nerves?"

"Those are drugs used in the treatment of mental illness. He knew he was in grave danger of losing touch with reality."

"And so he did."

"First reality lost touch with Tuleborné," Mary Burgess said dryly.

"Come again?"

"You must understand that living at Tuleborné was like living in a frontier prison. In 1920 there were no pontoon aeroplanes, no wireless for instant contact with the outside world. Lives depended on the twice-monthly visits of the paddle-wheel river steamer. The yellow river was their only highway, and they were seven hours upstream from the nearest station. The permanent population of Tuleborné numbered less than four hundred, including Negroes. The hillside settlement consisted of the Catholic school and church, hospital buildings, mission bungalows, a barracks, a sawmill and a few ramshackle commercial and government buildings along the riverbank. It was only a hundred yards from the water's edge to the dense virgin forest, and continual clearing was in progress to keep the wild undergrowth from reclaiming the settlement. The trees of the encircling forest were everywhere more than a hundred feet high, and so packed together no breeze stirred in the stifling interior. A few trails used only by Negroes penetrated this wilderness. In the dry season when the river shrank below its sandbanks there was sometimes a mild breeze blowing upstream. But Eustace had returned during the wet season, when the sky looms incandescent and tons of water pour down on the red metal roofs of the station. The river smokes and swells dangerously and the teeming life of the forest is affected; from microscopic killers to the huge wallowing hippos, nature is in a frenzy.

"It is all any man can do, no matter how well fortified by experience and faith, to cope with a wet season in the forest. But at Tuleborné, as Eustace struggled with his medical duties as well as those phantasms that plagued him day and night, it seemed as if God had inexplicably focused His wrath on their little station. The afternoon deluge was accompanied by cyclonic winds, bolts of lightning that struck with earth-shattering power. When it wasn't raining, the driver ants were out in force, and the hippos fiercely attacked almost every Negro's canoe. Even the steamer was damaged by these brutes and had to lay up at Tuleborné for repairs. Two members of the crew went raving mad that same night and killed a fellow crew member with *sjamboks*; in turn they had to be shot by local soldiers. Children at the school fell one by one into lethal comas, the cause unknown. Eustace's own daughter was affected. The steadily worsening storms uprooted trees and dashed them into mission buildings.

"A local *feticheur* appeared and spoke of a heavy judgment to be visited upon the white man. That was enough for the majority of the Negroes, who began to vanish into the forest. The hospital was emptied almost overnight. The district commissioner roused himself from his usual alcoholic daze and ordered the entire station evacuated. Eustace, for the sake of the few critical patients still in his care, refused to go, as did the Jesuit priest and the nuns of the school."

"What about the young man?" Luxton asked. "Jackson Holley. Did he remain with his father?"

"No. He desperately wanted to stay, but his sister needed constant medical attention, which he could provide, if she was to live until they reached the military hospital in Libreville. So the steamer, packed with refugees and riding very low in the water, left Tuleborné in the rain. Hours later, as they were sounding the siren for a landing at the town of Zenkitu, the steamer was battered by giant logs that came flooding into the mainstream from a tributary of the river. It quickly capsized. Nearly twenty passengers, thrown among the grinding logs, lost their lives. Jackson, clinging to his sister with one arm, thrashed his way to a sandbar. But his mother was not seen again."

"Dreadful. One can almost believe there was a curse in control of their lives."

"For myself, I am willing to believe only in the impartial hostility of nature, a tragedy of coincidence; not in supernatural direction or villainy However—soon after their rescue from the sandbar the little girl died in Jackson's arms, without opening her eyes. Jackson, though he'd contracted a fever from his immersion, sought to return at once upriver. He was convinced that his father would die too, unless he could persuade Eustace to leave the forest forever. Without a steamer available, it was very difficult to reach Tuleborné through the floods and unpredictable currents. Nevertheless he spent a few coins he had in his pocket to secure provisions and a Negro's canoe, and set off alone on the hundred-mile journey. The *chef du poste* at Zenkitu, a young lieutenant, promised to follow within a few hours. Fortunately for Jackson, he was true to his word.''

"And Jackson made it to Tuleborné?''

"Quite a feat of navigation for one his age; also consider how weakened he must have been, how near delirium. Jackson's written account of his first hours at the ruined settlement is passional, well couched but almost certainly distorted by hallucination. He stepped ashore as the last rays of the sun flashed along the river with the velocity, the heliographic violence of day's end in the tropics; night overtook him before he proceeded a dozen steps and he was utterly alone in the shooting, shaking light of his acetylene lamp. The earth at his feet was as hot and wet as a living heart, and the air cooling like a blizzard across his skin. He called and called for his father, working himself into a convulsion of fright. He was not answered; yet Jackson was sure he was being watched. He had grown up in the forest, and its peaceful moods, the *fainéance* of the beast, were a part of his skin tone, a rhyming pulse in the innermost mind. He also knew when the forest was out of sorts, in a murk of badness, sweating evil and dangerous to be near. This night he was suspicious of its carnivore odor, unnerved by howls and whispers and a stupefying hiss of intimidation that flowed leaf to leaf and curled invisibly around him.

"Trembling with fatigue, hagridden, feeling the malevolence of the forest closing on his fragile light, nonetheless he searched the village as he had to. Prosaic horrors were everywhere. He found the priest and nuns at their prayers, but dead of bloat, in a blue shimmer of transmutation. More dead, those luckless Negroes too ill to have returned to their families, were moldering in the hospital's dormitory. And then Jackson saw his father.''

Her voice, from so much talk, had become a rasp, low for his ears. Lord Luxton leaned forward on the settee, unwilling to miss a word.

"In the outermost flicker of the lamp's reach Jackson observed eyes—great brooding orbs just above the level of a sill. Unmistakably his father's eyes, though boiled down to the last pip of intelligence, of humane intent. The

90

rest of his face, fringed in frosty white, parched by grief and sickness, was unfamiliar, a total shock to the boy as he advanced the lamp. When he'd last seen his father, less than a week ago, there'd been only a few streaks of gray in the full head of hair and mustache, and his face, though grim and heartbreakingly indicative of spiritual surcease, had not sunk into such a wretched appearance.

" 'Go away!' Eustace shouted, as Jackson took another step. 'It's too late. Nothing can be done, she has me!' And with that he darted away from the unscreened window, toward the forest.

"Jackson pursued him, running with the lamp, dashing its light into the suspirating darkness, a dark of wormwood, of belladonna. The lamp, faint as a starpatch on the limitless wall of the forest, provoked new sounds, almost like laughter. Shocking laughter; it stopped the poor boy in his tracks. His father was nowhere to be seen. He felt a tug at his right-hand sleeve and whirled—but nothing was there. Sweat streamed down his face. His knees collided as he shook. And then a light appeared overhead, separated into alluring parts, beaded and twined round the thickness of a mandarin tree.

"With rapturous laughter the light crawled into a shape. Womanly, yet it was a serpent.

"Jackson had never seen such eyes: teardrop-shaped, big as angelfish, but cloacal. The beast became full-fleshed and scaly tall. He watched without a qualm as it warped, arced, turned centrally, throwing down and down its gilded coils, seeing the air with a tongue precious as a lisp—all the while drawing flat-headedly near where Jackson stood, but with the lightness of a cloud, the continued fluency of appealing laughter."

Lord Luxton nearly fell off the setee when a lamp flashed on a few feet away. Without his being aware of the passage of time it had grown rather dark in the doctor's parlor: Outside there remained a few tinder glints beneath the heavy part-raised lid of eternity; the moon, having risen through blood, was a pearly crescent twice-squared by windowpanes. The old housekeeper whickered at his show of nerves and shuffled dimly away to lower the blackout shades.

Opposite his lordship Mary Burgess sat as if she'd hypnotized herself, eyes dormant, the composed body yielding a tremor or two.

"Dr. Burgess?"

"That's all."

"I beg your—"

"Nothing more the boy could tell, except: a scuttling presence behind him, a quick shadow, a severe blow to the head as he turned. But he's never been certain. He doesn't know what he dreamed in coma, and what he truly experienced."

"He's alive today. Then some sort of rescue was affected by—"

"The young *chef du poste* from Zenkitu arrived late the following day with troops; they found Jackson in hospital, barely breathing. His trephined skull was wrapped in bandages that could have been cleaner. His father they observed limping about the settlement, scarcely clothed and in very poor condition. One foot was rotting from sores. He offered no resistance, and said not a single meaningful word."

"What do you mean, the boy's skull was trephined?"

"Surgically opened; two round pieces of skull, each about the size of a shilling, had been taken out."

"Why?"

"To make a fetish."

A bell tinkled glassily in the dark hall outside the parlor. Mary Burgess looked up.

"There's someone at the surgery," she said, distinctly uneasy. She got up and went to the front windows to look out.

She was there for a long minute. Lord Luxton waited, impatient, wondering what he was to make of the unfinished story that had so powerfully affected his imagination—of a living mythology in the primeval forest. "Womanly, yet it was a serpent." And what had Eustace Holley scrawled, possibly in an abject state of fear, on the wall of his chamber? Luxton wished he had copied

92

down the words, which had a vaguely familiar ring. LADY/IN THY SERPENT/PRISON-HOUSE/SOME PITY SHOW. That sounded right. So the good doctor had died, done in by an unknown force, obsessed by—what? His belief in a spectrum of monsters, a full bestiary that ranged from androgynes to bloodsucking Truds and the Corpse-Eaters in the *Book of the Dead*? His lordship wanted to ask—

The bell was repeated.

Mary Burgess's head jerked toward him. "I have to go. Please excuse me."

"Of course. Will you be all right?"

"Why wouldn't I be?" she said crossly. "It's only a patient. Have more tea if you like, I shan't be long."

But it seemed a lengthy wait to Luxton. He amused himself by leafing through a few of the volumes on her leather-topped writing desk: Lucian's *The True History*, Ovid's *Metamorphoses*, Charles Gould's *Mythical Monsters*, Keats and Coleridge. She had recently translated an epistle from the eleventh-century Christian reformer Bernard of Clairvaux to the Abbé Guillaume de St. Thiery, which criticized the excessive ornamentation of medieval churches, especially representations of synthetic creatures. Considering the fate of Dr. Holley, a portion of the letter was germane.

> What is the meaning of these obscene monkeys and raging lions? And of the horrid centaurs, the wild men, the blaring huntsmen? Here you see many bodies joined to one head and there many heads on one body. There a beast drags a horse dragging half a goat after it, here a horned animal is the forepart with a horse forming the hindquarters. Everywhere there is a profusion of the most varied forms, as motley as they are astonishing, so that people prefer to read in stones rather than in books and spend the whole day gaping at every detail of these oddities instead of meditating on their prayers.

Interesting, thought Luxton, as he paced the creaking

floor of the parlor. Dr. Holley had survived his ordeal, real or imagined, but obviously he'd never been restored to the twentieth century, to his trust in God and the holy order of the cosmos. Or was it presumptuous to conclude that belief in fantastic organic entities was particular to the primitive state of mind? The creative imagination was timelessly replete with monsters, some evil, some benign, but always linked to reality, the world of natural forms. The human-headed snakes, for instance, Indian demigods called Nāga. And what of the part-crocodile griffins of the Nile, plentifully depicted in ancient papyri? Were they more fantastic than those primordial creatures of wing and claw which are, by their extant bones, verifiable? The cultured and sophisticated Egyptians worshiped the fabulous, the half-human—but they also were aware and made use of such creatures as the electric fish, living batteries that could generate enough power to knock down a horse. . . .

"Good God," his lordship said aloud, visualizing a brilliant flash, a chemical-electrical pulse of, perhaps, a million-million watts occurring in a millionth of a second, creating an intense but focused shock wave, strong enough to fling a denuded old man through the narrow crotch of a tree. Luxton knew of no manufactured device that could create such power without general and widespread destruction. Then conceivably a natural source, some kind of sentient generator, could be the culprit. We are, he thought, all creatures of electrical impulse—yet how might this crude, awesome power operate within the laws of nature? Indeed. And how many human deaths were contained within a single drop of cobra venom, or an invisible colony of pneumonia bacilli?

Down below in the surgery Mary Burgess shrieked in terror.

Lord Luxton was bounced from his entertaining speculations as if from the tailgate of a wagon. Nerves afray, disoriented, nonetheless he was on the move without conscious thought. The Scots housemaid he discovered crouched at the top of the steep stairs, one hand on the railing, her small old eyes quibbling from nervousness. There was cloudy glass in the door at the foot of the stairs, behind the glass a pale inner light. He heard nothing.

"Dr. Burgess?" he called.

"Go doon," said the housemaid. She would not budge.

His lordship descended, opened the door. At the end of the ground-floor hall was an empty vestibule not much larger than a telephone call box. On his left were two doors, the first locked, the second standing open.

As he hurried down the hall to the dark waiting room of the surgery, Medwick, his chauffeur, came banging in through the vestibule door.

"Everything all right here, m'lord? I was on my way back from supper when I heard—"

"I don't know; come with me."

A thin strand of light was showing beneath the examining room door. They heard the brittle clashing of swept glass. Luxton turned on a standing lamp.

"Dr. Burgess?"

The sweeping stopped.

"Come in," she said.

Lord Luxton glanced at Medwick, who nodded and dropped into a chair to wait. His lordship let himself into the examining room, and was assaulted by the heat. For some reason Mary Burgess had started a fire of cannel coal in the old-fashioned stove. She had no other company. As she stooped to brush glass from the linoleum into a dustpan, Luxton observed that there was another way out of the examining room.

She was wearing, unbuttoned, a knee-length white coat, stethoscope in one pocket.

"What happened to your patient?" he inquired.

"My patient? Oh—" She carried the pan to a dustbin and disposed of the pieces, what was left of a medium-size glass bottle. She walked obtusely, like a convalescent, between the bulky cabinets and quaint machines of her practice, her studded face a purse of closely held afflictions. "It was Simon Temple. Bloody bump on his forehead. Too much gin, all the lads, and careless at horseshoes. Didn't amount to much. He went the back way home."

The telephone rang; Mary Burgess flinched but took the receiver from the wall.

"Oh, yes. Quite all right. . . . No, nothing. Gave myself a nasty shock, is all. Thank you for calling, constable." She rang off, her eyes closing in exasperation as she leaned against the wall. "Roused the entire village, did I? Stupid old woman."

"What caused you to scream, Mary?"

"I suppose—if one has suffered enough anxiety, one is capable of projecting with the mind's eye all manner of insults to reason. Even an image of the living dead. I merely thought I saw"—she paused for air—"something out there in the dark of the waiting room."

"Eustace Holley?"

She blinked agreement. "But I do not fantasize. Nor do I believe in ghosts. I've never screamed before. Wouldn't have thought I knew how."

"I'm sure you'll be all right now. I've put you under considerable strain, and for that I—What have we here?"

Before she could protest, Luxton reached beneath the padded table and carefully picked up a number of objects that had spilled from a small leather pouch clumsily handmade and stitched and now coming apart. There were three nineteenth-century enameled bells of the type used for Christmas decorations; some animal claws and rather long feral teeth; a few feathers; and, finally, two shilling-size pieces of what appeared to be bone. Everything was covered with a coarse red dust. The porous bone pieces were splotched with dark stains of indeterminate origin. Perhaps they were bloodstains.

"Burn it," Mary Burgess said after he had carefully gathered the lot. "Throw it all on the fire, for my sake."

"First will you tell me what I have here?"

"The components of a fetish. Supposedly the most powerful that can be made by the sorcerers of the African forest. The teeth and claws are from a black leopard. The red dirt has some sacred meaning, I don't know what."

"And the bone fragments?"

"Human. Sections of parietal bone."

"Those which Eustace Holley obtained from the skull of his own son?"

"Yes, I believe that to be so."

"And why did he do it?" Luxton said, staring at the handful of curious junk, which nevertheless had a most distressing history. "Why did he have to nearly destroy his son in order to make the fetish?"

"As I understand it, no less a sacrifice is required when one is threatened by the loss of one's immortal soul. But it was *not* Eustace Holley who performed that cannibalistic operation. It was a lunatic, a man physically and emotionally broken by the demands of his calling."

She walked to the stove and raised the lid. "Dump it all in here," she demanded, her voice high. "I say I want to be rid of it!"

Lord Luxton complied. As soon as he brushed the last clinging feather from his perspiring palm, Mary Burgess clapped the lid down tight. Then she pressed fingertips against her temples. Her bared teeth chattered.

"Perhaps a stimulant," his lordship suggested.

"No."

"I'm amazed that the boy survived such crude surgery in the wild."

"Savages of antiquity recovered from similar trephinings performed under worse conditions. His youth and an exceptional constitution saved him. More surgery was necessary. The dura mater had become seriously inflamed. If the infection had spread to the spinal cord—As it was, Jackson had drains in his head for weeks following his rescue."

"It's your contention, then, that Dr. Holley was the victim only of his overwrought imagination?"

"Worn to the quick, defenseless in his fatigue, he experienced waking nightmares. He perceived gross apparitions in the most innocent forms of nature. And when his Christian conviction, his knowledge of salvation through the perfect love of God, began to fail him, he adopted the magic of the Negroes, with which he was quite familiar. He'd had to be, in order to treat them successfully."

"Obviously he suffered another, similar breakdown quite recently. Why?"

Mary Burgess shook her head in despair. "I can't be sure. There were no significant changes of personality. In his dealings with the other Hawkspurn residents and staff he remained cordial but rather aloof, as customary. His routine was the same right until—I mean, he took his morning exercise, he had his music, chess and books. But he was dismayed by the war, the threat of invasion, although as you know in East Riding we've scarcely been touched by the raids. Even secondhand I suppose it was terrible enough for someone of his fragile emotions: the war news on the wireless, the effects of the blitz which he could observe in the faces of the poor children placed in our homes for safekeeping. 'A beast is loose,' he said once to me. 'Naught will do but that we shall be scourged. We have summoned the beast of the buried mind and now nothing else matters—angel, vision, light and body; nor the little children who are the sun of our own souls.' "

"Certainly not the sentiments of a crazed man. But a voice of doom, regardless."

"He turned to the Romantic poets, his favorites, no doubt hoping to affirm the perdurable in a time of crisis. Instead he found a new obsession in the life and works of Keats."

"How odd. That ill-fated young genius. Let me make a guess. Dr. Holley's obsession had to do with the narrative poem 'Lamia.' "

"Quite perceptive."

"There've been clues. *Lady in thy serpent prison-house* . . .' Definitely Keatsian. Quoted directly from the poem itelf?"

"I don't know," she said. "I'm not that familiar with it."

"He was attracted to Keats because of this one poem?"

"Because he judged the poem written from experience, not imagination."

"In other words he felt that Keats truly believed—"

"No, no, had *encountered* such a creature, which eventually was to be the death of him."

98

"Consumption was the death of Keats, as I recall. Also his brother, what was the name?"

"Tom Keats. Yes, Keats the poet died of the wasting disease, in Rome, in 1821. But Eustace claimed his end was hastened by the serpent-woman whom he loved, who night after night in unholy conjugation drew the substance of life from Keats's body, resulting in a lingering death."

Lord Luxton smiled. "Analogous to Holley's own haunted life. But the life of Keats has been exhaustively researched, and he was a prodigious letter writer. He had two well-documented affairs of the heart, with Isabella Jones and then Fanny Brawne. How did Dr. Holley explain a third, hitherto undetected *amor*?"

"He wouldn't argue his case with me. But he was convinced 'Lamia' existed—that *they* exist, are everywhere as common as alley cats."

"Or doppelgängers?"

"Perhaps a month ago—no, even more recently, toward the end of May—something occurred that severely depressed Eustace. I don't know what it might have been, a broadcast, a news item, but his obsession took a new potentially disastrous turn. Out came the fetish, in a corked bottle which he had secreted God knows where these many years. Naturally I was curious. He owned nothing, had not a single photograph or momento to remind him of his long service in the African forest. Suddenly here was this—ghastly thing, wrought with his own bloody hands, which he clung to day and night. 'The beast is loose,' he said. 'This must keep her from my bed.' I fully believe he was personalizing the dread of the war that is everywhere around us. I was afraid then, afraid that his sinking spell would result in a permanent derangement. I was afraid of the fetish, which seemed to be the engine of his morbidity."

"So you took it from him without his knowledge."

"Yes, on impulse, night before last." She turned and jabbed a finger at the hot stove. "But if you believe *that* filthy token had anything to do with his death—"

"I don't believe it, no. However—"

"Eustace did. Quite right. And he was terrified, having

99

lost his—his power, his singular defense against the spawn of a destructive subconscious."

"Thus he placed those importunate words on the wall of his bedroom."

Mary Burgess made a choking sound, and turned her face away.

His lordship studied her. He noted that his pulse was fast, his face flushed, and it wasn't just the heat of the stove on a mild June night. He always felt this way moments before making the crucial move that could stop a bomb—or kill him: steady, at a miraculous peak of hazard, not afraid but in a state of almost toxic excitement or elation, as if he shared in a mysterious way the timeless secrets of the universe—ultimately what he experienced was a feeling of total freedom, a willingness to confront any truth.

"What are your conclusions now as to the manner of Dr. Holley's death?" he asked her.

"It was sheer chance. An unexploded bomb. My God, can't you let him rest in peace?"

"Mary, I've seen flora proliferating in bomb craters in the heart of London which resemble nothing known on this earth. These plants are mutants, created by intense heat and some sort of short-lived radiation of which we are totally ignorant. Likewise I know that atrocious mutations of human nature are common in wartime. Is it so difficult to believe in strange animal forms, born of the enormous energy of human hatred and aggression that now threatens to destroy us all?"

"Yes. It is impossible to believe. I will *not* believe—"

"But you accept the longevity and reported ferocity of Gen Loussaint, who at best seems to have been half-mad, and at worst a Gorgonish mutation herself, ritually created by her cult of reptile-worshiping savages."

"She was old; on the verge of death. She could not have had anything to do with Eustace Holley's breakdown."

"Unless he was seduced by her, in the form of a ravishing serpent-woman that waxed and grew powerful as a consequence of his sexual desire."

"Sheer—bleeding—insanity!"

"What actually happened to him in the park this morning? Why were his genitals so ruthlessly ripped away? What caused those marks on his buttocks? Were sharp fingernails sunk into his flesh at a moment of ecstasy or release—before she blew him straight to kingdom come?"

Tears flowed unnoticed down Mary Burgess's cheeks. "Why—*why* should she come back to him, after all this time?"

"Revenge, perhaps. Or a necessary culmination: She needed his death to be free to roam at will."

They stared at each other. Her eyes were red with pain. Tears dripped from her rumpled jaw.

"Even with the world gone berserk, choking on blood, there can be no such thing. God would not permit it. There must be something left we can hold fast to. Safe, familiar. How difficult it is already to heal the sick, to bring comfort into the lives of the incurable. It taxes me to the utmost. I'm not entirely well myself. I beg of you. I haven't the strength to accept responsibility for his death. Such a meaningless thing—claws, bone, a few feathers. It *was* a bomb. My lord? Wasn't it?"

The lag set in, the vital sense of mission thwarted by circumstances beyond his control. His pulse idled; he sighed. "Yes, Mary. It was a bomb. So I shall report to the Department of Scientific Research."

She nodded dumbly, then unselfconsciously dried her face on the sleeve of her coat. There was a knock at the door. Sir John opened it. Medwick stood outside.

"The young lieutenant, m'lord. Says it's urgent."

Luxton turned to Mary Burgess and excused himself. He left the examining room. Mary Burgess closed the door again. She went directly to her autoclave, took out a sterilized hypodermic syringe. From the drug safe she obtained a quantity of morphine, and shakily prepared an injection. She peeled back her left sleeve, but then put the syringe aside. After turning off the lights she raised a blackout shade and just stared through the window at the rooftops of Nuncheap, the faint brew of northerly stars.

Within a couple of minutes Lord Luxton returned and

knocked. She glanced at the syringe, hesitated, grimaced, rolled her sleeve down and joined him in the waiting room.

"I'm afraid I must leave at once," he said.

"There's a bomb?"

"Something with a new type of fuse I've been keen to have a look at. This is only the second one that's survived intact."

She didn't know whether to feel relieved or apprehensive, but suddenly she was in control of herself. They walked outside together.

"Thank you so much for your time, Mary."

"I'm glad we talked. Dispelled the nonsense."

"Yes, reckon we've cleared the air."

"We're not children, after all, to be frightened by shadows, boggles or omens. How far must you travel tonight?"

"Portsmouth. Rather a lengthy drive."

"If it's wanting immediate attention, shouldn't you fly?"

He smiled sheepishly. "Oh, no, I never fly. Petrified at the idea of leaving the good old terra firma."

She smiled, too, skeptical but fond. "You're a most unusual man, my lord. Should you come this way again—"

"By all means."

"I'll say a prayer."

"Well, goodbye."

She thought she had seen the last of him, but as she was about to open the front door and go back in he came hurrying from the gate, not using the shielded flashlight.

"Mary, by the way—"

"Yes, my lord?"

"The young man? Jackson Holley. Can you tell me what's happened to him?"

She felt an irrational charge of cold fear. "Yes, he—he became a physician himself. But I'm afraid he's quite removed. He practices in one of the western provinces of Canada. Or is it the U.S.? I could look up his address for you."

Luxton thought about it. Mary Burgess said, "From the tone of his letters he seems to have achieved peace after many years of living rootless, shifting from place to place. Perhaps he's married now, settled in. News of the death of his father will come as a shock, of course. But I'm certain that if Jackson can accept his death as another tragic consequence of the war, then that shock will pass quickly, and there'll be no tormenting aftereffects."

Moonlight was meager, and because of the blackout there was no light from the house behind them. Mary Burgess couldn't read the expression in his eyes as Lord Luxton lifted his head.

"Yes. Does make sense. Well, it was a notion I had—actually no need for me to contact him."

They said no more goodbyes. Mary Burgess watched as he climbed into the passenger compartment of the long Rolls Phantom. When it was gone she bolted the door and thought instantly of the waiting hypodermic, her mouth sticky-dry from longing. Her body pained, every inch of it, her nerves were shreds of hot wire dangling from old bones. It would only be twice today—no, she wouldn't lie to herself, that was demeaning. Admit it; three times. But she *needed* it, the limpid twilight, the deceptive bliss. She knew what she was doing, so—no. Definitely no, she had to establish firm limits or all would be lost. She could get along without that third injection. Her head nearly splitting from anxiety. If she went upstairs immediately to lie down she could get by. Till morning clinic. The worst over now. Wasn't it? Just till morning, dear Lord. Her head coming apart in a long rip of agony, front to back.

At 2:15 the next afternoon Mary Burgess was in the garden dusting her roses with lead arsenate to kill the chafers when Lieutenant Kellow arrived at her gate. Mary straightened and took off her gardening gloves, narrowing her eyes against the bright sun reflected from the windscreen of the lorry as the bomb-disposal engineer approached her.

"Dr. Burgess?"

"Good afternoon, Mr. Kellow. Still grubbing for devices in the park of Hawkspurn?"

"No, we've packed it in. We're returning to Driffield, but it occurred to me that—perhaps you haven't heard the news."

"It was on the BBC this morning. Dreadful."

"Yes. A tremendous jolt. He was a hero to all of us."

"The report was sketchy at best. How did it happen?"

"An unexpected patch of fog in the Chiltern Hills, a cow in the road. Lord Luxton's driver managed to avoid the animal, but we can speculate they were traveling rather too fast for the road, so he lost control and smashed into a tree. His lordship died just before dawn of a broken neck in Radcliffe Infirmary."

"I had a feeling—such an awful feeling—shortly before he left here. But I thought it would be the bomb, you see, the one he was anxious to inspect."

"A sad twist of fate," Kellow said, with a look of distance in his eyes, as if his own fate had come into view and he was finding it rather lacking in swagger, shabby and unfitting. A cow in the road. He licked a corner of his mouth; he was at a loss. Mary Burgess let him off with a placid smile and a nod of thanks.

Then she put her gloves back on and kneeled to study more closely a developing case of chrysanthemum fasciation. She carefully removed the infected plant with a trowel and set it aside. Foolish, she thought, to be so fond of flowers when she ought to be raising cabbages on her plot of ground. But no one could hope to endure without an extra dimension to life, something frivolous to beguile the senses. There was no joy for her in a neat row of cabbages. She had her needle and her flowers and they represented peace of a sort, even comfort. And now Eustace was protected forever. A cow in the road. No damaging inquiries. No slurs on his competence. The lilac was splendid this year, having come back bountifully from the rigorous pruning of the previous fall. Looking around, she planned again the tribute for his bier: dozens of the scarlet peonies which he'd looked upon with favor, and lots of wallflowers. Then mums and roses for the

104

gravesite, every three days till fall. What she would do this winter without him she simply didn't know. Interior blooms, the nightlong winter, prick of the needle, Eustace gone. She found a green worm about to invade a tender young rosebud, foul thing to grow fat on another's heart, and then take wing—she dislodged it, crushed it methodically with a rock against a rock, lifting, striking. Her wide-brimmed gardening hat fell off with the jerking motion of her head. The sun was hot on her uncovered brow. Sweetness all around. She hummed quietly to herself as she pounded her rocks together.

III

KANSAS CITY, MISSOURI

August 2—3, 1944

They brag about their heat waves in this heartland city, but the last of July and the first days in August were something out of the ordinary. At six o'clock in the morning it was nearly as hot as it would be all day. Clouds rimmed the horizon all around, swelling fat as eunuchs on the midday humors of the sun. Toward dark they turned lushly blue with rain but kept their distance and there was no rain, only a crumple of thunder now and then, a rattled pane of glass. The daytime streets lay drenched in asphalt; children played tamely in the shade, but even the shade of a deep side porch came to weigh a ton. Weekends their fathers had beer breath before noon. *It was so hot.* Seemed hotter than '36, they said. And that was a record year. The river was down, lacking current and eddy. In the fashionable parts of town there was a charnel taint of stockyards, of sunburnt Kansas prairie. The sun gave dogs running fits and struck down those men who were overdrawn at the heart. People stood in long lines to get into refrigerated movie houses and avoided the touch of each other's skin. Everyone felt overripe, punky as melons. They seemed passionless but, paradoxically, in the steeping night, in flyblown neighborhoods raddled with neon, there were constant outbreaks from bad blood, razors trimmed their pounds of flesh, guns flashed rimshot to a tempo of screaming sirens.

Nevertheless Kansas City wasn't what it used to be. Now it was a cleaned-up town, reduced in scoundrels, somewhat moral and far less jaunty, no longer in love with its epic badness, its great jazz musicians banished for

109

lack of steady employment. Occasionally, when the Negro jazzmen came back to KC, passing through north to south on jalopy tours or just indulging spells of homesickness, some of them gathered briefly and memorably; they played all night in drab roadhouses in the sticks south of Grandview, just over the line in Cass County.

Jackson spent most of his afternoons at Union Station, though he wasn't going anywhere, and three or four nights a week at such places as Starr's Turquoise or Buster's Roxy Club (where the crawdads were especially tasty), listening to those artists who happened to be in town: He caught Big Joe Turner and Billy Eckstine's new, barnstorming band featuring Sarah Vaughan and Diz, and a husky homegrown kid called Yardbird who was the most amazing alto sax player anyone had ever heard. On those nights when he was sleeping alone, Jackson made his way back to the house where he'd rented a room for the summer. In bed at 4 A.M., he would sleep until the first streetcar came up the line at 6:24 and passed beneath his windows, moaning northbound to the huge railroad terminal on Pershing Road.

By 6:45 Mom Trutler was up and around, but she was so quiet he seldom heard her. At seven o'clock Dad Trutler came thunderously awake and spent half an hour in the bathroom trying to clear his sinuses, which particularly bothered him when the humidity was high. He was followed most mornings by his brother Rawley, a fifty-year-old bachelor with high blood pressure and a liquor problem. The Trutler brothers were druggists. They owned a pharmacy, on Locust Street below Hospital Hill, that grossed better than seventy-five thousand dollars a year.

Shortly before eight o'clock everyone was at breakfast and the front of the house was quiet, except for the now-frequent streetcars; Jackson could doze again if he wished.

He was in Lindy's room. Lindy, the youngest boy, had enlisted in the marines after his graduation from high school a year ago and was now somewhere in the Pacific. Mom and Dad Trutler had three other sons, all in the service. Bob was a flying instructor at the Pensacola Naval Air Station. Kenyon was stationed at the Frankford Arsenal in Pennsylvania. Donnie Trutler, who was good enough at baseball to pitch in the American Association in 1941 and 1942, had seen combat in Italy. He was now in the General Army Hospital in Memphis. He had lost his eyes when a clip of cartridges exploded in his face, detonated by a hit on the chamber of his M-1 rifle.

The bedroom, smallest of the five on the second floor of the house, was just as Lindy had left it last year. Mom Trutler had offered to clean out the closets and take down all the high-school memorabilia, but Jackson wouldn't hear of it. He was just renting for the week, he said. He was just passing through. That was in June. Now he was very much a part of the family. Three weeks ago they'd all gone south to visit Donnie, leaving him alone in the house with Sirje the maid, who was getting up there in years and more like a permanent houseguest than a servant. Jackson had the run of the kitchen and the use of the family's C-card Pontiac Six when he wanted it. They were completely trusting, but Jackson was accustomed to immediate and uncritical acceptance by total strangers.

Dad Trutler had asked around and come up with a couple of likely situations for him. A packinghouse baron's widow wanted a live-in physician. She was in the early stages of Parkinson's, the rigid kind, and had a few other, minor problems. Little would be required of him: Take her blood pressure several times a day, test her reflexes, dole out medication and inspiration in equal parts and try to avoid dying of ennui. Jackson had met with the woman and genuinely liked her—there was immediate rapport and probably he would end up in her will. But he'd also met Son and Daughter, a draconian pair of guardians, and was made aware of their implacable hostility. They weren't about to let some limey outsider get cozy with their mum. They would examine his life with a microscope. If nothing deleterious turned up they'd rig something to discredit him; they looked the type.

Then there were the eminent doctors Meadow and McShane, who owned a prosperous clinic but wanted a third, younger man to shoulder some of the load. Good young doctors were scarce in wartime. Jackson was

111

wanted for general practice, some light surgery, all of which he could handle with ease. He became well acquainted with Meadow and McShane, while they scrutinized him and tested his knowledge, which was all it should have been considering his certificates: Royal College of Physicians, St. Bartholomew's, Edinburgh Medical Faculty. Jackson was invited to each of their homes and introduced to friends and colleagues, who also looked Jackson over closely.

For that part of what had become a familiar initiation rite he was always at his best. Jackson was nearly forty-one years old, but appeared ten years younger. Blessed with a compact and athletic build, he stood just under six feet in height. He was like nothing the ladies were used to, an oddment in town, to their eyes mildly dandified; they were impressed with his poetic curls and blue eyes, his bittersweet humor and unmannered manners. They couldn't hear enough about his formative years on the Dark Continent. Jackson, also charmed by the pleasant company, decided that KC might not be the worst place he could choose, granted that he had a minimum of choices left. It seemed to be all set. He tried not to think about his dwindling cash reserve and awaited the bid of Meadow and McShane to join them.

Then a gruesome scene at the best country club in Kansas City made it clear that the hoped-for situation was far from ideal.

Meadow, the distant, patrician partner, the master of the studied impertinence, went haywire in the locker-room shower while the two of them were lathering up after several spirited sets of tennis. He couldn't have been drunk and there was nothing calculated or remotely sophisticated about his advances; perhaps he'd mistakenly judged Jackson's postmatch exuberance to be flirtatious. They were alone in the shower at the time. Suddenly it was like being penned up with a bull. Both men were bruised as Jackson fought to avoid being screwed on the slippery floor, under the needle spray. When Meadow ejaculated on the tiles, instead of calming down he became obscenely hysterical. He accused Jackson of having a clandestine relationship with the portly McShane. He followed Jackson at a jog into the locker room, not caring how loud he was. Several members of the club got a sizzling earful. Meadow made a pathetic attempt to improve himself in Jackson's eyes by assassinating McShane's character. He claimed that his longtime associate and lover was guilty of grossly unethical practices.

While Meadow disinterred all the bodies, Jackson grimly pulled on his clothes, then departed with what dignity he could still preserve. He already knew he was finished in Kansas City; ultimately his reputation would suffer, not Meadow's. This shouldn't have dismayed him—what was Kansas City to him, after all? Just the last stop of a train he happened to catch in a hurry. But he got drunk three nights running, and when he didn't take excellent care of himself the dormant malaria organisms in his blood brought him down with chills and fever.

There was no effective medicine for his chronic condition. This time he spent two days in bed, too sick and discouraged to raise his head or go to the bathroom.

An angel looked after him while he lay muttering or chattering, manufacturing despair between episodes of nervous sleep. The angel, a ten-and-a-half-year-old stripling named Nellie Trutler, emptied the bedpan, spoonfed him bland soups and cherry-flavored Jell-O, added blankets or ice bags as required and sponged his face often. Nellie was a shag blonde, rubbery-faced, slightly popeyed girl, a comedy-beauty with a disarmingly rational mind and a crush on him which they could both manage quite well. She maintained a menagerie in coops and pens under the elm trees in the backyard, and there was a constantly shifting population of dogs, cats, birds, rabbits, turtles, coons and undeodorized skunks. More often than not Nellie came to his bedside with animal dander clinging to her skimpy summer clothing, but she always remembered to wash her hands.

His fever broke on the third of August, a Thursday, and soon it was as if the attack hadn't occurred, except for a certain listlessness and tremor of the hands. Jackson mustered enough interest in life to sit up on the side of the bed and shave, using a pan of warm water placed on a whatnot in front of him, and a hand mirror. The evening light outside was bronze and dying rose. A blue spark from a streetcar flashed in his mirror as he scraped away with the straight razor. Children chanted skip-rope cadences and neighborhood radios were tuned to the war news, to Bing Crosby. The Trutlers had eaten overdone rib roast for dinner, and the odor would linger in the torpid air of the house for hours. After a curt quarrel with his brother, Rawley Trutler went out to a bar.

Nellie came in damp from play, her cinnamon-flake cheeks turned ruddy, half a dozen mosquito welts aglow on her bare skin. She had gathered a mason jar of lightning bugs to amuse him. She crawled across the end of the bed to set the jar on a windowsill, then slumped in a chair to watch him shave, her long legs outstretched, idly flipping a torn sandal on one foot to see if it would break all the way.

"You okay?"

"Getting there, chum."

"Want me to read the paper to you?"

"No, thanks."

Nellie picked up the *Star* anyway and leafed through it.

"Dorothy Dix says that the use of tears by any woman for a goal is con-temp-tible."

"Well, well."

"Can I turn the lights off so you can see the lightning bugs?"

"I might shave off the end of my nose."

"Why don't you use a Gillette safety razor?"

"They're vastly overrated."

The telephone rang down the hall and Nellie sprinted to answer it. She came back slowly as Jackson wiped lather from an earlobe.

"It's her again."

"Who?"

"The lady that called this afternoon. I told her once already you were sick. Do you want me to tell her again?"

"What lady are we talking about?"

"Oh, I forgot to ask! I'll go ask."

"I'll ask her myself," Jackson said. It was too hot, but he put a threadbare dressing gown on over his pajamas and went along the hall to the telephone stand by the stairs. Nellie followed and sat on the top step with her back to him and her ears flapping.

"Jackson," said Beggs, 'how are you getting along?"

"Just a bout of malaria. I'm feeling my old—"

"Malaria! My God. In Kansas City?"

"I came down with it in Equatorial Africa. That was a long time ago, but I'll never be completely free of the organisms."

"I've seen some of the boys coming through here with the shakes. Must be awful."

"I'm feeling my old self again," he repeated, sounding a bit too evenhanded and patient. The inevitable awkward pause resulted. Jackson heard her exhale, as if she were smoking. There was background noise, an echoing clamor, sepulchral tannoy announcements, outside the booth from which Beggs was calling. She was at the station.

"I guess you're wondering why I phoned you. I don't want you to get the wrong idea. I'm not trying to get started again. Uh. It was. Well. Sorry I called you a rat. You know, just got in too deep before I looked where I was going. Surprised both of us, didn't it? Uh."

"Beggs. You know I'm very fond of you." On the steps Nellie was picking at a fresh scab on one shin. Jackson gave her a nudge with a slippered foot so she'd stop. Nellie turned and looked at him with a facial twitch that was a cross between a squint and a wink: Call it a squink. Nellie was witty and she was exasperating, and Jackson was happy that she was far from a marriageable age. *Thus it will go on as long as children are gay and innocent and heartless,* he thought, and tried to concentrate on his stalled conversation with Beggs, wondering, with a gritty sense of resignation, if next she would start to cry.

But instead she said wistfully, "I believe it. Otherwise I couldn't—to get down to brass tacks, there's a favor I want to ask."

Oh-oh. "Huge, or medium-size?"

"Maybe a little complicated to explain on the phone, and anyway I have to get back to work, the troop trains are really pouring in here tonight. I'll be off at nine-thirty for a while. Meet me in the Westport Room? No kidding, Jackson, I'll be on my best behavior. This time."

She sounded on the level, and he was bored, and not up to amusing Nellie until bedtime. "Okay, Beggs."

"And bring your medical bag," she said, hanging up before he could ask why.

"Got a date?" Nellie said.

"The lady's with the Red Cross, Nellie-Nell."

"Oh. Are you going to work for the Red Cross?"

"It's a thought."

"Well, good news," Nellie said, an all-purpose expression for her these days. "Are you going out?"

"For a little while. Have to talk to the lady."

Nellie lazed against the banister, her head falling this way and that. "Do you know her very well?"

"Might call her a good chum."

"You said you were vereh fond of her," Nellie retorted, trying out her English accent. Then her foot slipped on a step and she nearly fell down the flight of stairs. She picked herself up, momentarily infuriated. But her eyes were clear when she looked up at Jackson, who fortunately wasn't smiling.

"I don't have to go to bed until midnight."

"What makes you such a privileged character?"

"Dad said. Do you think you might be in before midnight?"

"Yes. Why?"

"No reason. I might see you then. Have a good time." She started stiffly down the stairs.

"Where're you off to?"

"I'm going to Saint Joseph's. To light a candle for Donnie. Every time I think about Donnie I want to *throw up*. Somebody in the family better pray for him. And Lindy too." By then she'd turned on the waterworks.

"Hey, Nell?"

"Oh, what?"

"Thanks for the lightning bugs."

116

She reached the bottom of the stairs and sprang to the front door without looking back. "How'd you like a porcupine for a pillow?" she muttered, just loud enough for him to hear. Then the screen door banged as she went outside to the covered porch.

A USO band was playing passably good boogie-woogie in Washington Square when Jackson got off the Grand Avenue streetcar. Not wanting to sweat, he walked slowly across Pershing to the station plaza. He sweated anyway. At this time of night there were still double lines of customers waiting to get into Harvey House, which was located just inside the east entranceway of Union Station. Jackson made his way across the patterned marble floor of the lobby to the crowded Westport Room, where he checked his hat and medical bag.

Beggs was waiting where she wouldn't be conspicuous in her blue and gray uniform, at the banquette table for two which was hers whenever she wanted it, despite the fact that the Westport Room currently was the most popular dining spot in Kansas City. Jackson declined a menu and ordered a double scotch from Joe Maceil, the maitre d'. Beggs was already sipping a sloe gin fizz.

She was only a year or two older than Jackson, but her husband had been a cradle-robber and by the time Beggs was twenty she'd borne two children, both girls. Her daughters were now married and living on the West Coast. Her husband, a full colonel, was on active duty with Patton and she hadn't seen him for over a year. Beggs put in a sixteen-hour day as director of Red Cross services at Union Station, barely enough work to take the edge off her energies. She had a chunky firm body with an unusually trim waist, coarse bunned hair streaked three or four shades from wren brown to a tawny raw turpentine color. Her face was full, her mouth red and full and loquacious with a little predatory gleam of tooth showing in one corner; she had the thickly lashed, swart, knowing, almost brutally sexual eyes of a peasant sorceress.

The eyes were somewhat at variance with Begg's true nature. She needed men but was not aggressive in obtain-

117

ing them, content to let the chemistry of her many contacts work itself out. Nor was she as lusty in bed as her looks led one to believe. Beggs was just an ample, soft-hearted lay who wanted a lot of patting and stroking and nuzzling, the rest of it not all that essential to her well-being, though she'd happily employ any erotic device in her desire to please. Unfortunately Jackson, just one of a hundred men who'd come along in three years' time, had made her heart ache. And Beggs had reacted badly to the dilemma of the lovelorn; made demands he couldn't fulfill even if he'd had a mind to.

But Jackson saw at a glance as he sat down with her that they were going to be on good terms, with no awkward review of the recent past.

"I really expected you'd be gone by now," she said.

"KC isn't as bad as all that."

She shrugged. "Making yourself useful?"

"I've looked into a situation or two. I just don't know yet."

She studied him with her sexual eyes and he had an intuition of what she'd be like at sixty, gone white in the head but with her whore-mother memories intact and still wanting to fiddle. "I wonder what makes you the foot-loose kind," Beggs said. "You must have had a good practice, out there in Washington—"

"Oregon."

"You could have a good practice anywhere. Doesn't matter what kind of a doctor you really are. Not that I think you're a *bad* doctor."

"Thank you."

"When you're sleeping—when your hair falls a certain way, you can see the scars. Those terrible scars on your—"

"Beggs, let's not. Shall we?"

"Did you have an accident, or did someone put them there?"

"They're surgical scars."

Beggs took another Raleigh from her cigarette case. Jackson lighted it for her.

"If you're looking for someone in Kansas City," she

mused, blowing blue smoke away from him, "sooner or later you'll find him at Union Station. Particularly if he's the footloose kind, and a hit with the ladies."

"What are you getting at, Beggs?"

"Two men have been around, asking about you. They have a snapshot. Good likeness, and the girl you're with is a real beaut."

Jackson's scotch was brought by a waitress in a white uniform with a black bow tie. Beggs and the waitress chatted briefly about their respective families. Jackson drank half of his scotch and licked his tingling lips unobtrusively.

"What did they look like?" he asked Beggs when the waitress had gone.

"Plug-uglies, but not gangster types. A certain rawboned rectitude about them. They didn't wear city clothes very well. Rumpled suits, cheap white shirts open at the neck. They do outdoor work. Boats? I'd say they could be fishermen—their hands were rough and broken-looking. A lot of fistfights, those two. There's a family resemblance—and one of them has a crooked back."

"A tree fell on him a few years ago. He's in constant pain but devoted to some shabby religious sect or other and won't take so much as an aspirin or a shot of whiskey to ease his suffering. I *was* able to do him a bit of good through my knowledge of balneology."

"I'd say you know them very well."

"Adam Easterlin is the cripple; the other one might be a brother or even a first cousin." He finished the scotch and wanted another. "Good odds more than two of them are on my trail. It's a large family. They're lumbermen, primarily, on an epic scale. But not a bit of flash to show for all their money. True sons of toil."

"Sounds as if you resent them."

"No, why should I? Almost married an Easterlin."

"The girl in the snapshot?"

"Evelyn, my—former—fianceé."

"Really?"

"Entire bloody clan seems to have missed that distinction. It's *over*."

"Her idea? No, of course not, assuming she's of sound mind."

"Don't cheapen me, I feel quite bad enough. Fact is we didn't discuss it. I simply bolted."

"When the walls started closing in?"

"A matter of not wanting to bring Evelyn to grief. As I would have done, sooner or later."

"Why, dear?"

"My life has been plagued by—unexplainable disorders. What does the poet say? I attract hard events as height does lightning. At the last moment I decided I was not ready to give fate another crack at me, and in the bargain destroy someone I truly care for."

"Love."

"Yes. Well—yes."

"Oh, Jackson. You know, there's something so sad and doggone tragic about you. That's part of your appeal—we all think we'll be the one to lick it, whatever it is. But why have they chased you halfway across the country? To drag you back for a shotgun wedding with kiddyboots? You *couldn't* have been so thoughtless."

Jackson surveyed the crowd waiting in the vestibule of the Westport Room for a table, and wondered bleakly if someone he couldn't see was staring at him. There were a lot of Easterlins, and he didn't know them all. Just pure luck he'd been flat on his back for the past two days and not in his usual haunts, the restaurant or the cocktail lounge.

"No, she isn't pregnant. It's a matter of family honor. My timing was rather too fine, they were all but filing into the church when I took to my heels. Their honor will be satisfied once they've chained me to a tree in a lonely place and done my back to bloody ribbons."

"Well, don't worry about that. They may have left Kansas City by now."

"Depends on what you told them."

"I said we'd had a few dates back in June. And that I'd scarcely seen you since to say hello to. Just the bare truth, that's all. Oh, I did leave them with the impression you'd gone up to Chicago to look around."

Jackson frowned, not sure he trusted her. "You could have put them onto me very easily."

"Why should I?" Beggs said, both eyebrows rising; but her mouth was amused. "Go on, relax," she said, one hand placed ostentatiously over her heart of gold. She puffed away at the cigarette, a habit that he'd warned her to give up after listening to her lungs.

"And I thought I was here to do you a favor," Jackson said, catching the eye of the waitress. He held up his shot glass.

"Better eat something, don't you think?"

"Still queasy from the jungle bug."

"Oh, sure. About that favor, since you mentioned it."

"Ummm-hmm."

"There's a man staying with me I need to do something about."

"Staying with you?"

"Sleeping in my bed when I left. But it isn't that. He's sick. He needs help."

"A serviceman?"

She nodded.

"Well, aren't you the Red Cross?"

"Yes, but it isn't so simple, if you'll just listen."

"Who is he, then?"

"Major Charles Bradwin, U.S. Army. Cavalry."

"Didn't know they still had any."

"Mechanized, I think. Anyway, he was in the Pacific and saw a lot of fighting earlier this year. He must have been good, he has a Silver Star *and* a DSC, personally awarded to him by MacArthur. I found the medals while I was looking through his luggage. He wasn't wearing them when I picked him up outside in the lobby."

"Oh, you did pick him up."

"Not what you think. I literally took him out of the hands of the MPs yesterday evening about seven o'clock. They thought he was drunk, and he sure was abusive. Another few seconds and they would have delivered him to the provost marshal."

"What possessed you to interfere—"

121

"He looked as if he'd seen enough trouble in his life. Oh, hell, Jackson, I just couldn't resist him."

"What seems to be his problem? Battle fatigue? That sort can be extremely dangerous."

"The major was wounded in action—bayoneted. Apparently his regiment fought hand to hand with Imperial Marines on some godforsaken little island nobody ever heard of, but which we need to occupy at all costs. Until just recently he was at Letterman General. Now he's going home."

"Where is home?"

"Chisca Ridge, Arkansas. But he can't make it on his own."

"Then surely it's a matter for his family. Does he have a wife?"

"I think so. When he was half-asleep last night he talked about someone named Nancy. Only—I doubt if she can help."

"Why not?"

"He hasn't been crystal-clear about that, but he seems to believe she's in some kind of big trouble herself. That's why the major needs to get home in a hurry, and why he made such a fuss when he couldn't buy a ticket on a southbound train yesterday."

"All the railroads have a policy of accommodating sick or wounded servicemen on a priority basis. And the Red Cross Home Service Department will gladly arrange for a companion to travel with him."

The waitress came with a refill for Jackson and a roast-beef sandwich for Beggs.

"Sure you aren't having any?"

"Don't mind me, dig in."

"I will."

"Beggs?"

"Umm?"

"Your major friend is AWOL, isn't he?"

"I think so. I couldn't find any papers—emergency leave, travel orders."

"Which means his condition is such that they felt he shouldn't leave the hospital under any circumstances."

"He's not in the pink," she admitted between mouthfuls, "but I don't think he's going to die on us. What if he didn't apply for a furlough? He may have been so anxious to get home, he just walked out of the hospital and caught the first train eastbound from Oakland. And I have a hunch he didn't want—someone to know where he was going."

"Doesn't make sense. He's a major in the U.S. Army, perhaps a career soldier. Even if he *is* a wounded war hero, he can't ignore basic regs without jeopardizing that career and risking a court-martial."

"Then there are more important things than career on his mind."

"His wife, you said. Assuming there's trouble at home, wouldn't a phone call or a telegram clarify matters? Perhaps it isn't as urgent as he believes."

"Jackson, I spent nearly all afternoon on the phone! You'd think I was calling Tibet. That Chisca Ridge must be some little dump of a town. We don't even have a chapter there. But the local telephone operator, when I was able to get through, said that she would have someone who knows Major Bradwin call me back. Waited and waited. About five there was a long-distance call. Terrible connection. It was a woman. I didn't catch the name, I assume she's a relative. She had an accent, but not the hominy-and-hog-jowl I expected. European. She was delighted to hear that 'Champ'—which is what she called him—was in Kansas City and on his way to Arkansas. She said arrangements would be made to meet the Ozark Scenic when it stopped at—I forget the name of the town but I wrote it down—tomorrow night at seven forty-five."

"What about the major's wife?"

"You have to understand just how bad our connection was. Her voice sounding a million miles away in space, fading in and out. I think she said something like, *'But how could he know? How could he possibly know?'* Then she said, *'Tell Champ everything that can be done is being done. Tell him—'* Fuzz fuzz fuzz, click, and that

123

was all; next thing I knew I was talking to a supply officer at Camp Shelby, Mississippi, who thought he was talking to the Defense Department."

"The upshot is, you don't know a great deal more than you did before you made the call."

"But I know, I *feel*, that something's mighty wrong down there, and that he's expected. Tomorrow night at seven forty-five on the MoPac. That train leaves Kansas City early in the morning."

"Beggs, the only legitimate thing for you to do now is contact your director and arrange for an emergency furlough."

"Jackson, the red tape! They'll have to know everything about him. He's been AWOL for at least three days, maybe longer. Under the circumstances the most he could hope for would be detention in a hospital prison ward. He'd be a long time getting home, and he's come this far, and—"

"Very likely he *should* be in the hospital, Beggs. Do you really think you're doing Major Bradwin a good turn?"

"Yes," she said stubbornly, and took a big bite from her sandwich.

"There's more you haven't told me."

"Narumph frissent. Promise."

"What is it you want me to do?" Jackson asked suspiciously.

"Go up to my place and find out if he's in shape to climb aboard the Scenic tomorrow morning. I'll handle the rest."

"That's all?"

"Cross my heart."

Jackson tossed his second whiskey down. "What if I can't certify him as travel-worthy?"

"Then—I'll just have to go by the book, I guess."

"I hope so. I can't afford even a minor run-in with the U.S. government. I'm not a citizen."

Beggs dabbed her lips with a napkin and reached for her purse. "Take my car," she said. "It's parked on the plaza." She handed him the keys to her car and her apartment.

Jackson began, rather deliberately, to pull a dollar from his undernourished money clip.

"Get out of here," Beggs said good-humoredly, giving him a little push. "The drinks are on me."

Jackson looked at his watch. "I should be back in an hour."

"Why don't you stick around the apartment? Sort of keep an eye on the major. I'll get a lift home about one."

Jackson retrieved his Cubatan straw and his medical bag from the hatcheck girl and left the station. Servicemen with girls strolled toward the Liberty Memorial on the heights across the road, where cheap seclusion was available among the trees and dark shrubbings. Lightning glinted in the sky around the city, but without potency.

Beggs had parked her car on the west side of the plaza, facing Broadway. The lot was poorly illuminated and Jackson had to scout around for the black '39 Ford coupé; every other person in Kansas City seemed to own one. More cars were circling slowly on the plaza, a familiar rhythm which did not intrude on the rather cheesy, downfall mood he was in. He kept wishing he had laid that dollar on the table, despite his near-poverty. Just a grace note he might have used in orchestrating some sort of return to basic self-esteem.

Ah, there it was, dent the size of a hen's egg in the right front wing beneath the bullet headlight.

Of course he'd never intended to pay, and *she* knew it as well; wasn't the big mistakes one made in life that rankled so, it was the tiny chippings of deceit and evasion that eventually had the underpinnings of the soul in a state beyond repair.

Jackson heard an engine gunned harshly as he bent to unlock the door of Beggs's coupé. Now this matter of Beggs's wounded war vet, which he felt sour and uncertain about, obviously Beggs had reacted with her glands to Major Bradwin's predicament. No telling what the man had been through in the combat zone and it was just possible he wasn't safe to have around the house, did she ever give that a thought? No. And while he was at it, *damn* the mucky weather, his head felt like a throbbing sump.

A 1936 LaSalle 8 made a loud screechy turn off the drive in front of the station and Jackson's head popped up as the car bore down on him, strong headlights coming around full in his face.

He stood there almost too long, dumbfounded and squinting in the glare. Then he ducked into the coupé, knocking his hat off. The blue LaSalle jolted to a stop right in front of him, neatly trapping him inside the parking space. Jackson slammed his door and locked it.

The interior of the expensive LaSalle lit up as all four doors seemed to spring open simultaneously. A lot of big, homely men were piling out of the LaSalle, which looked as if it had been driven hard, many times, through a cow wallow. They left behind a young woman in the middle of the back seat who clutched her silken head in a lush lonely pantomime of hysterics, like a prima donna on a tiny stage, and Jackson through his shock felt a jab of contempt for the Easterlin men: *Had to bring her along, did you?*

The evening seemed to be going to hell with a vengeance. He rolled the window up tight and started the engine, though they were massed in front of the coupé and he couldn't drive two feet without doing someone serious injury. They were more than just a pack of primitive boors, they were sadistic. He wondered if, after all, Evelyn could be pregnant—but that was out of the question. Clearly they'd forced her to come.

"Oh, don't!" she cried, hanging half out of the LaSalle over a high back fender, wild light in her eyes, that face he'd doted on, rosy with youth and blissfully enigmatic, now so blubbed up out of proportion she was scarcely recognizable. *"Don't hurt him, I love him!"* Worse than salt in his wounds, more like crystallized acid, and to further his shame she began vomiting a yellow stream to the pavement like a drunken, degraded slattern. This had been a thoughtful girl whose nerves were not strong, who needed space and time and dreaming shade to neaten all

126

her days. Easterlins were rocking the coupé, pounding on it with their fists, baying incomprehensibly, where were the fucking police tonight?

Jackson was already over his fear of being hurt; at this point, suffering so keenly for the lover he'd abandoned, he didn't mind the prospect of the unavoidable brawl. In fact there was a joyous reckless heat bringing steam to the blood, though he knew it would be a costly way to vent his anger, couldn't hope to get in more than a solid lick or two before they stomped him to a greasy lump.

His head bounced painfully against the roof as his car was bucked up and down. *Come out of there you queer.* Charming. I can't marry your sister so that makes me . . . in a moment someone's fist would plunge through the windshield. *Kick your balls off.* God, Evelyn, if I could only have a moment to say how sorry . . . *Dick-licker. We'll get you out.* He saw a black lug wrench, wielded by Adam of the crooked back. They would smash the glass, then pick up the car and shake him out of it like a nickel out of a piggy bank. A plugged nickel, which was about what he was worth nowadays. Poor Evelyn, squashed for days between these hobgoblins, sheen of bloodlust in their righteous eyes, we're doing it for you, honey, sweatbox of a car rolling through the bleak furnacelands of the high plains, no wonder she was retching now.

The car directly behind the Ford roared to life and was backed hard out into the aisle, the chassis laying over on two thin tires as the driver frantically cramped the wheel. In the rearview mirror Jackson had a glimpse of a frightened couple who until a few moments ago had been snuggled down together and now were running for their lives, inspired by images of another Kansas City Massacre.

Jackson reached out with his right hand and ball-cocked the coupé into reverse, stepped on the gas. Two of the huge Easterlins had to leap back from the side of the Ford to avoid having their feet mashed as the coupé shot backward through the space just vacated. Jackson braked to avoid slamming into the other car, whose driver was

127

having difficulty changing gears. Metal ground against metal and then the other car jerked away, burning rubber in sprint parallels.

The thrown lug wrench shattered the window opposite Jackson, who ducked a prickly hail of glass and downshifted. He drove straight at those Easterlins who had come running after him. They had the good sense to realize he wasn't going to stop, and there was a spirited split-second scramble for precious inches in the roadway, Easterlin against Easterlin. Even so, Jackson nicked one of them in passing, a hearty hip shot that sent the brute reeling off balance into the spare-tire mount of a roadster.

As he drove away he had a last flashing glimpse of Evelyn that puzzled him. She was standing by the left front door of the LaSalle, body twisted at the waist, one hand desperately outflung as if she were waving goodbye. But she wasn't facing him, and it took Jackson a few moments to realize she must have plucked the keys from the LaSalle's ignition and hurled them away. The Easterlins might be a few minutes hunting the keys, or all night; but a minute or so was all he needed to get away, and Evelyn had given him that time.

Jackson trembled and gripped the wheel tighter as he sped down Pershing beneath Signboard Hill; then his eyes filled and he began to sob. It was wrenching sobs and soupy tears until he was barely able to see, to control the momentum of the little car. He had never thought it possible to die of grief, though he'd seen men die of terror. But he became convinced that if his convulsion of grief didn't quickly subside he would strangle, or blow an artery, or simply wind down to cold, breathless meat and bone.

He came out of it south of 46th on Wyandotte, rutting down the middle of the trolley tracks with an irate bell binging behind him for right-of-way. He pulled over to the curb in a no-parking zone opposite the Fox Plaza Theatre and stayed there, slack in his seat, pulse galloping from the base of his throat to the top of his head, numbness in the extremities. He might have thought a heart attack was in the works, but he also knew very well
128

the symptoms of acute self-loathing. No, he wasn't going to die, that was wishful thinking. People walking by stared at the crusty remains of the right-side window, and at Jackson, who was then made aware that he'd been swearing out loud. He decided he'd better move on.

Beggs lived nearby, around the corner on 51st, in a brick apartment house that was typical of the architectural style of the neighborhood, massive Greek columns in front, railed balconies up and down. It wasn't a very quiet street, too many small children with working mothers. Everyone slathered on Jitterbug to keep the mosquitoes off and slept out on their balconies in the summertime. When they weren't sleeping they were promiscuously minding each other's business.

Jackson found a parking space for the Ford and walked toward the apartment house with his medical bag. Lightning was nearer than before, touching off the roofline and community of windows, announcing him in a saturnine glare. He went in through the screen door and up the steps to Beggs's door, which he opened, making almost no sound, with the key she'd given him.

Inside there was a foyer with a night-light burning, an electric candelabrum mounted on one wall. Jackson passed by his reflection in a moody mirror and went through an arched doorway into the living room. The room was furnished with dumpy stuffed chairs, a sleigh-shaped couch covered in green velvet the color of the skin on a drying-out pond, standing lamps with ball-fringed shades offered at right angles to the perpendicular, and a collection of vasa murrhina displayed on shelves, window-sills and the mantelpiece. A clock was ticking on the mantel between ebony-framed photographs: Beggs and the girls, each of whom had her faithless dusky eyes, that attitude of artless promise and the unaffected come-on; Begg's husband, with tankers' goggles on his forehead and a cigar stub between his teeth, looking devil-may-care and pleased to be at war. Flocked curtains were joined over the closed windows and glass doors to the balcony, and the shades had been pulled down as well. As a result the temperature in the apartment may have been close to a hundred degrees. Jackson turned on a lamp with a forty-watt bulb in it and wondered why Beggs had left the place closed up.

Facing him was another arched doorway, draped and overdraped with more of the green couch velvet Beggs was so stuck on. Beyond the doorway was the dining room, with a small kitchen on the left, another short hallway straight ahead to the back bedroom. Holding the drapes aside, he stepped into the dining room, his mind on the liquor cache in the sideboard, what Kansas City folk called the old Ignorant Oil. A long shadow came out of the kitchen, followed by a tall, thin, glistening, nearly naked man with a glass of Coke in one hand and an army-issue .45-caliber automatic in the other.

He aimed the pistol at Jackson, who came to a standstill, sweat popping out all over his face. Major Charles Bradwin of the unhorsed U.S. Cavalry? Too bloody right.

"Beau?" said the major, in a crude voice that was only slightly above a whisper. "I'll kill you, Beau, if I have to."

For a weightless moment they were close in the matter of this threat, as close as longtime lovers. The major's eyes were earnest and unwinking but not too well fixed on Jackson himself, an indication that emotionally he was out the back door of the mind somewhere, balancing, in the dark, on a high thin wire, with only a pencil spotlight to show him the way.

While he was trying to put together an answer that would neither startle the major nor give credence to his worst suspicions, Jackson took professional inventory of wounds recently healed. Two-inch scar on the right upper quadrant of the abdomen, penetration wound, most likely the result of a bayonet thrust. The tip of the bayonet undoubtedly had gone through the diaphragm and the pleura and may have holed the right lung, resulting in a pneumo-thorax. Serious but not often fatal unless untreated for a long period of time.

The other wound, the one across his throat which was responsible for his lack of voice, had come close to killing him. Since he was alive today it meant there'd been a field hospital on the perimeter of the battlefield, because a sur-
130

geon who was both lucky and good had had to do a fast job of tying the artery in the neck. Even so, if the major's brain had fasted without blood for more than a few minutes, then today he would be in a vegetable bin instead of running around loose. Also possibly credit an alert medic who'd pounced on the major shortly after he went down with his throat slashed and spurting blood.

Though he was now ambulatory and seemed to have normal reflexes, he could still be permanently crazed by reason of his ordeal, or by a crucial loss of oxygen to the part of the brain that did most of his thinking for him. He'd established right away that he was no one to trifle with.

"Major," Jackson said, "I'm a friend of your friend Beggs. A doctor. She asked me to look in on you tonight to make sure you were comfortable."

"I see," Major Bradwin replied, with no indication in his face or voice that he'd even been listening. That was bad. Somehow he gave the impression, without speaking again or batting an eye, that he was willing to shoot Jackson just for practice. The hammer was cocked and it wouldn't take much, only a minor miscalculation on the major's part. Jackson felt his lips about to twitch, in mirth or high hysteria. Jackson Holley, unemployed sawbones, died last night in Kansas City of a minor miscalculation. His last words, which will be distributed along with his personal effects to the Salvation Army, were: *I don't even know what I'm doing here.*

With economy and a touch that said he knew his weapon intimately, Major Bradwin pointed the .45 at the ceiling and lowered the hammer with his thumb. He placed the gun on the dining-room table, but within easy reach.

"You're British, aren't you?"

"Yes," Jackson said.

"What's your name?"

"Holley. Jackson Holley, Major—"

"Forget that. Just call me Champ if you want to. I've been Champ all my life."

"Okay."

"Would you care for a Coke?" There was, in his phrasing of this inquiry, the suggestion of a man of quality, a West Pointer, perhaps, though he wore no rings, only dog tags like every other soldier. "There's no ice," Champ added. He drank from the glass in his hand. "I learned to like it without ice while we were at Oro Bay. That's in New Guinea."

"Oh—yes."

"Too hot in here for you?"

"I think so."

"I closed up after she left today. That was the only way I could sleep. Knowing the place was closed up."

"Who's Beau?" Jackson asked imprudently.

Champ's quick eyes had ice picks in them. Then he smiled, but his smile was out of sync with his guarded manner.

"Someone I'm having trouble with. What about a drink? Whiskey? She probably has some around here."

"In the sideboard."

"Fine. Why don't you help yourself? You must be more at home around here than I am. Sorry about the way I sound. It's better than it was, though. They did more surgery at Letterman, the vocal cords, and my voice is coming around."

He cleared his throat, almost bringing up a cough, which he was able to suppress by tensing muscles all over his body. Then he looked down at his glass as if something rare and interesting had fallen into it. Jackson walked gingerly to the sideboard, put his medical bag down, opened the doors and took out a bottle of Teacher's and a shot glass.

"We'll sit in the living room," Champ said when Jackson had measured out his drink. Jackson looked at him. "Go ahead," Champ said, his eyes dead level, his mouth grim again. He picked up his shooting iron.

"You can trust me, major," Jackson said hopefully.

"I know that. You're a friend of a friend, aren't you? Go ahead, friend."

They went into the living room and, after some minor skirmishing, body English and shifting eyes, chose oppos-

132

ing chairs. Champ in his olive-drab skivvies sat with his back to the corner nearest the fireplace, art glass like a church window all around his head. The .45 he placed in his lap. Every inch of his body gleamed, it drizzled sweat. His hands, forearms and face were much darker than the rest of him, the tropical tan like a permanent walnut stain with a yellowing glaze that showed in the jaw hollows. He was clean-shaven. The eyes were brazen in their private darkness, the forehead high and broad at the temples, giving him a brainy, high-caste look. An archdruid, but the angular slatted body was that of a country man and so were the wide, penurious lips, the bony chin and the hint of a cowlick, though he kept his coarse brown hair short.

He fingered the well-raised scar at his throat, it was like a pink exclamation mark lying almost on its side: first the nick on the left collarbone, then the broad and upward slash, his assailant having attempted to hack his head clean off. It was obvious he had a fever that was worsening, and he had to drag for breath, which hurt him.

"Where do you come in?" Champ said hoarsely.

"Angel of mercy, and all that."

"I can get along without a doctor. What I need——" He went into a fit of coughing, his face going darker with effort and a heartfelt anguish. Jackson tasted his whiskey and looked calmly at the struggling man. Tears were running down Champ's face by the time he got himself under control.

"I'm trying—to get home. She said—she'd fix it. Confidentially. So where do you—come in?"

Jackson got up, took off his wrinkled jacket and headed for the dining room.

"Where do you think you're going?"

"Just sit there and shut up." Jackson brought back the bottle of scotch and a clean glass. "Drink it," he said to Champ, "it won't do any harm. Then I'll get to work."

He rolled up his sleeves, opened his medical bag and set out what he would need. Champ sipped the whiskey cautiously, then eased back into his chair. Jackson made a trip to the linen closet for a clean towel, found a brighter light bulb Beggs had squirreled away and replaced the

133

bulb in the lamp by Champ's chair. He cleaned his hands in alcohol, then took Champ's temperature, listened to his heart and lungs. He opened his bag again and got out a sterile hypodermic needle and a Squibb ampule filled with a chalky liquid.

Champ studied the needle and the drug. "What's that?"

"It's called penicillin, but it's not legitimately available in this country. The military is getting all of it, and it's saved a great many lives. May well have saved you from a lethal infection, assuming they had it at the field hospital where your throat was stitched together."

"I don't want any drugs. I told you I had to get home right—"

"Now see here, major, you're walking around with what I believe is a serious case of pneumonia, involving both lungs. With a course of penicillin and plenty of bed rest you'll pull through. Otherwise you could be dead in a week."

"If penicillin is so scarce, how did you get hold of it?"

"There's a small black market in the drug. Very small. You have to know the appropriate shady characters." Jackson filled the hypodermic partway, swabbed Champ's bicep with alcohol and injected the penicillin. Champ flexed his arm and sipped more whiskey.

"You don't look as if you ought to know shady characters."

"I could be a shady character myself. Now that I've saved your life, and I must say that's bloody expensive stuff, how about letting me have the gun?"

"Why?"

"If you should nod off while you're sitting there, I wouldn't want you to start slinging lead in your dreams. I'm not the Yellow Peril."

Champ nodded, picked up the automatic, shucked out the magazine and handed it to Jackson for safekeeping.

"Also the cartridge in the chamber, if you don't mind."

Champ smiled and pulled the slide back, ejecting the round. "You know about weapons."

"I know a little about a lot of things," Jackson said,

134

pocketing the loose cartridge. "Could you stand a refill, major?"

"Some water this time." He began coughing again, but not so violently. "So it's pneumonia. I feel as if there's a hot horseshoe stuck in the middle of my chest."

"I've given you a miracle drug, but even miracles take time. With further treatment you'll be feeling a new man in forty-eight hours."

"Lord, I hope so."

They sat together for another hour without much being said. Champ wanted to know why Jackson wasn't serving King and Country, and Jackson showed him the scars on his head and mentioned the long-standing case of malaria. Why wasn't he working back home, then? Personal reasons. Jackson continued to water down Champ's scotch, and Champ drank a lot of it.

After a while Champ's eyes closed, and presently Jackson heard a tentative snore. He went quietly across the stifling living room, opened the drapes and cracked the French doors for a draft of air that was surprisingly cool. There was a brighter burst of lightning than he'd noticed earlier. Maybe at last it was going to rain.

He approached the chair in which Champ was sitting with his head thrown back and took the nearly empty glass from Champ's big hand.

Champ opened his eyes and his fingers closed on Jackson's wrist. He had a painful grip. Jackson stared down at him. Champ looked awake, but Jackson sensed he was merely somnambulistic.

Champ's other hand encircled his own throat, but gently. There was panic in his eyes; he gasped. "Wasn't the Jap," he said in his husky voice. "I killed the Jap. It was Clipper who did this to me, Clipper came back with Boss's saber in his hand! You think I'm crazy—but I swear it. I know what I saw. Clipper came back from the grave to get *my* head too!"

Jackson flinched. "Major, you're dreaming. Major— you're going to break my wrist!"

Champ rose half out of his chair, trembling, holding Jackson fast, eyes on Jackson's face but no recognition in them. "Having trouble with all of them. Can you beat that? First Clipper, now Beau. Wonder what Beau's up to. He touches Nancy, I told him I'd kill him."

"Wake up, major."

"I've never done anything to Beau. I don't even know him. What does he *want* with me?"

Jackson pried himself loose from Champ's grip, leaving skin under the other man's fingernails.

Champ looked around Beggs's living room, bewildered. "What'm doing here?" he muttered, chewing his lower lip. "Nhora? God, help, *help me*, Nhora! You're the only one I can—"

"Major Bradwin!"

Jackson shook him. But instead of waking, Champ stood there in a daze so effective he seemed posthumous.

"Bloody come *out* of it, major. I'm Dr. Holley, and I'm looking after you now. No one's going to bother you. Are you listening? Talk to me. Tell me that you hear me."

"Hear you," Champ breathed. He had a partial erection through his shorts. He touched it meditatively. His eyes focused in a dingy way on Jackson's face.

"Need to piss."

Jackson guided him to the bathroom and hung around to be sure the major didn't pass out while at the toilet and injure himself.

"Bed," Champ said, coming out of the bathroom with a smile tight as a tourniquet. He pushed past Jackson and went in a rapid shuffle down the hall to Begg's room and sprawled diagonally across the bed, facedown.

Jackson opened a window and covered Champ with a sheet. He placed his fingers in an armpit, then on the back of Champ's neck, found him cooler, not sweating as much. Jackson returned to the living room, took off his tie, his durable old Peal shoes and his socks and poured another drink for himself.

Beggs came in at a quarter past two.

"What the fuck happened to my car?" she said crossly.

136

"Ah, Beggs, top of the morning to you," Jackson said, wiggling his toes at her.

"Having a swell party? I *asked* you about my car."

"I ran into the Easterlins outside Union Station. Would you believe, they behaved very badly toward me, Beggs."

"I'll bet."

She was too annoyed to say any more. She disappeared into the dining room and returned ten minutes later, more cheerful, having changed into a chiffon blouse, Huck Finn slacks and rope-soled sandals. Beggs had also made herself a Tom Collins from Orange Crush and gin, which she nipped at while sorting through her considerable collection of jazz recordings. She settled on Jay McShann's "Vine Street Boogie," which Jackson particularly liked, and put the record on the Victrola, keeping the volume low.

"I guess those roughnecks didn't hurt you. Just broke up my car."

"Well, it was only a window. I'll gladly pay the damages."

"Skip it. I know you don't have a pot to pee in. Anyway, I'm insured." Beggs did some improvised jazz steps in the middle of the living room, and smiled. "He's sleeping like a kid back there. Means he's okay, doesn't it?"

"He's got those walking pneumonia blues, Beggs."

"Oh-oh. Damn."

"I'm ninety-eight percent certain. I'd like to see a set of X-rays."

"Can you handle it?"

"I gave him an injection of penicillin, much more effective than the usual sulfa— What do you mean, can I handle it?"

"Get him well. Get him home."

"Now just a second there, Beggs—"

The night turned suspensefully incandescent, and thunder jarred the house. The French doors blew open all the way. There was a quick patter of rain in the leaves of the elm trees along the street, then a heavy silence. Then the sky broke and rain gushed down. Beggs ran to secure the balcony doors.

137

She walked back to Jackson and sat on the arm of his chair, mooching over companionably until her haunch rested against his low shoulder. Swigging her soda-pop Collins, she looked fondly down at him.

"Lover, you need to take a trip."

"Do I?"

"Those Easterlins may have missed you at the station, but they won't leave too many stones unturned until they find you. If they saw the license plate of my heap, well . . . How are they connected back home, do they get along with the local law?"

"There's a cozy symbiotic relationship. The sheriff must be an in-law."

"So much the worse for you. It wouldn't be a bother for the sheriff of—what's the name of the place—"

"Big Sugarpine."

"—to swear out a warrant for your arrest—take your pick of charges, and I'll bet she's just a wee bit underage, okay?—then notify the KC police. They'll come straight to me, and what can I say this time?"

"Evelyn was eighteen on the Fourth of July. What *would* you say?"

She gave him a slit-eyed, challenging look. "What about the major, hon?"

"He needs to be under a doctor's care. He must have quiet and bed rest, a minimum of seven days."

"But he won't die on the way home."

"It would be very foolish to let him travel in his—"

"Can he make it, though? That's all I'm asking."

"Risking all sorts of complications."

"That's a strong young guy, even if he is a little under-nourished right now. Bless his heart, they'll take the best of care, down on the old plantation."

"What plantation?"

"I forgot to mention. When I was chatting with that local telephone operator in Chisca Ridge, she let me know that the major's family owns the whole town—"

"That could be one Flying Horse gas pump and a general store."

"—*and* the best part of three counties surrounding the

town. I called a friend who's in the grain busines here in KC. It took him a couple of minutes to look them up in his Dun and Bradstreet, and almost five minutes to read the entry to me. There's a twenty-five-thousand-acre plantation, with another ten thousand acres under long-term lease. Bradwin and Company had its beginnings way back in 1823. The main plantation is fifteen miles long and eight miles wide. There's a railroad, an agricultural experiment station, a mule market that handles ten thousand mules a year, cotton gins and processing plants. What I'm trying to say is, if you take care of the major those goodhearted southerners will take wonderful care of you."

"There's too much about this I don't like, Beggs."

"You won't like anything at all about the Jackson County Jail. Which is where you're headed if you don't wise up."

"I just can't believe you would take advantage of our relationship—"

"God, that *does* things to me! When you get a little stuffy and *so* British-sounding. Just hearing you talk, I'm in hog heaven. I'm really going to miss you, Jackson."

"I absolutely refuse to be maneuvered into—"

Beggs squirmed delightedly against him. "Just keep it up," she said, "and I'll have to pull down my pants."

"Now, Beggs—"

"Let's do bananas tonight! I'll load up my twat with two medium-sized ripe bananas, and then we'll have a nice tussle, and by the time we're horny enough those bananas will be mashed to a fare-thee-well."

Jackson flung himself from the chair and reached for his coat. He put it on, sat down and stolidly laced his shoes. He put his tie in his coat pocket. It was still pouring outside. Beggs clicked her empty glass against her teeth, thoroughly enjoying herself. She went over him and over him with her steamy and hugger-mugger eyes until he felt as if he were wearing a sticky coat of varnish. But he couldn't be angry with Beggs. She had sensed that he wanted to be raped. One way or another.

"Sending me out into this rain," he grumbled.

"Try to be back in an hour."

"Don't worry."

"Also I'd advise you to be a perfect mouse going in and out. Then tomorrow when I send the Easterlins or the cops around, the Trutlers won't be able to tell them anything. It'll look as if you sneaked away in the dead of night."

"Jesus wept," Jackson said, picturing this humiliation.

"If the major wakes up, do I give him anything?"

"Sugar tit."

Beggs showed him a well-cured tip of tongue. "I covered the broken window with a piece of tarp, you'll be dry enough in the car. Now scram."

The streets were awash as Jackson drove the few blocks west to the Trutler house. It was a quarter to three and he met few cars along the way. He drove by the house once, trying to see, through the fogged windows of the coupé, if the Easterlins had somehow tracked down his rented digs. But the blue LaSalle was nowhere in the neighborhood. On his second watery pass he lurched into the driveway and parked beneath the little roof over the side door of the screened porch.

The Trutlers had left a porch light on for him. He wished they hadn't. He preferred full darkness in which to sneak his belongings from that front bedroom. It wasn't as if he was doing them out of the rent money, but he felt ungracious and would miss them, particularly Nellie; it mattered that she would be stuck with a poor impression of him, police at the door making inquiries, his reputation in default. He might write her a letter later on, when it appeared safe to do so. *Dear Nellie, free advice is cheap at the price. Stay full of yourself. Give sorrow its day, but never a day and a half. Invest nothing in a traveling man's smile. Be a soft villainess. Yr. chum—*

Close lightning gave him a slash and a jangling scare. He got out of the car and let himself into the unlocked house, then turned off the outside light. He walked up the stairs with lumping thunder all around, muffling his dim tread. Turned right. Walked down the carpeted stretch of hall to Lindy's room. The door stood half-open. Lightning

140

glared in at the the windows as he entered. The first thing he saw was Nellie, in her pajamas, huddled in the easy chair, toes curled, sound asleep, her blonde head celestial in the playing-out light. When the light vanished, there was a residue of fireflies moping in tint glass, a splatter of rain along the inch or so of breathing space between the window and the sill. Nellie was a complication, but she was a dependable sleeper in the dead of night. He had only to pack a few things and empty his part of the closet and be on his way.

His own pajamas had been folded neatly at the foot of the bed. He turned to pick them up. In the next blue, crackling wave he saw the serpent curled on the counterpane, its oiled moody head rising like doom toward his outstretched hand.

Sometimes he had a precious moment, or two. This time the screaming started at once. He had thrown up his hands but he was locked in that attitude, couldn't budge a muscle. Out of the corner of a dazzled eye he was aware of his own crucified shadow and of Nellie, windmilling up from the chair as he pumped out scream after scream, already feeling the whispery fatness of the great serpent rounding on him from knees to waist, ranging upward with its gripping speed, immense head radiant in one armpit, then sliding free and touching the root of his naked throat. Which stopped the screaming abruptly but left him breathless, seized up from the waist, jelly, jelly below and a noxious cloud of shit as his bowels misbehaved and the temperature of his extremities plummeted toward absolute zero.

Nellie reached in between him and the bed and picked up her dangling pet, turned holding it protectively against her chest and away from the source of their distraction, the energumen. Too late. Jackson was already dying in another's brawny embrace.

"Out," he whispered, shaking. "Afraid. Take it. Away."

Nellie fled the room and he began his slow collapse, knees hitting the floor, head hitting the soft side of the

141

bed. He tried to stay upright but slid to the floor and lay there in a gut-level heap, knees drawing up tightly, seat of his pants sticky. He gasped.

The ceiling light in the room came on. Trutlers everywhere. Sharp voices asking questions. Nellie whined. "I just wanted to *show* him—"

Jackson lifted his head, daring to look at her. Nellie's hands were free, wiping a snotty nose. She'd put the snake away in her room. She was quivering in the doorway. Big tears stood out on her cheeks. But it was a voluptuous fright she was enjoying; she could be enamored, like any child, of a show of freakiness.

"Oh, Jackson. It wouldn't bite."

He tried to smile. "Sorry. It's phobia. Ophidiophobia. Can't help. Myself. *Everybody.* Get out. Leave me alone. Please."

Nellie sniffed the air he'd fouled, put her hands over her mouth and retreated. So did the adult Trutlers, with muttered regrets and dumb felicitations. The door closed.

Like a little mouse, Jackson thought giddily, *I'm.* But he felt the beginning of his release. Out of danger, for now. The telephone rang. Dad Trutler spoke apologies to disturbed neighbors. Shortly after he hung up, Nellie yelped in pain and indignation, her bottom smacked hard. When the house was quiet again Jackson got to his feet and crept winded down the hall to the bathroom, where he took care of himself.

He packed beneath the falling rain in a nearly total emotional vacuum, adrenal glands now just reviving but still as useless to him as language is to a tongueless man. He left the house at five minutes past four. He was as wobbly as a hammered steer. He had the impression that they were wide awake, and listening. All save little Nell, whom in parting he imagined pillow-stuffed and deeply into her windup dreams, safe at the heart, darling, almost chastised but with a cruel beginning of sensuality in the deepening corners of her mouth. Her eyes enchanted, cold with wiles behind the plummy lids. Seeing him. Each plausible breath turning now to scales, to a poisonous filigree invading like heavy mist the clement dreamlight round her head.

Thus he fantasized. Young or old, in the end they were meant to bring him down.

IV

SOUTHBOUND—
KANSAS CITY—
CHISCA RIDGE

August 4, 1944

The Missouri Pacific railroad's Ozark Scenic train, Kansas City to Little Rock and Memphis, was made up of some of the oldest equipment on the line: A black, mountain-type locomotive provided the power for four mixed coaches, baggage and grill, two of which were for colored and two for white. The train, a milk run, stopped almost everywhere from sunrise to well after sunset, in places called Cricket, Yellville and Zinc. It took twelve and a half hours to travel the 271 miles from KC to a division point in eastern Arkansas where the arrival of Major Charles Bradwin was anticipated. None of the coaches was air-conditioned, but all were crowded. The luncheon available from the grill was meager.

It rained all day, off and on, local thundershowers. Sometimes there was just one cloud and a cylinder of gray rain, heat and light all around while the rain bored through. Once they were below Carthage, Missouri, there was something to be said for the scenery. The air was cooler through the mountains. The coaches carried plains heat with them like a Thermos into the cool of an Ozark gorge, green byways. Peaks gave off smoke into the gold of the upper air; smoke was dense where the rivers churned white as paint. Settlements appeared. Wagon roads, a raw and slumping hillside, the screaming flash of a sawmill blade in a dark shed. Men stood on branch-line platforms where even this train wouldn't stop. They wore hats of brown or black felt that looked crafted by munchkins. Many of the men were crippled in some profound way: crutches, pinned-up sleeves, eyes filled with the glare of frost, frozen forever, arctic in their solitude.

147

The women with baskets, brooms. Bareheaded. Looking up in doorways, baleful with the sun gone red. Stark hollows, the train whistling, a singular hawk before the day goes winking like a coin, and out.

Supper wasn't much either. Jackson ate a warm orange and some Cheezits and then stood between coaches and watched for the fullness of the night. The hills were slowly giving out to farmland, to a richness, alluvial; the air different now, just faintly redolent of the coming delta, of still water and decay and crushing heat. They were passing a narrow bog, splintered trees emerging in the window light from the train. This air was far from tropical, but it was enough to make him uneasy.

For a while the stops had come less often. In the coach Champ Bradwin slept undisturbed. He'd slept most of the way, pumped full of penicillin and aspirin, waking only to take liquid nourishment or go to the bathroom. There were a few servicemen on the train, no one of his rank or better; they'd glanced respectfully at the scar on his throat and the Silver Star which Beggs had decided he should wear for his homecoming. She'd pressed his tailored uniform and taken it in here and there, and the major looked just fine.

Jackson's mood had gradually advanced from plumbbottom to the point where he could hold his head up and look people in the eye again. He was wearing his best Palm Beach suit and Beggs had given him one of her husband's hats, a Stetson Baku straw, very snappy, to replace the one lost at the railroad station during his Dillinger-style getaway from the Easterlins. It was a little too large, but 'he had to have a hat, he felt unmanned without one, and vulnerable; along the African equator a white man whose head was uncovered to the sun for more than a few minutes was likely to be a dead man, and although he'd been nowhere near the torrid zone for over twenty years the headgear habit was ingrained, unbeatable as nicotine.

He'd hoped to get better acquainted with Champ during the long trip down, but during his wakeful periods the major was untalkative, tense despite his medication, and obviously wary of the company he was keeping. Jackson had used an idle hour at Beggs's apartment before their departure to read through the journal the major kept while in the Pacific. The journal did confirm the fact that he had a wife named Nancy, that she was not writing very frequently and had been ill, the nature of the illness undisclosed. A further, clandestine search of the major's possessions turned up a likeness of his lady, a studio portrait so overcolored her complexion was that of a ripe peach, her eyes impossibly blue. She was pretty, but without glamour; a trace of wistfulness in her smile. She looked kind, patient and obedient. The sort who would worship a stalwart chap like the major.

There was no mention in his journal of the mysterious "Bo," or "Beau," who seemed to be a threatening presence, at least in Champ's mind. The journal was almost exclusively about war, or the lack of it, since his regiment, primed for combat, had been underutilized for nearly a full year after clearing Fort Bliss in June of 1943. For a time, early in '44, they'd been employed as labor troops unloading ships in New Guinea. Degrading work (according to the major) for the oldest surviving cavalry regiment, whose first commanding officer was Robert E. Lee and whose troopers always had been in the thick of the Indian wars on the American frontier.

But at last they had all the action they could handle, on a group of mountainous little islands called the Admiralties, situated at the head of the Bismarck Sea and just below the equator. The major's squadron was the first to go ashore at Los Negros, in a seeping rain. The Japanese were well fortified around the cavalry's principal objective, personally selected by General Douglas MacArthur, an airstrip called Momote. They were for the most part Imperial Marines—the very best fighters, picked for size, condition and fanatical courage. Many of them spoke excellent colloquial English, which was to be a problem later on. Apparently Major Bradwin's work in securing the beachhead had been outstanding, for the next day when MacArthur came ashore for the record books Champ was singled out, promoted on the spot from captain and awarded his DSC.

149

The fighting, however, had just begun. The worst of it went on at night for weeks—close, tight, bloody combat in dugouts and in the midst of shattered coconut palms with the sky in a continuous rip and blaze of tracers, many thousands of enfilading rounds fired by both sides. Even when an area was thought to be secure there was no way to keep the Japs from filtering through at night. Some of the Imperial Marines tied bandages around their arms at pressure points so they could go on fighting even if an artery was severed. That was real dedication.

For the first three weeks in March the cavalry and their reinforcements slowly mopped up the island. Champ had been in battle off and on during that period, sustaining two small wounds, when, according to the account in his journal, written a couple of months afterward, he experienced the vivid hallucination that nearly cost him his life.

Manus, March 19

At 2200 hours Japs breached our weakened left flank at the edge of the strait, their best counter-offensive since the first days of Hyane Harbor. They must have been resupplied from a cache of arms and ammunition in the jungle highlands west of here. G Troop suffered heavy casualties, and the CP was overrun within minutes, there was little warning and no place to retreat. It was a case of stand and fight and die, to the last man. But nothing we have been through before prepared us for this. Confusion, a rush and tangle of bodies, screams, shots, blood. We went at it hand to hand in the flickering dark, so strangely lit by the jet flashes of rifles, the bright haze of machinegun fire. In their panic, Americans were mistakenly killing Americans; I only hope the same was true for the enemy. I don't know how long it lasted. After the first assault there could have been a dozen survivors on both sides. The brutal fighting continued elsewhere as our other troops repelled the wave of shrieking Japanese. In our little pocket of the jungle, stinking of guns and slaughter, wounded men cried or pleaded for help in the dark while we, the survivors, groped toward each other, firing erratically, lashing out with bayonets at the touch of another's flesh, or at nothing more substantial than a sharp odor of fear clouding the night in front of us.

I may have killed one man, or several. I know I was wounded, and I reached the point where my legs would no longer hold me up. I fell, and a body lurched beneath me; I struck at the groaning thing with the bayonet in my hand until I was soaked all over from his blood.

Then I crawled a few yards and fainted.

Before there was light there was the sound of birds, sporadic firing far away, a crackle of static on a broken radio. A man weeping. That was me. Crying before I was fully awake, shivering in the tropic, predawn coldness. My chest was on fire, and with each breath I heard a raspy snoring sound, as if I was pulling air into my lungs through a skewered rib cage.

Someone, I sensed, was watching me. I could barely make him out against the starless sky, which was only a shade keener than the pitch-black of the fringed trees that stood all around the clearing. There was a faint, corrupt shine where his head would be, but that may have been due to my own faulty vision. His presence was not of great concern, because I believed I was already dying. The stuttering guns sounded closer, heavy machine-gun fire. There was a pitiful high-pitched scream, then silence. I tried to get up and fainted again, not because of pain, but from the sudden draining of blood from my head.

The birds, piercingly cheerful, woke me a second time. My uniform was stiff with gore, unmalleable. Now it was early morning, a silver mist hovering a foot or so above the ground-lumps of the dead all around. The broken radio was whistling and chatting in the Sioux language; there are six of these Indians in our regiment and we had pressed them into service as radio operators, because too many of the Japanese were sending false messages in English to confuse us.

And he was still watching me from a distance of a few feet, gross with pollution, nastily luminous, one hand on his hip, his weight cocked against the saber he had planted in a decaying log. The blade of the saber was dulled and pitted from neglect, but I recognized it anyway, the functional hilt was of 18-karat gold and could never tarnish. The Blue Ridge uniform in which he had been buried was caked with mold. His face was aged meat, grayed, bristly, giving off that highly poisoned, scaled glister. But this was no ghost, he was as solid as the curse we bear. Curiously, I was not afraid. And I wondered if I had died without realizing it. But then I knew if that was true I wouldn't be sobbing for breath, hurting so much.

"Brother," said Clipper, "you've been lucky at war." He looked across the battleground to emphasize his point. "But I can't wait any longer."

"What do you want?" I asked him.

But my heart was breaking because his eyes, and only his eyes, were just as I remembered them, unaffected by the long night down under, clear, youthful and full of the Old Nick, as Boss used to say. And why not? They were Boss's eyes too. Fear began to seep through me, though I had thought I couldn't care.

"Why, I need you to come with me. I missed you at the chapel, and you can see the consequences for yourself. I'm neither here nor there. So with your co-operation I'll just finish the job now." And he stepped back, pulling the point of the saber from the wood.

I heard voices, American voices I thought, coming along the trail into the clearing. I opened my mouth but I didn't have the breath to scream for help. Clipper's expression, as he measured me for the cutting, was hateful.

152

"We're all just getting what we deserve, don't you see?"

I turned my head and became aware of the clotted bayonet in my right hand. Somehow I found the strength to stand, and lunge. The blade sliced rottenly through his side. Clipper disdainfully knocked it down with one hand and cut my throat with the other. I felt nothing after the first knock of the blade against my collarbone; then a gloomy choking sensation in my throat. I instinctively clamped my left hand on my throat where it gaped, trying to minimize the damage. Clipper had me by the other hand, and was pulling at me impatiently.

"Let's go," he demanded.

Instead I fought, even as my life gushed away, I tore my hand free of his grasp. And in that instant he lost his power and strength, and changed, before my eyes . . . to a charred, tottering mummy.

"Bonefort's next," the conductor said, passing between coaches. He pronounced it "bony-fart."

"On schedule, are we?"

"No, sir. 'Bout forty minutes late this evenin'. You catching the Texan?"

"Meeting someone," Jackson said. "I think."

"That's good. 'Cause the Texan'll be long gone time we get to Bonefort."

"Any other trains after the Texan?" Jackson asked.

"All depends on whur you want to go. Now there'll be the Sunshine Special southbound to Houston at twelve-oh-five, then the northbound Sunshine hour after that, arrives Saint Louis eight-thirty tomorrow morning."

"Thank you," Jackson said, and followed the conductor into the coach where he'd left Champ.

Champ was now wide awake, but Jackson was concerned about his appearance, the tart pallor of a just-cut lemon, and his eyes were deep in his head.

"Thought you told me I was going to feel better," he complained.

"You may be having a mild reaction to the penicillin.

153

Or it could be simple nausea." Jackson gave him Drama-mine with a sip of water.

Champ licked his lips. "Where've you been?"

"Getting some air."

"Talk to anyone?"

"Just the conductor."

"Well, have you *seen* anyone, I mean?"

"I still don't get your drift."

Conversation was an effort; Champ swallowed again. "Seen anyone who looks as if they might be following us."

"You suspect we've been followed? All the way from Kansas City?"

"I don't know. I was just asking."

"Going in circles here, aren't we, major?"

"The hell with you," Champ said bitterly, and closed his eyes.

Before long Jackson felt the train slowing. He gave Champ a cautious shake. "It's Bonefort. We're getting off. Can you walk?"

"I'll make it okay." He didn't seem eager, now that the long ride was ending. He gazed out the window at a thin scatter of lights along the track.

The train crawled now, through a switchyard filled with cattle and tank cars. Jackson, with a porter's help, assembled their luggage. The train crossed the straight and narrow of the main line to the southwest and fetched up on the north side of the one-story brick station. Jackson and the porter piled the luggage on the station platform.

Jackson had a long look around. A pfc, taking leave of his family, stood so small in his oversize uniform that he seemed to be nothing more than fingertips, ears and Adam's apple. The family members leaned against each other and clutched each other desperately and said not a word. A heavy farmer in bib overalls was supervising the unloading of many cardboard cartons of peeps and tiny feathers that floated upward in the mild cones of light along the platform. To help him he'd brought along a Negro, whom he insulted or threatened in a jocular tone whenever the man's pace slackened enough to displease him. *Goddam you, Ezzard, 'ffun they was swappin' pussy*

154

for sweat down at the whorehouse, you couldn't work up enough to get French-kissed. Haw, Ezzard would laugh, every time, haw-haw, showing the gold in his teeth.

The porter hopped aboard to help Champ get off. But no one, apparently, was going to be there to greet the major; no one had ordered up a brass band for the occasion.

Whut I heard, Ezzard, you was borned five months late 'cause your mammy couldn't wake you up from your nap.

Haw! Thass truf. Mos' likely.

Jackson gave the porter a dollar. The Ozark Scenic went on its way. The sparse activity around the station thinned down to nothing.

Champ stood on the platform looking neither left nor right.

"No one's come, major. What now?"

He seemed, in a complex way, relieved that he had not been met. "Ask inside," he said. "Ask about a private railroad car."

"Yes, sir, major," Jackson replied, suddenly and extravagantly angry. Because what he'd seen thus far of Dixie didn't please him, and he still had a very sick man on his hands, when he'd been half-hoping for an excuse to break away. There was a sweet ripened moon overhead that failed to impart glamour to his surroundings. Bonefort, Arkansas, smelled like pig shit. He kicked open the door to the waiting room and went inside, and when the door didn't close fast enough to suit him, he turned around and kicked it shut.

A ticket agent took in his display of temper with a sidewise look. Then he went back to work in his lighted cubicle, pigeonholing slips of paper. He looked around again when Jackson approached him.

"Haow yew?" he said.

"I beg your pardon?"

The agent looked past Jackson, taking time to study the figure of Champ on the platform outside.

"That the war hero?"

"One of them. Are you acquainted with Major Bradwin?"

155

The agent consulted a sheaf of notes and telegrams on a clipboard, extracted one.

"Major Charles R. Bradwin, from Chisca Ridge?"

"Yes."

"Family's sorry they couldn't be here to meet him. They did send a private car by way of the Delta, Saint Francis and Dasharoons."

"Where is it now?"

"Siding over there by the anhydrous-ammonia tanks. You don't know where that is. What you do, you go outside on the platform and look for a nigger named Walter. Don't have to look too hard, you don't see him, just call 'Walter!'—like that. He'll turn up. He's always somewheres around. Walter'll take you and the major to his car. I expect one-two-seven will pick it up around eleven, twelve o'clock tonight."

"Thank you," Jackson said, mollified. He took the telegram from the ticket agent and handed it to Major Bradwin outside. Then he went looking for Walter. He had three Negroes to choose from. He had not noticed them before, getting off the train, but he had a feeling they'd been in their particular spots for hours, if not all day. Now that he wanted one of them, they were suddenly visible.

Walter turned out to be a ricketsy runt with a spry manner once he was in motion. He quickly gathered up the luggage and pushed it on a hand truck across several sets of rails to a far corner of the switchyard, Jackson and Champ trailing slowly behind him. Champ just wasn't capable of much more exertion. And he was wheezing almost inaudibly, which disturbed Jackson.

The private car, which undoubtedly dated from the turn of the century, was mammoth and dirty. Its blue and gold colors were hard to distinguish beneath a spray of dried mud. The windows looked blacked out from the observation deck forward, but there were small outside lights at the head end of the car. They walked that way, the hand truck rattling along beside the rails, Walter caught up in a nearly wordless song, moaning and humming like a man with a toothache.

Jackson felt an almost inescapable sense of gloom. Much as he disliked Bonefort, Arkansas, he didn't want to get aboard this disconnected railroad car that was waiting for the one-two-seven. He didn't believe in ghosts and he wasn't prone to hallucination; nevertheless he felt a sympathetic tremor as the champ hung back, then put a hand on Jackson for support or reassurance. Jackson helped him up the steps and inside.

There were a number of surprises: first the odors of freshly cooked food in the butler's pantry, then the rosewood-paneled parlor, which was clean and well lighted and furnished in the style of one of the better gentlemen's clubs in London, with an exuberant dash of Creole charm. There were paintings of the French Quarter of New Orleans by unknown artists, and several works of French postimpressionists, the names not overly familiar to Jackson.

The air inside was warm but not stale; Major Bradwin turned on the air conditioning right away. A table had been set with crystal and china. There were full decanters on a sideboard, whiskey and sherry, red wine on the table. Jackson opened the door to the bedroom and looked in. A woman's room, Italian Renaissance, and also in good order.

"You don't need to go in there," Champ said curtly.

Jackson closed the door again. Walter had come aboard with the luggage, which he left in the butler's pantry. Jackson paid him. When he returned to the parlor Champ was slumped in a chair and his eyes were closed.

"How are we feeling?"

"Woozy."

Jackson gave him another shot of penicillin from his dwindling stock. He hoped it was beginning to do the major some good; obtaining a fresh supply would take weeks, even if he had the money.

"Drink, major?"

Champ opened one eye. "What can I have?"

"Sherry, if you've a taste for it."

"Fine. What I really want to do right now is lie down."

Jackson found lap robes in a closet and arranged pil-

157

lows on a long sofa. Champ took off his shoes and unbuttoned his collar.

"Too hot," he complained, when Jackson insisted on covering him.

"You won't be; and I don't want you coming down with chills. Not malarial, are you?"

"No, I was good about taking Atabrine."

Jackson poured sherry for Champ and whiskey for himself. There was a folded note on the table which he'd overlooked before—heavy, stiff cream paper with edges like razor blades. *Darling,* the note began, and he read no further, handing the note to Champ along with the stemmed glass of sherry.

"From your wife, I believe."

Champ made no comment. He took the note and began to read.

"I'll just help myself to chop," Jackson said.

In the butler's pantry he found a baked ham keeping warm in an oven, fresh breads, wheels of imported cheese. He drank the rest of his whiskey, made a sandwich and went outside to sit on the steps of the car to eat. Mosquitoes weren't a problem here, perhaps because of the train smoke. A long freight train was rolling north on the main line. He heard the far-off percussions of a juke joint. He was less hungry than he'd thought. He had a sense of being watched, studiously appraised. The lights of the rail yard had softened and were smearing. Peculiar, he'd forgotten how to chew. His tongue was getting in the way, and swallowing was hard. Coming down with something? No, he felt all right—just lazy and aimless, a little uncoordinated, strain catching up at last.

He threw half the sandwich into a nearby ditch for stray dogs to find and went back inside, always just a shade off balance, blinking his eyes to focus them. There was a haze in the parlor. The air was now pleasantly cool and dry. Champ snored on the sofa, fingers of one hand trailing on the carpet, his empty glass nearby, the twice-folded note in his other hand. Jackson rubbed his eyes and looked at his watch. Half an hour had gone by very quickly. He took the note from Champ's unresisting hand

158

and glanced at it. The words climbed the paper at an odd angle and seemed to drip off the edge before he could make sense of them. He threw the note on the table and turned to sit down. Instead he crossed his feet and fell.

Wasn't much of a fall: he couldn't be alarmed by his appalling clumsiness because he'd somehow, instantly, acquired the knack of floating on air. *Chloral hydrate?* his professional mind inquired, getting a little panicky, but Id promptly rose up and told Ego and Superego where to stuff it, he was having a jolly good time. Jackson floated facedown for a while until the carpet seemed near, then he just flipped over on his back and continued to float in the softly wavering, jelly air. Thoroughly comfortable, no other way to describe his situation. Holding one hand before his eyes, he studied the deep grooves, particularly his life line. It looked like a road to him, curving gracefully through the long palm valley. He imagined himself walking slowly on this road in sunlight, coat hung carelessly over one shoulder, in no particular hurry, just whistling his way along. All by himself on the road, nothing ahead that worried him, and for once nothing behind that was gaining on him.

At a quarter to twelve a MoPac locomotive hauling a baggage car and three empty chair cars with all shades drawn backed up the siding to the private car and coupled with it, not gently. With the new car hooked on, the train pulled slowly out of Bonefort, Arkansas, heading south.

A man who had been sitting on an upturned cement block in the shadows of the anhydrous-ammonia storage tanks got up and extinguished his half-smoked cigar in a tin cup that still held a little cold coffee. He threw this liquid away, put his cigar in a shirt packet and the cup in his bindle and walked out to meet the departing train.

Early Boy Hodges was about six-one and thin, but his shoulders were broad and high. He limped, though not badly. He wore a herringbone cap and a long-sleeved shirt, the sleeves peeled back to just below his elbows. The GI shirt was so durably waxed with grime and body oils it could shed water like a slicker. It was no trouble

159

for him to board the moving train, he did it with a sort of offhand elegance that told of long experience.

Before opening the door to the middle car he paused to remove his jackknife from a scabbard on his belt. The knife had a deeply scored handle carved from staghorn, a blade five inches long and a blade three inches long, each blade sharply silvered from a daily whetting. With this knife Early Boy could cut off a man's ear, or a thumb, at a stroke. He placed the opened knife inside the band of his cap where he could get at it quickly and entered the car, which had begun to sway as the train picked up speed.

Early Boy was certain that the only other passengers aboard the train were the unconscious men in the private car, but he moved with instinctive caution into the almost pitch-dark coach: A couple of shades had popped up from the lurching of the train, and just enough moonlight came in to show him the way down the aisle. There was nothing in this car of interest, and nothing in the first car either. But he went into the baggage car with his knife in his hand, the blade just behind his right leg where it wouldn't catch the light too soon.

The baggage car was almost empty, except for the polished mahogany coffin midway, between the rollback doors on either side of the car.

Early Boy braced himself and studied the coffin, dismayed, touched by sorrow. Then he put his knife back in his cap and went to open the top of the coffin. By moonlight and the flickering roadside light of several hamlets he studied the remains. The train was moving much faster, like a runaway; probably it would not stop until it reached Dasharoons. He had to hold on to the coffin with both hands so as not to lose his balance. Heavy as the box was, he felt it shifting uneasily when the train leaned hard into the curves.

"Never had a cut dog's chance," he said under his breath, feeling an emotion that wasn't far from fear, though he was sure he was the least fearful of men. Nothing to lose, nothing to gain, no one to care for. At least not anymore.

160

He closed up the coffin then and went back to the middle car and picked out a seat for himself, raising a shade partway so he could look out if he had a mind to. He took an apple from his bindle, began to peel it with the jackknife. The apple turned out to be bitter, but he ate it anyway, chewing slowly because of bad teeth. After a while he was forced to sing to his anger. He sang a couple of Carter family standards in a half-aloud voice that couldn't have been heard half the car length away: "Little Darlin' Pal of Mine" and "Thinking Tonight of My Blue Eyes." He sang that last one especially for her, with true regret evident in every word. Meanwhile anger kept snapping the big blade of the jackknife into the handle, thumbing it out, snapping it back. Gradually his throat turned to stone, and his songs were just a whisper.

Anger won finally. It always did.

The rocketing train brought Jackson back to consciousness by gently but repeatedly banging his head against a leg of the dining table in the private car. The headache he woke up with was out of proportion to the amount of punishment he was absorbing from the table leg. His eyes wouldn't focus. He felt as bad as if he'd been on a prolonged ether drunk. Rolling over was an effort, but it was slightly better lying on his stomach with his fingers hooked into the carpet; he didn't feel so much at the mercy of the careening momentum of the train.

For half a minute, before he started retching, he had the chance to think about where he might be going and what he was doing on the train. But he was disoriented and confused by a large body of guilt that shared his skin, guilt that could not be resolved into specific accusations. So he'd done badly again. Taken the wrong way out. If only the goddam train would stop for a minute, two minutes—didn't they know how sick he was?

While he was throwing up, the pain in his head was excruciating, causing a free flow of tears. Then as he lay helpless, cold and nearly syncopic, the pain diminished. Guilt also edged away and he was touched, as if from a distance, by fear. Someone else's fear.

It had a galvanic effect on Jackson. He was able to sit up and then to stand, leaning on a chair. The sofa on which Champ Bradwin had been sleeping was empty; Champ was gone.

Cutlery and glassware rattled on the table. Jackson wet his dry mouth with water from a carafe and sniffed the scotch he'd been drinking for a clue as to what might have knocked him out. The whiskey smelled okay, but he wasn't about to taste it again.

Physically he'd begun to improve, his vision sharpening, his heart settling down, he could move and maintain his balance. With damask napkins he cleaned up after himself and threw whiskey on the carpet stains to disguise the smell. But now that his senses were more acute he was aware of another odor in the air, raw and foul, like that of an unclean human body.

Jackson wondered if Champ's sherry had been doctored. If so, he wouldn't be up and around, because he'd drained his glass. Which prompted an interesting speculation: Why had he been drugged, and not Champ? Perhaps because Champ alone knew what Jackson would be drinking, and only Champ had had the opportunity to doctor the carafe behind his back.

Now all he had to do was think of some plausible reason why Champ would want to knock him out. Or he could just forget the whole thing, pull the emergency cord and get off the train before he suffered a worse fate than a headache and an upset stomach.

No reason for him to be worried about the missing Champ. But he was.

The crystal of his Marks and Spencer watch had been cracked but the expensive timepiece was still ticking; it was now almost one in the morning, so he'd been unconscious for three and a half hours. During this time someone might have entered the car, walking over him like a carcass, a dog in the road, to take Champ away.

Jackson raised a window shade and looked out at the land, the stars, a tin-roof town cheaply lit and playing out at high speed along the track. The train swayed and curved outward in a way that made Jackson queasy all

162

over again; he saw the glow from the firebox of the locomotive, with nothing in between but a string of dark cars carrying no passengers.

He began his search in the bedroom of the private car, just to make sure Champ hadn't wandered back there and passed out in the small bathroom. He also checked the door to the observation platform, but it was locked on the inside, and the lock was corroded from disuse.

It was possible, Jackson thought as he went forward, that Champ was no longer on the train, which could have stopped and started a dozen times while he was sleeping off the drugged whiskey. Nevertheless he felt compelled, by the unelaborated anxiety that had been with him since he woke up, to look through the rest of the train.

The chair car just ahead seemed as empty as he'd anticipated, but it was uncomfortably dark inside. Again he noticed in the stuffy air the taint of an unwashed body, so strong the proprietor might have passed that way only a few minutes ago. A seedy trainman, perhaps—or a hobo enjoying unaccustomed luxury.

Jackson reached across a seat to raise a shade and provide more light in the coach, but he quickly reconsidered. An ordinary bum, nosing around the private car, would have found it impossible to resist the free booze. So either he was lying unconscious in one of the three cars, or—the man, despite his wretched body odor, was no ordinary bum. In which case, Jackson thought, he might be traveling in greater hazard than he'd imagined. But if he was going to continue there was no way to proceed from one car to the next without calling attention to himself, he'd just have to risk it. By now he was convinced—a new twist to the old anxiety—that Champ Bradwin *was* aboard, and in desperate need of him.

The middle car. Jackson, yearning for light, unbalanced by the headlong sway of the train, stepped on something slippery in the aisle and tumbled backward into a seat, icy with alarm, hands up to protect himself from whatever might come flying out of the dark at him. But again he was alone; the vivid terror quickly vanished. He scraped at the sole of his shoe with his fingers. Apple pulp and

163

seeds, fresh juice. There were peelings in the seat where he was sprawled, and the air all around was much too familiar, rancid as a flophouse.

Jackson scowled and sat up, struggling against the momentum of the train, hearing a long whistle as the lights of another town pierced the worn-out shades of the chair car. He'd wrenched his neck in falling, and it was painful. Light flickered on the back of his hand as he reached up to massage the stiffened muscle.

He turned then and he saw that the shade covering the window had been slit by a sharp knife, many times, to achieve a complex design. The headlights of a stopped auto struck the shade at an upward angle, revealing a coiled serpent. The fabric of the eyes glowed, a virulent yellow: his imagination prompted the serpent to weave and hypnotize.

He bolted just in time, and was midway through the first car before his lungs unlocked and he could draw a breath.

Only the baggage car lay ahead. Jackson hesitated, but going on was better than going back, past the emblematic serpent, mistress of his disordered life.

The windowless door to the baggage car seemed to be locked, but the handle responded freely when he tugged at it. He put his full weight against the door. Then the baggage car lurched and the door popped open. Jackson fell inside just as the bum he'd been seeking was about to throw Champ Bradwin off the train.

Or so it looked to Jackson, but he had no time to sort out his impressions. The side door of the baggage car was open; the train was rushing across a long trestle; both men were dangerously near the door, locked together and struggling. Above the clatter of the train Jackson heard Champ scream.

He moved toward them, but was distracted by the sight of a dark-haired young woman in a satin-lined coffin— and by the coffin itself, which moved to the sway and roll of the train as if it were on casters.

Early Boy, wearing a cap that hid half his face, had Champ in a forearm vise and was choking him, forcing

164

him down on one knee. Champ's own grip had loosened, and now a hard shove could send him bouncing along the trestle track and into the dark slough below.

Jackson caught Early Boy by the collar of his shirt and hammered him in the kidneys. Early Boy, jolted loose from Champ, turned in surprise and pain.

"Not me, doc," he gasped, but Jackson hit him a second time, and Early Boy doubled up on the floor of the baggage car. His cap fell off. Jackson, momentarily paralyzed by surprise, stared at him. When he turned his attention back to Champ he saw Champ at the doorway on his hands and knees, so close to falling out that the next hard sway of the train would throw him beneath the wheels.

Jackson reached him quickly, but he wasn't prepared for Champ's reaction. Champ fought desperately while Jackson dragged him back toward the middle of the car. Jackson bumped into the coffin and Champ tore himself free, made a lunge for the moonlit doorway——there was no doubt he intended to jump, but Jackson grabbed him again. Both men banged hard against the wall next to the door. As they struggled, Jackson had a close look at Champ's eyes. He appeared to be demented by grief.

"What are you trying to do?" Jackson shouted.

The train bent into a long curve. The coffin immediately slid another two feet, to the edge of the doorway. Champ looked around in horror. Early Boy was getting up, reaching back to a hip pocket, his eyes gravely fixed on Champ. Both Champ and Jackson tried to get hold of the coffin to keep it from falling off the train.

Early Boy took one step and sapped Champ rather delicately behind the left ear.

Champ collapsed to the baggage-car floor as the heavy coffin, with Jackson still clinging helplessly to it, dipped out the door and tilted slowly toward the vertical. Jackson found himself being crushed between coffin and doorframe. The still-attractive face of the dead young woman rose toward his own like a cameo in a jeweler's revolving display case, her dark hair beginning to tangle in the rush of smoky air outside. Then the train lurched and ground

165

its wheels around the curve and he was spared the final bone-breaking weight of the coffin as it slipped away and fell from the train.

Jackson, breathless and stunned, dropped to one knee and saw the coffin strike the ground end-first midway down a steep embankment. The lower lid opened on impact and the woman, dressed in white, seemed to step lightly from her satin couch, turn in the air, raise her hands in a theatrical gesture of departure and disappear abruptly as a dark fence of trees came between her and the train. Jackson closed his eyes, cramped by nausea. He couldn't open them again until he felt a hand on his shoulder.

He looked around at the face of Early Boy Hodges.

"Give me a hand with him," Early Boy said curtly.

"The coffin—we must stop the train and recover the body!"

"She was dead when she fell off; what difference does it make to her? Come on."

Early Boy reached behind Jackson and pushed the door shut. It was quieter in the baggage car as Jackson got to his feet. He was so light-headed he couldn't stand without holding on to the handrail beside the door.

"What are you doing on this train?" he said.

"Going south."

"I heard you were dead."

Early Boy smiled derisively, the smile happening only on the left side of his face, pulling his mouth askew as if a fishhook were caught in the corner. A gunshot wound, untreated for too long years ago, had paralyzed several of his facial muscles. Early Boy glanced at Champ, then stooped to take hold of the unconscious man.

"I can carry him," he said to Jackson. "You lead the way."

"Why did you hit him, Early Boy?"

"You saw yourself. He tried to jump. Would've broke his neck, or worse. I just did get hold of him when you come along." He smiled again. "Looked to me like you was good for a couple hours more shut-eye back there. What's the matter, doc, can't hold your liquor anymore?"

166

He tested Champ's weight, grunted, changed his stance and grip and lifted him without too much effort, using the fireman's carry. Champ groaned and breathed through his mouth. Jackson wasn't too concerned about the effects of the blow he'd received; he had respect for Early Boy's technique with any kind of blunt instrument. But he didn't move out of Early Boy's way.

"Why was Champ trying to kill himself?"

"The way I get it, that woman in the coffin was his wife."

"Oh, for God's sake, I don't believe it!"

"Ask him yourself. If he makes any kind of sense when he comes around. Enough to drive a man crazy, what he just been through."

"He may have suffered worse than that these past few months."

"That a fact? Why don't you tell me about it, doc? But not here. He's getting heavy, and my back hurts."

Jackson anticipated that Champ would come around by the time they reached the private car, but he was still unconscious when the sweating Early Boy lowered him to the sofa. Jackson first examined Champ's eyes with a penlight and found that the pupils reacted normally. There was no lump where he'd been struck. Jackson proceeded to carefully monitor Champ's pulse, heart and lungs.

"He's asleep, that's all," Early Boy said, sounding churlish. "You know me better than that, doc."

"The major has pneumonia." But Jackson had reached the same conclusion: Champ wasn't doing badly and probably wouldn't have more than a sore spot on the back of his skull and a mild headache when he awakened.

He looked around at Early Boy, finding him even more distasteful in a good light.

"Really hit the skids, haven't you?"

Early Boy winked at him. "Don't be too sure. Sometimes it's the only way to get around. The yaps don't look all that close at a man who smells as bad as me."

"Is the FBI still after you?"

"Everybody's looking for Early Boy. But I told you a long time ago I'd never do a day's worth of federal time."

167

"There's a stall shower in the other compartment. Borrow my razor if you'd like. And for Christ's sake throw that bloody shirt away."

"I'm traveling kind of light these days."

"The major has a blouse and trousers to spare. I'm sure you're not particular about the fit."

"Skivvies too?"

"I'll lay everything out," Jackson said desperately. "Just get away from me."

Early Boy nodded amiably, then stopped short of the bedroom door. "Better not have any more hooch to drink. It's all bad, doc, every drop."

"How do you know that?"

"I know what I have to know, to stay out of jams. Maybe you're a better man than I am, doc. High-toned, let's say. But it seems to me like you're *always* trying to pull your tail out of a crack."

Jackson appropriated some of Champ's clothing for Early Boy, which he left in the bedroom. He held his breath while he made a thorough search of Early Boy's things. Then he went outside to stand between cars, where he smoked a cigarette and stared at the dark landscape.

How much further did they have to go, to reach this place called Dasharoons? He was unable to forget the sight of the dead young woman in the falling-away coffin, the terror and anguish in Champ's eyes. Obviously it was no accident that the coffin had been aboard this train. Someone, very callous or possibly demented, had wanted Champ to see her like that. He wondered how Nancy Bradwin had died.

The image of her lying in a weedy ditch beside or beneath her coffin many miles up the line was almost more than he could bear. He regretted not pulling the emergency cord to stop the train, a simple and rational act. Had he been in a state of shock himself, befuddled by events? Jackson couldn't remember.

Perhaps the coffin had fallen near enough to the road to be discovered by the first passing car. Not much comfort in the thought, but it was the best he could do.

Jackson went inside and glanced at the note addressed to Champ. It was lying on the table with Early Boy's grimy fingerprints on it. Jackson decided he might as well read it too.

Darling Champ,
It's so wonderful to know that you'll soon be home! I wish I could be with you now, but I felt that I shouldn't leave Dasharoons even for a few hours in the event we do hear from Nancy. Please try not to worry, and God grant we will have her back before long. I'm sure this latest episode will be the last; seeing you again should make all the difference in her recovery.

My love,
Nhora

It was a letter that might have been written by almost anyone: Champ's mother, his sister, a mistress. In referring to Nancy Bradwin the writer seemed depressed, and not particularly optimistic despite a cheerful choice of words. Obviously Champ's wife had been missing, and not for the first time—*this latest episode*—therefore if she was ill, the problem most likely had been emotional rather than physical. . . .

Early Boy came out of the bedroom in skivvies. "Pretty fancy," he commented, toweling his hair dry. Washed clean, his hair looked two shades lighter and was heavily streaked with gray, although Jackson felt certain that Early Boy wasn't much older than he was. He hadn't touched his five-day growth of beard, which was patchy and white around the pitted bullet scar, but it was no longer difficult to linger downwind of him.

Early Boy cast the towel aside and touched the bullet scar.

"Remember, doc?"

"Very well. You shouldn't have let it go so long before you came to see me. I'm not a surgeon, but I might have been able to do something."

"You did okay. I always thought you was a swell doc-

169

tor. Saved Jake McGinness, didn't you? And Petey Gailor, he might've lost that leg, it looked bad and smelled worse. Come as a real surprise to me, seeing you aboard this rattletrap."

"Where did you get on?"

"I don't know. I was sitting by the side of the road, first train along, I hopped it. I heard you was fixed up pretty good out West. Seattle, maybe."

"And a couple of other places."

"Oh, I get it. Always just one jump ahead of the dicks, like me."

"Not a bit like you, Early Boy. I treated your kind when I needed the money, but the law's never been interested in my career. It's the desperadoes who earned all the headlines."

"They tell me Hoover's thinking about a list. The ten most wanted criminals. You want odds I'll be at the top of that list when it comes out?"

"Don't flatter yourself. You don't matter anymore, Early Boy. You're a curiosity now, and all you ever had was a vulgar flair for publicity—"

Early Boy laughed. "When they talk about banks, I'm still number one."

"Is that so? When was your last job? It completely escaped my notice."

Early Boy began to tick off the years on his fingers, then looked up with an expression of exaggerated surprise. He shrugged.

"Been a while since I seen anything I liked. When I do, you'll read about it in the papers. *Before* I pull the job."

"You did get away with that stunt more often than not." Jackson tapped his own lip with a forefinger approximately where Early Boy had been shot in a near-disastrous escape from one of the banks that he had announced he would rob. "I've always wondered why you deliberately made life so difficult for yourself."

"Saw Harry Houdini when I was a kid. Never forgot it."

"What? Oh, yes. Many men can escape from handcuffs,

even a corset of chains. But when you're holding your breath underwater at the same time—"

"Just make it simple," Early Boy said impatiently. "*Any* jerk with a gun can stick up a bank."

"Or break in the night before. But it requires a certain feeling for high drama to arise from a good night's sleep rested and refreshed, to shave and greet the officers when they appear, wearing a starched collar and a new tie—"

"With a corsage for the ladies and cologne for the gents."

"And a tommy gun cradled in one arm. No, it was never the money, was it?"

"I look like a lot of money to you, doc?"

"Only the stunt mattered. The notoriety. But where's the limelight now? What happened to you?"

"It's the simple pleasures that count the most, didn't nobody ever explain that to you?"

"I think you're a liar. It's one of two things about you I've been able to depend on. You're a splendid actor, and a habitual liar So I suppose it *is* dense of me to ask you what you're doing on this train. But I want to know. And you goddamned well had better tell me."

"Getting a little agitated, aren't you, doc?"

"I can cope with it. I can cope with *you*. If you're looking around for that marvelous skull-knocker you carry, I disposed of it. I found the knife, too. Did some whittling on the shade in the chair car, did you? But why a serpent?" Jackson took Champ's duffel bag from a cabinet and produced the army automatic. Early Boy looked pained.

"Oh, doc, what the hell's got into you?"

"Getting agitated, ain't you? *Ain't*. That's the word you should have used. After all these years of effort, turning yourself into a picaresque gangster, the breeding still crops up. Aren't. Ain't. Herodotus."

"Her what?"

"Who, not what. Herodotus was a Greek historian who specialized in military affairs. Once in a delirium you quoted him to me. At length, in the ancient Greek."

171

"Could have been double-talk you heard. Guy out of his head, what do you expect?"

"I was a Greek scholar myself when I was a boy; in addition to most of the medicine I know, my father also taught me the classics. I understood you very well. You're an educated man."

Early Boy said, with a hint of contempt, "And between us, we ain't good for a bowl of beans." He looked at Champ, who was moaning quietly in his sleep, then again at Jackson. "You ain't too steady with that automatic. How about you just put it down, and no hard feelings? I don't know a thing more'n I told you already. But any cluck can see the bad news ain't all in yet."

"Put two and two together, have you?"

"What's *your* interest in the major, doc?"

"I'm paying off a favor for a friend. The hard way."

"Well, I don't owe nobody no favors. So I'll just get off at the next stop and go my way."

"I'll decide that."

"Better decide soon. This train's slowing down, in case you ain't noticed."

Jackson had noticed. "It could be Dasharoons."

"How would I know? I'll step outside and have a look."

"I'm not sure yet that I can do without your company. Leave your trousers behind."

Early Boy winced but unbuckled the loose uniform trousers and let them drop. He stepped out of them and left the car.

Jackson felt uneasy and looked around. Champ's eyes were half-open, but unfocused. He had raised his head from the couch. The train was rolling to a stop.

"Do you hear me, Champ?"

Champ said nothing. His head turned as Early Boy reentered the car. The two men looked at each other. There was a slight apprehension in Champ's eyes, a heavier pulse in the hollow of one temple. Early Boy smiled slantwise at him.

"Coming around okay, huh? Hello, big stuff."

"Do you know this man, Champ?"

172

Champ made no reply. The train stopped with a small lurch. His head sagged in response and he almost fell off the couch. Jackson propped him up with one hand. Champ rolled back with a sigh, apparently exhausted, and closed his eyes.

"Home yet?" he asked.

Jackson glanced at Early Boy.

"Siding. Signal down the line. Waiting on a redball freight, maybe, coming the other way. How about it, doc? Do I get off this rattler now?"

"You can go," Jackson said. He put the .45 automatic on the table.

Early Boy, who was buckling the khaki trousers, paid no attention to this gesture. He nodded but failed to move.

"Well, what else do you want? Get going."

Early Boy said with a beggarly whine, "Saved his life, didn't I? Now that's worth something."

"How much?"

"Ten bucks cash."

"I'll give you five," Jackson said contemptuously.

"Forget the sap, but I put in a lot of work on the blade of that jackknife."

Jackson reached into a pocket of his coat and handed the knife to him. Then he counted five singles from the few bills left in his money clip and gave those to Early Boy.

"Didn't leave you much."

"I'll have my true reward in heaven."

"Let me get my cap and bindle, then I'll say so long."

A Frisco Mountain, flying white flags, was passing and shaking them; Jackson and Early Boy went outside as the lights of the redball's caboose dwindled to the magnitude of stars and the 4-4-0 at the head of the Dasharoons train began to move back onto the main line. Early Boy dropped without difficulty to the ballast, adjusted his bindle and walked along beside the departing train.

"If the major don't die on you, then you ought to make out okay, doc!"

"I intend to!"

"One thing you need to be careful about!"

"When I want your advice—"

"For a quack you're as good as any real doctor I ever met!" Early Boy had begun to lag behind the train, limping from the aggravation of the pace he was obliged to maintain. He raised his voice, but not enough for Jackson to hear him clearly; the train whistle was blowing. Early Boy said something else about real doctors, and about things even the best doctors couldn't understand. Then a blackish comber of locomotive smoke swallowed him to the brim of his herringbone cap.

With the back of his hand Jackson dashed at a cinder caught in the lashes of an eye.

"Son of a bitch!" he yelled, looking back at the siding, but Early Boy wasn't there anymore. Thoroughly angered, and nauseated again by his anger, Jackson went inside.

No reason why that last-minute remark about "real doctors" should have upset him. From Early Boy's warped perspective every man's life and motives were suspect—life itself was a bad play in which he was the only actor of stature, always slyly in control, improvising brilliantly, manipulating his fellow actors, misdirecting them for his greater glory. So Early Boy had constructed for Jackson a puzzle within a puzzle and bowed off stage to applause only he could hear, leaving Jackson bumbling and uncertain before a stony and possibly sinister audience that awaited explanations he was inadequate to provide. He couldn't hope to escape from himself for a little while, thanks to good-hearted Beggs.

In his own grip he uncovered the bottle of Teacher's scotch—seal intact—which Beggs had given him. Champ Bradwin's face was dry and warm to the touch, and he snored comfortably on the sofa. Jackson took a crystal goblet to the bedroom of the private car and sat in a chair beneath a swarm of dingy cherubs painted on the ceiling.

When he was halfway through the bottle Nancy Bradwin made an appearance, leaving her coffin, stepping lightly through the air like a child going from stone to stone across a wide brook. Back and forth in front of him, trippingly. But her head dangled crudely, as if from a broken neck. The audience sharing this apparition with him seemed to love it. They murmured to each other in a dialect he scarcely remembered. Jackson watched Nancy Bradwin unflinchingly and treated his fear with fresh drafts of whiskey that he could barely swallow. With each drink Nancy became less substantial; but he was close to the bottom of the bottle, and she refused to entirely disappear.

"I'm sorry," Jackson told her. "I can't raise the dead."

"You raised 'em in Peoria; you raised 'em in Saint Paul," Early Boy sang. He had reappeared wearing a window-pane-check suit and a shaggy red wig. In one hand he carried a horn with a rubber bulb that made rude noises, and there was a flower in his buttonhole that squirted a stream of water into Jackson's face. The audience ate it up.

Jackson stood grinning sheepishly in the glare of the key light. His tricky trousers ran up and down his bare legs. Whistles; rimshots.

"Folks," said Early Boy, mugging his way to the front of the stage, "if it walks like a quack, and has feathers like a quack, and quacks like a quack, WHAT IS IT?"

"QUACK QUACK QUACK!" they screamed. Early Boy turned and hit Jackson over the head with a pig's bladder. It made a farting sound.

"Tell me," Jackson pleaded. "Tell me how you know so much about me."

"Stick to the sketch, you chump!" Early Boy hissed in his ear. He flashed his crooked grin at the audience and gave Jackson a squirt from the fake flower. "Oh, doctor!"

"Yes, yes. That'll be five dollars."

"Five dollars! But you haven't heard my complaint."

"That'll be ten dollars. Now you really got something to complain about."

"The problem is my wife."

"Yes, I can cure the common scold."

"Doctor, my wife thinks she's a lamppost."

"Shed some more light on that for me, will you?"

"She hangs around the street corner all night."

"Take two aspirin and walk your dog someplace else."

They're not laughing, Early Boy whispered. *It's all your fault. They'll never book us anywhere after this. Do something!*

And suddenly he was gone, leaving Jackson alone before his auditors. A single work light burned feebly, throwing his shadow to the pit.

He could hear but not see them; they were dangerously restless out there, in the tropic dark. Jackson was streaming wet from that last squirt of the flower in Early Boy's lapel, from his own nervous perspiration. He advanced cautiously to the foot of the stage; sure enough, they were making the sound he most dreaded hearing.

Hisssss   Hissssssss

"Impresario!" Jackson called. "Please, sir! I want to get off. Let me off now."

He was soon aware of the old man's eyes, truculent orbs shining coldly in the dark. The rest of the face gradually came clear, and Jackson, quaked, dismayed by the revelation of time's cruelty, by the absence of love, by the pain of yet another judgment.

"Drunk," the impresario said.

"Oh, no, sir," Jackson protested.

"Dis-rep-u-ta-ble."

Jackson's mouth was too dry for him to speak.

"And a disgrace to my profession."

"You taught me everything," Jackson said. "I'm as good as you."

"How dare you compare us?"

"Don't," Jackson croaked. "I would have *died* for you. Let me have what's left of my life."

Hisssss

"Play," he begged the silent orchestra. But they'd packed up and gone home, leaving only the odd oboe glinting in the dark. He turned frantically upstage. "Lights!" He was ignored. The filament of the single bulb high on the brick fire wall was turning red. Soon it would die.

"Early Boy!" Jackson shouted. He heard the thunderous clang of a steel door closing somewhere off stage.

In the dark nothing was left but the gleam of an old man's vexed eyes.

"Help me, father!"

"I can't."

Hissssssssssssssssssssssss.

"Can't you hear? Don't you know what's coming?"

At last there was a hint of sympathy in his father's voice.

"I prayed to God, but she took me anyway. Just as she will take you. I have no advice to offer. We're an unfortunate lot. But I'm not telling you anything you don't already know."

Jackson whirled again. The work light flared briefly, and exploded.

In the last red trace of illumination before the world completely closed down on him, Jackson ran.

He ran, in the open air, down a weedy slope away from the railroad track and the standing, steaming train, beneath a moon that was red and as low as the treetops in the sky behind him. Big mosquitoes swarmed around his head. He splashed through the muck and shallow water of a drainage ditch with the noise of hounds baying in his ears. He came to a rutted clay road and angled across it, falling twice. Each time he scrambled to his feet the hounds sounded closer. They scared him. He knew he'd been drunk aboard the train, and dreaming. He was no longer dreaming but he was still a little drunk, and unable to get his bearings. Not knowing where he was or where he was going or what was after him worsened his panic. Flight was harrowing, but to stop was unthinkable.

Across the road there was a field, then a stand of bare, jagged trees that seemed close-by. Jackson, hoping for the best, made for the deadwood and undergrowth. But the dogs were coming, followed by horsemen cutting around in front of the locomotive, plunging down the embankment in pursuit. Almost out of breath, Jackson floundered between tufts of coarse matted grass, his shoes laden with mud. But he forgot the pain in his chest when he heard the crack of a rifle.

He plunged into the eerie wood, too busy to be apprehensive about night-dwelling snakes that might be hanging around the windfalls. His clothes snagged in the prickly brush, and he soon found it impossible to flog himself through any more of it.

The dogs were having no trouble. Jackson heard them crashing and panting not far behind and at last he gave up, using his remaining strength to shinny up a leaning tree trunk, where he clung to a few broken stubs and shuddered, wrapping his head in his jacket for the protection from mosquitoes it afforded. By then all the dogs had gathered in bellicose ceremony at the base of his tree.

The lead horseman had a light Jackson perceived through the cloth of his jacket. The horseman had to shout to be heard over the barking dogs.

"You want to come down, Early Boy, or do we shoot you down?"

Jackson wearily unshrouded his face. The light from the electric torch stung his eyes. He blinked and shielded them and looked at the Negro on the horse below. The Negro had eyes pale as looking glass, and other features that told of mixed bloodlines. There was a rifle in the crook of his right arm. He laughed in a disgusted way and shook his head and called back over one shoulder,

"Take a look here at what we got."

The other horse appeared, a big roan gelding. Jackson turned his head and squinted at the rider, a tall woman who wore a shooting vest. Her hair was pulled back tightly from her face. Despite the poor light it was possible to tell that she was an extraordinarily handsome woman. She carried a pump-action shotgun, finger on the trigger. Obviously she was not happy, but to her credit she looked concerned about this case of mistaken identity.

Jackson slapped at a bitten ear and attempted a jaunty smile. But the concern he glimpsed in her green eyes reminded him that he'd had about all he could take for one night. He couldn't smile. Instead a tear slipped down his cheek.

"Good God," Nhora Bradwin said, as the Negro hushed their dogs. "Who are you?"

V

"DASHAROONS"

August 5, 1944, and after

Don't ya know God gwine keep 'er punishin' white folks—keep 'er sendin' dem floods, win' storms and lettin' disasters come to dier chillun, an' dier chillun's chillun in dis day an' time.

—ISHREAL MASSIE, *former slave interviewed at the Petersburg, Virginia, City Home in 1937*

"Dr. Holley?"

Mosquito netting. Heat. A rank sweetness in the air of the room. The face of the elderly Negro, three paces beyond the bed, indistinct in a pearly light that could have been dawn, or dusk. The bedsheets in which he'd slept were clammy from the sweats of his anxious dreams. Jackson's throat was raw; he felt a touch of ague, there was a run of chills. It was all too familiar.

"Dr. Holley?"

His father was urgently needed. But the terrifying black men in snakeskins and crocodile masks had taken him away. Weeks ago. With the help of the tireless Sisters of Radiant Hope and the Negro orderlies his father had trained, Jackson had managed to keep the hospital open, functioning in a limited way. But there were too many seriously ill patients and not enough drugs, there were surgical cases he dared not touch, despite his precocious skill at excising tumors and repairing strangulated hernias. And his mother, going slowly mad with fear, inconsolable—how could he save her?

"What do you want?" Jackson said.

"My name is Hackaliah, suh. Miss Nhora ask me to look in on you."

"Miss Nhora?" Jackson rubbed his sore head. Memories of Tuleborné were fading, but his skin still tingled from the dreamlike impact of déjà vu. "Oh, yes." He sat up in the bed. "How long have I slept?"

"I reckon about fourteen hours."

"What time is it, Hackaliah?"

"Seven-thirty the even'. Is there somethin' I can do for you, Dr. Holley?"

"Light a lamp. And my robe, please. Is that coffee I smell?"

"Yassuh. Is."

Jackson parted the mosquito netting and got down from the four-poster bed. The air of the room was like a warm bath. Balcony doors stood open, but there was no evening breeze. Torch light was reflected in the glass of the doors. Jackson heard tree frogs, and the crunch of automobile tires on a gravel drive in front of the plantation house.

Hackaliah turned on a lamp and brought Jackson's silk robe, which had been painstakingly pressed for him. Hackaliah wore a gray cloth jacket, a string tie and striped pants. He was a large, stooped man with a palsy. Parkinson's, Jackson decided, but it was affecting only his head and not his hands, so he could go on working. He looked the sort of man who'd rather die than be considered useless.

"Have you seen a doctor recently, Hackaliah?"

"No, suh. I don't bother."

"Why not?"

"There's no doctor hereabout anymore. Just Old Lamb. He says I shake 'cause I's old." Hackaliah chuckled humorlessly.

"How old are you?"

"I's told I was born the last year of the war."

"The Civil War? Let's see, that's roughly eighty years."

"Yassuh. Is. You did tell me coffee." Hackaliah poured from a service that looked to be five or six pounds of pure silver. The china was eggshell-thin and very old. The coffee was bitter. That was the chicory in the coffee, Hackaliah explained. A southern tradition. Jackson decided the taste would require getting used to.

While Hackaliah ran his bath and laid out his clothes for the evening, Jackson finished his coffee, standing on the long balcony that overlooked the drive. Traffic was fairly heavy on the hundred-yard horseshoe of pure white gravel. Men, women, a few children, calling at the designated hour to pay their respects to the family. Torches burned at intervals along the boxwood hedges, and there were more torches on the lawn. The sun had set, the sky over Chisca Ridge was yellow, smoke drifted across the mirror surface of an artificial pond. There were endless neat white fences running to the horizon, groups of barn-like buildings with metal roofs. He saw settlements and woodlots. He had a glimpse of the coiled river a mile away to the east across a flood plain of great richness, black soil eighteen hundred feet deep. Now a levee controlled the Mississippi's flooding. The wealth of Dasharoons would last forever.

"Hackaliah, have they found Nancy Bradwin's body?"

"They brought her home before noon today."

"The body's here, in the house?"

"No, suh. At the funeral home."

"What did she die of, Hackaliah?"

For the first time the old man's eyes touched briefly on Jackson's face; then his gaze faded away as if he feared empathy, or involvement. He spoke reluctantly.

"I don't know."

"But she was ill months before she died."

"Yassuh."

"Bedfast?"

The palsy seemed more pronounced. "Sometimes, Miss Nancy—she would sleep just like dead womans. Three, four days a spell. Nobody could get her up. Then, when she did wake up, she was most ways like her old self."

"I see. What do you think of that?"

"I don't know," Hackaliah said again, staying scrupulously shy of opinions.

"What did her physician have to say? Was he able to make a diagnosis? Oh, I forgot—you told me there's no doctor here. But surely the family would have sent for—"

"There *was* a white folks' doctor in Chisca Ridge, five months back. Dr. Talmadge. Younger mans than you. He looked after Miss Nancy, day and night." Hackaliah hesitated, then said softly, "Cared about her."

"I'm sure you all cared, very deeply. I'd be interested

in talking to Dr. Talmadge. Could you tell me where he's practicing now?"

"Dr. Talmadge died."

"Oh, that is a shame. And so young. What was the cause?"

Hackaliah hesitated, then looked at the ceiling. Slowly he brought a gnarled hand to his throat, encircling it; his head sagged suggestively. His old eyes shone in a contemplative aside to Jackson. It was a bitter pantomime, evoking mystery and a sense of dread not easily put into words.

"Hanged himself! But why?"

Hackaliah dropped his hand. His voice rasped as if he'd squeezed his throat too hard. "Didn't say."

"There wasn't a note, you mean. Was his health poor?"

Hackaliah was thoughtful but uncommunicative. Jackson mused, "There'll be a case history of Nancy Bradwin somewhere. I'd very much like to see what sort of treatment—" Hackaliah had turned and was walking slowly away. "Where are you going?"

"Bath water's cold by now."

"Good, just the way I like it."

"I believe I forgot to lay out your razor."

"Hackaliah, when you were telling me about Nancy Bradwin, you said she slept for 'days at a spell.' Why did you choose that word?"

Hackaliah paused in the doorway. "The way I talks sometimes."

"How much do you know about spells, Hackaliah?"

"Spells?"

"Magic spells; sorcery. I believe it's also called voodoo in this part of the world."

Hackaliah said with a grimace of disgust, "None of that around here; we'uns all washed in the Blood of the Lamb."

"I also had a Christian upbringing—in the midst of an African forest."

Hackaliah looked around at Jackson; the ceaseless shaking of his head seemed to contradict a gleam of interest in his eyes.

184

"I was raised to be a medical missionary, and in the course of my training I had experience with magic, both white and black. I respect its power. I saw strong and apparently healthy men lapse into comas and die, for no logical reason. It was magic that killed them; the power of suggestion. Nancy Bradwin slept like a dead woman. What you mean is that she *seemed* dead."

"Yassuh."

"Did she stay in one position for hours? Was she cold to the touch? Was she visibly breathing?"

"I don't know; I wasn't 'lowed in the room. Only Miss Nhora and Aunt Clary Gene."

"She had no medical attention after Talmadge hanged himself? Why wasn't she taken to Little Rock, or Memphis?"

"Couldn't nobody make her understand she needed help. When Miss Nancy wasn't—sleeping, or doing them other things, she felt just fine."

"What other things?"

Hackaliah closed his eyes for several moments of pained contemplation. "It ain't decent for me to say."

He shuffled on into the bathroom. Jackson, mildly exasperated, followed.

"Who *can* tell me?"

Hackaliah tested the bath water with his fingertips, then used force to shut off the leaky faucet. " 'Bout some things, you should talk to Miss Nhora. If you needs to know. But what good it does now? Miss Nancy's gone."

"There are questions about her death—and the last few months of her life—that want answering. Of course it's family business, she was Champ's wife, but he's in no condition to make a proper inquiry."

Thinking of Champ, Jackson felt a twinge of remorse for having slept through the day; Champ might have had a setback without his knowing.

"Hackaliah, where's the major now?"

"In his room. Had hisself a mighty poor day."

"I shouldn't wonder. Who's with him?"

"Aunt Clary Gene."

"And who is Aunt Clary Gene?"

"Nursemaid to all the boys. She's old now, but she had powers in her day. Spiritual powers. She could heal the sick. No need to worry about Champ, long as Aunt Clary Gene is there."

"That's reassuring, but he needs a regular course of penicillin. I'll just be a few minutes. Hackaliah, that razor could use a touch of the strop."

"Yassuh," Hackaliah said, closing the blade in the ebony handle and departing.

Jackson had bathed and washed his hair and was back in his robe when Hackaliah returned with the honed razor.

"Miss Nhora ask if you would come down to the front parlor after you see Champ."

"Delighted. Oh, Hackaliah—"

"Suh."

"There was a young man riding with her last night, a Negro. His skin is light with a kind of smoky cast to it, and his eyes are as pale as dry champagne. Do you know who he is?"

"That be Tyrone. My youngest."

"Oh."

"Takes after his mama," Hackaliah said, a moment before the silence might have become mean and uncomfortable. His head shook and shook. "She was quadroon, a pretty smoke color, yassuh. And the eyes: honeybees, just full of that sting. She wasn't no good for a settled-down mans. I was fifty-some. Well, Lord, I ought to have leave it alone, but I still had some kick back then, and you could see the heat come off her skin like a tar road in August." The old man grinned unexpectedly, a hearty, evil grin that hardened into an expression of self-mockery.

"What happened to her, Hackaliah?"

"Soon after the baby come, she up and left. Didn't hear nothin' more about her." His tone indicated no regret. "If you needs me for somethin' else—"

"Not at the moment, Hackaliah. Where will I find Champ?"

Hackaliah told him. Jackson shaved, dressed quickly and went upstairs to his patient.

The three-story house had been built with wide center halls and palladian windows at each end. There was a bright green runner the length of the upstairs hall; the oak floorboards creaked comfortably underfoot. Renovation was under way. Woodwork varnished to a dull·chocolate shade over the years had been stripped, painted white. The hall windows were open; there was a mild, not very cool draft. Screening kept out the bugs. In the shaft of the center stairs the wrought-iron framework of a small lift was also getting a paint job. Above the stairs there was a skylight well, the glass shrouded with moonlit moths. Voices rose from the ground floor. The bedrooms and baths on the third floor were square, modest in size, interconnected if suites should be needed. All but one of the doors stood open, all the lamps had been lit.

A maid carrying a tray backed out of Champ's room as Jackson approached. She wasn't immediately aware of him and nearly dropped the tray in fright when she turned around. A glance at his medical bag reassured her.

"Has he eaten anything?" Jackson asked.

"Some soup; he didn't hardly touch the breast of chicken."

Jackson went in. An old Negro woman dressed in rusty black looked up from the tea she was fixing, a pinch of this and a pinch of that from dingy jars and small sacks. Her stockings drooped and she wore thick glasses. She was about five feet tall and looked as frail as a paper box kite. But there was an attitude of beatific endurance about her, the round little face, wreathed in kettle vapors, expressing the homely serenity of a backwater saint as she ministered to the sick man.

Champ was reclining on a padded deck chair still faintly stenciled with the name of the ship from which it had come: *Lusitania*. The room was a boys' playroom, with an emphasis on things military: campaign maps and a mailed glove mounted on one wall, lances, Civil War swords, model aircraft suspended on wires from the ceiling, lead soldiers in disarray on a tabled battlefield. Champ's head was turned toward the open doors of the balcony, beyond which he could see departing vehicles in

187

the torchlight: a 1933 chauffeur-driven Packard touring
car, a smoky pickup truck with standing children in Sunday clothes bunched together like tenpins. He didn't look
around when Jackson spoke.

"Aunt Clary Gene? I'm Dr. Holley."

"How do you do, doctor."

Jackson put his medical bag down and smiled as Aunt
Clary Gene took the kettle from the hotplate and poured
boiling water over the tea maker in a china cup.

"What have we here?"

"Coltsfoot leaves; fever weed; witch grass. Some pep-
permint to give it savor."

"Any tansy, mother?"

She looked around patiently at him. "Not 'less I likes
to kill him."

"Know your plants, do you, mother?"

"Knowed them all my life. Never made nobody worse.
Made lots of folks better."

Jackson got out his stethoscope and a thermometer.
"Champ? How do you feel?"

Champ moved his head. His eyes were bleary from
grief, or shock.

"All in."

"Do you remember the trip home last night?"

Champ licked his lips. "No." He turned his head
toward the balcony. "Nancy's dead," he said quietly. "I
didn't make it, did I? Just didn't make it in time."

"You tried."

"Get hold of Murph; let Murph straighten it out."

"Murph?"

"General Murphy T. Givens, War Department. He'll
take care of it."

"Take care of what?"

"I'm AWOL. Not that it really matters a damn."

"There shouldn't be any problems, once they know the
circumstances. We do have more important things to
worry about."

Champ abruptly tried to sit up, to force his way past
Jackson. He nearly fainted from the effort.

"Major, you can't—"

188

"Take me to her!" Champ pleaded. "Oh, for Christ's sake, Nancy, Nancy, *why?*"

Jackson held him until the momentary charge of panic and shock failed. Then Champ lay back, weak and palpitating, perspiration breaking out all over him.

"I haven't found out yet," Jackson said. "But I will. Please cooperate with me now."

The lungs seemed clear, but Jackson wanted X-rays. The recent presence of a physician in Chisca Ridge argued for some type of clinic, perhaps a well-equipped surgery. He gave Champ a shot of penicillin, doubling the usual dosage. That left only a two-day supply. Just enough, he hoped, unless Champ took an unpredictable turn.

"What is that you just give to him?" Aunt Clary Gene inquired, skeptical of the chalky liquid in the bottle.

"It's called penicillin, mother. A recent discovery. They obtain it from the mold of bread."

"All kinds of molds is good for healing. Why, I always knowed about that."

"Keep giving him your tea, mother. All he'll drink. He needs the liquid. Champ, I intend to have a look at the local medical facility, if there is one. I'll be back in a couple of hours. Do you need assistance getting to the bathroom?"

"No."

"I'd rather you be in a bed, you can't be too comfortable in this old deck chair."

"I'm comfortable," Champ said, frowning. He drew a light blanket closer to his chin, as if he'd sensed the swift approach of one of the German torpedoes that had sent the liner to the bottom of the North Atlantic. He stared at a wavering biwing model airplane overhead: One wing was broken, hanging down. "I love this room," he said, voice just above a whisper. "Our rainy-day room. Used to dream about being here—you know, playing toy soldiers again, making up war games—all the time I was trying to get off that bloody Jap island, going round and round the island, tracers in the sky all night long, and men blowing up, *shit,* just never getting off. Not till this happened." His
189

fingertips explored the slash across his throat; his lips parted, bloodless simulacrum of the wound. "I fixed that wing twice after Clipper broke it. Clipper broke a lot of my things. Have to fix it again, damn it. God knows I'm tired."

"Try to rest."

"How do I do that?" he asked. Two tears rolled down his cheeks, but his voice was still bare, dry and unemotional. "I don't sleep. I just go straight back to that island Mac wanted so bad and *do it all over again.* There's no getting off. The only way off is dead."

"Champ, I'll be back soon."

"Oh, are you going? Tell Nancy—"

He flinched and rolled his head aside and gestured with one hand, like a sorcerer trying to pacify an unexpected demon. "They keep telling me. She—but then I forget." He seemed exasperated, then frozen with dismay.

"Oh, Champ, Miss Nancy's asleep in the bosom of the Lamb. By and by she'll wake to glory. Trust in Jesus to lift this curse from our house. Abide. Abide."

Jackson looked around at Aunt Clary Gene, obscure in the shadowland of her great age. He felt a chilly apprehension: In this house he kept waking from dreams, his own lonely dreams or Champ's version of the circles of hell, to confront stern dark faces. Frail as she was, Aunt Clary Gene had a moralistic force as compelling as gravity. Jackson was drawn to her. He touched her arm, but she felt no need to look at him.

"Poor boys," she murmured. "Poor boys."

"What curse, mother?" Jackson asked.

Champ answered him. "There's no curse. We've had our share of bad luck, that's all. What family hasn't?" He had propped himself up and was staring at Jackson, for the moment both demanding and rational, yet he seemed to be slipping in and out of dense cloudy moods, some charged with lightning. "Bad luck with Clipper. Couldn't hold himself together. I know all about that now. Almost gave way myself. Maybe it'll still happen."

"You'll soon be back on your feet, Champ. Don't worry."

190

Aunt Clary Gene had turned away and removed the tea maker from Champ's cup. She took the tea to him and spoke in a voice toothless and so soft as to be almost without words, a kind of communion hymn. Champ drank for her and lay back, her hand on his forehead. Jackson had further questions but felt out of touch now. He left them alone and went pensively downstairs toward the remaining voices in the front parlor.

Nhora Bradwin looked up as soon as he entered the room.

"There you are, Dr. Holley."

The night before he'd been too exhausted to fully appreciate her. Because of her exceptional height she dominated the few older men and women in the large parlor. She wore midnight blue instead of black: jersey, vest and skirt. Her uncovered hair was severely bound up, almost penitential in design, and her face had no coloring except for skin tone and the startling, marbleized green of her eyes. As she approached Jackson she still looked mildly embarrassed by the circumstances of their first meeting. She took his arm, momentarily turning her back on the room. It seemed to come as a relief to her.

"I hope you were able to get some rest."

"Yes, thank you." A servant appeared; Jackson helped himself to a glass of whiskey from a tray.

Nhora lowered her voice and tightened her grip on him, as if to draw him more securely into her confidence. "You've seen Champ? What do you think?"

"He's not in serious danger from the pneumonia. His mental state concerns me. He's suffered repeated shocks to the nervous system, going back to his experiences in combat a few months ago."

"I know, it must have been awful for Champ. That scar on his throat . . ."

The whiskey turned out to be bourbon, which had a sweetish resonance he didn't really care for. "Very simply put, it's a miracle he's alive. But he may have endured a critical period of oxygen deprivation which—"

Nhora released him, looking around and smiling at the others in the parlor. They had everyone's devoted atten-

191

tion. Her voice continued low. "I want to talk to you about that; about everything. Thank God the calls are almost over."

"Was it meant to be a wake? The deceased isn't present."

"No, there was cosmetic work that had to be done because of the—the accident, the coffin falling off the train. Anyway, with this behind us we can bury her in privacy and in peace. Let me introduce you. I hope I have all their names straight. Most of them I never see except at weddings and funerals."

Jackson wondered, as he'd wondered shortly before falling asleep that morning, about Nhora's position in the family hierarchy. Unquestionably she was mistress of Dasharoons, though she couldn't have been more than thirty years old. Her speech was not southern, nor was he certain, as he had been earlier, that she was French-born, despite the telltale sibilance (*Sshamp*) and Gallic inflections. Perhaps she'd been raised bilingually, in some distant corner of the world.

Aunts, uncles, cousins. Nhora introduced him as the physician who had accompanied Champ from San Francisco in this emergency. And how was Champ? Too ill to come downstairs, but recovering. No, he wouldn't be going back to war. Thank the Lord, said one besotted old gentleman with drooping mustaches. What Dasharoons needed was a man around the place. "Not that we don't love *you*, honey," he then said to Nhora, who smiled gallantly. There were other smiles, from the women, with no appreciable measure of sincerity. By and by it was over. Only then did Nhora allow herself to pick up a glass, of red wine.

"You must be starving," she said to Jackson. "There's supper. I don't think I could eat. But if you wouldn't mind company—"

"By all means."

A table had been set for him in an oak-paneled drawing room; servants came and went with covered dishes and chilled wine. The drawing room was dominated by full-length portraits of patriarchs and their

192

women. The largest, most impressively framed portrait took up nearly half of one wall. In the painting a full-dress mounted parade was in progress on a western army post. A turn-of-the-century cavalry lieutenant occupied the foreground, facing away from the dusty parade ground, strong chin sharply drawn against a pale blue sky. He was mounted on a dangerous-looking black horse. He looked equal to the danger. Despite his youth, it was obvious that the arrogance of command already had been fused with a sense of duty and high calling, producing this masterpiece of the martial temperament.

In the planes and angles of the lieutenant's face there was something of the sick man upstairs. But Champ, at roughly the same age, had been humanized by self-doubt, by true fire and bloodbath and pain.

The painter's style and artistry were unmistakable, but Jackson checked the signature to be certain. Frederic Remington.

"When was this painted?"

"In 1903, at Fort Riley, Kansas."

"Who is he?"

"Sylvanus Bradwin the third. He was my husband. No one ever called him by his given name. After he was discharged from the army he was just plain Boss. Like his father, and his grandfather before him."

"Boss Bradwin. I assume that he's no longer——"

"Boss died a little over two years ago." Nhora helped herself to more wine and looked at the untouched tureens with a faint smile. "You're not eating."

Jackson politely uncovered a clear soup and picked up his spoon.

"I shouldn't pry into family relationships, but I can't help being curious. Obviously you were not the first Mrs. Sylvanus Bradwin."

"No, the third. I married Boss when I was twenty-four years old and he was——let me think about that——sixty-five. He already had three grown sons."

Outside there was a passing voice, indistinct. The landscape had blurred into darkness. Nhora looked sharply out, away, then out again.

193

"A difficult situation for a young bride," Jackson said.

"It *was* trying at first. I was overanxious and anticipating real bitterness. But Champ and Clipper treated me with intelligence and courtesy. They never tried to make me feel ashamed of my—my need for their father. Hardly anyone else reacted so well."

She sipped her wine and prowled restlessly beside the glass veranda doors. "Would you mind if I closed them?"

After closing the doors she also drew the drapes. There was a ceiling fan in the drawing room, and the door to the hall stood open. Nevertheless Jackson quickly felt overheated. Nhora, still restless, didn't seem to notice how stuffy it was.

"And what was the attitude of the third son? Beau, is that what they call him?"

Her reaction was delayed; startled. "Where did you hear about Beau?"

"Champ mentioned him. Apparently he's very worried about Beau—he implied some sort of threat. 'Someone I'm having trouble with.' Those were his words."

"What? When was this?"

"Night before last, in Kansas City."

Nhora came back to sit opposite him at the table. "My God. Do you suppose he's actually *seen* Beau? Talked to him?"

"I don't know. Would that be unusual?"

"Beau left Dasharoons in 1920, when he was seventeen. He had a violent falling-out with Boss. As far as I know, no member of the family has had any further contact with him. Champ told me once he believed Beau was dead. But Boss never thought so. Boss seldom mentioned Beau to me, but I'm sure he was hoping—someday Beau would come home."

Jackson buttered a crusty slice of bread. "I told you how Champ and I happened to meet."

"Through that Red Cross worker, the one I spoke to."

"Champ was in rather a bad state when I first saw him. Not so much from the pneumonia. But he was drifting in and out of touch with reality, possibly hallucinating. How old was Champ when his brother left Dasharoons?"

194

"He couldn't have been more than four or five years old."

"At first Champ mistook me for his brother, before I spoke to him. He was holding me at gunpoint, I might add."

"But what was he *afraid* of? If he thought you were Beau, then obviously he couldn't have seen Beau recently. Yes, he must have been hallucinating."

"Still—he was specific about his fears. He felt that Nancy was in danger and that Beau, somehow, was responsible. So far his fears have been realized."

Nhora bowed her head. "Poor Nancy. Oh, God, I felt so helpless! There was no way I could describe to Champ—and I hoped each episode would be the last."

Jackson sampled a Creole dish, diced veal and mushrooms with a rich herb sauce. "Tell me about Nancy. How long was she married to Champ?"

"Five years. But of course they saw very little of each other after Pearl Harbor. When Champ was assigned to Fort Bliss in the fall of forty-one, Nancy came to Dasharoons to live. She'd lost the baby only a few weeks before, naturally she was depressed. She needed rest and quiet, not the strenuous competitive life of a military post."

"What was she like? I've only seen a photograph."

"Photographs don't do her justice—she looks fragile and sort of dreamy or inconsequential, her bone structure doesn't hold up for the camera. But her skin was exquisite, translucent, sunlight seemed to pass right through her. She was a *very* bright girl. Phi Beta Kappa at the University of Virginia. History. She and Boss would go on for hours, but other people thought she was shy, standoffish. That's a capital offense in a place where *socializin'* takes up so bloody much time. It was just that Nancy hated the gossipy invective that passes for conversation around here. She much preferred to listen and observe. When she talked she was never boring. She had a knack for defining someone's personality or style with a few words. A lawyer friend of ours with a really good mind

195

has been going to the dogs lately—Nancy said he ought to stand trial for 'self-embezzlements.' "

"You really liked Nancy."

"I loved her. I wanted to. I tried." Nhora paused in exasperation, unsure of how to neaten the contradictions.

"But you couldn't fully respond to her, is that it?"

"Nancy was an exceptionally good person, but sheltered and unsophisticated. An only child. Her parents were schoolteachers. They lived decent, calm lives in a decent, dull town. No serious illness, no family upheavals or moral dilemmas. She never had to push or shove to get to the front of the line like—some of us. So I think she lacked the fortitude for the life she eventually chose."

"And the man?"

"Champ is not the warrior his father was. He was gentle with her. And too protective. When Clipper tried to kill Nancy, she wasn't equal to the—the irrationality, the sheer horror of it. Something gave way in her mind and she was never the same—"

"Clipper did *what?*"

Nhora stared across the table at him as if looking into a newly opened tomb. "Went berserk on his wedding day. It was a military wedding, full dress uniform, sabers. The cadet chapel at Blue Ridge Military Institute. Clipper drew his sword on the altar and ran it through the throat of his bride-to-be. He then came down into the aisle and beheaded my husband with one stroke. Nancy apparently was to be next. Somehow Champ prevented—more slaughter. Only God knows why Champ wasn't killed. Instead Clipper—swallowed his own sword and plunged through a window, thirty feet to the pavement below."

Jackson was speechless, food caught in his throat. Perspiration stood out on Nhora's face. She continued to stare at him, and through him. Jackson cleared his throat with a swallow of wine.

"Champ said something about his brother 'giving way,' but I—that's a terrible tragedy. No wonder he still has nightmares about it."

"Does he?" Nhora said quietly, coming back into focus. "He isn't the only one. And I wasn't there."

"Why?"

"I was sick the day of the wedding; it might have been food poisoning, or an inflamed appendix." She reconsidered an earlier judgment. "I didn't mean to sound so critical of Nancy. Of course she went to pieces, I probably would have done the same. I was hysterical just hearing about it. I can't tell you much about the rest of the day—I drifted, trying to make myself useful, but it was one dreadful scene after another at the hospital."

"When did this happen?"

"May, two years ago." Nhora suddenly jumped, almost upsetting the chair, and turned on a maid who had quietly reached in front of her to remove a plate of melting butter. "Lillian!" Momentarily her face was transformed by an expression of such ferocity that Jackson was shaken. So was the maid. She had jumped back a good three feet.

"I'm *sorry*, Miss Nhora."

Nhora softened, lips thinning in wry apology. "You gave me a scare, Lillian. Let the butter melt. And please leave us alone."

The maid nodded and turned quickly away, but Jackson observed that she was still in shock, as if there'd been other nights like this, occasions when Nhora was not so forgiving. During their brief time together Jackson had found Nhora intelligent and humane, not the sort to abuse servants. On the other hand, one would not expect to encounter her night-riding with a shotgun and a Negro companion.

"What happened after the tragedy, Nhora?"

"As the surviving son, Champ could have been discharged or transferred from the cavalry and come home. He was needed here—Nancy badly needed help. We argued about it, but he was under such a strain I couldn't reason with him. Champ felt dishonored by what Clipper had done. He wanted to fight this war for all of them."

"So you and Nancy were here alone."

"Yes. I had more than enough to occupy my time. With Boss gone, everyone at Dasharoons was demoralized. There was talk the plantation would be broken up and sold piecemeal. That kind of talk had to be stopped

197

right away. Champ couldn't be here but he approved of my taking over, for the duration. We have excellent foremen, but someone has to have the final word, often a dozen times a day. I'd learned a thing or two from Boss. Make up your mind quickly, and stick to your guns. I can't tell you how scared I was, the first few weeks."

Outside a dog bayed deeply and Nhora lifted her head, listening with great concentration. But the dog soon stopped.

"And Nancy?" Jackson asked.

"She brooded. I guess the word is—languished. She began sleeping long hours, then days at a time."

Jackson loosened the knot of his tie and dabbed at the perspiration on his throat with a handkerchief. He looked at his food without interest, and drank the rest of the now-tepid wine in his glass.

"Are you too warm?" Nhora said absently.

"It does seem—"

"If you've finished your supper, why don't we go outside? It might be cooler on the lawn."

A heavyset Negro man leaned against a pillar of the veranda by the steps, smoking a corncob pipe. He slowly removed his straw hat at Nhora's approach, gold winking around the stem of the pipe. There was a bulge on one hip that had to be a gun, and a formidable one.

"Even,' Miss Nhora."

"Good evening, Bull Pete. This is Dr. Holley."

"How do you do, doctor? How's our man Champ tonight?"

"Improving slowly; don't worry."

Bull Pete shook his head several times. It was an old, hard, wearing-down head, like a stone in a Mayan jungle, stony solitude about the flat eyes, the nose pebbled by lupus.

"Yas, suh! That the best news we could have around here. All that man been through. Sure is good to have him home. Good to have you here too, doctor, hope you likes it at Dasharoons."

Nhora was on the top step, scanning the lawn. Torches were still burning here and there along the drive. Strong lights had been turned on in the trees, cutting the mild ground haze. The lush grass looked pale but fiery beneath the haze, like a carpet of phosphorous.

"Bull Pete, what was the dog?"

"Runned across a fox track, mos' likely."

Jackson saw other Negroes, some with hounds, walking leisurely under the trees and along the drive. Each man had a rifle with him.

"Expecting Early Boy tonight?"

Nhora turned her head. "I'm *never* expecting him. That's the trouble."

"Aww," Bull Pete said in disgust, "that Early Boy thinks he's slick. But we'll get him."

"Haven't had much luck so far," she said with a disconsolate air, and walked down the steps to the lawn. Ginkgo trees tinkled as a breeze stirred from the northwest. They followed a path toward the willow-enclosed pond.

Jackson brushed a buzzing mosquito away from his ear, and another, then reconciled himself to the occasional bite. Nhora, who was bare-armed, seemed unaffected. "I'm sorry. We've sprayed all summer, there can't be many left around here."

"Mosquitoes don't bother you?"

"They never bite. I can walk through a swarm of them and not be touched. I don't know why. Some people say I have a very thick skin," she added, with a glint of vexed humor.

"What does Early Boy want around here?" Jackson asked.

"I don't know. If he's such a good thief, he could have looted the office safe. We keep a good bit of cash on hand for day-to-day business, as much as five thousand dollars. No, it isn't money. He seems to take some sort of morbid pleasure from——hanging around. He was fascinated with Nancy."

"He's been in the house?"

"Weeks ago. I got the shock of my life when I walked into Nancy's room late one night. She was in one of her sleeping spells; we tried not to leave her alone for more

199

than a few minutes at a time. He was standing at the side of the bed, just looking down at her. He was wild with anger, as if he wanted to kill her. But *why?* Poor Nancy, she never hurt anyone."

"He may have been looking at her, and thinking of someone else."

Nhora wasn't listening. "I just panicked, I almost brought the roof down screaming. He looked at me then and actually smiled. It's a twisted sort of smile that goes up one side of his face. Hideous. Just like the first time I saw him, standing in the rain in Virginia, keeping his demented deathwatch."

"When was that?"

"The night after Clipper went crazy. Champ and I were having supper in General Bucknam's home. I looked up and there was this face at the window. Rain dripping down. No telling how long he'd been standing there, watching, feasting on us."

Jackson heard a train whistle, and turned his head to follow the progress of the distant locomotive. He felt a lingering chill across the nape of his neck, as though he'd walked through a web on the lawn and part of it was still clinging to him.

"Just one of the family," he said.

"What do you mean?"

"There couldn't be a better explanation for all the attention you've received. Beau Bradwin has finally come home."

Nhora faltered and looked stunned. "Oh, no, no, I can't believe that! Early Boy Hodges is—he's—"

"A wanted criminal."

"I mean he's insane! He must be. If you saw him, just once—"

"Fortunately all I know of Early Boy is what I've read in the newspaper. But that was some time ago. As I recall, he's never been in custody. Nor very much photographed. There *is* one famous photo of him, nervy and grinning, posing inside a bank with his tommy gun and a group of very unhappy-looking bank officials—"

200

"I've seen it. That was how I identified him, after he told me who he was."

"He wanted you to know?"

"Yes, he boasted about what a notorious character he was. Urged me to get in touch with the FBI."

"Did you?"

"Two agents came down from Memphis, but of course there was no sign of him for the next two weeks. The FBI gave me the impression that they would be happy to take him off the sheriff's hands once he was apprehended, but they really had more important things to do. I was told to call if he showed up again. They went back to Memphis. An hour later I was getting ready for bed. I opened the balcony doors, just a little. I smelled cigarette smoke. He was out there in the dark, enjoying himself. He must have climbed up there, but it's not an easy climb. I couldn't see him well, but he could see me perfectly. I was just—rooted with fright, but shaking. Have you ever had such a chill you thought your bones were going to break? Couldn't speak, couldn't run. Early Boy laughed. 'The FBI,' he said. 'What a bunch of jerks.' Then he told me he'd be seeing me."

"You didn't call the FBI again?"

"I don't need them anyway," Nhora said determinedly. "There are plenty of men here. Men who can shoot well."

A Negro youth with a rangy red hound on a leash passed by and Nhora murmured a greeting, paused to rub the dog behind the ears.

"Perhaps you shouldn't kill him. Not until you're certain of who it is you're dealing with."

"But if it's Beau, then why—this is his home, why should he have to hide and prowl at night and terrify us?"

"He *was* Beau, twenty years ago. Now he's someone else, but something of Beau must have survived intact all these years—feelings, longings, loyalties. A sense of loss. How old was Beau when he had his falling-out with Boss?"

"Oh—seventeen, I think."

"Then there'll be photos of Beau when he was a young man."

Nhora shook her head. "I've never seen any. Boss destroyed them."

"Somewhere an aunt or uncle has an old snapshot tucked away. Hackaliah, Aunt Clary Gene—there must be others nearly as old at Dasharoons. They should remember Beau very well. Early Boy bears scars, doesn't he? He can't be all that pleasant to look at, but if they saw him—"

"They *haven't* seen him, as far as I know. I've seen him; Tyrone has had a few glimpses."

"He could purposely be avoiding them," Jackson said. "Which brings us back to Champ."

They had stopped near the shore of the pond. There was a small dock, and some rowboats sitting perfectly still in the water. Something flickered down magically from the high willows and struck at the surface, leaving oiled rings. Nhora drew back with an expression of distaste. Bats. Jackson wasn't quite touching her, but he thought he could feel the tremor that went through her body.

"Early Boy. Beau. Well—I suppose it makes as much sense as everything else that's happened to us. What *about* Champ?"

"How much was he told about Nancy's illness when he was overseas?"

"Very little. We knew so little ourselves, I didn't want to alarm him. And Nancy was writing regularly, during her good spells. He wouldn't have known what to believe."

"Did you call him at the hospital in San Francisco when Nancy disappeared?"

"No. There'd been other occasions, I thought we'd find her in a day or two. Sometimes she came home by herself. Not very clean. Not caring, either. Exhausted, like an animal that's been run half to death. It made me sick to think about the men she'd been with—"

Nhora looked swiftly at Jackson, eyes darkening, as if the emotional price of trafficking in family secrets was coming too high for her. Jackson ignored both the look and the implied lack of trust in him. Nancy Bradwin was dead, but Champ was alive—precariously so, and possibly in danger from a living ghost. He recalled vividly his first meeting with Early Boy Hodges, a busy three hours. He'd cut away the stiff bloody gauze mask with which Early Boy had sealed the lower half of his gun-shot face. Early Boy's eyes, sunken and crazed from the agony of facial neuralgia, were fixed on Jackson, they never wavered while he worked. There were shattered teeth to be pulled; then he made a deft incision and severed a tiny nerve to end the pain forever. Early Boy was left with a palsied mouth, a memorable grin. Despite the dogs and gunmen patroling this part of Dasharoons, he wondered if Early Boy was watching him now, and remembering.

"Did Nancy know Champ was back in the States?"

"Of course. We tried to put a call through to him at Letterman as soon as he arrived, but there was some problem with his throat, he'd just had corrective surgery and couldn't speak at all. So we made plans to fly to San Francisco. It'll be two weeks this Thursday."

"Nancy was all right then?"

"Perfectly all right, very concerned about Champ, but *so* excited. Her mood was so good I couldn't help thinking—all the trouble was behind us. I'd been fooled before. But this time when she slipped, it was heartbreaking."

" 'Slipped'?"

"I don't know just how to— Imagine a pretty girl, in a pretty dress, in a backyard swing. Not going very fast or very high. Balmy skies and flowers and peace. Content to sway gently back and forth. That was Nancy when she was—right. Now imagine the scene darkening, like a bad dream. Nancy suddenly flying higher and higher, as if she's being pushed. Kicking her feet and struggling, frightened, but still trying to appear calm, to maintain her balance, smile, and graciously reassure you. Then falling, taking a very long time to fall out of that swing to the ground. Getting up. But the dream is really ugly now, sullen and dark, because it's not Nancy in the dirty, torn dress. The eyes are coarse, wild, and blue, full of contempt for everyone. Her manners are street manners, shack-sassy. Her morals would be shocking in a crib."

"When did she disappear for the last time?"

"Eight days ago. The longest stretch so far. And—" Nhora paused, her throat tightening; she had to massage it to force the words out. "She was found dead yesterday morning in a sleazy mountain motel room, about sixty miles the other side of Little Rock."

"Who identified her?"

"Everett John Wilkes. He's the family lawyer, one of them."

"You didn't go?"

"I—I couldn't. I suppose—I'd been expecting this for a long time, whenever she wandered off. But when I heard the news the shock was so great I took to my bed. As they say."

She had made a rather fast recovery, Jackson thought. Within twenty-four hours she'd gone riding in pursuit of the elusive Early Boy Hodges, who wasn't there and couldn't have been there, unless he'd found a way to beat the train to Dasharoons. *But if he intended coming back here, why go to the trouble to deceive me?* Thinking about the curious ways of Early Boy Hodges was enough to give Jackson a headache, the equal of the headache he'd had after drinking doctored whiskey aboard the train. And he was already troubled enough by the circumstances of Nancy Bradwin's death.

"How did she die? A woman alone in a motel room, a young woman with a history of picking up men? Wasn't there a proper inquest?"

"The sheriff of Kezar County is an old friend of the family's. A local doctor examined her and said she died of heart failure. He signed the death certificate. Everyone was anxious to cooperate, to get her home as quickly as possible. Evvy made the arrangements, and the coffin was put on the train last night." She smiled bitterly. "He could have come with her, instead of stopping in Little Rock to drink with his cronies at the capital. How do you suppose that heavy coffin—"

"A freak accident," Jackson suggested. "The door wasn't securely closed and it jolted open in transit."

"We can be thankful Champ didn't see her. What a

gruesome coincidence, both of them on the same train coming home."

"Could it have been planned that way?"

Nhora stared at him, distressed and a shade less friendly than she'd been up to now. "Of course not! As soon as I knew Champ was coming, I had the private car thoroughly cleaned and refurbished and sent on the way. At the time I was still hoping to hear from Nancy, I just couldn't go myself."

"The car was handsomely stocked. Cold wine and a warm meal. But no one was waiting for us when we reached Bonefort. I found that somewhat odd."

"Tyrone volunteered to go along and see that Champ had everything he needed. But as soon as I heard about Nancy, I wired the Bonefort station. Tyrone hired a local Negro to cook and stand watch and came home right away. I suppose the other man got tired of waiting and left before you arrived."

"You felt that you needed Tyrone here?"

Nhora's eyes narrowed; she didn't answer right away. The insinuation became more obvious with each passing second. "I depend on Tyrone," she said. "He's my friend—and he was Nancy's friend, too."

"I see. Do you happen to know if Nancy's body was embalmed before it left Kezar County?"

Apparently she was still thinking about Tyrone; Nhora needed time to focus on his question. "I—she must have been. Isn't there a law?"

"There are always laws. And ways to avoid them, when one is anxious to please, as you say the sheriff was in Kezar County. Assuming Nancy was properly embalmed, it still isn't too late to discover the true cause of her death."

"What do you mean? The doctor said—"

" 'Heart failure' is too convenient a diagnosis, when someone of Nancy's age is involved."

"Well then—she—I don't understand. What do you think happened to—"

"Forgive me, it's almost a certainty Nancy Bradwin was murdered."

A car had turned off the road into the drive and Nhora's face was blanched by the powerful headlights. She made no move to shield her eyes, and something about the pained nakedness of her face in this glare caused his heart to pound unexpectedly. The car was stopped by a Dasharoons guard. Jackson heard a sleepy-sounding bass voice that carried well across the expanse of lawn.

Nhora winced, and began moving toward the lights and the voice as if she were lured. Then she stopped and swung around, rediscovering Jackson.

"Nancy?" Nhora said harshly. "Who would want to kill Nancy?"

"Someone as disturbed as she. Someone like Early Boy Hodges."

Nhora planted her fists on her lips as if to deny his intuition, but she quickly dropped the pose. "There just couldn't be any reason for him to—".

"His reasons may defy logical analysis. Judging from his actions, I agree with your conclusion that he isn't sane."

"All I have to do is think about him and I start shuddering."

"You didn't alert Champ in San Francisco when Nancy disappeared. Who else might have called with the news, the lawyer?"

"Evvy Wilkes? *Not* without asking me."

"Then it could have been Early Boy—but I think it was Nancy herself. This time she may have run away out of fear."

"Nhora! Tell your nigger to get away from my car before I run him over!" The voice was now sounding a little drunken.

Nhora glanced at the waiting car, a Cadillac. "Oh, God," she said, "why tonight? I guess I'd better go talk to him, but he's *not* coming in the house and upsetting everyone. Would you come with me, Dr. Holley?"

"Jackson, please."

"Jackson." Nhora set such a pace across the lawn that

206

he had to concentrate to keep up. "You must enjoy reading detective stories," she said with a thin smile.

"*Nhora!*"

"All *right,* I'm coming!"

"I am a detective of sorts, all physicians are. When I was a boy I was fascinated by the exploits of Dr. Bell."

"Who?"

"Dr. Joseph Bell of Scotland, the model for Sherlock Holmes. Dr. Bell had an incomparable ability to observe and make deductions from the minutiae that are invisible to the untrained eye, sounds that the bored ear never hears. It isn't random curiosity when I propose that an autopsy be performed to determine just how Nancy died. It should be done without delay. When is the funeral?"

"Day after tomorrow, at ten in the morning. Just the immediate family."

"Good, there's time. Who is the local coroner?"

"Coroner? I have no idea. Evvy will know."

"*Nhora! What's keepin' you, Nhora?*" His tone was bellicose, but there was a hint of rude playfulness, as if he enjoyed baiting her. Nhora was still smiling, without pleasure.

"But I don't think Evvy will be of much help to you tonight," she said as they reached the car. A chauffeur was behind the wheel. He smiled uneasily at Nhora, as if afraid she might blame him for his employer's excess of bile. The Negro men Jackson had seen so far were either too young for military service or defense plants, or, like the chauffeur, verging on the ancient. Leaving aside the question of their marksmanship and the stalking quality of their hounds, it wasn't much of a rear guard to defend against the likes of Early Boy Hodges, who obviously had the run of the place when he felt like it.

Jackson looked back at the house, vibrant in the dark surround, but he was unable to single out the third-story playroom where Champ lay virtually unattended, and unprotected. Something should be done about that, and soon.

He raked at a mosquito bite on one cheek as Nhora opened a rear door of the Cadillac.

"It's good to have you back, Evvy," she said dispassionately.

"Where's Champ? I want to *see* that ol' boy. Goddam, it's been two years since I set eyes on him!"

"May I introduce Dr. Jackson Holley? He's Champ's physician."

Everett John Wilkes leaned forward in the seat, squinting at Jackson. He was a heavy man in a seersucker suit, jowls on his chest, graying hair tumbling down into his eyes, a florid complexion to match his rummy disposition. There was a pair of crutches beside him.

"Doctor?" he said loudly, as if they were still on the other side of the lawn. "Where from?"

"I'm with the Red Cross," Jackson replied, now at ease with the convenient lie.

"*American* Red Cross? You sound British to me."

Wilkes's accent and diphthongs were a puzzle to Jackson, but the rhythm of his speech was seductive.

"I am a British subject, but I've practiced in this country and in Canada for many years."

Wilkes continued to look him over. "How *is* Champ? I heard he was dying."

"He has pneumonia, but I'm still confident he'll recover."

Wilkes nodded, his eyes filling as if he were about to weep. Instead he smiled and bellowed, "Now that's some piece of good news, doctor! Yes, sir. Happy to hear it." He fumbled for a handkerchief and used it, then shifted his attention to Nhora, unable to conceal a gleam of malice. "Well, there's business I want to talk over with Champ; need to bring him up to date. No time like the present."

"Surely business matters could be postponed for a week or so," Jackson said, as Nhora hissed softly in exasperation. "Champ is quite weak, he's been on the road for days trying to get here. And emotionally he's in a precarious condition: the war, the death of his wife. He still hasn't fully accepted the fact of her death."

Nor had Wilkes, apparently; at the mention of Nancy Bradwin he winced in pain. Jackson had studied the law-

208

yer closely as he spoke. Without doubt Everett John Wilkes was a heavy drinker, perhaps he was chronically drunk. In the available light it was as difficult to calculate his degree of sobriety as it was to fix his age. If he was an alcoholic, then he was one of the rare ones whose wits never failed them until the lights went out. Jackson decided to test this observation.

"But we have business that shouldn't wait," he said. "You and Nhora have to make a difficult decision tonight."

"Decision about what?" Wilkes said suspiciously. "Champ's back; Champ'll be runnin' things from now on."

"When he's fully competent. In the meantime an autopsy must be sanctioned."

"Autopsy? You talkin' about *Nancy?* What the hell for?"

Nhora drew a little closer to Jackson, touching him, whether to give support or reassurance he didn't know. "Dr. Holley thinks Nancy may have been murdered," she said.

Wilkes's eyes widened slightly; he sank back out of the light, exhaling, his body reacting in nods and jerks to the implications of the word "murder": He spoke for the first time, in a normal tone of voice, phrasing a question that was becoming too familiar to Jackson.

"Jesus," he said. "Just who the hell *are* you?"

The clinic in Chisca Ridge, a three-story brick house without distinction, was two blocks south of the one-street business district of the small town. It occupied an overgrown acre at the intersection of Des Arc and West Pine streets; similar houses, separated by victory-garden plots, filled the neighborhood. There was a deep front porch, a porte cochere and too many shade trees, which would serve to keep the interior dark even on the brightest days. The lower windows were shaded, the upper windows vacant. A child had left a broken roller skate on the front walk. A cat studied them from beneath a drooping branch

209

of a giant mimosa tree. As they walked up the steps to the front door, Nhora morosely jangled the ring of keys she had received from Flax the undertaker.

"Henry was unaccountably brilliant, considering his background," she said. "He came from one of those impoverished mining towns where children rarely go to school past the sixth grade. Henry was spindly from birth, and if that wasn't enough of a handicap, when he was ten a coal truck ran over him. That accident put him in the hospital for two and a half years. His father was a minor union official, so fortunately there were medical benefits. He needed seventeen operations in all, and still some of his bones wouldn't knit properly. To take his mind off the pain he educated himself, reading nearly every book in the local library, taking college-level correspondence courses. Somehow he put himself through medical school, but he never made up the cost emotionally.

"His record was sensational—I saw the transcripts—but the prestige appointments he wanted didn't come his way. Henry had no social graces, and he was totally at a loss on any level of give-and-take with other people. Also he had the sharp, antagonistic manner of the man who knows his superior mentality isn't going to pay off for him. Henry had a minor breakdown from overwork; nothing serious, but his psychiatrist recommended an undemanding practice in a town like this one. He wasn't experienced, but we needed a doctor badly."

Jackson struck a match while Nhora searched for the right key to unlock the clinic. There was a tarnished brass nameplate beside the bellpull. *Henry F. Talmadge, M.D.* A breeze pushed its way through the heavy mimosa, and shadows came to life the length of the porch.

"The practice turned out to be more demanding than he anticipated. Because of Nancy?"

"Yes." Nhora put a key in the lock. "His interest was—far too personal. I think he fell in love with Nancy. He should have looked for help, he could have taken her to Memphis or New Orleans. But after a while he became obsessed, he had to find the cure all by himself."

The door opened and they went in. Nhora paused to

210

turn on the dim overhead light in the foyer. On the left a mahogany staircase went up to the second floor. Nhora turned and looked at the top of the stairs with visible apprehension.

"What's the matter?" Jackson asked.

Nhora pointed. "That's where he did it. He tied his rope to a baluster, then jumped or threw himself over the railing."

"When did it happen, Nhora?"

"The end of March; March twenty-sixth, I think."

"No one knows why?"

"He was under a strain, spending so much time with Nancy other patients were neglected. There were complaints."

"That isn't enough to drive a man to suicide. Is it?"

"I don't know; I told you he was obsessed. He had no tolerance for frustration, for failure." She led Jackson down the linoleum hall. "This is the white reception room, the colored is in the back. There's a colored doctor in town, Old Lamb, who has his own office. When Dr. Gilgo was alive Old Lamb saw patients here three days a week, and he could use the facilities now if he wanted to. But I don't think anyone's been in this house for months."

Nhora massaged the base of her throat. "I can't breathe in here," she complained.

"I'll find what I need."

"You won't be long?" she said hopefully. "I'll wait outside on the porch."

The clinic had been well designed and was more modern than Jackson had anticipated. One room was fully equipped for emergency surgery. Shelves of pharmaceuticals were still usable. The previous tenants had purchased the best instruments and machines available. Jackson found a chest of unexposed X-ray plates purchased within the year. The laboratory was adequate for routine tests—blood counts, pregnancy—and the medical library was up to date, thanks to Dr. Henry Talmadge, whose nameplate was in two-thirds of the volumes.

And someone had kept good records through the years;

in the doctor's private office he found Nancy Bradwin's file and pulled it.

Jackson couldn't resist taking an extra few minutes then and there to look through the file. He switched on a desk lamp with a green glass shade and put the file on the blotter, bending over it as he turned to the first page. But he couldn't concentrate; a faint, sourceless odor in the room distracted him.

He looked more closely at the desktop beneath the lamp. Dust, of course, thick enough to gray the darkly finished wood. But the corner of the desk had been scrubbed clean, as if someone had sat there to read.

The odor was identifiable, now that he was giving it some thought: apples.

Jackson found two apple cores in the wastebasket, and peelings. Fresh no more than three days ago. He got down on his hands and knees, discovered more apple parings and a couple of spat-out seeds on the carpet. In the desktop there was a thin gash, where Early Boy's knife had been stuck close to hand.

"What's keeping you?" Nhora asked from the doorway. Everett John Wilkes came up behind her, straining on his crutches, dragging the dead weight of his left leg.

To tell them of his suspicion that Early Boy Hodges had been making himself at home in the clinic while going through the medical files would have invited sharp questions from Wilkes. How could he be so certain it was Hodges, and how had he become acquainted with the outlaw's habits? Jackson had known Wilkes for only a short time, but he was already wary; it was obvious that the lawyer was not a fool despite his prodigious, compulsive drinking. He had the vision of an owl in the besotted darkness of his mind. Having paused outside the door, he was already twisting the cap off his silver flask of bourbon. Jackson had concluded that Wilkes didn't crave whiskey for its own sake; he drank it austerely, in measured swallows. Neither was the lawyer courting oblivion, like many other heavy drinkers. There seemed to be a massive fear behind his grip on the bottle. In the

212

dark which he created for himself he found courage, and relief from demons.

"Coming," Jackson said with a smile, and turned off the desk lamp. He brought the file with him. Wilkes coughed to clear his throat, leaning to his right, on his good leg, and recapped his flask. "What's that you got there?"

"Everything Dr. Talmadge knew about Nancy Bradwin's condition. I should study it before the autopsy."

Wilkes nodded. "Judge Romney'll have that court order ready, nine o'clock in the mornin'." His voice was thick with booze; it sounded to Jackson as if he'd said "coat odda."

"Is this where you're going to do it?" Nhora asked as they went down the hall to the front door.

"No, Flax and Dakin have better facilities for an autopsy. Because Flax is the county coroner, I'll just be assisting."

"And you're sure she won't be disfigured—I mean, autopsies are really brutal, aren't they?"

"You won't notice a thing," Jackson assured her.

Wilkes was adroit with his crutches, but in going through the door he hung a rubber tip on the sill and nearly took a hard fall. Jackson and the Negro chauffeur caught him in time.

Wilkes swore under his breath. He was sweating heavily, his pride suffering. "Goddam deadwood. I'd make out better with it cut off!" When they had him upright he shot a look of special pleading to Jackson. "Maybe there's somethin' you could do?"

"The leg is paralyzed?"

"Yeah. Woke up one morning about a year ago and it was numb all over, like I might've slept on it wrong. My two oldest boys had to cay-ruh me into the house, you'd think I was senile. Well, I hoped it would get better by and by, but it's just deader'n *hell*. Looks bad, too, like that time I had a broken arm when I was a kid, after they took the cast off."

"Have you seen a specialist?"

Wilkes snorted. "I've seen forty of 'em. What they

specialize in is bad guesses, and big bills, and no help at all. About all they had to say was that some nerve is affected—"

"The sciatic nerve."

"That's the one; they said the nerve sheath just disappeared, like it was eat up overnight. How can a thing like that happen to a man without any kind of warnin'?" There was fear in his look this time—tomorrow it could be the other leg.

"I don't have a good answer, either," Jackson said reluctantly.

Everett John Wilkes brooded over this admission as they went down the walk to his Cadillac. The chauffeur hopped ahead to open the back door for him. But instead of getting in, Wilkes swung around on his crutches, stopping Nhora and Jackson as they were walking back to Nhora's car.

"Well, what do you think about it?" he demanded of Jackson. "Could you make do with what we got to offer here?"

"Excuse me?"

"Don't be deceived by the looks of the town, it's small but it's decent rich. Dasharoons ain't the only plantation in the county. We do need a doctor here, in the worst way. What do you say, Nhora?"

"It's a wonderful idea, but Dr. Holley hasn't been here long enough to make a decision about—"

"I know it; I *know*: I'm merely askin' him to keep us in mind, if he thinks the Red Cross could spare him for the duration."

"I'm immensely flattered, Mr. Wilkes."

"Evvy. Chrissake."

"Evvy. It's a fine clinic. But you've taken me by surprise."

"We'll have a few drinks soon—talk it over. Y'all take care." He lowered himself into the back seat of the Cadillac, reaching for the flask in his coat pocket as soon as he was settled. The chaufeur closed the door.

"He drinks a lot, but he's only as drunk as he wants to be," Nhora said. They watched the Cadillac drive away,
214

then turned to her own car, a modest Chevrolet coupé.

"I don't believe he likes you very much."

"He was patronizing when I married Boss, and shocked when Champ put me in charge of Dasharoons. I suppose he thinks I have—grand designs. I don't. I love Dasharoons, but it belongs to Champ. I wouldn't have it any other way."

Nhora opened the Chevy door and went blank for a vital second. Jackson saw the reflected gleam of a streetlight on the point of the sword that was aimed at her head and reached around her to slam the door shut. Nhora backed slowly away, mouth working, staring at the car. She backed all the way across the street and into deep shadow. Jackson heard her groan.

He opened the door again. There was a gardenia stench, cheap perfume, which he hadn't noticed before. It smelled inside the car as if a bottle had been uncorked and drained on the floorboards. The sword, or saber, had a straight blade about three feet long. It had been wedged hilt-first through the steering wheel. Jackson tested the edge of the saber with the back of his hand; it was sharp enough to shave with. He went around to the other side of the car, got in and worked the saber free. Nothing fancy about it; a duelist's weapon. A single gold star, wired to the hilt, dangled in the palm of his hand. He placed the saber in the trunk of the coupé and went to Nhora.

She looked bloodless when he drew her out into the light; her skin was predictably cold as her body continued to adjust to the shock she'd received.

"What is he trying to *do* to me?" she cried.

"Clipper's?"

"Yes!"

"How could Early Boy get his hands on it?"

"The saber originally belonged to Boss, it was one of his cherished possessions. He gave it to Clipper for graduation. It should have been buried with Clipper, but Champ said no. The saber was in the attic at Dasharoons with all of Clipper's things. I don't know why we didn't just throw it away. Clipper was nothing but a vile, de-

215

mented little monster, *and he killed my husband with that sword!*"

Jackson looked back at the Chevrolet, trying to fathom what Early Boy had in mind when he placed the saber there. No matter how hasty Nhora was about getting into her car it was unlikely she would have been hurt. Still, this seemed to be more than a scary prank; might there be some meaning in it, according to Early Boy's deranged logic?

"There was a gold star wired to the hilt; does that have any significance?"

Nhora shook her head in anguish. "I don't know, I can't think. Could we get out of here?"

Jackson drove. The odor of perfume was still strong in the car, even with the windows wide open. Nhora had a cigarette and said nothing other than to give directions until they reached the boundary of Dasharoons. Then she was able to relax, and to breathe without gulping air.

"What frightens me most is the way he gets around, and no one ever sees him."

"Early Boy has spent years living like a shadow. And he has a flair for the dramatic, as you know."

She turned her head to look at Jackson. "Do you think he wants to kill me?" she said, her voice even but a flare of panic in the eyes, like an animal with one foot in the grip of a trap.

"No. If that's what he wanted, he's had opportunities. He seems to be testing, challenging you. It's like a brutal club initiation, ritualistic in design. That's all I can make of it."

"But why?" she said, hopelessly, almost inaudibly. "I haven't done anything to him."

"Champ is very ill now, and unstable. For all practical purposes you're the boss at Dasharoons, and Early Boy may resent that."

"No matter what he thinks, or any of them think, I've done the job my husband would have done. I'll go away, for God's sake! I'll pack my bags tonight if that's what he wants."

She was a woman who cried suddenly, and violently

216

and got over it within a minute or two. Afterward she didn't touch her face; she angled the window vent and her tears dried in a slipstream of warm air. Her hair waved and tangled becomingly. Jackson glanced at her more than he needed to during the final mile home.

"You asked about the gold star," Nhora said, as if she'd been thinking of the saber again. "It meant that Clipper was first in his class at Blue Ridge for four years. Only a few other cadets have won it. Clipper led an exemplary public life. No one knew about the rot underneath, until it was much too late."

"What do you mean?"

"Just as Beau was—*tried* to be—Boss's conscience, Clipper was the dark side of Boss. No bones about it, Boss was a hell-raiser in his time. He had a good, honest streak of lust and he indulged himself, colored and white. But he treated his women with respect and affection. Clipper's sexuality was twisted, he used young girls shamefully. He left a diary behind that described orgies and sick fantasies. Champ and I both read it. Clipper expressed such contempt, such loathing, for sex, for what is human and necessary in all of us."

"Was there a clue in the diary to his maniacal behavior?"

"He made frequent references to girls of fourteen and fifteen, his favorite ages. Their pain and fear and—virgin blood intensified his pleasure."

Jackson nodded. "And his first victim in the chapel was his own fiancée. Then he ran wild."

"Yes, with all the guests screaming and trying to get out, and the old chapel shaking to pieces; they had to pull it down afterward——"

"What caused the shaking?"

"The chapel bell. It hadn't been rung for years, wasn't safe, there were cracks in the belfry. But the bell was somehow set in motion during the ceremony. It pounded away, dead silent they tell me, but so powerful the roof started to fall in. Champ told me later that he thought Clipper was all right up to the moment that bell began to toll—"

217

"But he couldn't hear it."

"He could *feel* it, all the guests could, the chapel shuddered with each stroke. When the panic began, people were trampled and smothered and cut by flying glass. All I know of it is the aftermath, the victims lying everywhere on the hospital grounds. I was in a dream state all that afternoon. Shock, I suppose. I felt—outside of myself, walking two paces behind someone I didn't know. I was afraid I was going to have a breakdown. Champ got me through the worst of it, and I'd lay down my life for him now."

There was a plantation pickup truck—orange, with a white block letter D on the door—parked in front of the house when they arrived. Tyrone was sitting with his booted feet on the running board, holding the crudely bandaged left hand with his right.

"Even', doctor," he said with a strained smile. "I was waitin' on you."

"Tyrone, what happened?" Nhora cried. Dark blood was showing on the bandanna in which he'd wrapped his injured hand.

"It's that donkey engine at the number two gin. I reached around in the dark where I shouldn't put my hand anyway, and the pry bar slipped just a little. I think the knucklebone on the little finger's gone, and she's all tore up for sure."

"Come in the house and I'll have a look," Jackson said.

One of the maids brought his medical bag to the kitchen while Jackson soaked the bandanna loose from Tyrone's lacerated hand. The little finger was broken in two places and he would lose the nail, but not the use of the finger. Jackson cleaned and dressed it and applied a splint. Tyrone drank coffee with the other hand, holding his handsome head high and ignoring both the treatment and the pain while he listened to Nhora tell of her latest scare from Early Boy Hodges. She concluded with Jackson's hypothesis that Early Boy and Beau were the same man.

Tyrone looked at Jackson with new interest. "That would explain some things," he admitted. "I've chased him before, you see, horseback, times when I thought I just might have him. Then he'd disappear, like a fox that knows every bolt-hole and hollow tree on the plantation." He turned thoughtfully to Nhora. "If daddy Hackaliah could just get a good look at him—"

"That's another reason to suspect he's Beau," Nhora said. "He's been careful to avoid anyone who might recognize him."

Tyrone shrugged, unable to make up his mind. "Well, it's a long shot, don't you think? I wouldn't be so quick to believe it; too many questions need to be answered first." He winced and held up his left hand, studied the splinted finger. "How long before it stops throbbing? I can feel it all the way up the back of my neck."

"It'll hurt for a few days, I'm afraid. Try not to use the hand at all. Would you like a sling?"

Tyrone shook his head disdainfully, then smiled at one of the colored maids who had been hanging around the kitchen and sneaking looks at him. "Lillian, I haven't seen you to meeting for about a month now."

"My mama's been visiting from Belzoni, reverend. And you know how she likes the Antioch Baptists."

"I know. Well, come on back and bring your mama too. Maybe we can *persuade* her away from the Baptists."

The women giggled and his smile got bigger, feeding on their admiration. Tyrone had the graceful carriage and sexual self-esteem of a Moorish prince, but he lacked maturity, which tempered his confidence and subtly devalued his poise. He was at home here, but he seemed to glance around too much, as if anticipating a ghost of hostility, whispers of disapproval from dead generations.

"I didn't know you were a preacher," Jackson said.

"Oh, yes. Preacher; school principal; full-time mechanic now that everybody else has gone off to war. Thanks to Boss I graduated from Fisk University up in Nashville. I remember how he come across me when I was just four years old, back when daddy Hackaliah had that big old shady place on the Forked Deer. I had me a handful of manuscript, some book Boss was writin', pages he threw

219

out in the trash. And I was tryin' so hard to puzzle out the words my eyes were bugged.

" 'You can't read that, you're too little.

"I just looked him right straight in the eye. 'I'm goin' to, though,' I said.

"Well, he laughed. Said, 'Listen, my little judge'—from then on, that was always his name for me—'you get to where you can read what I wrote there, and by God I'll send you to college.'

" 'Course I couldn't accomplish it all by myself, but I'd get people to read me bits and pieces, and I'd work on the little words till they was familiar, then go on to the big words. That was *all* I did: Other kids come around to play, I'd tell them, 'Can't play with none of you now, I'm too busy.' Eighteen months later I sat Boss down, those pages was fallin' apart by then, but I read it all to him. He didn't say nothing, just took a key off his ring, the key to his private library. 'Don't never let me catch you outside loafin' when you can be in my library.' He spent a lot of hours with me there, too. I knew Latin by the time I was ten. No matter that he didn't owe me nothing. He kept his word about the college."

Tyrone shook his head as if he still couldn't believe Boss Bradwin's generosity. "There are days when I'll just be out walkin', all wrapped up in myself, and somethin' steals over me. My skin begins to prickle, I'll look up real sudden expectin' to see him ridin' his horse at me across the fields. But times have changed. Times have changed."

His mood shifted abruptly and there was a look of outrage in his remarkable eyes. Often they were almost colorless, pools of liquid glass, but they were quick to pick up the soft hue of lamplight, the deep color of Nhora's blouse when she stood next to him, the dark or light of his emotions. Such was his intensity and appeal that they were all silent while he brooded. Then Tyrone flexed his left hand carefully, and looked up.

"I hope you plan to stay awhile," he said to Jackson, with the smile of a preacher winning converts. "A few days ago this would have meant a twenty-mile ride to the next-nearest doctor."

220

"I understood there was a colored doctor in town."

"Old Lamb?" Tyrone looked sad. "He won't be with us much longer."

"Why, what happened?" Nhora asked.

"Just old age. Too many things wrong that can't be fixed. Two weeks ago he took out his teeth and refused to eat. He'll sip a little water, that's all. Nobody can reason with him. He just sits on his front porch in that old cane rocker, day and night, rain or shine, his eyes fixed down the road, like he's waitin' on the Angel of Death."

"That's terrible."

"It may be," Tyrone said thoughtfully. "But when a man feels he's put in his time, and there's nothin' left but to suffer, you can't blame him for wantin' to die." He got down from the stool he'd been sitting on. "Don't suppose I could look in on Champ for a couple of minutes?"

"I'm sure it's all right," Nhora said, then looked to Jackson for confirmation.

"I hope he's asleep, but we could go up."

Jackson had suggested to Nhora that a man be on duty near Champ at all times. Bull Pete was guarding the third-floor hall when they went upstairs. Everything was peaceful, said Bull Pete, smiling like a man who knows how to keep the peace. He bummed a match from Tyrone for his pipe. Aunt Clary Gene, shoeless, was sitting in a chair by the playroom windows. Her eyes were closed and she didn't open them, but she acknowledged their presence by nodding and smiling.

Champ, on his back, breathed through his mouth without distress. His skin was dry. He was drowsy but responsive when Nhora sat down beside him, taking one of his hands in hers. Tyrone stood behind her, out of the light. In this room his force seemed blunted by intimations of trespass. His eyes roved.

"Not too long now," Jackson cautioned them.

"Hello, Champ."

"Nhora. What are you crying about?"

"I'm just h-happy you're going to be all right."

"I'll pull through."

"So good to have you home."

"Yeah. Good to be here." He lifted his eyes, straining to see. "Who's that with you?"

Tyrone jittered, perhaps unconsciously, as he looked down at the sick man.

"Champ, it's Judge."

"Who?"

"You know, Tyrone."

"Oh, Tyrone. Haven't heard you called 'Judge' since we were kids."

"Don't know why I said that. Somethin' about this playroom bring it all back to me."

"Did you ever come up here?"

"Few times, I snuck up when I knew there wouldn't be nobody else around."

"That's right. Clipper caught you once, didn't he?"

"No, I outrun him. I expect he chased me a good two miles, cussin' all the way." Tyrone laughed. "Clipper never liked me much. He was little, but he'd fight."

"He sure would." Blacker memories of Clipper intruded, turning Champ's tentative smile into a grimace. "How are you, Tyrone?"

"Can't complain. I hear they awarded you the Silver Star. Champ, I just want to let you know we're all real proud."

Champ didn't have anything else to say. He swallowed hard and closed his eyes. Tyrone looked uncertainly at Jackson, who shrugged.

"I think we should go."

"Couldn't I sit here a little while longer?" Nhora pleaded. "I won't disturb him."

Jackson agreed, and went out with Tyrone.

"That scar," Tyrone said. "They just about cut his head off."

"He was very lucky."

"Sometimes I wonder what it's like, to fight the war. I was set to go the day after Pearl Harbor, only they found scar tissue on my lungs. Scars like Boss had from tuberculosis, which got him discharged from the army. I never knew I was that sick. One winter I had a bad cough that hung on past spring, I was down to skin and bone by the

222

time it wore off. But I wasn't more than a day or two in bed, nobody paid no mind."

They started down the stairs, and Tyrone looked around with satisfaction. "Nhora's fixin' this old place up. She's made plenty of changes around here, this plantation is better run than it ever was with Boss in charge. Would you have a brandy with me, doctor? I could sure do with a brandy night now."

"Thank you," Jackson said, fascinated by Tyrone's unabashed show of proprietorship.

"I'd like for you to see Boss's library. Four thousand books, more or less. He catalogued them all by himself. His papers are there, too, and manuscripts—seldom a day went by Boss didn't write something. Down this hall here."

They paused before a pair of mahogany doors ten feet high. Tyrone produced a single key on a chain.

"This key? It's the same one Boss gave to me a long time ago, when I proved to him I was somebody worth his time. Nhora has the other key. No need to keep the library locked anymore, but it's like a sacred trust to me. Nhora, we been goin' through his papers in our spare time, see what there is might be published. When he died Boss was working on a biography of General Jo Shelby, and a history of Dasharoons plantation that makes good readin'."

The library was a cramped, dusty, untidy oblong two stories high. Bookshelves and wooden filing cabinets stood everywhere, even in front of the draped windows, but the shelves couldn't contain all the accumulated volumes. They were stacked on the floor like aimless pillars from a ruined culture, piled on and under a big antique writing table; books were asprawl in the seats of two leather reading chairs. Even at high noon only streaks of sunlight would penetrate this monkish stronghold. But the artificial light was good and mellow, and Tyrone turned on a standing fan to circulate the warm air. He left open one of the doors to the hall and took a dark bottle of Napoleon brandy from a liquor cabinet beside the Louis XV table.

"Eighteen ninety-four," he said, "and still goin'

strong." The glasses were clean, fragile crystal. Tyrone poured generously from the bottle, which was two-thirds empty. "Boss only touched this when he was in a celebratin' mood," he said. "It's lasted a good many years. But I'm of a mind to believe he wouldn't begrudge us tonight."

He savored the brandy, swallowed, rolled his tongue around inside his mouth. "Most of the time," he said, "I don't have an appetite for liquor. It would make a wrong impression on my flock, don't you see? I tell them prayer will pacify. And that's good advice. But I also recognize that when a man is so wrought up he don't know if he wants to laugh or cry, only strong drink will do."

"Amen," Jackson said with a smile.

Tyrone held up his splinted hand. "I wouldn't have got this if I'd had my mind on what I was doin' tonight. I was broodin' away about poor Nancy. I'm happy Champ's landed home in one piece, but Lord, he's suffered so, with no end to it that I can tell. Such a change come over him when we talked about Clipper. It happened more than two years ago, but how can any man forget what we all saw that day? My own faith was sorely tested."

"You were there, Tyrone?"

Tyrone nodded. "Standin' at the very back of the chapel. The wedding day was sultry, and overcast. The Blue Ridge mountains were on fire a few miles away. You could smell the smoke inside. Not a breath of air was stirring. No human hand moved the chapel bell, but it began to toll. There was a supernatural presence in the chapel, we all felt it. By 'supernatural' I don't mean the Almighty. I believe in a God who is just and righteous in his anger. My God would not put innocent people to the sword, 'less he had some *plan*, a greater purpose in mind. That's why I said to Nhora, and I say unto you, God in his anger just turned his back so that the evil in Clipper would burst like a boil—all the corruption was allowed to spew forth as a lesson for us to study, and profit from."

"Unfortunately it would seem that Boss had little time to reflect on the moral lesson being offered. And what about the poor girl who had her throat sliced open?"

224

Tyrone said confidently, "Their blood was shed so that Clipper would stand revealed in all his wickedness. Wasn't a revelation to me, but I grew up with Clipper."

"As did many others."

"Yes, but Clipper always had a special dislike for me; he showed me early what a devil he was. Never liked to have me come around the house, it killed his soul that I had a key all my own to the library. He couldn't ever lay a hand on me while I was in here readin', Boss just wouldn't stand for it. As long as I stayed around the library I was safe, but like I told Champ, I'd get the urge to sneak upstairs to the playroom. I never saw toys like those boys had! I could have helped myself to a few lead soldiers, they had hundreds, but I never stole a thing from nobody. Only Clipper made out like I did.

"Caught up to me one day in a field when I was comin' home from school. Clipper had a friend with him, one of the Skinner boys, they was just looking to pass the time by makin' me miserable. Clipper was three years younger but almost as big as I was, and strong for his age. I wasn't much of a fighter, never saw the sense of it. He got me down and roughed me up, like always, but no matter how much I was hurt I never showed it. That always frustrated him, then by and by he'd get bored and just go away. But this time he pretended to find one of his lead soldiers in my pocket. He must have put it there while we wrestled.

"Well, Clipper went crazy. It was a lie and he knew I wasn't a thief, but he hated me so much in no time he got worked up to where he believed it. Because he wanted a good reason to do me real harm, you see. The other boy, by then he didn't want no part of what Clipper was up to. I swear to you Clipper was frothing at the mouth like a mad dog, and his face was scary-white like I never did see before. My tongue dried up to the roof of my mouth, I couldn't talk, let alone try to reason with him. What he did was fetch a bale of barbwire, rusty barbwire, and bind me to a tree with it. Out there in the middle of a big field, tall grass in every direction. Wasn't no way I could move without gettin' pricked bad.

"Now that should have been enough for him, might've

225

been long after dark before somebody come out to look for me and hear me holler; my own daddy was so used to my bein' up at the big house he wouldn't have paid no mind I didn't get home for supper. I did holler for a while, but there wasn't another sound except the birds in the tree and the dry grass cracklin', and when I smelled smoke I knew what *that* was. On his way home Clipper had set fire to the field. I don't mean just tossed a match: He'd gone to the trouble to set a fire a hundred yards wide, and it was comin' up behind me mile a minute.

"I couldn't take my eyes off that fire. I think I went a little crazy, snortin and rollin' my eyes like a horse in a burnin' stable. Just as well I didn't pay attention to what was happenin' to my poor hung-up body. Clipper had left just enough slack so that if I wanted to bad enough I could get loose, but I had to pay the cost. I paid. I left hide and meat on those barbs, and I got the marks to this day."

"I'm sure Clipper had reason to regret his actions, when Boss found out."

Tyrone smiled, but his dilated eyes looked hard as ice. "I never told Boss that it was Clipper. I did have some privileges around here, but tellin' on the boys wasn't one of them. I could've got Clipper punished, but Boss would have thought a lot less of me. I knew that, so I kept my mouth shut. Anyhow, I wanted to prove to young Clipper"—Tyrone drank the last of his brandy and closed his eyes peacefully, leaning against the edge of the table— "prove to him I was better than he was, even if I didn't have all his—advantages."

Observing Tyrone in profile—the prideful chin, the look of the conqueror—Jackson was reminded of the Remington portrait of Boss as a young man. Tyrone's true paternity couldn't have been much of a secret at Dasharoons; but it was the sort of thing no man, out of respect for or fear of Boss, would ever have acknowledged. Fortunately Tyrone had inherited, in addition to his physical resemblance, Boss's sharp wits and bookishness. So Boss had casually accepted him, within
226

well-defined limits. Tyrone had even won a cherished nickname: little Judge.

"Did Clipper realize you were his half-brother?" Jackson asked.

Tyrone didn't answer, and he looked so relaxed against the table Jackson thought he might have gone to sleep. Then Tyrone stirred, picking up the bottle of brandy. He looked at Jackson with a hint of admiration.

"You do keep a sharp eye out," he said. "The more I get to know you, the better I like you. Have another, Dr. Holley?"

Jackson nodded. Tyrone poured them each a dollop.

"It was never spoke of around here, but he knew. Picked it up from what wasn't said. Everybody understood Boss to be a lecher with a keen interest in poontang, and he joked about that too: There'd been two, three babies turned out lots darker than me. Well, those chillun just never had no significance for Boss. Never saw himself in them. But my mother, Boss really doted on her. She was light, not even high-yella, kind of smoky cream color. He set her up in business down in New Orleans a little time after I was born. She got run over by a brewery wagon one fine day, but that's another story. There never was a joke about her *or* me. Still, Clipper knew what— who I was, and so did Champ. Now, Champ was older, and never gave me trouble, but he always did have a lot on his mind. He wasn't Boss's favorite by a long shot; that made him anxious and eager to please and he had to work hard to get Boss to notice him at all. Clipper had *plenty* time for me. Clipper had all his great-granddaddy's hatred for black people stored up inside—and Sylvanus Bradwin the first was a slavemaster with a fearsome reputation. This house was built on the bodies and blood of Africans. Clipper was just naturally *bad* to niggers, but the fact that he was related to one—and had to look that nigger in the face almost every day—drove him wild."

"Did he give you more trouble, after the fire in the field?"

"Dropped a rock off the roof that knocked me out for

227

two days. Put a baby rattlesnake in my bed— What's the matter, doctor?"

Jackson had shuddered involuntarily, almost spilling some of the brandy from his glass. He was able to smile. "Snakes. I don't like them."

"They don't bother me as much as Clipper thought. I just plucked that little rattler up by the hackles and tossed it out the window. Oh, I was glad to see Clipper go off to school, his thirteenth year. But from what Nhora tells me, his meanness didn't stop. He was bad with the little girls—and some grown-up women, too, who ought to know better. He was a devil, and that was never more plain to me than the day he died." Tyrone's head tilted forward moodily, and he sniffed deeply of the brandy fumes. "Because he didn't die, you see. Not like he should have."

"What do you mean? Nhora said he committed suicide by swallowing—"

"Swallowed his saber and crashed through a window to the ground. When I got to him, and I was the first one there, he was still alive, his gory teeth clenched on steel. But he was *grinnin'* at me; there was hell-light shining through his eyes. I'm a strong man, doctor, strong in my faith, but I couldn't bear that sight. My knees shook and I was cold to the roots of my heart. There was a pile of paving stones nearby covered with a tarpaulin. I pulled off the tarp and threw it over him. Last thing I saw was his eyes blazing, and I still dream about them. His eyes in my dreams are hotter than the fire he set, the fire that was meant to burn me black, blacker than all the other bastard babies Boss brought forth, black as the nigger I refused to be. Then I see him lyin' in his grave, eyes open, blazin', schemin' to get even with me. And I wake up like a little child in my bed, cryin' for the mama I never had."

Tyrone's hand, however, was steady as he lifted his glass to his lips. "Champ and Clipper and little Judge," he said. He seemed to be talking to himself. "And Beau— maybe we should think about Beau now. What if it's true, and he has come back?" Tyrone studied Jackson, trying to take this notion seriously. "Beau was the best of them, from what I hear, but that was a long time ago. What's left of old Beau now?"

"Not much, perhaps. He seems to be holding a grudge against everyone who lives at Dasharoons. That could be the result of some twisted ideas about patrimony."

"The only way to get at the truth is to run Early Boy to ground. Easier said than done." Tyrone gave a start, flinching from a movement in the doorway. Jackson turned too. Hackaliah stood there, nodding almost imperceptibly, his face without expression.

"Heard voices," he said to Tyrone. "Didn't know it was you."

"Who else, daddy?" Tyrone said, taking a deep breath. "No need for you to stay up."

"Somethin' happen to your hand?"

"Caught it 'tween two gears. Be okay. Long as you're here, maybe you could answer somethin's on my mind. I don't remember Beau, I just barely remember the night he left home, all the killin' that was goin' on across the Ridge. But you and Beau, you were real close, daddy."

"That's so."

"Spared your life, didn't he?"

Hackaliah appeared to draw himself more closely together, as if anticipating a hard knock or two. His yellowing eyes were decidedly unfriendly, but he looked at the floor and his tone didn't change.

"No tellin' what Boss would've done to me, didn't matter to him how I was in the right. His blood was up, he was a wild man. So I got horsewhup, and I could've been shot. Beau stopped him the only way he could: knocked his own father down with the butt of a rifle. Ruint his mouth for all time." Hackaliah's own mouth twitched in satisfaction; then he wearied of the emotion, held tight to his shaking head with one big hand.

"What chance Beau's alive today?"

"Ain't give much thought to Beau in a long while."

Hackaliah's voice had faded to a whisper. He also had the ability, Jackson noted, to fade into the background of a room so completely he was like a piece of battered furniture one is accustomed to having around and can't quite decide to throw out.

"Shit you ain't, daddy," Tyrone said, tense and angry not to have the old man's eye. Jackson glimpsed what it must have been like for so many years, the two men linked to each other in a sham of propriety that was humiliating to everyone but Boss, and possibly his mistress. "You do think about him. You think about how good it'd be here now if Beau never left. Don't you, daddy? Well, suppose he is alive."

"I don't know. It just can't be, that's all."

"*Suppose*. You wouldn't let him slip back without lettin' us know, would you?" He said this with a smile, but the implication of a threat brought the old man's eyes slowly back to him. Hackaliah seemed more perplexed than frightened.

"Crazy even to talk about such a thing," Hackaliah said at last. "Can I go now?" The obvious note of servility matched the deadness in his eyes, as if he had a blind spot where he was now looking.

"You could stay and have some of this brandy with us," Tyrone proposed, slipping into indifference.

"I don't believe so. I never have taken a drink in Boss's house. And I never will."

Tyrone yawned. "Times change, daddy. Want me to coax you, is that what you want?" His voice became almost a falsetto. "Have some of this de-licious fifty-year-old brandy, daddy Hackaliah. I know you ain't never tasted nothin' like it in your whole life."

"It's not your place to invite me to drink in *this* house," Hackaliah said ruthlessly.

Tyrone turned and smacked the tabletop in annoyance.

"Oh, get on out of here then, daddy! I don't want to fight with you. I know my place better than you. I always known my true place, and don't forget that."

Hackaliah went out the door without comment, leaving Tyrone rigid with tension. He busied himself clearing the leather chairs of books, flopped down in a chair, waved his hand for Jackson to sit. "Brings out the worst in me,' he muttered. "Don't know why. He never treated me all that bad, no matter how much sass I gave him."

"Was he married to your mother?" Jackson asked, sitting on an arm of the vacant chair.

"Oh, sure. But nothing ever happened in bed, you understand. She was reserved for Boss. But I suppose daddy Hackaliah wasn't so old he didn't get a letch now and again for what he couldn't have."

"Perhaps his desire did get the best of him on occasion. After all, Boss horsewhipped him."

"I don't think that had to do with my mother. Happened the night of the Chisca County War."

"What was the Chisca County War?"

"A massacre; that was just the name they gave it afterward in the newspapers. Wasn't too many colored men shootin' back that night. I suppose you learned in school how slavery was abolished in this country after the Civil War, but don't you believe it. Oh, a colored man works for wages or shares now, but shares can't buy him nothin'. He's still always in debt to the big boss man, and all he's ever got is shacks and dirt and the cold wind in February. Even with the war on, there's six, seven hundred men workin' this plantation, and twenty-five years ago there was over a thousand. Dasharoons was the biggest mule market in the South, maybe in the world. But it was the human mules who had all the grief. Thank God there's always been a colored man with gumption, willing to stand up and declare for the rest of us. In 1920 his name was Elias Pearman. And what he said was, 'If you don't get paid enough to eat right or wear shoes on your feet, don't work till you *do* get paid.' That's just a commonsense philosophy, but it didn't set well with the boss man, at Dasharoons or anywheres else. White trash tried to kill Elias Pearman, but he was cool and nimble under fire, as well as lucky. All the boss man did was stir up sentiment in favor of Elias, which probably wouldn't have happened if they'd just allowed him to speechify. No speech made in the history of the world has had the power of a single drop of shed blood, and coloreds hereabout were so sunk in misery very few recognized a savior in their midst. And, it's true, there were colored men dead set against Elias, because they feared the wrath of the boss. As you might know, Boss Bradwin was the most powerful boss of all."

"You mentioned a massacre; is that how he chose to exercise his authority?"

Tyrone shook his head. "From what I've been able to learn, talkin' to those that was there, readin' Boss's own journal, I don't believe he had a thing to do with the attempts on Elias Pearman's life. Boss was the biggest, but he was the smartest too. He had to realize that in the long run Elias couldn't do him much harm. Boss was rich, but times was poor, and when a poor man was reachin' for a dollar you didn't offer him two. I don't condemn Boss, because he was a man of his times. But he took pride in the fact he'd been a soldier, he thought he was a born general and only bad luck had held him back from a brilliant career. The truth is he wasn't good enough in the only real fight he ever had on his hands, and a lot of innocent blood got spilled because he lost control, of himself and the men he tried to lead."

"How did the confrontation with your people come about?"

"Because of Beau, who was not like his daddy at all. He had ideals, and true concern for sick and hungry men. He was a young Bolshevik, at a time when folks around here was not too well acquainted with that word. Through Hackaliah he met Elias Pearman, and was swayed by his radical arguments. Beau thought it would be sensible for Boss, a scholarly man who studied history and knew about revolutions, to meet a genuine revolutionary. Not the evil-minded anarchist he'd been hearing about, but a prophet of the change that was surely going to come.

"Boss finally agreed, after a couple of all-night discussions that hotted up enough to keep my daddy wide-eyed awake in his bed up under the attic. Boss must have loved Beau a lot, because he wasn't impressed with the boy's political philosophy. In fact Beau caused him considerable pain and embarrassment among his peers. But you have to hand it to him, he was willing to let Beau think his own thoughts and make his own mistakes in life. 'The hard way is the way that sticks,' Boss wrote in his journal. And he went forth to debate with Elias Pearman, an angry man who could handle the language ever' bit as good as Boss himself."

"It was a public forum?"

"At the Vauxhall community church on Chisca Ridge. It's all colored there—except for Boss and Beau there wasn't another white man in the church that night. Tension was high. Took courage for Boss just to walk in without so much as a peashooter on his person. After all, Elias was a radical man despised by whites, and shots had been fired in his direction. But Boss knew what he was doing. He knew he had the respect of most colored, even if they didn't love him. And he knew just how to ease the tension. Held out his hand to Elias and fixed him with a keen eye. 'Been lookin' forward to this.' Ooo-wheeee! Everybody relaxed. Then the two of them, two giants, commenced to talk. They had at each other, but it was fair; it was clean. I do wish I could have been there that night, before the flames and the killin'."

Tyrone broke off and abruptly got up to rummage in the cabinet next to the table, like a hungry man in search of a midnight snack in the kitchen. He brought out a majolica humidor.

"Boss left these fine Havana Upmann cigars behind. Now and then I get the urge to smoke one. How about you, doctor?"

Jackson, impatient to hear the rest of the story, declined. Tyrone, awkward because of his injured hand, finally got the cigar going, drew on it fiercely and sat down again. He was a greenhorn with a cigar, however; it didn't suit him and emphasized a certain callowness of manner. He seemed to be smoking it only as an expression of obscure privilege.

"Their debate lasted a good three hours. The trouble started away from church. Maybe Boss didn't know his men were out there. I expect some of the white sharecroppers at Dasharoons got worried and came to keep an eye on things, and brought along their shotguns for company. Then word got passed around in town: 'Boss Bradwin gone up to Vauxhall tonight, and there's a thousand niggers layin' for him.' That kind of twisted story. So they came on horseback, and they came in flivvers, armed and mean. They gathered just outside of Vauxhall. It was a dark night. Just imagine what the colored people, those that wasn't in church, thought when they got wind of this mob on their doorsteps.

"Nobody to this day knows if a colored man opened up with a gun in the dark, or if it was one of the mob that was millin' around got spooked and lost control of his trigger finger. But a man named Griffin Albright, who was Boss's top foreman at the time and a personal friend, pitched down off his horse, back of his head shot away. The church all of a sudden emptied out, everybody runnin' to see what had happened. Boss was right up front, highly visible in his white suit, else the mob would have cut down on 'em. Griffin Albright's brother Bob had the dead man in his arms; he was screamin' and carryin' on. It was an ugly situation, with colored men faced off against white across the road, only a little bit of a yellow streetlight shinin' down between. But Boss took the upper hand right away. He calmed Bob Albright and sent him and a couple others away with the body, a smart thing to do. Then he turned to Elias Pearman.

"I want the nigger that did this," he said.

" 'It looks to me,' says Elias, cool as always, 'like all the guns are in your hands.'

"There was a growl from Boss's men, but Boss stared them down. Then he turned back to Elias. 'Does that mean,' Boss said, 'you think one of these men shot Griffin Albright in the back of the head?'

"Elias nodded. 'Check your own guns for one that's just been fired.'

"That was a good suggestion, but Boss never had the chance to act on it. All the armed men held their guns in the air, firing round after round. It must have sounded like the crack of doom. A panic would've started, but Elias shouted at his people not to run.

"When the gunshots died away Boss said, 'You have

one hour to hand over the nigger that killed Griffin Albright.'

"Some say Elias smiled at Boss, but it was a bitter smile. "I'll ask about this matter. And then I'll come and tell you what I know. Will you accept my word if I tell you it was not a colored man who did the shooting?'

Tyrone paused and rubbed his eyes, pondering the long-ago confrontation as if it were an invisible chessboard set in front of him.

"I think Boss's nerve failed him then; he had all those men behind him loaded for bear, their weight was on his back. But still he had control, and time to lead them all back from the edge of the abyss. 'I've got to know you some tonight, Elias, and I think you're a righteous man.' He could have said it simple as that, and walked away with his dignity.

"What he said was, 'Bring me a nigger in one hour, or you'll regret it."

"After that, there was no backin' down for either of them."

Tyrone sat smoking and brooding over the climax of his story. Jackson said, "Where was the sheriff while this was going on? Or was there no pretense of law in Chisca Ridge?"

"There was a good sheriff back then, and he kept the peace. Happened to be away on a fishin' trip. Boss had all kinds of badges from state authorities, gave him the right to make arrests. All he wanted was to come up with some poor colored boy to shut away in jail for a while. It could've been settled Boss's way. Colored people knew when they had to cooperate with the boss man, so lynch fever wouldn't take over. But Elias Pearman was there, and Boss made the mistake of puttin' it to him on a personal basis, 'stead of takin' Elias aside and kindly explainin' how things had to be done to cool the heat from the murder, if that's what it was.

"Elias didn't say another word to Boss; he led his people back to the church. Boss probably thought he'd got his point across. He left a few dependable men there on the street of Vauxhall Community to keep an eye on

235

things and withdrew with the rest to a higher point up the ridge, in a pasture that overlooked the church. A couple of jugs got passed around and there wasn't much ugly talk, it was dark and chilly up there and the men just wanted to go home. Boss and Beau sat on a runnin' board and talked to each other. It was quiet in Vauxhall for almost an hour. Then commenced singin' in the church, soft at first. 'By and by we will see Jesus.' Boss checked his watch once or twice, gettin' worried, I don't doubt. It was no time for hymns.

"They heard it then. *'There's a nigger runnin'—there's two of 'em!'* Lanterns flashed in the street and the woods below; the chase was on. More gunfire. Screams this time. Boss stood up.

" 'The lyin' son of a bitch,' he said. He meant Elias Pearman. 'Let's finish this.' "

"Who ran?" Jackson asked.

Tyrone shrugged. "Elias had everybody in church, and he told them they needed to stay there, until daybreak or longer, stay until reason could be restored. He promised nobody would be hurt, long as they remained calm and prayed. A couple of boys—they weren't more than fourteen—may have got scared thinkin' about what could happen. Or else they were just bored and wanted to see if they could slip by the guards and get home undetected. Both boys were chased down and shot dead when they didn't have breath to run another step. A lantern was thrown, a house fired up, more people left the church. Some were hysterical with fear, some in a mood to kill a white man. A few ran for their guns; others just kneeled in the street, petrified, and they were run over like toads when Boss's little army swooped down from the pasture.

"In all the madness Elias Pearman was helped to escape from the church. When Boss found out, he flew into a rage. I think the smell of blood had all but unhinged his mind. 'We're goin' after him, and we'll find him.' He didn't try to organize a search, just turned his men loose in packs to roam wherever they pleased.

"As the night wore on, destruction spread across the ridge: Vauxhall, Tambourine, Tchula Bend. Some places
236

they were met by gunfire, colored men tryin' to protect their homes and families. That was the excuse for slaughter that numbed the soul. The sun rose the next morning on smoke and grief and ruin. Bodies laid out in rows in the fields. The national guard had to move in to prevent an uprising. But Boss claimed a victory through his bloody mouth. Had the gall to say it was all necessary to preserve order and the southern way of life!"

"What happened to Elias Pearman?"

"He was on his way out of the county in a truck driven by daddy Hackaliah when Boss caught up with them. It was dawn by then. Boss turned them both out and unlimbered his big old horsewhip. Beau had been at his side all night, pleadin' with Boss to let up. But Boss was like a drunken man. He shook off Beau and lashed out: Once, twice, three times, the blood flew. Daddy Hackaliah sank to his knees in agony. Beau just couldn't take any more. Grabbed a rifle from one of the men and drove it buttfirst into Boss's face. Boss dropped like a sack of wet meal, and that was the end of the Chisca County War. Over fifty dead, includin' white. By the end of the day Beau was nowhere to be seen. I don't believe Boss mentioned his firstborn son again, not as long as he lived."

"I'm surprised Hackaliah was allowed to remain here."

"He had the good sense to lay low for a time. It's a big plantation; you can go weeks at a time without seein' a man if you don't want to see him. Just about everybody ignored daddy, he was like a pariah. But he's been with Boss for a long time, and he did suffer a whippin', so Boss gradually allowed him back into his good graces. If I'd been daddy, though, I don't think I would have been so quick to forget and forgive. He should have gone away when Beau did."

Tyrone got up out of the chair, looking powerfully troubled by his lifelong ambivalence toward Boss Bradwin.

"Oh, I forgot to mention. Elias Pearman took his proselytizin' across the river, and the next year he was murdered in Greenwood, Mississippi, by the Ku Klux Klan. Only skin left on his body when they found him

237

was behind his ears and on the soles of his feet. In the old days that was called 'blanching.' It turned a disobedient black slave white by parin' him down to the—what do you call it? The subcutaneous tissues."

Tyrone held out his hands as if inviting inspection; his hands trembled. "Some of us, as you see, been *blanched* in other ways; more enjoyable for the boss man, and not near so bloody." He smiled bleakly. "Not a pleasant way to end this conversation, but I better had get along. Sometimes I just can't shut my flap, and your ears must be fixin' to drop off."

"I find everything about the Bradwins intriguing, particularly Beau's story. What a sad end to his youth. Mine ended rather abruptly, too, but under different circumstances."

Tyrone wasn't listening. He took a fair-size roll of currency from his twill work pants. "Let me pay you now for patchin' this finger."

Jackson waved the money away. "Nonsense. I´should look at it again in two days, and change the dressing."

"Appreciate your kindness, doctor. I'll just shut the light then and lock up."

It was after eleven o'clock and the house was quiet. Hackaliah or one of the maids had turned down the counterpane of Jackson's bed and laid out his pajamas. The balcony doors had been closed against the sultry night. It seemed cooler in his room than it had been in the library, a welcome relief.

Jackson unknotted his tie and put on his slippers, then placed on a Chippendale secretary the late Dr. Talmadge's case history of Nancy Bradwin. As he leafed through the dog-eared and sometimes illegible pages he mulled over what he already knew of her strange metamorphosis from a rather shy and quiet woman with not very great emotional reserves into an aggressive trollop. Successive shocks—the loss of a baby, Clipper's terrifying patricide at Blue Ridge—apparently had brought on the change in Nancy's personality. Or could there have been a pathological reason? Her pattern of wanderlust following a term of unnaturally deep and prolonged sleep seemed to

238

indicate emotional imbalance rather than a lesion of the brain. . . . There was, of course, a third possibility, rooted in the preconscious, in race memory, plausible only to someone of Jackson's particular background and experience.

Once more Jackson witnessed the dark fall of the coffin from the speeding train, her body loose, wraithlike, supernal in the moonlight, free from the sorrows of a troubled house and ill-fated family, free of hex, released from the spell of tainted blood. In the forest of his youth, a place of heat and deep moody silence and terrors swifter than the eye can follow, he had learned that none of us belong to ourselves, but to spirits good and evil.

Jackson shuddered and bent to his work, but the atmosphere of the house distracted him. Nancy Bradwin, by circumstance, had been committed here—eventually to die, beside herself, dispossessed. In this house people walked with guns and jumped too easily, looked sidewise down the dark hall, eased around corners and blamed their nerves on the threat posed by Early Boy Hodges. But something else was in the house: something dark, swollen and miasmic, threatening to explode. Jackson felt thin-skinned and vulnerable, a child in the forest again.

Devoting himself to the chicken tracks of Dr. Talmadge afforded some relief from the unevenness of his emotions. There was nothing in Nancy's brain or bloodstream to account for her malady. Talmadge had tried heavy doses of scopolamine and paraldehyde, but after tentative success, some encouraging periods of brightness and normalcy, Nancy Bradwin had gone back to her cold, deathlike slumbers. In the end Talmadge, admitting in the dry language of the report that he could not help her, returned to his clinic and hanged himself.

Of his final hours only the act was known, not his thoughts. Was he motivated by despair, or had he found an answer that, instead of enlightening him, had driven him mad?

Perhaps it wasn't Nancy after all, Jackson speculated, but the unhealthy atmosphere of this house where Talmadge had spent so much time, neglecting the rest of his practice. . . . Jackson rubbed his throat, as if in sympathetic response to the pressure of the rope that had killed Henry Talmadge. He took off his shoes and lay down on the bed. Just for a few calm minutes, a period of meditation; it was almost time to go up and look in on Champ again. But he was more tired than he had thought. Almost as soon as Jackson reminded himself not to forget Champ, he fell asleep.

In the Negro settlement, a neighborhood of plain board houses and big trees, fenced chickens and dilapidated automobiles sitting on rusted axles, the women attending Old Lamb came and went faithfully. Past midnight the air was still humid in this place, where the Forked Deer river slowed to a heron's roost and seemed dankly finished, directionless, beneath the live oak. From where Early Boy crouched in concealment he could make out a high shine of moisture on the aged man's untroubled brow. A kerosene lantern was hung beneath the porch eaves where the light wouldn't be in his eyes. The porch and steps were heaped with barbarous flowers. Static crackled from the radio, with an occasional clear passage of half-sung blues as some gifted stranger played the bottleneck.

The women changed his nightshirt twice, tenderly stripping him naked without appearing to disturb him very much as he sat in his rocking chair. At least he never complained. They knotted white handkerchiefs soaked in cold water around his head and gave him frequent drinks from a gourd dipper. The water flowed through him and the slats of the chair and dribbled onto the worn boards of the porch. He rocked from time to time, when he was alone. That disturbed the cur dog which slept by the radio, one eye partly open and glowing redly like a doomed tube.

After the last appearance of the women from inside the house, when the moon had begun to set, the lamp burned low and finally flickered out. Not another light showed anywhere in the settlement. Early Boy rose from his couchant position and popped his stiff joints discreetly, then went about his business.

The old cur heard him as he trod the first step to the porch; he tried to spring up, but his back legs wouldn't untangle and he flopped foolishly across Old Lamb's bare feet. He was whining his way up to a growl when Old Lamb put down a hand to silence him.

Old Lamb turned his head in Early Boy's direction. "You come to hymn and Bible me?" he said crossly, gumming his words.

"Not my style."

Old Lamb sniffed the air, as if finding his odor unfamiliar. A change came over him. He spoke in a stronger, educated voice. "Oh, it's you, Beau. Had yourself a bath?"

"Early Boy, if you don't mind."

"Glad to see you, whatever you choose to call yourself."

Actually Old Lamb couldn't see much of anything: Of one eye there were only bluish glints beneath a heavy lowering lid; the other eye was dormant in a bristle-bog, buggery growths all around it. He smiled at the fierce, particular clutch of Early Boy's hand on his shoulder. "Sit," the old man said.

Early Boy glanced at the screen door, listening to snores inside the house, the heavy sounds of one of the women turning over in her sleep. Then he hunkered down near the rocker, his back against a pillar of the porch.

For several minutes neither of them said a word. Early Boy looked as if he were napping with his eyes open, but he had taken inventory of every shadow, and no sound escaped analysis. Old Lamb began to rock. Then he stopped to pee in his wholesome shirt. He rocked again.

"Nephritic kidneys. Renal failure."

"I noticed that. You in pain?"

"No. The breath of starvation is like the odor of fresh bread. Did you know that?" A mild complaining note crept into his voice. "But it takes a long time to die this way."

"How long you gone without food?"

"I don't know; when did you come the first time?"

"Two weeks ago."

"Since way before then. I'm weaker than I was; sometimes I can barely detect my own pulse. But it's taking so long, Beau."

"Call me Early Boy. You could've give yourself a shot of something, end it quick. Why didn't you?"

"Early Boy, I had a dream." A smile formed. The dog at his feet whistled in his sleep. "I walked with my neighbor Jesus to a door that opened in the earth. And he carried all my bones packed in a little gold keepsake box, small and round as an egg or an eye."

"That's some dream. I wonder what it has to do with my question?"

"Easy. Before I can walk again with Jesus, walk the straight and narrow path, I have to give up all my corruptions. And I've been a corrupt man. So I take in nothing but pure spring water. I piss out all the poisons. I grow weaker, but exalted. In the end I'll step down from this old rocking chair, light as a feather, and Jesus will be waiting in all his shining glory, his hand outstretched for mine."

Early Boy looked both ways along the deserted road in front of Old Lamb's house, thinking of Sunday school long ago, and Bible lessons. His mother had been a soprano in the Baptist church choir. It was about all he remembered of his mother: singing solo in the choir loft, her voice eerily perfect, but without passion.

"Have you thought about what I asked you?"

Old Lamb nodded. "I have."

"Well, then?"

"It's too late. It won't do any good to kill him, he's just the *N'ganga*, a *feticheur*, and not a very good one at that."

"What if I do kill him?"

"It's the *loa* you should be concerned about. She must be the Ai-da Wédo—the most powerful of African goddesses. She has, she is, eternal life."

Early Boy turned his head and spat. "Horse shit."

"Have you seen her?" Old Lamb asked him patiently.

"Told you what I saw. A ritual, and a goddamned bunch of snakes, more snakes than I ever seen in one place before."

"Of course. The Ai-da Wédo is a serpent, goddess of the moon and wife of the sun. In Africa she's called Mawu, in Haiti Erzulie—she's dark, and as beautiful as the queen of Sheba. Those who want to change their fortunes, their station in life, invoke her. But there's a danger in that, as you already know."

"Didn't they wring all that voodoo crap out of you in medical school?"

Old Lamb was amused. "For many years I set aside my faith. I didn't truly believe again, not until I saw her—the Ai-da Wédo. Beautiful as a rainbow, forbidding as the adder." The brightness of his mind seemed to fail abruptly, leaving him a soiled mummy, his voice fading into querulous dialect. He spoke to unseen intruders: "Git yore hands off me now, tol' you I jus wants to be left 'lone. Don't do that, niggers, I ain't et nothin' and I won't, jus' tend to your ownselfs and let me die!"

Early Boy sighed, putting a fist against his wrecked mouth to stifle the sound, wondering if he would have to come back another night, or if there would *be* another night for Old Lamb. He waited, not sure what to do. But Old Lamb spoke again, brisk and sure.

"It's an old religion, you know, older than our own. Moses was a voodoo initiate, a student of Ra-Gu-El-Pethro, the sacred Midianite teacher. Moses, according to the voodoo tradition, married Sephora, daughter of Pethro, and she bore him two mulatto sons. All of the social and religious teachings of the Bible, codified by Moses, had their origins in the Negro theocracy." He chuckled richly. "I do wonder what all the sanctimonious white preachers around here will say when the truth is finally revealed. Thousands of years before Jesus, the beauty of ancient civilizations was the beauty of their blackness. Their wisdom was Negro wisdom. Who knows? If the Ai-da Wédo has chosen Tyrone to be the prophet of the ultimate Truth, the dawning of the new age of the Negro

243

race, it must be that he's a better man than I thought he was."

"Tyrone's nothing but a crazy nigger, and you know it."

"Tyrone always had time to sit and talk. There was little he couldn't absorb quickly: medicine, philosophy, religion—though his Christian faith had become a shell, riddled by contempt for the white man's pompous religiosity, his own refusal to abide meekly outside the Jim Crow door to heaven. I was flattered by Tyrone's attention, renewed by his vigor, seduced by the quality of his mind. In return he seduced my daughters. He must have thought I owed them to him, for the time he spent with me. So Tyrone was never a true friend of mine. But I believed his cause was just. I believed in his right to all the lands of Dasharoons. Why not? You no longer wanted what your father, and his fathers before him, purchased with the blood of slaves. Tyrone's cause was just, but his pursuit of it seemed hopeless enough to turn him into a crazy nigger, like you said. So I took pity and helped him—"

"You taught him voodoo. Like giving a little kid a can of gasoline and matches to play with. So he raised the devil with his voodoo. How did he cripple the lawyer, by sticking pins in a doll?"

Old Lamb began to shake his head. "No, no, you don't understand—I taught him voodoo, not to fulfill his fantasies but to take his mind off them. I hoped he would become absorbed in its complexities and possessed by the right spirit, one who would serve as his mentor. Voodoo is not primitive witchcraft, as so many white men want to believe. Its rituals and symbolism are as complex and meaningful as anything in Christianity. The pantheon of voodoo gods rivals those of the Greeks and Romans, with whom they have many deities in common."

"Where did you learn about voodoo?"

"My mother was a mambo in Haiti. Unlike so many of the priests in an overcrowded profession, she seemed to have an authentic calling, which must include reverence for the *lois*—the laws of creation."

"But Tyrone didn't have the call."

Old Lamb sighed, and Early Boy caught a whiff of his yeasty breath.

"Tyrone was mounted too soon, before he was prepared for the responsibility. One must have power over the *mystères*—the spirits—in order to drive out the unruly ones before they can do harm. But the Ai-da Wédo—that's different. She has no earthly master."

Old Lamb began to cough and rock and clutch at his chest. Early Boy couldn't tell if he was in pain, or laughing. His sentient eye blazed with ardor. When the cough subsided his mouth chewed soundlessly for a time. There was a nugget of phlegm on his lower lip. As he resumed speaking, he reverted to guttural dialect.

"You know de Ai-da Wédo, she can fly twice round de worl' in smoke an' fire, tail like a comet, 'fore you whispers her name. She got power like de earthquake, but she can strut, too, jus' like some fancy whore. Tyrone, he think 'cause she play de flirty womans wif 'im, he got control ober her. But you don't fuck wif de Ai-da Wédo and live to tell no stories, no, sah! De big boss man, you knows who I mean, be alive today iffen his boy didn't fuck wif de Ai-da Wédo." Old Lamb broke down in a sweaty wheeze of laughter. "Jezebel! She try to fuck wif me too 'cause she's afraid, jus' a little bit you know, of my dead mama's magic! Strong *baka!* But I don't let Ai-do Wédo mount me, and not jus' 'cause I's old. No, sah, never gets *dat* old. But I's plenty careful 'bout what I dips my wick into."

He slumped sideways in the chair, still laughing, until tears ran from his burdened eyes. Early Boy looked at the screen door, ready to melt away from the porch if anyone stirred inside and came sleepily to investigate a dying man's mirth. But Old Lamb had to stop laughing in order to breathe. After a while he became very still, his gray head sagged down onto one shoulder.

Early Boy reached out and touched a meatless black wrist. "Hey, Old Lamb."

Old Lamb made a snoring sound. Then his voice came bleakly. "Who's that?"

"Beau," he said, with the greatest reluctance. "It's Beau Bradwin. I need help."

"I know you. I always liked you. Beau, you shouldn't have run away."

"Smartest thing I ever did. Now tell me what happened to Clipper. Did the Ai-da Wédo get him?"

"She seized his mind and body."

"How?"

"Through sexual intercourse."

"Here's the sixty-four-dollar question. What can I do about her?"

"I'm cold, Beau. Shut out the light, please. It's a cold light."

Early Boy arose and blew out the feeble flame of the lantern suspended overhead. He went back to his position. Old Lamb spoke as if he hadn't moved.

"The light, Beau."

"It's out."

"Then what is that I see? Can't be an angel of mercy, coming after me. It's too small, too far away. Like an eye, staring. No lid to the eye. Yellow. It burns me. I'm dry and cold and still corrupt. Too late, Beau. *Uncle Guardian, neighbor Jesus, give me your baka!*" As if suddenly afraid of the indifference of his Christian god, he broke into a moaning Creole chant. "*Yahwé, Yahwé, Bossou mrin! Empéchez lan-mò prend-m'* "

The dog lifted his head in a nervous way, a tremor running through the gaunt and frowzy body.

Early Boy glanced reluctantly over one shoulder. Clouds were on the run across the dark bayou, blinding the moon.

"It's nothing," he said. "The moon. But it's gone under now." Yet he felt a prickle of unholy excitement at the nape of his neck. The dog gasped and whined. The tops of the big trees in the bayou, at the edge of the settlement, had begun to roll toward them like ocean combers.

Old Lamb started up from the chair, then fell back in frail defeat, his face wrinkled and as solemnly glazed as a newborn child's.

"Tell me!" Early Boy said harshly.

The word was faint, and frustrating. *"Baka."*

"What the hell does that mean?"

Old Lamb's heavy-lidded eye opened like a sunrise. His mouth was open too; his breath rushed in and out.

"Protection. Strong magic. Ai-da Wédo must respect—the power of your sacrifice."

Grit stung Early Boy's cheek; he threw up his hands. A few feet away, in the dirt dooryard, a dust devil had appeared. As it moved closer, soundlessly, the air was filled with the rush of flowers lifted from the porch steps, whirled, then flung with such velocity they had the impact, on bare skin, of tiny mad fists. Carmine petals clung to Old Lamb's starved face, they flocked to the screen door and stuck there. The dog had disappeared from the porch. There was a sweetness in the air, garish, like the cheapest kind of nigger perfume.

Early Boy got to his feet, stiff with alarm. Old Lamb gripped the rocker arms and rocked for dear life, but his feet weren't touching the floor. His head jerked up and down with the violence of the rocking. In the botanically sweetened air of chaos, the porch roof shook and rattled and revealed sharp edges in an upsucking wind.

"The Ai-da Wédo!" he screamed. "She scald yore skin, she poison you. Get away, Beau, get away!"

Behind the screen door a child had appeared in her nightgown, a girl about ten years old, her head shapely as a kidney bean, clipped to a summery quarter-inch of fuzz. Her eyes, a glowing, liquid bronze-green in the changing light, were open, but she looked fast asleep. Her hands jittered, pawed nervously at the flower-matted screen; air pressure kept it closed against her. She opened her gaptoothed mouth as if to howl or cry. Instead Early Boy heard from her the bony, chilling sizzle of a calabash, or a canebrake rattlesnake.

Enlarging on this dreamwork, other women of the house slowly appeared behind her. They looked dumbstruck, mute but charged with apprehension, like the chorus of an antique passion play. As the women gathered, the little girl pressed more urgently at the

247

screen, throwing her slim body against it. The rattling sounds from her throat grew louder.

Flowers flew at Early Boy's head and brought tears to his eyes. The fragrant air had a bitter aftertaste and burned his throat like quicklime. His skin had begun to smart and sting as the night turned sickly from fluorescence. His jaw sagged under pressure and he felt spiked, through his gut, to the pillar of the porch, unable to free himself. His eardrums ached until he clamped his jaw shut; there was no sound of wind, just windless pressure upward and outward. He felt squeezed and contorted as the roof sheared and flew away. The house groaned from strain, and big trees leaned frighteningly near, attracted to the vortex. It seemed they must come unrooted, and smash the house to kindling.

As he fought to breathe, to think, Early Boy heard feminine laughter. Old Lamb had stopped rocking. He had pulled off his nightshirt and was sitting slack, emaciated but unexpectedly prominent in the groin, sticking up almost a foot. What looked like a limb of a tree had come loose and smacked against the front of the house. When it fell to the porch Early Boy saw that it wasn't part of a tree at all, but a big blacksnake. The snake lay stunned, or dead. While he struggled to free himself another snake came hurtling and wrapped itself around his upraised arm. He flung it away in revulsion. More laughter. Then the perfumed air was filled with twisted snakes and puffs of rioting flowers.

Early Boy had lived a hazardous life and survived pain as bad as a man can know; nothing in his life had ever made him scream. But he screamed now, helpless and tormented.

Suddenly the pressure slackened, the whirling air was momentarily still. The screen door opened and the little girl ran out. With a squall of delight she mounted her grandfather, pulling up her nightgown, exposing her immature pubes. She tried earnestly to impale herself on his erection.

Early Boy, his eyes streaming, reached her in a bound and snatched her away. He knew there was a deep cistern

248

on a slab at the rear corner of the house. He stumbled toward it, half-blinded, the girl clamped under one arm. Now dark was light and light was dark, like a photographic negative. He was scalding to death, as Old Lamb had promised. The air was unbreathable, thin sweet fire in the lungs. But he couldn't resist a backward look, prompted by the taunting laughter of the Ai-da Wédo, temptress and eternal serpent.

He looked quickly, and away, an image of the eyes of the basilisk burned forever on his brain. He fell against the cistern, reached up, pushed the cover off and dropped the Negro girl into the rainwater. As Old Lamb shrieked, Early Boy followed her, plunging headfirst into the cistern. Early Boy was aware of an intense flash of green light. He lay low in dark clean water with the struggling girl, a hand over her nose and mouth. He half expected a concussion that would rock the cistern on its foundation, split the tarred boards and spill them, along with a cubic yard of water, to the ground.

It didn't happen. When the girl became frantic in her efforts to breathe, he let her pop to the surface. She gasped for air and began to cry, clinging with both hands to the lip of the cistern.

Early Boy was surprised to see that Old Lamb's house was still standing. The little girl's racking sobs were answered by whimpers of terror from inside the house. A woman groaned. "Oh, Lordy, my eyes on fire! Help me, please!"

The night was comfortably dark again, starry, windless and humid, the air fit to breathe. Not a trace of viridescence, or the cloying perfume. Chickens, awakened by the flash of artificial dawn, squawked and fretted. Every dog in the neighborhood was yowling, announcing death. A snake, possibly a cottonmouth, stirred on the littered ground and slithered away. Early Boy's blood ran cold, but there was no sign of the Ai-da Wédo.

He heaved himself from the cistern, pulled the girl out and stood quaking with an arm around her, for the moment unable to take a step. He looked around at the scattered, withered flowers, the twisted sheets of metal from

249

the porch roof. It had been a pocket-size tornado, silent but devastating. The broad leaves of the oaks facing the house looked bedraggled and dead, as if hit by a killing frost. So did the tomato plants staked along the south wall of the house.

Old Lamb had disappeared from the porch, but the rocker moved almost surreptitiously. Up and down the street, lights had appeared in other houses. Men were coming, possibly with guns, and he was in danger. He released the girl, who sank trembling to the ground and refused to budge when he urged her to go into the house with the women. His skin still smarted, but bearably, as if he were suffering from a mild sunburn. He turned, dripping wet, and stumbled away, trying to run.

Near the hen house he came across the body of Old Lamb.

At first, because he still couldn't see very well, he didn't know what it was. Grotesquely elongated and flattened by stress, it was spread against and deeply embedded in a framed section of sagging chicken wire. It looked like an effigy made of wet black mud and bits of mica and shiny, splintered sticks. But the sticks were bone and the wetness was blood dripping down into the chicken yard. In a beam of light from an adjacent back porch he saw the distorted face of Old Lamb, and the shocking hole in the body where the genitals had been joined.

A dog was loosed and it came after him, making little whuffing sounds of effort. It was one of the lean, savage killers of the neighborhood and not to be fooled with. He wrenched a narrow fence pole from the ground, turned and met the charging dog with the pointed end. The impact, as the point drove deep into the animal's throat, jarred him against the body on the chicken wire. He left the skewered and kicking dog on the ground and ran, a manic hop-skip-jump because of one stiff leg. A shot was fired, then another. Unworried, Early Boy changed direction, leapt a ditch, entered the bayou, grinning boldly in the dark, leaving pandemonium behind him.

It was five minutes after three in the morning when Nhora awakened Jackson. She was wearing a peignoir. She seemed dazed with sleep herself; there was a blue, taut, inconsolable look about her.

"Excuse me for coming in; your light was on and the door was open."

Jackson got up quickly. "What's wrong? Is it Champ?"

Nhora shook her head. "No, I just looked at him on the way down. He's sleeping. But there's been a tragedy, a fire or something down on Little Fox Bayou. They need a doctor there badly. Would you go?"

Jackson pulled on his shoes. "How far is it?"

"Three miles. I'll drive you. Give me a minute to change."

She turned and almost ran from the room, agile for such a tall woman. There was something blissfully erotic in her flight, creating a field of energy in which he was momentarily trapped, feeling both charmed and cheated. The lively fullness of her breasts in silk, a shadow cleft or two, explicit inner curves—the peignoir covered her from neck to ankles, but it was not a modest garment. He popped a shoe-string under tension and swore to himself, then made the repair with shaking hands.

They rode in the coupé, which still smelled of the perfume which Early Boy Hodges had dumped inside. As if to mask the odor Nhora smoked cheap strong cigarettes, Spuds, one of the wartime brands. Jackson thought about the saber that he'd placed in the trunk, wondering if it was still there. Perhaps she'd finally rid herself, and the unlucky family, of this weapon. But he didn't ask. Her eyes were narrow, rimmed in mourning blue, her lips bloodless; the anxiety with which she had awakened seemed not to have left her.

In Little Fox Bayou two of the county's cars had been parked so that the angled headlight beams partially lit up a small house near the south end of the single street. Nhora drove cautiously past groups of Negroes along the road. Everyone was outside but keeping their distance.

"My God," Nhora said. "Old Lamb lives there."

Sheriff Lydell G. Gaines and several middle-aged deputies were checking, with flashlights, the ground outside the house. They were all armed, with rifles or revolvers.

Gaines came over as soon as Nhora stopped. He was a small old crew-cut man with a wiry salt-and-pepper mustache and eyes that bulged coldly behind the thick lenses of his glasses. He wore khakis and a soiled gray Stetson, a revolver under his left arm instead of on his hip. He was not a man who fussed with words. He used as few as possible.

"Mornin', Miz Bradwin." To Jackson he said, "Gaines. You're?"

"Jackson Holley. What's happened here?"

Gaines tugged at his Stetson, looked up and down the street. Next door a rope creaked as a small boy, nearly invisible in the dark, rode a swinging iron hoop suspended from a tree limb. Jackson heard sounds of women weeping, then the crack of a pistol that no one seemed to take much notice of; but Nhora flinched as she came up beside him.

"Dynamite," Gaines said. "Maybe. Big flash. Porch roof blew off. Screen door off the hinges. Front and back. Blew him in one door, out the other."

"Old Lamb?" Nhora said unbelievingly. *"Why?"*

Gaines shrugged. "Klan." He looked at Jackson. "Doctor? Two, three hurt bad inside."

Jackson started toward the house with his medical bag. In the glare of headlights he saw withered grass, blighted shrubs and dead leaves on an oak tree. The porch roof was gone, all right, and the screen door was caved in, but a rocking chair had survived intact and untouched. Dried or dead flowers and leaves littered the porch.

A gun flashed in the dark off to his left and he froze, Nhora bumping into him.

"Snakes," the sheriff called to them. "Big'uns. Place is crawling. Watch your step."

Nhora sucked in a breath and went more slowly, but the dooryard was nearly bare, no hiding places for reptiles. "I can't believe the Klan would murder Old Lamb, he never made any trouble—" She turned, realizing he wasn't with her. "Jackson? Jackson!" She came back, staring uneasily at him.

"Sorry," he said between clenched teeth. He had closed his eyes. His heart loped but the rest of his body was going numb. A pall had spread across his rational mind.

"What *is* it?"

"Phobia."

"Oh, God, really? Snakes? How bad?"

"Very bad. I—lock up. Sometimes I—I can't help myself, I start screaming until I black out."

"Fight it," Nhora urged quietly, taking hold of his arm.

"I'm trying." But he was cold and his tongue had thickened as he imagined what might be crawling across the ground toward them.

"Walk with me. To the house. You'll be safe inside. You believe that, don't you? Think about something else, *anything*. People are hurt, maybe dying. You're needed."

She leaned closer, imposing her weight; he felt her breath on his cheek, her own heartbeat. He was still dazzled and filled with a sense of doom, but he could look at her. Nhora smiled.

"I know what you're going through; I can help. Come on."

"You know—?"

"I'll tell you all about it; *come.*"

Steady in her grip, focused on her calm strength, he walked—like an aged man with a double hernia—to the porch. As soon as he was safely up the steps the phobia lost its power. He paused to get his breath. Nhora squeezed his hand reassuringly as she let him go.

"Dynamite," he muttered. "I don't think so."

"What, Jackson?"

"There's no lingering odor of explosives. And half the house would be in ruins."

"I see what you mean."

He peered at the stars through the joists, the scrap remains of a metal porch, then approached the smashed-down screen door. Hinges had been ripped from the frame, but otherwise the frame was intact. They stepped over a jumble of rusty mesh and went inside.

There was a sharp odor of medicine in the house. Furniture was upended, smashed. A tall, stooped Negro man with slick hair like Cab Calloway's led Jackson into a small bedroom. They heard another gunshot. A kerosene lamp burned at the foot of the bed; shadows dragged across the ceiling. The granny woman, stretched out with her swollen hands loose on her breast, was obviously dead. She had hematomas the color of eggplant and had bled from the nose and ears. So many of her bones had been broken, including both wrists, she might have been struck by a speeding car. Jackson made a cursory examination, then drew a sheet over her.

He turned to a younger woman in a chair, held down by two friends. Their fingers were biting into her plump arms to keep her from thrashing. Her eyes were blindfolded, by a makeshift wet cloth bandage.

"Kill it," she raged, grinding her teeth.

When Jackson tried to unknot the bandage the woman twisted away.

"What's her name?"

"Arabella."

"I'm a doctor, Arabella. Let me look at your eyes."

Arabella could open them only for an instant. She screamed in pain.

"Hold her tightly," Jackson instructed the other women. They were all sweating profusely in the hot room. He carefully pried open a suppurating eye to examine it.

"Kill it, kill it!" the distraught Arabella pleaded.

"She be blind?" the tall man asked.

"Only if there's extensive retinal damage. The corneas should heal without scarring. I'll apply a salve to ease her pain, but you must drive her immediately to a hospital where an ophthalmologist can treat her. Do you know what happened?"

He shook his head. "I live over thataway. Something blew up. Big flash, like a propane tank."

Arabella strained forward in the chair. Cords stood out in her neck. "For God's sake, git de hoe and kill it! Don't let it in de house, it bite us all

Nhora, looking over Jackson's shoulder, put a hand on

254

him, which prompted him to ask, "What is it, Arabella? What did you see?"

The woman stiffened, letting out her breath in a hiss of anger, or fear. Then intense pain carried her off a little distance, momentarily separating her from danger as if she were in a frail boat on a rocky coastal sea. It was no one man or group of men in white sheets who had frightened her—*Git de hoe and kill it . . . it bite us all!* Was she phobic too? The explanation wouldn't serve. A raw and powerful force had burned her eyes, wrecked half the porch, hurled one body the width of the house through two screen doors, and mangled the old woman lying under the sheet. Jackson felt hard pressed and heavy with dread, as if the violence could flare up again, supernaturally—from the well of the smoking lamp, from a tame shadow on the wall. He fumbled in his medical bag for morphine and gave Arabella an injection before working on her eyes.

Sheriff Gaines came in as Jackson was reapplying bandages with pads of gauze soaked in a solution of boric acid. Arabella, released from the worst of her pain, was peaceful now, half-asleep. She muttered unintelligibly when spoken to. The other women were anxious to get her dressed and on her way to the nearest large hospital, John Gaston in Memphis. Jackson and Nhora left the room with the sheriff.

"Where is the other body?" Jackson asked.

"Out back."

"Have you killed the—are there many—'

Gaines looked at him with a hint of amusement. "No snakes. Scared 'em all away."

Jackson, his pulse racing, forced himself to go outside. The back screen door, on a line with and twenty feet from the front door, was also wrecked. They walked down railed wooden steps and across the yard, past a grape arbor and a vegetable garden. Someone had hung a lantern at the corner of a tool shed. Two Negro men in bathrobes were talking to deputies near the hen house. A dead hound, apparently killed by a thrust of the sharp-pointed pole that protruded from its throat, lay in the dirt.

A deputy with wire cutters was hacking old Lamb loose from the fence. Nhora took one look at the blood and chicken feathers and returned to the car to wait.

"What happened to the dog?" Jackson asked.

"Caleb—he's the nigger inside the house—saw a man runnin' through here after the dynamite, or whatever it was, went off. Caleb let his dog off the chain. Man killed the dog."

"What did the man look like?"

"Too dark. He ran with a kind of a limp, Caleb says. Skipped along kind of stiff-legged. But he was fast anyhow. Caleb had a couple cracks at him with his rifle. Didn't hit him. He disappeared into the bayou."

Sweating deputies lowered the body of Old Lamb to the ground. They spread a tarp and shone a light on the body. Insects were swarming. Glossy red chickens strutted around aimlessly.

"Well, what the *hell?*"

"Looks like his pecker was blowed off, Lydell."

"Looks like it," Gaines said glumly. He applied a match to a fat cigar.

"Must have shoved that stick of dynamite hard up his ass," another deputy said.

"Dynamite, hell," Gaines said. "Cover it up till they come with a box for him." He stared at Jackson through a blue billow of cigar smoke. "Unless there's something else you need to see."

"Sheriff, I'm puzzled."

"Know exactly what you mean."

Jackson turned and looked at the house, which stood thirty feet away. He reckoned the distance from the front porch to the chicken-wire enclosure as more than fifty feet.

Gaines said, "My daddy was an old powder man. Now I know dynamite just don't act like that. Old Lamb been standin' that close to a good-size blast, you could pack what's left in a fruit jar. It would've blowed the front of that house to smithereens. Bust windows up and down the street. Fumes hang in the air, specially on a still night like this one. What was it then? You know where he stood

256

and you see where he is now, stuck like a wad of chewing gum to the chicken wire. He must have shot through that house like a goddam human cannonball in a circus. Hit his own wife hard enough to break near every bone in her body. Jesus Christ. Maybe it was a lightning bolt. A tornado. I don't know what else has that much power."

"I don't either," Jackson said.

"Some kids was fooling around the federal transmission line last spring. Storm blew up. One of them was on the pylon, maybe fifteen feet off the ground. He caught a big surge; there was a flash and it flung him a ways. Broke his back, but he was probably electrocuted already. There's only one little AC line connects up with this house, and it's nowhere near the front porch."

"I noticed that."

Gaines stuck out his hand. "Thanks for comin'. How's Champ?"

"Holding his own."

"That's good. You get a notion about this, come around to see me. Lewis, swing your light over here. Doctor's goin' back to his car now, and he don't want to be steppin' on a dead cottonmouth."

More Negroes, relatives of Old Lamb, had arrived. A woman wailed as Arabella was half-carried to a waiting car. Nhora was sitting sideways in the seat of the Chevrolet coupé, head heavy in her hands. She looked up at Jackson's approach.

"Sorry. I couldn't take any more."

"We can go now. I've done everything I can."

"Wait," Nhora said, getting out of the car. "Old Lamb's granddaughter was in the house, or near the house, when it happened. A neighbor is taking care of her——she's afraid something's wrong with the child, that she's hurt but won't say anything."

Jackson yawned. "Okay." They walked together down the road to a house with a picket fence, lamplit windows. A teen-age boy let them in.

It was a clean house, the furniture dilapidated, lace curtains turned crumbly as brown sugar at the windows. A woman wearing an orange bandanna sat holding the girl in her lap. The girl was wearing an oversize nightgown and appeared to be asleep, but she was convulsively sucking her thumb. The woman in the bandanna crooned to her.

"What's the little girl's name?" Nhora whispered to the boy.

"Loretta."

The woman cradled the back of Loretta's head with a big hand as Jackson came near.

"Is she cut or bruised?"

"No, doctor. Jus' scared out of her wits. They found her 'longside the cistern, half-drowned. But she won't say a word."

Jackson hunkered down and studied Loretta's pretty, glazed face. Her eyes were open, blank and empty as a couple of walnut shells. He smiled at Loretta, then replaced the woman's protective hand with his own. Loretta didn't resist. Her skin was cold, her heartbeat and pulse too fast. Snakebite? He gently removed the nightgown and looked everywhere for puncture wounds. No. He then felt for lumps or broken bones, watching her unresponsive eyes. He found nothing suspicious and dressed her again in the nightgown.

"I think she'll be all right. She's in shock. Stay with her, hold her, talk to her. I'll leave a mild sedative to help her sleep."

"Yes, doctor."

As Jackson rose the child's eyes moved with him, and focused for the first time. She was looking at something behind him.

Suddenly she moved, scrambling from the woman's lap, nearly knocking Jackson over in her haste to get away. He reached for her, but missed. The boy also attempted to get a hand on her. Loretta changed direction effortlessly, raced for the front door. Nhora blocked her way. Loretta flung up both hands, spun from Nhora's grasp and crashed into a curtained window next to the door, breaking the glass with her elbow.

At the sound of shattered glass, Loretta's eyes rolled

258

back in her head and she fainted, falling weightless as an autumn leaf to the carpet. Nhora picked her up.

"My God, what happened?"

"Lay her on the sofa," Jackson said.

Loretta was unconscious, but her breast heaved. Then saliva bulged at one corner of her mouth, ran down her chin. There were blood drops above one wrist, from a shallow cut or scratch. Her heartbeat was arrhythmic, respiration forced and shallow. Jackson was preparing an injection of scopolamine when she had her first convulsion. The second one tossed and doubled her and she died rigidly in his hands.

During the next fifteen minutes Jackson tried every life-saving device at his disposal: digitalis in the heart muscle, artificial respiration. He was exhausted and shaking, his suit soaked with perspiration, when he went outside. A hearse from the Negro funeral home had come for the bodies of Old Lamb and his wife. Jackson told the undertakers about the dead girl, then went in search of Sheriff Gaines.

"Heart give out?" Gaines asked. He was down to the stub of his cigar. In the yard a cock crowed. The sky had drained to silver in the east.

"Very unlikely. I've heard of cases of extreme fright where the vagus nerve becomes paralyzed. Then the victim can't breathe, the heart stops. More common in animals than it is in humans. The convulsions were symptomatic of strychnine poisoning, but she had nothing to eat or drink while I was there—I just don't know what happened."

"I reckon you did all you could."

"*That bloody doesn't bring the child back, now does it?*"

Gaines took a step out of the way, as if he didn't want to be contaminated by Jackson's anguish.

"Can't go blamin' yourself. Get some rest, doctor."

"Good advice," Jackson said, still red-faced from his outburst. He turned and walked back to the house where Loretta had died.

The living room was filled with neighbors, a great

brown bulwark. Psalms were spoken, coffee was brewing. Nhora had her arms around the woman in the orange bandanna, who sobbed quietly. Nhora was staring at the blanketed corpse on the sofa. Jackson walked toward her. Hands touched him kindly. A pint bottle of whiskey was slipped into his coat pocket; he didn't know who the benefactor was. He smiled numbly and stopped in front of Nhora.

She shifted her gaze.

"We might as well—" He held out a hand. She came with him, eyes puffed and red, hair in a wild tangle.

Outside they met Tyrone as he was coming through the gate. He was wearing a dark suit and had a Bible under his arm. Two other men, perhaps deacons of his church, trailed behind him. Nhora and Tyrone stopped and looked at each other. He seemed touched by her powerlessness in grief. He nodded gravely to Jackson, and went on past them to the house.

In the car Nhora asked, "What time is it?"

"Twenty past four."

"I don't want to go back to Dasharoons just yet. Unless you're worried about Champ."

"No."

"Let's drive, then."

He put the car in gear and they left the settlement. Nhora pointed east, where the bayou tree line was clear and stark against the dawning sky, a few lingering bright stars.

"I think I'd like to go to the river. It's peaceful there. I've always loved Dasharoons, but lately I have to get out of the house, I feel I'll go crazy sitting around."

They took a paved road to the levee, then a dirt road down through slash land cut by backwater channels livid in the brinking light, channels numerous as the lines in the palm of an ancient hand. A larger channel which the river had made for itself years ago was silting up, loaded with swept-down trees that composed a naked, broken, dangerous-looking thicket 200 yards deep. Between this thicket and the body of the river lay a gentle brushy sandbar. Nhora showed him where to leave the car. Then she led the way, picking her path with certainty 300 feet to the edge of the river.

From the top of the levee the river, then a quarter-mile away, had looked dark and as quiet as a vein in the throat. This close he experienced its rude, tugging power. The air was milder, even cool at water level. The river lapped at a partly submerged log. It was the mightiest river on the continent, longer than but not as wide as the K'buru—river of the mind, his own, vital life stream.

Jackson felt the jolt of his rage leaving him; he was given over to interior currents, deep forces, a bewildering sense of having traveled endlessly to arrive at a point more than twenty years in the past. The same root terrors, the same questions waiting to be answered. He felt slow, witless, demoralized by grief. Low bluffs on the other side, roof lines, the galumphing bark of dogs, the sky a transparency unmarred by cloud or star fleck, prepared for red thunder, the upcoming sun, stupefying radiance and heat, another torpid day in the tropics.

"Jackson?"

He looked around at Nhora, who was standing a few feet downriver, holding her dress bunched at her thighs. She had taken off her shoes to cool her feet in an eddy. There were frozen points of light in the full pupils of her eyes, her smile was strained.

"You were making—sounds. You scared me."

Jackson exhaled slowly, but there was still a binding pressure on his chest. "Some boyhood passion come to mind. We lived totally at the mercy of a river like this one." He looked at the looming boneyard behind him. "Lived with the forest at our backs, and often at our throats. Or so it seemed." His throat was parched now. He remembered the gift of whiskey and took the bottle from his coat pocket. But he just held it, feeling awkward about needing a drink so badly.

"Oh? Where was this?"

"A missionary station and logging town called Tuleborné. On the K'buru River in French—"

"My God, you don't mean it! I lived in Equatorial Africa, in Zenkitu."

"When?"

From 1921 until about 1926. My father was a civil servant, not a very happy man. He died young. His health went very quickly in that climate. Of course part of his decline was due to me, the strain of not knowing if I was dead or alive." She moved closer to Jackson, shyly lowering her dress. "Is that whiskey? Could I have a taste?"

Jackson uncorked the bottle and handed it to her. She tilted it back with relish, drinking like a man, eyes closed in contemplation, her face faint ivory against the lightening sky. She handed the bottle back, lips pursed and rueful, a hint of tears.

"Probably homemade," she said, her voice coarsened by the fiery stuff. "But it isn't—half bad."

Jackson didn't care about quality. The whiskey bit away tension and settled down to a slow pleasant burn in his stomach. "Dead or alive?" he inquired.

"Oh—when I was three years old I was kidnapped from a carriage of the Ocean-Zenkitu train. It had stopped just before that famous tunnel, the one where so many thousands of Negroes died—"

"From trapped gases in the mountain they were trying to dig through. I know the place. Dense forest all around. Who kidnapped you?"

"I barely remember what happened; my mother was so terrified by the experience she had to be institutionalized. Many years later it was still an ordeal for her to tell me the story. It seemed that the train was raided by a band of men from a decimated tribe called the Ajimba. They wore—"

"Crocodile headpieces. And S-s-s—" He turned, shaking, toward the river

"Jackson!"

"*Snake*skins. It's all right, I'm not going to have another of my bloody seizures." He drank a little more of the whiskey for safety's sake, held out the bottle. Nhora declined with a shake of her head. She put a hand on his elbow; then, after a reflective few moments, slipped her arm loosely around him.

Jackson stared at the flowing river, and continued:

"I've had—experience with the Ajimba myself. They were a warrior sect, a secret society going back many centuries before the white man set foot in Africa. I believe at one time they were heavily involved in the slave trade. Their rituals incorporated human sacrifice. Throughout the nineteenth century the Ajimba were at their most powerful, ranging ferociously from the K'buru highlands to the sea. According to one legend, a demented Frenchwoman of unbelievable longevity ruled them for more than a hundred and sixty years. Her name was Gen Loussaint. Have you heard of her?"

"No."

"How many others were taken from the train?"

"I don't know. Half a dozen. I was the only European."

"And how long were you a captive?"

"Nearly three years."

"*What?* Didn't the government make an attempt to ransom you?"

"They tried everything, but they never heard from the Ajimba. Mother told me it was assumed I had been murdered, something to do with their bloodthirsty ceremonies. The truth is not very interesting. After I was kidnapped, the Ajimba seemed to lose interest in me. They had their hands full just staying alive—it seemed as if we were always on the move, dodging soldiers, the *gard indigène*. I never saw the men wear crocodile masks again. They hunted for their food. Kept wild dogs trained to kill. They were a rather sad, pathetic people. No one was ever cruel to me. I was part of a family—I had several 'brothers and sisters.' I remember that one of my brothers was playing too near the dog pens, he was snatched inside and torn apart. I still have vivid nightmares about that. And—there was a lot of sickness, we were always in mourning. I don't know how I survived, but when I was finally returned to civilization I was in perfect health. Not a blemish or a missing tooth. I had to relearn English and French, though."

She nudged Jackson for the bottle as he was having another swallow. He passed it to her.

"How were you returned?"

"I was given to an Arab trader in exchange for a bolt of cloth or a goat or something. I suppose they just got tired of me. The Arab made a very shrewd deal. He collected a reward of two thousand dollars."

Nhora drank until the bottle was half-empty. She had tightened her arm around him.

"Gets me weak in the knees," she said. "I *think* this is what has me so weak all of a sudden." She tucked the bottle into his jacket pocket and laughed, quite loudly. The sound echoed across the river. Nhora seemed as stunned as if she'd farted; she buried her face against his arm. "Where did that come from? Everything is *dreadful*—dying, dying. But I don't know what to feel. Jackson—how long do you think you'll be staying? There, I finally said it."

"I just take one day at a time. Always."

"Is that a good answer? It was a sincere question. From the heart. Jackson, remember when you were petrified in Old Lamb's yard, and I told you I understood how terribly you were suffering? Because I'm afraid so much of the time myself."

"Of Early Boy Hodges?"

"Nothing that easy to explain. You saw the dog by the chicken coop, his eyes glaring and dead, his bloody mouth locked open, the jaws and teeth around the pole he swallowed—what a nightmare. I just walked away, I couldn't take any more. All my life something like that has been coming after *me*. I dream of wild dogs, catching, throwing me down and pulling at me with their sharp teeth until I—I don't have hands or feet or arms, all torn off, my breasts too; all I can do is wriggle and crawl to try to get away. But they sniff me out and pounce and then the only protection I have is to coil like a sn—God, I'm so sorry! How you jumped."

"Never mind. That's certainly one of the most compelling dreams I've heard. A psychoanalyst's delight."

"Do you know the meaning?" she asked timidly.

"I've had only minimal exposure to psychiatry. How often does the dream recur?"

Nhora sighed. "Too many nights, lately." She studied him. "Are you thinking something you don't want to tell me?"

Jackson smiled, demurring.

"Well—Henry Talmadge said I was afraid of being a woman. It's the sort of thing he *would* say." She thought this over and regretted the churlishness. "I doubt if he knew much about psychiatry either. Henry thought there might be a physical reason for my restlessness and bad dreams, so he did a complete examination. Very complete: He took strands of my hair and even nail clippings for analysis, can you imagine? And *two* samples of blood—he came back for more, saying he'd mislaid the first vial. By then Henry looked awful, he wasn't sleeping himself, and he was at the end of his tether with Nancy. I never found out what he learned about me; it was only two days later that he hanged himself. And I'm still having those nightmares."

Dawn was shrilly alive with birds in the derelict trees behind them. The sky, like fine bone china, showed a rim of gold on the horizon.

"Let's walk," Nhora suggested, keeping her arm around him. He was lulled by the pleasant suspense of wondering just when he would kiss her, and what would follow. "There's something I want to show you, and it's almost light enough."

They went slowly along the glistening river toward the narrow south end of the sandbar, where saplings had taken hold, and the deadwood was laced with vines.

"It was a common practice," Jackson said, "for the Ajimba and other tribes to feed puppies minute rations of a deadly poison every day. By the time they matured and were trained as hunters, their tissues were permanently saturated with enough of the poison to paralyze an elephant. Just a scratch from a fang or a claw was enough to kill a small animal in a matter of seconds. But the dogs themselves were immune."

Nhora shuddered. "You know a lot about the Ajimba, Jackson."

"They carried my father off after one of their raids. He

was a doctor. He'd spent eleven years in Tuleborné, which realistically can only be described as a hellhole, often working twenty hours a day to keep up with the demand for his services. He doubled the size of the hospital and trained many Negro assistants. The meager professional help he received was from the Sisters of Radiant Hope, a tiny Catholic nursing order—and he had my help. What ability I have today I owe to my father."

"How old were you?"

"Seventeen, when our luck turned bad. That was in 1920."

"Your father was killed?"

"No. By his account, they took good care of him. He was missing for three months but when he returned his memory was clouded, he thought at best he'd been away three weeks. He was confused in other ways, disoriented, and, I believe, severely frightened by his experiences in captivity. He claimed he was taken for the purpose of treating an ancient hag, a white woman, who convinced him that she was the legendary Gen Loussaint."

"You mentioned her."

"Stories about Gen Loussaint were always fantastic and frequently chilling. One met old-timers, traders who were on the river long before the turn of the century, and some insisted they had dealt with her. In her prime she was said to be very beautiful—what else?—but inhumanly cruel, unequaled in wickedness, a priestess of butchery among savages infamous for their bloody dealings with other tribes. Her cruelty so pleased the evil spirits of the forest that she was given the power to change her shape, to vanish in a twinkling and reappear miles away. Familiar rubbish. She became—reptilian, after the fashion of the Ajimba gods, but not less beautiful. Her other-worldly self was a kind of succubus, common in African folklore."

Jackson smiled. "When I was a boy, alone at night in my bed, I could work up a case of shivers in no time just thinking about such creatures swooping down on me. Symptomatic of the buried terrors of puberty, I suppose. At the hospital we were accustomed to seeing patients who seemed to have nothing organically wrong with them,

266

yet inevitably drifted into comas and died. Sometimes the cause may have been untraceable poison administered by an enemy—Africans poisoned each other at a prodigious rate. Other victims were frightened into believing a succubus was having intercourse with them while they slept, draining the life force from their bodies. It's not difficult to look back with objectivity, but I grew up among primitives besotted with superstition, and the fantastic seemed commonplace then. Like the Shadow, the primeval forest clouds the minds of men. Insignificant spiritual wounds became gaping sores infested with the bacteria of unreason. My father was an educated, disciplined, God-fearing man. But eventually he succumbed."

"He was convinced that he'd actually met Gen Loussaint. But she was dying, and not very beautiful. Did she fall out of favor with the gods?"

"Oh, she didn't exist: I am sure my father imagined her. He must have fallen quite ill after he was captured. He may have been delirious for long periods of time, lying in a hut surrounded by talismans, relics of the Ajimba's beastly religion, dreaming the legends with which he was already familiar."

"You're shaking; are you cold?"

"A little." Jackson produced the bottle of whiskey and opened it.

"You first," Nhora said.

He drank. Then she had a swallow, watching him, her green eyes coming clear against the sunburst of a perfect morning. Jackson clamped his teeth to stop the chill that plagued him. He took the offered bottle and finished off the whiskey, pitched it to the current.

"Well, he s-seemed all right when he returned to us, but shortly thereafter he began to break down emotionally. Nothing but overwork: father s-should have been persuaded to take a long holiday. And the rainy season that year was the worst in memory, intolerable. The river was out of its banks. Brutal storms swept over us, collapsing buildings. At the same time there was an epidemic, a mysterious sickness that struck nearly everyone at the station. If that wasn't enough, a crackpot *feticheur* began to announce the end of the world, and blamed the white man. Negroes deserted us in droves. The damned rain just wouldn't stop. My sister became critically ill, and my mother was ill too, from incessant worry. Father asked me to accompany them to Zenkitu on the steamer. I begged him to go with us; by then we all had the feeling that s-s-something disastrous was overtaking Tuleborné. But I suppose you'd have to say the real tragedy, for the Holleys, took place in Zenkitu harbor."

There was a crisp breeze off the river; Nhora brushed hair from her eyes and said earnestly, "Jackson, this is upsetting you. Don't tell me any more, you don't have to."

"It's important. Because I have an explanation to make, an apology to offer. And if you're going to accept my apology, you must first understand what—who—"

"Apology?"

"Just listen," he said, eager to get on with his divestiture. "The steamer was near Zenkitu, jammed with refugees from the flood and very low in the water, when a surge of giant logs from a tributary stream battered and capsized it. It happened in less than a minute. I couldn't save my mother, she was swept away before I could get a hand on her. I swam to a bar with my sister in tow. She was unconscious then, and never came to."

"Jackson, I'm so sorry."

"I went back upriver after my father. By then I had a fever. I don't remember much of the journey, which I made alone in a small boat. A miracle I didn't drown. Eventually I reached Tuleborné. The rains had ceased. I found my father. At least I had a glimpse of him. In less than a week his hair had turned snow white. He was totally mad, mad, mad. He—attacked me, then nearly killed me during some impromptu surgery."

"Surgery?"

Jackson pushed his hair aside to show her the scars. "Yes." He was trembling, from indignation, pain and disgust. "It seems father removed pieces of my skull, quite without permission, to make a fetish strong enough to protect him from his—his dismal obsession."

"Gen Loussaint?"

Jackson nodded tautly.

"I don't understand what you mean by a fetish."

"In the simplest terms it's a good-luck charm: a rabbit's foot, a silver dollar, a four-leaf clover. Civilized men pay lip service to superstition. But an African's life is circumscribed by his religion, his belief that he is powerless to survive without magic. He is surrounded by human enemies and at the mercy of swarms of hostile spirits eager to snatch his soul away from him, to possess his body. When dealing with these spirits there are rules to follow, daily appeasement is a necessity. The faithful are rewarded by being left alone, because the spirits also must obey the occult laws of creation set forth by Legba, god of the sun."

"But why did your father risk killing you? Why was it so important to have a piece of your skull?"

"He thought he *had* killed me—and so much the better; there's no more powerful magic than to sacrifice a member of your own family to complete a fetish. He succeeded in banishing his nemesis, I'm sure. Unfortunately he never recovered his sanity."

"What happened to you, Jackson?"

"I spent nearly a year in hospital. Complications. My father was returned to England, to a rest home for burned-out or deranged missionaries called Hawkspurn House, in Yorkshire. I caught up to him there autumn of 1921."

"He must have been happy to—"

"He refused to see me, insisting that I had died the night he trephined my skull in Tuleborné. It was thought that the shock of an unexpected confrontation might prove beneficial. But he looked right through me. I didn't exist for him."

"He was faking! Wasn't he?"

"How will I ever know? I was profoundly shocked by his implausible treachery. I still don't recall very much of the year that followed, the psychic storms I weathered, the desolation. Because I had worshiped my father. I was inspired by his knowledge and art; the brilliant improvisations he wrought with limited equipment, under frequently

269

desperate conditions; his energy and spirit. I devoted my life to *his* work, *his* service. I was diligent, responsible, obedient—and always fearful that I would never be good enough to fulfill his expectations. I had to become a man before my time. In return for this abiding loyalty he nearly succeeded in killing me."

"He was mentally ill. He couldn't have known what he was doing."

"That's why I was unable to admit to myself how angry I was. He had no *right* to do this to me—to become a tired, broken, prematurely old man. I didn't give up hope easily. I made many trips back to Hawkspurn. But it was like stirring a dead fire until I was shrouded in ash. Slowly my rage began to have an effect. I belatedly caught up with my adolescence. I had a rather wounded, romantic, Rupert Brooke-ish air about me that was not yet out of style, the war having so recently ended. Also I had a certain amount of mother's money to spend. I discovered I was attractive to women. I was sullen, rebellious and frequently drunk. I abused the hospitality of those relatives who kindly took me in.

"Before the money came to an end I was persuaded to take up my medical studies in London. Of course, what else was I to do with the rest of my life? I had no natural talent for pub-crawling and roistering, it was all a bit thin and unsatisfying once the first good shock of perversity wore off, and there was no one girl I was particularly attached to. I was talented, my father had said so, and I knew that in due course I would become a great surgeon. But I no longer had his faith to sustain me, and by the time I reached London, not knowing a soul there, my cloak of self-assurance was ragged with terror. I now had to accept the fact that I was virtually alone in the world, I would never again see him look upon me with love and approval."

They had come to the end of the sandbar: the jumping-off place. There was a golden sheen on the roiled surface of the water. A small whirlpool was spinning fifty feet from shore. Jackson stared at it and recalled, for the first time in many years, his K'buru baptism, by Fullerite tradition a rite of the ninth year. Going down dazzled in song and heat, embraced by the love of the multitude, bent over backward from the waist, suspended in the river, his head held under by the weight of his father's hand, nostrils pinched together, mouth sealed against the thrilled outcry in Jesus' name *amen*. . . . Where had his faith gone? It had all drained into the austerity, the sucking dryness of a drab, dotty, unresponsive stranger, a man who had never sung, laughed, prayed, cradled him in tenderness. A cipher, a long-lived cripple, a failure.

The breeze changed direction. Nhora was standing close behind him and her hair whipped fetchingly against his cheek. He turned and took her face in his hands, to calm himself. She looked patiently at him, waiting, not smiling but radiant.

"Medical school was a disaster. I already had experience and skill which my fellow students would be years in acquiring. After my training in the bush, having learned in hazard highly unorthodox technique, I was not adaptable to the grinding routine of classroom and laboratory. I knew already what I felt I had to know, and disdained the fine points I was expected to learn. I refused to assimilate mountains of information that would be useless in practice. I was not reluctant to feel superior, even to my instructors. This attitude fast discouraged friendships.

"To relieve my boredom and win acceptance I became the class hell-raiser. Because of my father's considerable reputation I was granted a certain amount of immunity from official reprisals. But when I openly conducted an affair with the wife of the chief of surgery at Saint Bartholomew's, they were forced to expel me. Thus I achieved two aims: My feelings of superiority were reinforced, and I was relieved of the necessity of ever having to prove how good I could be if I wanted to."

"But you *are* a doctor. A good one."

"I possess certificates from the most distinguished faculties of medicine in Great Britain. I am acknowledged to be a member of the Royal College of Physicians. All of my degrees and certificates are among the best that money can buy. What I mean to say is, they're forgeries."

Nhora's eyes widened.

"I'm an imposter, Nhora. A charlatan. I spent less than a year in medical school. All I have by way of qualification for my adopted profession is the knowledge that my father gave me, plus what I've observed and read during the past twenty years. I've knocked about two continents, often working on the fringes of society where no questions are asked, somehow just missing serious difficulty with the law. Making abrupt changes of residence out of fear that I'll be investigated, and exposed. I have no right to be looking after the health of Champ. If he died, I'd be open to criminal prosecution. Men go to prison for such quackery."

He let go of her then, because he saw that she wanted him to.

Nhora walked a few feet away, head down, leaving sharp footprints in the muddy sand. She looked sideways at him, her lips compressed, and banged a fist against one hip. She appeared to be seething.

"Could another doctor have saved that child tonight?"

"I don't think so. I used all the accepted resuscitation techniques. I've been successful before in such emergencies —cases of electrocution, drowning and so forth. This time I failed."

"Then you have nothing to apologize for. Do you know what killed her?"

"I've been over every possibility in my mind. She was poisoned, I think. I don't know how."

"Jackson, how many lives did your father save?"

"Thousands, I'm sure."

"You worked alongside him for years. Would you be willing to take some of the credit? That is, if you were inclined to be halfway generous with yourself?"

"I suppose so."

"And in all the years you've been practicing medicine without a license—how many saved, Jackson?"

"I don't know."

"*One* life, Jackson? Just one?"

He forced a smile. "At least that."

"And how many have you killed from simple bungling, because you didn't know what you were doing?"

"I always know what I'm doing. Or I don't do it."

"Then clearly you're not a quack. You're a trained physician, by any reasonable standard. Years ago it was legitimate to learn medicine the way you've learned, through apprenticeship."

"This is the twentieth century. The laws have changed."

"I'm sure they have. And how many unqualified, splendidly incompetent doctors are turned out by our medical schools each year?"

"Who knows? I've met general practitioners I wouldn't trust to swab a septic throat, surgeons who gave me cold chills whenever they picked up a scalpel."

"Champ's going to live, isn't he? But he might not have, if you hadn't given him that new drug." She walked back to him. "No more apologies from you, Jackson. Not now or ever. If you've been looking for a place where you don't have to worry about the past catching up, then I think you may have found it." She smiled strangely. "You looked so woebegone up in that tree last night. Tears in your eyes. My heart fell out of place. Not right away, about two hours later, I was just lying in bed thinking about you, the way you turned up in my life. What do you want to do, Jackson?"

"I still don't know. For now all I care about is being with you."

Nhora's face was pleasantly reddened by the rising sun; she shielded her eyes with one hand to see him. She smiled again, with more confidence, and beckoned with her other hand.

"Let me show you the *Stephen Mulrooney*."

"The—?"

"It's an old stern-wheeler, dating from the great age of steamboats on the river. Most of them went out of service or were destroyed before the turn of the century—they were particularly susceptible to fire—but the *Stephen Mulrooney* was rescued from dry rot by a millionaire cotton planter in Helena. Until a few years ago he used it as

273

a kind of floating clubhouse for his cronies and his women. The big flood of 'thirty-nine swept the *Mulrooney* from its dock and downstream. Somehow it wasn't destroyed by the floodwater or the weight of all those trees. You can still see one of the stacks from here—" She leaned companionably against him, pointing to the vast thicket which stood half in sunlight, half in darkness.

"It's in *there?*"

"Battered, but well preserved. The backwater is shallow and acid, and that's saved most of the hull. Some of the staterooms on the portside boiler deck silted up during recent floods, but the forecastle and the Texas deck have stayed high and dry. Children don't go near the boat. It's not easy to find your way through the thicket, and there are a lot of—you know. A boy was fatally bitten two years ago. Then there are rumors of haunts, phantasms floating around at night. But the decks are in sunlight nearly all day. It's cozy and almost dry and not too buggy. Bugs don't bother me anyway. The *Stephen Mulrooney* has been my getaway place, when I'm fed up with people and circumstances. But I haven't been aboard for a few months. Come on."

Jackson was rooted. "You must be joking."

Nhora laughed. "You ought to see your expression. Jackson, I'm not trying to be cruel. You won't see anything you shouldn't see, or don't want to see. I'm serious. I have power over animals. It's almost as if they know my thoughts, and I know theirs. I've had this power since I was a little girl." She held his head delicately and kissed first his ears, then his eyes. His face tingled from the mild pressure of her hands. He felt a rush of blood, lingering heat, a sense of fulfillment and ease. "There. That's all. You're protected."

"I'm tempted to believe you. But I'm not—I can't—"

Nhora frowned. "How long have you been phobic? I don't see how you could have lasted for so many years in Africa if you were that afraid of—"

"I didn't have it when I was growing up. I first became aware of the phobia in the garden of the dispensary in Kisantu, where I was recovering from my head wounds and subsequent infection. What I saw was just an ordinary nonpoisonous type of snake—slithering through dry grass. I wouldn't have given it a second glance in Tuleborné; I could identify the deadly ones at twenty paces. It wasn't even headed my way. Nevertheless I was suffocated by a tidal wave of atavistic terror. I imagined the thing—crawling on me, enfolding me. I shook and sobbed. Two of the nursing sisters had to half-carry me back inside."

"Something must have happened in Tuleborné, when you went back to your father, to make you phobic."

"My memory of that day and night is very dim."

"Aren't there ways to find out?"

"A down-and-out 'colleague' of mine, a defrocked Freudian analyst, once suggested the therapeutic use of sodium pentothal."

"What would that do?"

"Unlock the past, as they say. With the aid of sodium pentothal I could relive what I've willfully forgotten, my every move from the moment I returned to Tuleborné."

"But you don't want to."

"I think I'm better off with my phobia."

"The cure is worse than the disease?"

"It may be."

Nhora put a hand on Jackson's shoulder to steady herself while she slipped back into her shoes. Without speaking she walked unhurriedly toward the great thicket. He could now make out one thin rusting smokestack, its crown askew, of the *Stephen Mulrooney*. The stack was inclined at an angle of about twenty degrees from the vertical, caught in a net of branches.

"Jackson," Nhora called, "is your father still living?"

"No. He was killed in the spring of 'forty-two by an unexploded bomb in the park at Hawkspurn. Concussion dashed him against a tree, I'm told. Fortunately there were no other fatalities. I should have returned to England for the funeral. The truth is, I felt he'd buried himself, years ago."

Nhora reached the thicket and paused, as if trying to

remember the best way to penetrate. She strolled to her right for a short distance, stopped and looked back.

"Won't change your mind?"

"Nhora, I can't."

"I'll just see how the old tub is getting along. Won't be a minute. Don't go away."

With that she stepped up onto a mossback trunk, posed vividly in a streak of sun, then pushed aside a hanging mat of vines and jumped blithely out of sight. Jackson stared after her, his teeth on edge. Then he turned and unzipped his pants and stood moodily pissing into the river.

"Jackson! Jackson!"

He put himself in order and ran to the mossback log where he'd last seen Nhora. There had been no terror in her voice, she couldn't be in serious trouble, but she wanted him urgently. He vaulted to the top of the log and stood peering into the thicket, unable to locate her. Birds chittered. He could feel the sun on his back, but it was still somber steeping twilight inside the thicket.

"Where are you?"

"Here." Her voice was more distant. Then Nhora appeared, disquietingly featureless, as if there were a wall of opaque glass between them. She was about a hundred feet from Jackson. "Just walk straight to me. Remember, I'm protecting you. It's squishy underfoot, but there's nothing in your way, nothing that will hurt—"

"Nhora, what do you want?"

"You have to see this for yourself," she said impatiently. "Come on, please, I'm getting a *little* scared, I don't understand what it all means."

He heard a mourning dove, and a faraway dog. His throat had hardened intolerably. He couldn't do it, she wasn't fair. The very suggestion produced a narcoleptic heaviness in his limbs. And then, with the kind of mysterious, abrupt transition common in dreams, he discovered himself well into the jagged thicket, shoes sucking in the bog. He was suffering as much as he'd ever suffered in his life, but moving, moving blindly toward her soft and reassuring voice.

276

Nhora's hand reached out and touched him; she gathered him in. His eyes were stinging from sweat or tears. He clung to her, panting, feeling disgraced but also obscurely brave.

"Hello, Jackson. Was it so bad?"

"For a while there."

She kissed him, restoring partial sight and sensibility. "Now you're right in the middle of it—all your fear. What do you do?"

"I—I start screaming and black out. Or, just possibly, I get stronger."

"What will it be?" she asked, leaning back and gazing stringently at him.

"Stronger," he admitted, pleased by his slowing pulse. "But still susceptible."

"I told you. From now on I'm looking out for you."

There was a small sound behind them, like a ferret plunging into shallow water. Nhora glanced around. Jackson could see part of the derelict *Stephen Mulrooney*: a railed upper deck, the glassless pilothouse.

"I think somebody's moved in," she said.

"Is that what frightened you?"

"No." She took him by the hand and led him across slippery, close-packed logs that formed an adequate corduroy road through the muck. They stopped at an arch formed by tree roots, with a hundred cavities suitable for nesting cottonmouths. Jackson felt a shudder working up from his bowels, but Nhora, oblivious, stood staring raptly through the murky tunnel.

There was a familiar odor in the air which overpowered rot and dampness: a blazing stink of whorish perfume.

And Jackson, as he eyed the forbidding gateway to the *Stephen Mulrooney*, became aware of other curiosities: small white candles in crude holders wired to the tree roots, a pair of hanging Congo drums.

"It's touchy," Nhora murmured, "but we can go through." She led him into the trembling, clinging roots, some almost invisible in their delicacy. Jackson felt as if he were edging deep and raw into his own nervous system. A couple of times he glimpsed, out of the corner of his eye, something light-skinned and sluggish stirring in the overhung hideaways, but Nhora increased the pressure of her hand in his and pulled him through, into unexpected sun.

They stood blinking at the sharp light, looking around. Several years of backwashed silt had created an earthwork which someone had troubled to beat firm and level with the steamboat's partly entombed forward boiler deck.

"Good Lord," Nhora said. "What *is* this?"

A pavilion of sorts had been erected alongside the *Stephen Mulrooney*: four crude posts supporting a pyramidal, shingled roof. There was a central post surrounded by a large, stone-paved platform. On the stone lay rattles, bells, other stones with inscriptions or drawings, necklaces, more drums and a number of covered pots and jars. A wicker ship model hung from a crossbeam of the roof. Other artifacts suspended from the roof included calabashes, baskets and a few homemade banners adorned with skulls, astrological symbols and swords.

A pit had been dug in the ground; it was covered with what looked like half of a radiator grill from an automobile. Wisps of smoke arose from buried coals. A swordlike iron bar had been plunged through the grill and into the coals. Jackson touched it tentatively and snatched his hand away. He looked more closely at the center post, where a black-snake whip was knotted to an iron ring. Nhora picked up some of the pots and opened them. They were empty. She stared at Jackson, starkly curious.

"It's an oum'phor," he said. "A temple of voodoo. The place where we're standing is the peristyle. This is the altar stone, the *kpé*, if I remember correctly. The rattles and bells are used in the ritual. Some of the jars are called *govis;* the voodoo gods reside in them while waiting to be summoned during a rite."

Nhora hastily replaced the jar she had been examining.

"The center post is the most important feature of the temple. The top is considered to be the center of the sky; the bottom, of course, would be the center of hell."

"Who would go to all this trouble?"

"It's an ideal location for secrecy. Notice the design on the center post: The spirals represent two serpent gods, Danbhalah Wédo and Ai-da Wédo. The wooden post itself is the chief god of voodoo: Legba. And the whip is a substitute for a live snake. It represents faith in voodoo, mastery of its powers."

"But who's practicing voodoo here? And why?"

"It's the religion of the African Negro. Contrary to the reputation voodoo has, there's nothing intrinsically harmful in it. But there are sects outside the tradition in which the motive power is human sacrifice. The Ajimba were members of a criminal sect. They believed they became superhuman when they wore the representational skins or masks."

"Human sacrifice?" Nhora said, grimacing as she looked around again.

"I doubt much blood has been spilled here, other than that of a goat or a lamb."

"Then why do they want to hide what they're doing?"

"I suppose your Negroes are reluctant to let their neighbors know they hanker after the old religion. It must be a small sect; perhaps this is even a private oum'phor."

"That perfume. It's foul. Like the perfume Early Boy dumped in my car."

"I know."

Nhora stared at Jackson, perplexed. "Do you suppose *he's* involved in this?"

"White initiates are rare, but not unheard of. Anyone with a knowledge of procedure can perform a voodoo ceremony. The perfume is homage to Mawu, as she's called in Africa—mother serpent, the Ai-da Wédo, who is symbolized by the model ship hanging there. Long ago the altar was always hollow. There was a—a live snake inside, its body supposedly inhabited by Mawu."

Jackson turned toward the buried fire. "That iron bar in the coals—the forge of the gods—can have several meanings. In legend the iron fell from the sky and is a symbol of cosmic sexual desire. The bar also represents a sword, or dagger, the serpent-in-iron. A weapon that kills.

279

The so-called red sects, those who go in for murder and cannibalism, have as their emblem the avenging sword of Saint Michael."

"Then what was the meaning of Clipper's sword in my car? What was he trying to say?"

"I have no idea, Nhora."

Nhora glanced up at the Texas deck of the steamboat, as if she'd seen something moving there. She looked back at Jackson and shrugged, but her smile was strained.

"Now I'm—jumpy. We ought to get out of here. But I'll never be satisfied. If Early Boy *has* been hanging around here, the sheriff should know. Do you think he could be on the boat?"

"Shall we have a look?"

Nhora's fingers fastened on his arm. She lowered her voice. *"No.* What if he is? I've changed my mind, Jackson. We'd better go."

"Somehow I can't believe Early Boy has anything to do with this; even if he's mad as a hatter it's an unlikely bent. But something occurred at Old Lamb's tonight that was so strange I'm tempted to call it supernatural. And Early Boy Hodges may be an eyewitness."

"He was there?"

Jackson nodded.

"How do you know that?"

"He was seen running away after the explosion, or whatever it was. A Negro who took a shot at him said he ran with a distinctive limp. That describes Early Boy well enough for me."

"He does limp—Tyrone said something about it weeks ago. But how did you know?"

"Early Boy and I go back many years, to a time when I was keeping body and soul together as sawbones for the criminal element."

"You didn't tell me that!"

"I didn't know how, before. Oh, and you can blame me for his distinctive smile. He was shot in the mouth by a bank guard and I had to sever the nerve that was causing him agony."

280

"How well do you know him?" Nhora asked, still astounded.

"I mistrust the public personality. I've never had reason to fear him. He's not a hoodlum and I doubt he's murdered anyone. He hews to a personal code chivalric in its complexity, which a logical mind couldn't hope to fathom. I think, now that I know who Early Boy really is, that I'd welcome a chance to talk to him."

Nhora shuddered. "But not here."

"I'm certain we're quite alone. I'll just have a quick look aboard."

Nhora stayed behind, near the center of the peristyle. Jackson found the deck planks still reasonably sound—and tracked with muddy bootprints. An area in front of a louvered stateroom door had been swept clean recently. The door was warped, sticking to the frame. He put his shoulder to it and the door scraped open. A shaft of sun lit up the dry, musty room inside. The odor of perfume drifted out. Jackson hesitated, then entered and was immediately blinded.

The room, apparently, was the holy of holies, dedicated to the worship of a particular god. Jackson shielded his eyes against the reflected glare of a broken mirror, part of a bulky old bedroom dresser that stood near the middle of the small room. The walls had been draped in faded, water-stained red velvet. The dresser served as an altar. Ritual designs, called *vèvès*, decorated the bow front. There were amulets, bells and candles on the dresser top, along with an *asson*, a calabash rattle containing small stones and the vertebrae of snakes. It symbolized both the power of the priest and the voices of the ancients, the *loas*.

Nothing unusual in all this. Jackson yawned and turned, glimpsed something hanging on the back of the door. It startled him until he realized it was little more than a scarecrow on a wrought-iron cross, mounted so that it could be carried during ceremonies. But it seemed worth a closer look, because the scarecrow obviously was meant to be a woman.

There was a glossy wig on top of the cross, blatant red

281

curls hanging down the front of an old-fashioned, petticoat-stuffed dress, an heirloom from another century. The dress was of lace and silk, with belled sleeves and a high neck. The silk had been a rich brown, but it was now sun-spotted, and the serpentlike effect was disquieting. So were the snakeskins that had been wrapped around the cross-piece; shreds of skin dangled from the ends of the bar like wispy fingers.

The only other object of interest was a gold locket on a chain, half-hidden by the sprawl of wiggish curls. He picked the locket up, found the catch with tracing fingers, opened it, stared at the oval portrait inside. He was swept by nausea. His hand tightened on the locket; he snapped the chain and bolted from the room.

"Nhora!"

She was waiting for him in the peristyle, eyes glazed from shock or rapture, lonely as a saint at a stake: But this stake, more terrifying than the flames of hell, was slowly twining itself around her.

Dun-colored, and of the earth. But the gaze of the giant was remote, far-reaching as starlight. It looked at him with towering arrogance, freezing the will. King of the gods. His mind shrieked, but no sound issued from his throat. Nhora's hands slid glibly along the snake's body, urging it upward, head-high. Jackson tried to push himself away from a pillar of the steamboat, but his legs were unworkable, he was forced to cling. Thinking: *I know what it must mean.* But intuition was fouled by darkness that crossed the mind like a swift-running cloud shadow.

Nhora began to turn away, her body seeming to undulate, to move metachronally with the winding-around horror in her hands. They stood eye to eye, open-throated. Jackson heard the faint gush and rattle of a calabash. Shock bolted through him and the rotten pillar snapped in his embrace. He fell, fell a long way, striking the deck with his chin almost as a painless afterthought. There was an instant of awful, artificial clarity, a sensation of release from life—discontent, elation, self-pity—before he was tumbled under in a rocketing flood.

Champ awoke alone, in a cool skin, breathing passively, focused without sorrow on a wall of new sunlight, his mind like brand-new. He was half-alert to the danger he believed himself to be in, wondering coolly about it though he didn't have an inkling of what had warned him, or what to expect; he had no dream or premonition to go by. He lay there, on the steamer chair in the playroom, covered with a thin yellow blanket, light streaming healthily through his mind. His body felt neutral. He didn't have to go to the bathroom, he wasn't hungry, there was no pain. He felt as lightly strutted as the model airplanes overhead, his body ready to be used, with reasonable caution.

Each physical act—sitting up, placing one bare foot on the floor, then the other—called for introspection. Demands to be weighed, and met. Sense of blood tilting deep, wobbling in the belly, a heaviness, like mercury finding a level. Standing was moderately suspenseful. He grasped the back of the chair. He heard a tractor in a field, morning moves of the house coming alive. He felt, then, curiously pressed for time, although still there was nothing definite, just an awareness of being the last in command. Boss watching him from a wall, shadow of his pith helmet eclipsing all but the jaunty grin and grizzle of safari beard, '32 or '33, the tall barrel-chested man beside him none other than Ernest Hemingway.

Champ moved flat-footed along the picture wall, nudging his shadow before him. Visions of a family half-destroyed. Duty to fulfill. Weight of reckoning to bear. He was in command. His heartbeat rang in his ears. He had to stop and lean against the wall, head floating precariously. Then he went around the room again. Heavy in the lungs. No breath. Like trying to squeeze air from stones.

He stopped again and, without knowing why, took down one of a pair of Civil War sabers crossed beside the mantel. He unsheathed it.

Hadn't been cleaned in years. The edge nicked and dull. He and Clipper, inflamed by the movies, by Douglas Fairbanks, having at each other mindlessly in duels. Could've been seriously hurt, despite their lack of power and technique, even with these heavy dull blades. Boss never put a stop to it. He preferred wounds to timidity.

Tears sprang to Champ's eyes. He made a conscious effort to hold the saber high and steady, but his arms trembled. He snuffled from weakness, and let the blade drop, the point narrowly missing bare toes as it struck the hearthstone.

In command, but not ready. And so he would be killed like the others. Knowledge that had awakened him so early on this cheerful morning. Death was coming, he would fall.

He replaced the saber in its tarnished scabbard and laid it on the mantel. It was no good to him anyway; too damaged to repair.

But there was another, useful saber. Not far away.

His old bedroom was next door. Nothing had been changed during his years away from Dasharoons. His metal locker from Blue Ridge Military Institute was at the foot of the bed. Champ opened it. He took out neatly packed cadet uniforms. Mothballs rolled along the floor. Near the bottom of the locker, blade protected by a soft and elegant jewelers' cloth, was the dress saber he had received from the company on graduation day. The hilt was gold, the blade unflawed Swedish steel.

With his weapon in his hands he felt nerveless again, satisfied that, whatever his fund of strength, he need not die disgraced.

He took a whetstone from the locker and, sitting on the edge of the bed, placidly concentrating, seeing nothing but his own quick reflection in the mirror surface, he began to work.

"Jackson!"

He heard her faintly, as if she were years away, separated from him by time rather than distance; it might have been his mother's voice. He was conscious then of the radiance of the sun, his eyelids glowing and warm. Something moved, he felt a shifting weight against his ribs, the sun was blocked. He heard himself groan. Drops

284

of ditch water pattered on his face, collected in the hollows of his eyes. He trembled in irritation and raised a hand to skim away the lingering drops.

Nhora caught his hand and held it tightly.

"Be careful, you're still bleeding."

Pressure against his chin, he couldn't open his mouth to answer. He grunted something.

"Here, let me help you sit up."

As he was lifted, supported by an arm across his back, pain arrowed from a cut and throbbing chin; he felt a chipped tooth with his tongue. His neck was stiff and painful too. Nhora's face, when he opened his eyes, was very close, somewhat blurred. He blinked to clear his vision. Didn't work. There were bits of leaf mold in her hair, a smear of blood—his?—on one cheekbone. A fly buzzed them both, then vanished.

She took her other hand away from his chin and he glanced down at the bloody handkerchief she was holding, darker blots in the crimson.

"How deep a cut?" he asked, moodily calculating stitches, not yet concerned about what might have befallen him. His memory was as bad as his eyesight. But there was a lump of foreboding in the region of his heart.

"I don't know. It's almost stopped bleeding now. For a few minutes you were like a—a gored ox, I was scared."

She turned her head to drop the wadded handkerchief into a rust-flecked coffee can filled with water. The sun jumped at him again. He traveled back an instant, to the flash in a bureau mirror, the stateroom aboard the tottering old *Stephen Mulrooney*. A room draped in shabby red velvet and oddly claustrophobic, like a chamber in a dead heart. The room had contained some kind of threat, and now he felt alarmed. What was it?—Just an old dress, a wig, some snakeskin. A childishly executed version of a voodoo goddess, but which one? That was crucial.

Another flash-jump, to a little piece of time slick as ice: His mind slipped and slithered as he tried to grasp the significance of the locket and the portrait which he had—

The next thing he knew he was pushing Nhora roughly

285

away from him. She sat down hard, heels in the air, almost going over backward. Jackson scrambled to his feet and swayed like a drunk. Nhora was very close to tears.

"Jackson, what's got into you? You'll start pouring blood again."

He leaned against the car and looked at the river; the sun was much higher than it had been back in the thicket. Now he was shuddering. His shirt was sticking to the hairs on his chest. He looked down. Bloodstains everywhere, drip drip drip to the cuffs of his trousers. He stared at his clenched empty hands, dimly aware that he was missing something. But the blood baffled him.

He looked at Nhora. She was standing but hadn't made a move toward him. She swam into sharper focus.

"What happened?" he asked her.

"Jackson, I don't know! You came running out of that stateroom and hit a post or something, then you fell facedown on the deck." She was trembling, from relief or fear. "Just good luck you didn't knock yourself out. I don't know what I would have done then. I stopped the blood as best I could, and led you back to the car—*now* what's the matter? Are you going to faint?"

"You had," he said carefully, trying not to shy away from the new horror occupying his mind, "a snake in your hands."

"Oh, God, is that all?" Nhora said with a look of irritation. She lowered her head and picked at bits of dried mud on her dress. "I don't know where it came from. I was waiting for you, I looked down, there it was right at my feet. I knew I had to get rid of it before you came out, or else—" She shrugged, raised her eyes. "Jackson, I told you, from the time I was a little girl I could handle snakes, even poisonous ones like the cottonmouth. I suppose I learned not to be afraid when I was with the Ajimba, they always had hundreds of snakes and lizards around. They prayed to them. Snakes were their gods."

"This one was a monster—tall as you."

"I think you're exaggerating, it's just your phobia." She spread her hands, indicating a length of three feet. "I don't give a snake any more thought than a june bug, now

286

can we change the subject? And I *hate* the way you're looking at me. I'm not unclean, or some kind of freak, just because I picked up a snake. Why don't you tell me what you saw in that room that upset you so badly."

"Nhora, I had a locket. What happened to it?"

Nhora reached into a pocket of her dress and came up with the locket. It spun on the chain, spraying the light of the sun at him. "I gave it to my mother when I was seventeen, a year before she died. There's a picture of me inside. I haven't seen the locket for a couple of years, I thought it was lost. Where did you find it?"

"In the stateroom. Hanging from the neck of a filthy ritual effigy."

"How did it get there?"

"Don't you know?"

"Of course not!" she exploded. "Somebody found the locket, or else it was stolen—oh, I don't know." She opened the locket and studied the tiny portrait of herself. Then, dismayed, she snapped the locket shut and put it away. She turned with a look of bewilderment and walked a short distance from Jackson, head down again, brooding.

Jackson waggled his sore jaw with care, but there was no grit and grind of a broken bone despite swelling on the right side behind the chin. He was no longer dizzy and in danger of losing his balance, and his vision was coming around nicely. He took off his jacket, stripped the ruined shirt, used a clean portion of it and water from the coffee can to scrub his chest, put his jacket back on. He made a pad for the cut and taped it securely in place, swallowed two aspirin and decided he would live.

"What was it like, the effigy?" Nhora asked.

"An antique dress, a wig, some snakeskin wrapped around a cross of iron."

"Was it supposed to be—me?"

"That's obvious. Still, it's quite unusual for someone other than a god to be depicted in the holy of holies—"

She came stalking back to him, mad and frightened. "I swear to you I have nothing to do with voodoo rituals!"

"Nhora, I believe you."

"Oh, yes, you *say* that, but your eyes look kind of sick and it's not just because you knocked yourself silly down there, you look as if you're afraid I'll *touch* you."

"I'm grateful for your quick thinking; I admire you tremendously and I've accused you of nothing sinister, so please don't go flying off the handle at me."

Nhora's face was dark red with anger; she was out of touch with reason as she raged, "I just want to know who's picking on me! And if I don't find out I'll get the sheriff, I'll come back myself with a can of gasoline and burn it, all of it!"

She brushed past him and went flying along the rutted wagon road to the top of the levee. The ignition keys were in the Chevrolet. Jackson backed it around and drove slowly after Nhora.

As soon as he stopped the car beside her, she got in. She wouldn't look at him. She was stiff with suppressed grief, eyes swollen but tearless. He drove on.

"I'm sorry. I shouldn't have attacked you. I guess I was getting back because you scared the wits out of me. I couldn't stand seeing you hurt. Going to the river was a bad idea."

"No, it wasn't."

Nhora smiled then, gratefully, gave him a glance. "How many of us have you told about yourself, Jackson?"

"You're the first."

"Why?"

"For the first time it's important—no, essential—that I separate reality from illusion at the beginning of a relationship, instead of saying nothing and encouraging the usual bad end, a spasm of conscience that's merely an excuse for skipping town with heavy heart and a full baggage of ego-serving remorse. But I can't give up my unsanctioned practice of medicine. My life is, and will be, based on self-deception, and I warn you that it's a habit of narcotic tenacity."

"You haven't deceived me," she said calmly. "We all lead unresolvable lives, Jackson. As for bad ends, I've had them, and I can't afford another one either. I still want you."

288

"Come what may. Nhora—delicate question, but I must ask—I saw the way you responded to Champ last night, and I know you care about him. I wondered if—"

"Yes. I did make love to him. Once. The night after Boss died. We were alone, bewildered, so deeply wounded by the murders, by the terrible revelations in Clipper's diary, that sleep was impossible. It was a way of sharing pain, diluting it. I'm not ashamed, but I wouldn't want to do it again. Even with Nancy dead, I haven't given a thought to the possibility of—Champ and me."

They jolted over a bump in the road and Nhora slipped easily to his side, clung to him. She sighed.

"I've been thinking about something, since we were at Old Lamb's. It can't be coincidence."

"What is that, Nhora?"

"The day Clipper went crazy in the chapel, something else strange happened near there—on Railroad Ridge, which overlooks the town of Gaston and the military school. A little boy named—Jimmy, I think—was on the ridge picking flowers for his sick mother. A terrible thing happened to him in the woods. No one is sure what it was, he died just a few hours afterward. But he told his brother that a huge ball of light came out of the woods at him. There was a wind strong enough to tear the clothes from his body. He was burned, yet there wasn't a mark on him. I saw Jimmy at the hospital soon after it happened. Tried to comfort him. He was in such pain that when I touched him he fought and screamed—I accidentally scratched him, there was blood and skin under my nails."

She looked at her nails now; they were dirty and broken.

"It wasn't determined how the boy died?"

"No. Do you remember what I told you about the chapel bell, swinging as if it were caught in a small tornado?"

"Yes."

"That was happening about the same time Jimmy ran into—whatever the light was, on the ridge. The next day I went to visit Jimmy's father and brother. We walked, in a drizzle, up the ridge and found the approximate spot where Jimmy had been gathering flowers. The flowers were all dead. Everything in a circle about fifty feet in diameter was withered, devastated, as if by frost. Even to the tops of the trees, dead leaves in May. I stood in the center of the circle, and looked across at the chapel on the campus a mile away."

"This was near a railroad line? Perhaps a piece of ordnance was stolen from a train, carried uphill by the thieves and abandoned in the woods. A timing device may have set it off just as Jimmy—"

"Don't you see? The same thing happened at Old Lamb's tonight! That powerful, withering light, Arabella blinded, the little girl dying like Jimmy in Virginia, twisted out of shape, her bones all but snapping from convulsions. Horrible."

"There are similarities between the events, but we're nearly seven hundred miles from Virginia, and two years distant in time. I don't see why you insist there has to be a connection—"

"I don't know either, but I feel so—guilty, as if I *should* know, as if the explanation's perfectly obvious and I'm willfully overlooking it."

Jackson started to shake his head, but pain in the back of his neck gave him pause.

"Nancy died in some mysterious way—*you're* not satisfied that she had a heart attack. It's as if we've been struck by lightning, again and again, wherever we go—the wrath of the gods. Why? Because of Clipper? Clipper paid, Boss paid. Who else has to pay? There's no refuge at Dasharoons. Will Champ be next?"

"Nothing's going to happen to Champ."

"Nothing good," Nhora said hopelessly, and was appalled. She made a small sound of distress and stifled further conversation by biting hard on a knuckle of one hand. She didn't speak again until they pulled up in front of the house. Servants were already at work, sweeping the veranda, watering flower beds. The house was filled with light and air, it had nobility in the morning: a monument to men, and an era, never to be seen again.

"Take the keys," Nhora said. "You'll need the car to get to town."

"Do you want to go?"

"No. Will you be seeing Champ?"

"As soon as I bathe and change."

Hackaliah must have observed their arrival; his bath-water—lukewarm—was ready when he reached his room. He scrubbed and thought of Nhora: her touch. Out of the bath Jackson studied the cut on his chin with a hand mirror and decided the scar would be trivial. He put down the mirror and stared vacantly out the window; the glass was loaded with light. Nhora's grave, elliptical eyes, shimmering with the same insubstantial daybreak gold. Eyes and the soul; vision and comeliness. The inevitability of his need for her. He tightened his buttocks in response to heated pressure in the groin, the thickening penis. But that wouldn't do, not yet. *We all lead unresolvable lives, Jackson.* His bloody suit had been whisked away to be cleaned. He put on a tan tropical worsted suit and went upstairs to call on his patient.

Champ was alone in the playroom, half-dressed, wearing an old striped robe over army pants and undershirt. He was skinny in the trousers, which were bunched at the waist. He had shaved himself. He was seated at a small table eating breakfast, doggedly because his hand wasn't steady. He looked up from the plate with eyes free of fever, looked through Jackson not as if he were absorbed in thought but rather steeling himself for something unpleasant that might also be coming through the door.

"Getting your strength back?" Jackson said amiably.

"I think so." He tried to refocus, but Jackson was made uneasy; it was as if a piece of Champ's mind had disappeared during the night, crumbling away from the mass.

He stared at the bandage on Jackson's chin. "What happened to you?"

"I took a tumble."

Aunt Clary Gene came in without a sound, very nearly sleep-walking. She unpinned a black hat with a veil. She looked grave-marked, thin as moon shadow, as if each death in the community reduced her closer to invisibility.

"Thank you, doctor," she said. "For all you did last night."

"I'm sorry I couldn't do more."

Champ put his fork down. "What about last night?"

"Old Lamb passed on," said Aunt Clary Gene. She began brewing tea, filled with her usual quiet passion for whatever small task was at hand.

"Oh." Champ gazed at his plate. "I don't think I can eat any more."

"I'll just listen to your lungs then."

As he was applying the disc of the stethoscope Champ said, "I need exercise. Too weak."

"You can walk up and down the hall. No stairs." He completed his auscultation. "You're sounding much less congested, Champ. I'd still like X-rays, but I think they can wait for a couple of days."

"When is Nancy's funeral?"

"Tomorrow, I understand."

"I'd like to go."

"You aren't strong enough yet. The ordeal could give you quite a rugged setback."

Unexpectedly tears began to drain from Champ's eyes, but his expression was more sullen than sad. "We only had a little time together. Now I'll never see her again."

"I know how difficult it is for you," Jackson said, preparing an injection of penicillin.

"Nobody's been kind enough to tell me what happened to Nancy."

"It was her heart, Champ."

"Her heart," he repeated, without emphasis, but a shudder flicked across his shoulders. "Where was she going, when she died?"

"She was on her way to San Francisco, to be with you."

"San Francisco," he said worriedly, making fists, testing his strength. A prolonged shudder this time. There was something black and threatening in his downcast brow. "That's a lie, isn't it?" he said, as if he were talking to a third person in the room.

Jackson hesitated, too long. "Why do you say that?"

"Because she called me, at the hospital. I don't remember when. Said she had to get out of here, because of Beau."

"She was afraid of Beau?"

Champ lifted his eyes. "Ask him," he said, smiling thinly and suspiciously, as if he had always been sure that Jackson and Beau were the best of friends.

"I can't, I don't know where your brother is. Could you roll up your sleeve for me?"

Champ's attention shifted to the syringe. "Putting something in or taking something out?"

"It's penicillin. I've been giving it to you right along."

Champ watched the syringe as if he were destined to be eternally fascinated by it. Then a dreary change came over him, he lost the keyed-up suspicious look and wandered from his line of attack. ". . . Okay. Just don't take anything out. Too much of me has disappeared already. You understand what I mean."

"Not exactly. Tell me more about Nancy. She called you in San Francisco and—"

"Had to find Beau. Nancy was trying to get to Beau. Or something like that. I meant to ask her what it was all about, coming home on the train last night. Was it last night? We talked for a long time. I told her how it had been for me, in the war. There are men who love war. But I'm not one of them. Found that out once and for all. Nancy understood."

He smiled, heartrendingly, at Jackson. "Or did I imagine all that? She couldn't have talked to me, she was lying in her coffin."

"Champ, you've been through so much. Give yourself time." Jackson withdrew the needle and swabbed the spot with alcohol.

Nhora came in smiling expectantly, high shine to her face, hair sleekly tied at the nape of her neck. She was wearing riding pants and a gingham shirt in brown and orange.

"Champ, you look—"

Champ thrust Jackson aside with a strength Jackson

293

wasn't prepared for. His other hand clamped just under Nhora's jaw with such force that her mouth was frozen open. Her eyes, glazed with panic, stared at the dangling airplanes. She staggered back, bearing his weight, until he got his other hand around her throat too and bent her savagely, thrusting her head far back as he tried to crush her windpipe. His body was against hers, groin to groin. He whined and shuddered like a dog in heat as he tried to kill her.

As Jackson grasped Champ by the wrists and attempted to wedge himself between them, Champ's charge of extraordinary strength failed. He suddenly released Nhora and collapsed heavily on the floor. She fell against the wall by the door, rasping for air, staring at Champ, ready to run for her life if he stirred. But Champ was out cold, eyes back in his head when Jackson turned him over, muscles twitching galvanically.

Jackson carried him to the padded deck chair and prepared a barbiturate for injection. Aunt Clary Gene stood dumbfounded at Champ's side.

"I want someone with him every moment. Someone strong enough to handle him."

"He was just the gentlest boy," she muttered. "Couldn't never do a hurtful thing like that. It's the truth. Champ just *couldn't.*"

When Jackson had sedated Champ he turned around and saw that Nhora was gone. He followed to her room. The door was locked. She sobbed inside.

"Please let me in! Are you badly hurt?"

Nhora's sobbing continued, but during the next few minutes as he stood there, intermittently knocking and calling to her, she sounded as if she were winding down. She wasn't hysterical, and if she could breathe well enough to cry so luxuriously, then probably Champ hadn't damaged her. Nhora knew he was by the door; clearly she didn't want to see or talk to him.

"Nhora, you're not in any danger now. He'll sleep most of the day. It's five of nine, I have to go into town. We'll decide what to do about Champ when I get back."

What to do? Jackson failed to come up with alternatives as he pondered the problem while driving to Chisca Ridge. It was evident now that Champ hadn't survived the ghastly throat-cutting in the jungle without permanent ill-effects. All but destroyed by the loss of his wife, he had become unpredictably violent, potentially homicidal. Perhaps the best answer was to turn him back to the military; he belonged, at least temporarily, in a prison hospital ward, where he could be examined by specialists. Another tragedy for the dwindling family to absorb. Nhora would have to make the decision. But she couldn't hesitate, not after his attack on her. He might try again.

In a thoroughly melancholy frame of mind, Jackson parked and entered Flax and Dakin's funeral parlor.

They were ready for him in a basement room where three electric fans stirred the clammy air. Flax was a big bluff man with Father Christmas spectacles and a messy unlit cigar that seldom moved from the center of his mouth. His shirttail hung out and his trouser cuffs covered his little feet. Dakin was a nervous dwarf in a business suit and polka-dot bow tie. The two partners, he explained, as Flax set out his tools, had not spoken to each other in six years; some sort of feud, Jackson gathered. They seemed to work well together nonetheless, revolving around each other like double stars.

The court order for the autopsy had come through. Flax, the coroner, listened to hillbilly music on the radio while he worked. The body of Nancy Bradwin had come unembalmed to him in the early afternoon of the day before; while Dakin made notes he described the condition the body had been in. Jackson soon discovered that Flax was a competent and thorough examiner, able to distinguish those marks and blemishes that had been on Nancy's body before death from those sustained when her body fell from the train.

"There weren't no penetrating wounds," he explained to Jackson. "Not even a pinhole. These four scratches on the left side of the throat might be from fingernails"—he positioned his hand, fingers spread, to illustrate—"if she

295

was in some kind of catfight. But she don't have the bruises I'd expect to see if she was beat up."

The autopsy proceeded, with the removal of the scalp and hair and, neatly, the top of the skull, high-speed saw whining and chittering as Ernest Tubb sang lachrymose songs about Texas on the radio.

"No scalp lesions or hemorrhage, new or old," Flax intoned. "No hemorrhage of the temporal muscles. No fracture lines new or old." Flax pried into the bloodless brain, separating the thready lobes, with Jackson looking over his shoulder. The brain looked normal, no clots or hematomas, but he hadn't expected to find that Nancy Bradwin had died of an aneurysm. It was her heart that interested him.

In due course Flax lifted the organ from the chest cavity.

"Heart killed her?" Flax snorted. "Not this heart. I hope mine looks this good."

Jackson examined Nancy's heart himself, and concurred. No occlusions or faulty valves, no wasted patches on the stout muscle that might have resulted in cardiac arrest.

Likewise the liver, lungs and spleen appeared normal. "Too bad we don't have blood," Flax said. "Blood could tell us a lot." He sectioned the vital organs and packed the tissue in dry ice. At that point it would have been difficult for anyone not in the mortuary business to understand how neatly Nancy Bradwin would be restored for viewing, prior to the funeral, now that Flax had finished his autopsy.

"Friend Dakin's on his way to Little Rock this mornin'. He'll drop the specimens at the state pathology lab and tell them we're in a hurry, should have some results by telephone tonight."

Everett John Wilkes was waiting for Jackson in the foyer of the funeral home when he went upstairs. Red carpet, ferns, the light of the sun diffused by stained glass panels.

"Know anything now you didn't know before?"

"Physically she was in very good condition when she died."

"Then she wasn't murdered." His face became congested as if in a parody of grief, but it was just a sneeze coming on. He reached into his back pocket for a handkerchief and stifled the sneeze.

"Not in a conventional way."

"Meanin' she wasn't stabbed or shot or hit over the head. What else is there?"

"Paralysis of the central nervous system, perhaps. I'll know more when we have the pathologist's report on stomach contents."

Evvy Wilkes turned his head slightly; a sunbeam trembled at the level of his brow, exciting one bloodshot eye.

"You think she was poisoned?"

"I don't know what else to think right now."

"Those long sleepin' spells of hers—maybe somebody was givin' Nancy pills to make her sleep."

Jackson shook his head. "Dr. Talmadge would have found traces of any barbiturate in her blood."

"That is, if you trust Dr. Talmadge."

"Do you have reason to believe he was guilty of unethical conduct?"

"Wasn't around here long. Nobody got to know him very well. Surly little bastard. Then he hanged himself. That's proof-positive he had an unsound mind. He just might also have had plenty to feel guilty about."

"I think he was in love with Nancy; frightened for her. And there was nothing he could do. He may have sensed that she was doomed, for reasons that are still unclear to me. I only know that bona fide Bradwins are getting scarce."

Wilkes sneezed again, and looked around uneasily "Ashes to ashes and dust to dust," he muttered. "But it's the kind of dust I'm allergic to. Had your breakfast?"

"No."

"The Turkey Shoot Café ain't bad. Let's get on out of here."

They walked a block and a half to the café. Wilkes, in

297

shirt sleeves, labored on his crutches. His left shoe was all but worn out along one side, from dragging. The day was heating up and he sweated buckets, but he seemed determined to ignore his physical handicap.

Jackson briefly weighed the bad news he had to tell and decided there was no gentle way to break it to the lawyer. He took off his straw hat to mop his damp hairline, and described Champ's attack on Nhora.

"Jesus Christ!" Wilkes shouted, and he stopped short in the street, hulking over his crutches, big drops of sweat rolling off his face. He did battle with his emotion, overpowered and shoved it deep inside and slammed a lid on it.

He said quietly, "In your opinion, doctor, should Champ be committed to an institution?"

"I don't know what's going on in his brain. He might well have seen, instead of Nhora, an Imperial Marine entering the room with a machine gun in his hands. In a few hours Champ could wake up all smiles and not remember a thing about it. But he's a soldier, it's wartime, and he's AWOL. As soon as he's strong enough to travel Champ should be given over to the military."

"Is it battle fatigue, or is he permanently brain-damaged?"

"Let's hope a case of battle fatigue, complicated by his emotional problems."

"You don't *sound* too damn hopeful," Wilkes said resignedly.

They reached the café. Two gold stars hung in a flyspecked window and there was a sign on the door: *No soft drinks for the duration—buy war stamps instead.*

"You didn't ask me how Nhora is," Jackson said, as he held the door for Wilkes to enter the café.

"That's right. I didn't."

"She wasn't hurt very badly."

"I figured she wasn't."

The Turkey Shoot Café was a long dim room repeating all of its bleak angles in too many mirrors. There were ceiling fans, and a ghostly beer smell. At ten o'clock in the morning they had it pretty much to themselves. They took a booth near the back of the café. Wilkes ordered a beer and a plate of hash browns for himself, recommended fried eggs and country ham with red-eye gravy for Jackson. He lit a cigarette and fidgeted with his GI Zippo lighter. A nearby radio was broadcasting yesterday's closing commodity prices on the Chicago Board of Trade. A tractor went by in the street. Two old men played dominoes in the shade beneath the tin roof of a machine shop. In the deep dark beyond them the brilliant tip of an arc welder wandered like a lost star.

Wilkes waited until he had a couple of swallows of beer before he spoke.

"You got any idea what Dasharoons is worth?"

"Millions, I presume. Who owns it all: Champ?"

"Nhora's got a one-eighth share. I tried to argue Boss out of it. Champ's will provided for his wife and children. But Nancy's predeceased him, and there ain't no children. Dasharoons, for all practical purposes, is intestate. That's why I was so anxious to sit down and have a talk with Champ right away. I *could* say that preserving Dasharoons is a sacred trust to me, that's partly true. But looking after their legal business has kept me, and my daddy before me, and a couple of old survivin' partners, in grits and gravy for the last sixty years. So I figure I owe Boss my best efforts now."

"What would happen to Dasharoons if Champ is declared incompetent?"

"Property is placed in trust, and administered by the trustees, of which I am one. When he dies, the property gets sold, piecemeal if we see fit. The money goes to a number of institutions of higher learnin'. Plenty of eager buyers been sniffing around since Boss left us. My legal fees from the trust or the sale would keep me well fixed in my declinin' years, so I ain't worried about income. What I *don't* want is for the plantation to fall into the wrong hands."

"Nhora's hands?"

Wilkes drained his bottle too quickly, frowned, signaled the waitress for another. "No court would give her another square foot of Dasharoons. I saw to that before the marriage ever took place."

"Beau, then."

"Beau's dead; he must be."

"Long-lost sons and heirs have a way of showing up unexpectedly."

"He's not the one I'm worried about," Wilkes said stubbornly.

"That leaves Tyrone, doesn't it?"

Wilkes looked startled, then impressed. "By God, you keep your ear to the ground, don't you?"

"I had occasion to treat his injured hand last night, and we became acquainted. Tyrone makes no bones about his paternity."

"He damn sure don't. Couple of times he tried to capitalize on his bloodlines. Boss was more patient with him than I was. Tyrone had been coached before he came to me. He knew, even though Boss chose not to legally acknowledge him, that he had a case. So I explained the true facts of the matter to him."

"Which were?"

"I told Tyrone that even if he got a respected, dedicated jurist to take his case, which I doubted, he'd still spend years in the lower courts losing on every technical point we could come up with. I reminded him that the judges of this state, even those who sit on the highest court, are obligated for practical reasons to influential men like Boss, and conditioned by their heritage to turn a deaf ear to niggers eager to exploit an accident of birth, which is not the same thing as a birth*right*. I told him that Boss might be inclined to make a small gift of money, supplementing his generosity in the past—"

"Sent Tyrone to college, didn't he?"

"Right. Make a gift of money, oh, say, as much as two thousand dollars, if Tyrone should decide to pursue his choice of vocation a long way from the environs of Dasharoons. He had the nerve to smile at me."

A bottle of Griesedieck Brothers beer, a pot of coffee and plates of food were set before them. Wilkes mopped
300

his heated face with a napkin. Jackson noted that his eggs were fried hard as hickory nuts.

"*Smiled* at me. So then I said, okay, son, get yourself a lawyer. Petition the court. Go right ahead and *embarrass* Boss Bradwin. Because that's all you'll be to Boss by then, a source of humiliation and embarrassment to him and his children. And let me tell you somethin' else about Boss: You can criticize his kids, kick his dog and kiss his good-lookin' wife, if you do those things privately. He'll bend over backwards makin' excuses for you. But if you have the bad judgment and the discourtesy to make your insults a matter of public record, then Boss will prove to be *unforgiving*. He banished his own firstborn son forever, the son he loved most dearly in this life. What do you think he'll do to *you*, you little darkie shittail? You misbegotten son of a yella whore? You clap-brain arrogant *jackass*."

"That was not a very gentle threat."

"I did manage to make my point."

Jackson ate some of the crisped egg white, a forkful of grits, which he found palatable, and stirred sugar into his coffee.

"So he's given up his claim to Dasharoons?"

"Not likely. I firmly believe, now that fate has dealt a hand or two his way, Tyrone's changed his strategy. Champ is home, and in a vulnerable position, and those two sure as hell have figured out a way to take advantage of him."

"Those two?" Jackson said, startled. "You're including Nhora?"

"Yes, sir!" Wilkes smacked the table top with the flat of his hand for emphasis, spilling some of Jackson's coffee. "She's been without a husband for more than two years. Why's that? She's young, healthy, and plenty of men have found her beautiful. But in all this time nobody's seen her with an eligible man. That nigger's always had himself quite a reputation with the ladies, married and unmarried. It doesn't require a great deal of imagination to know what's goin' on at Dasharoons these days."

"I doubt that Nhora and Tyrone are having an affair.

301

They're—friends, that's all. What could he gain? You said yourself that Nhora can't inherit Dasharoons."

"She could if Champ would just sign his name to a piece of paper handin' it all over to her. Then Tyrone, who's got her wrapped around his little finger, would have what he wants. The last legitimate Bradwin out of the way. And he wouldn't have to worry about wakin' up some night to find his nuts nailed to the top of a burnin' cross."

Wilkes waved more cold beer his way, a brace of foaming bottles this time.

"You see, I don't trust the woman. Never trusted her worth a damn. It was always instinct, though; nothin' I could lay a good solid bet on."

"You simply resented her for marrying into the family. You felt she was all wrong for Boss."

"He paid for his good times. She got that old pecker of his uppity again. So maybe it was worth one-eighth of that good black-bottom land. I don't like coincidence, I suppose. Who the hell is she? Where did she come from? Off a goddam boat. She marries Boss, then a year later Boss and Clipper are both dead, and Champ goes against all good advices by puttin' her in charge out there at Dasharoons, while he fights the war."

"By all accounts she's done an excellent job."

Wilkes sourly considered Jackson's defense of Nhora, and pulled on a beer. "Dasharoons can damn near run itself. But you're right, she's made it her business to learn the business. She just ain't been so shrewd about the company she keeps. And now she's made a mistake, and maybe I'll find out why all this time I haven't trusted her."

"What kind of mistake?"

Wilkes smiled good-humoredly, but his eyes were cold. "I could be makin' just as big a mistake trustin' you too much. You only got off a train night before last, yourself."

"Nonetheless I have access to Champ, and you don't. You need my help, I may be the only one who can help you now. Provided there *is* some sort of conspiracy afoot."

"That says it all."

"What about Nhora?"

"Stuck on her a little bit yourself, it seems."

"She's kind and lonely and frightened by the disastrous fortunes of the Bradwins. As baffled as you or I. Shall we get on with it?"

"Okay. Day before yesterday, about nine-thirty in the mornin', Nhora called me at home. She was cryin'. Couldn't get any sense out of her right off. Then she told me about Nancy. Asked me—no, she *begged* me to go up to Kezar County and claim the body. That's a two-and-a-half-hour drive. I left right away."

"Why do you suppose Nhora didn't want to go?"

Wilkes gulped beer and gave him a look of seething satisfaction. "No good for that kind of thing, I guess. Or maybe she was too tired to make the trip again."

Jackson was properly astonished. "What do you mean, again?"

"She was there the night before, sometime after midnight."

"How do you know that?"

"Some Bradwins twice removed live up Kezar way. They spotted her drivin' through, in that little Chevrolet car of hers."

"They must be mistaken."

"If you see her once, you remember her. She's that kind of woman."

"What would she have been doing in Kezar County?"

"Lookin' for Nancy."

"Well, then, if she found Nancy, surely she would have said something—"

"Found her dead, maybe."

"And drove all the way back to Dasharoons, in the dead of night, without having notified the authorities? That doesn't make sense."

"Some folks regard her as bein' a little *strange,*" Wilkes said deliberately. "Have all along."

"Oh, I see. Well, why don't you just *ask* Nhora if she

was in Kezar County. No sense in prolonging the mystery, if there is one."

"She might have good reasons for denyin' to me she ever went there."

Jackson felt his face stiffening from outrage. "Is that an accusation?"

"I'm purely speculating." He lifted his big head back, closing his eyes, letting the beer gush down his throat.

"This is something that does want clearing up," Jackson admitted, after taking time to think. "If you consider the eyewitnesses dependable."

"I do. Another reason why I wanted to chat with you this mornin'. You appear to have her confidence. And I surely don't. Lose your appetite?"

"I don't want to leave you with the impression that I'm worried about what Nhora may have to say on her behalf."

Wilkes hit his dead leg with a fist, feeling nothing except, perhaps, the repetitious shock of psychic pain. "If she and that nigger are in cahoots, *anything* could happen. Murder."

Preposterous. You may despise Nhora, but you can't seriously believe—"

"She wouldn't be the first white woman to lose her dignity, and her common sense, because of a handsome buck. Who knows what kind of hold he has on her?" Wilkes tested his logic silently; then, with a twist of his mouth as if he were about to spit, rejected it. "No. She's probably not capable of murder. But *he* is." He gestured at his crutches. "I'm a cripple and there's no damn earthly reason for it! Unless somebody fixed me up on purpose. I've run into the nigger a few times since this happened. He's polite, he smiles, but it's the smile of a man who knows more than he chooses to tell. Like he could do worse to me, if he really wanted to.

"Let me explain what I was up to the night I lost the use of my leg. I always have liked my liquor, although I been on it heavier than I should this past year. Anyway, I was drivin' home late at night from Judge Walker T. Murry's stag party at his fishin' camp. And I was okay to drive long as I had the road to myself but not feelin' any pain, you understand. I missed the turn at my gate in the dark—I'll do that cold sober sometimes—and the car slipped a little catty-corner into the drainage ditch. No way to get it out without the tractor, and I didn't feel like walkin' the three hundred yards to the house. I figured I'd have a nap there in the car, then go on up to my own bed. It was a warm night, so I laid down across the seat and corked right off.

"Don't know what it was woke me up. A dog, a train whistle. A hoot owl. Still dark. But the door on the driver's side of my Caddy was open, and I was hangin' half out of the car. I heard footsteps, like somebody runnin' away down the road but tryin' to be quiet about it. I sat up. Tears in my eyes. Head goin' round and around. Puke comin' up. I might've seen a man, just a split-second's worth, runnin' where there was a trace of sky light between the dark pine trees. I leaned out and puked, then fell back down on the seat and passed out. Next thing I knew, it was past dawn. I got out of the car to piss and my left leg wouldn't hold me. No feeling. It was already a goner."

Wilkes wiped beer foam from his lips and said, with beseeching clarity, as if he were asking mercy of a hanging judge, "You have any notion of what a man could do to take away a leg like that?"

"Yes, I'm afraid I do. The sciatic nerve sheath could be dissolved by chemical means. An injection of paraldehyde in the right place would accomplish it. But one must know just where to insert the syringe."

"How could Tyrone find out about that?"

"A doctor or trained nurse would have to show him how to do it."

Wilkes looked out the window. "They're buryin' Old Lamb today. I never trusted that old bastard. Too much education. I don't know what kind of a doctor he was, but sometimes he got the idea he was a nigger lawyer too."

He paused, flinching as the windshield of an auto making a turn in the street caught the sun and hurled dazzling white light at his face, unexpected and as nerve-racking as

305

a scream of fear. Wilkes ducked and looked oddly chastened, cleansed of his anger.

He said slowly, sounding depressed, "Sheriff doesn't know how Old Lamb died. Some scare talk this mornin'. The supernatural. Niggers love ghost stories, don't they? I hear you were out there. Any ideas?"

"He was as badly mangled as if he'd stood in front of a train. His genitals were—ripped away. Missing."

"Like some kind of animal got to him? Pack of wild dogs, maybe. There's a few wildcats left in the swamps." He dismissed his own explanations with an irritable grimace and wrapped his hand around the remaining bottle of beer. Three quick ones had slowed him a little; his drawl had become charmingly difficult to comprehend. "I was *they-uh* when Boss got hacked to *day-eth*. Clipper with that sword. A madman. Chapel fallin' to pieces. No rhyme or reason to it. I don't know, maybe we're up against more than the two of us can handle. Champ's just about helpless right now. If you're a man of integrity, and I think I can still rely on my good judgment in such matters, then I know you'll take good *cay-uh* him. When you want me to get in touch with the army?"

"Tomorrow; let Champ rest another day. I'll discuss the case with the surgeon-general if possible, have him speedily removed to a good hospital."

"Where Nhora and the nigger can't get their hands on him. They had time alone with Champ so far?"

"Nhora was with him for a while last night. But I'm still unconvinced that you have anything to worry about where Nhora is concerned." He was impatient to be gone, on his feet abruptly before he finished speaking.

"Just be careful," the lawyer said broodingly. "Between now and tomorrow noon I think I ought to visit with Champ. My observations might come in handy later on, in a court of law."

Jackson saw the wisdom in that. "Why don't you come to the house in the morning, about nine?"

"The Good Lord willin' and the creeks don't rise."

Wilkes wouldn't let Jackson pay for his largely uneaten
306

breakfast. He was off to the bathroom on his crutches when Jackson left the café.

Ten-forty in the morning. War Time. The sun not high yet, but the temperature, according to the car radio, was heading for a fierce one hundred. Negroes worked in bonnets and straw hats, chopping cotton in the mammoth level fields along the straight road through Dasharoons. Dun fields, row upon row cracked and bleeding, dense white bleed of bolls. Osage orange trees and shade rushing over him, blips of dark too quick for comfort, and out again into the vivid blue, car racing but not fast enough to out-distance the horsemen of the nerves. Heat had him by the throat; his damaged chin and head were throbbing, his shirt stuck to his ribs and back.

The house, in contrast to the wide-open road, was cool as well as bright in every corner. Hackaliah was coming down the stairs as Jackson crossed the foyer.

"Where is Nhora?"

"She gone out riding, half hour ago."

Jackson paused in his dash up the stairs. "She's all right, then."

"Yasuh. Champ, he ask to be moved from the playroom."

"Moved where?" Jackson was amazed that he was even conscious; he had loaded Champ with phenobarbital.

"To Boss's room." Hackaliah studied Jackson from two steps down, eyes expressionless; but a blood vessel throbbed nervously near the top of his bald head. "I didn't know if it be right or wrong to move him. Sometimes, when they was children, and bad afraid of the dark, Boss let the boys come into his bed. It was a comfort, I know. So Bull Pete and me, we carried him downstairs."

"What did Nhora say about that?"

"She was gone already," Hackaliah said, a shade indifferently.

"Show me where he is, please."

Boss Bradwin's room, at the opposite end of the hall

from his own room and next to Nhora's, was a tastefully furnished museum dominated by a four-masted bed with enough unsinkable oak to sail it across an ocean. There were works of art from every continent; rare books under lock and key; glass cases filled with medals, scrolls and other awards; photographs of Boss with all the presidents from a dour, paunchy Teddy Roosevelt to FDR in his prime. The room was elegant, rich and explained too much about Boss at a glance. Perhaps everything. His ego was deafening after two years in the grave. But Champ, easily overlooked in the bed, was as deeply asleep as Jackson had seen him. He took Champ's pulse, thinking of Nhora in this same bed, tumbling with the rugged, doting old man; he felt sick with longing and apprehension. Aunt Clary Gene, hollow-eyed, kept her vigil, and Bull Pete was parked in a chair just the other side of the door. Serenity, for now.

But there was trouble, too, in this room, Jackson didn't know just what. Champ had struggled back to his beginnings; what comfort was there to be found in the cold flash of medals, the cant of sabers and big-bore guns? He lay burnt-out, frail, of unsound mind, forever dominated by the tragedy of a murdered man, easy prey for the bumptious spirit still shadowing the outer edge of his domain. . . It was a haunting truth, too close to the flashpoint of Jackson's own existence, the unthinkable crisis of his narrowed-down life; he had to breathe and be free a little while longer. Desperation drove Jackson from the house and to the stables, in search of Nhora's green and willing eyes.

He inquired at the stables; the Negro stableboy was not sure where she had gone. He gestured in a southwesterly direction. Jackson took off his coat and loosened his tie and got back into the scorching car. He pulled the brim of his Baku straw hat lower, tilting it against the sun-bounce off the car's hood, the brilliance of the sky.

All the roads were dirt, for the most part straight and pale through the knee-high cotton, through dusty green soybean fields. Trees appeared in oasislike clumps, their shade closely packed with somnolent cattle. He stopped at
308

a cotton gin, but no one there had seen her. At a railroad siding he passed the private car in which he and Champ had completed their journey from Kansas City. Seeing it revived sensations rather than memories. The way behind him was laden with dust, impenetrable.

He drove fast and mindlessly, quartering the huge plantation, thinking only of the horse and rider, feeling the relentless pull of Nhora, erect and galloping, somewhere just beyond his reach. The car, needing only a robot's touch on brake or gas pedal, going slowly out of his control, an instrument of the destructiveness of time. Chutes and sloughs, low glitter of an oblong pond, willow trees, a spillway. The heat over all, shimmering. Then fallow ground, brush arbors, and, nearer the river, rise and fall of wooded ridges, limestone outcrops. Noon. Birds and shadowless pine trees, fencewire, the road dwindling to a muddy impasse. A gate. A sign.

DASHAROONS
PRIVATE HUNTING PRESERVE
TRESPASSERS WILL BE PROSECUTED

Silence, as he left the car. Galaxies of insects, spinning nowhere, lifespan of a single day. He saw the roof lines of some low rustic buildings through a stand of oak and tulip poplar, and walked that way, stepping into a clearing dominated by massive stone barbecue pits, a taint of old feasting. The riderless stallion, suddenly aware of him, threw up its head in alarm and snorted. Lofty trees here, interlaced branches, a hothouse stillness, the sun falling in glimmers across the moss-covered, swaggy ground. Green, damp scent of humus rising with every step he took. The horse's saddle had been removed and thrown over the railing of a long porch. There were shutters over every window.

As he was about to call, Nhora came around the corner of the main lodge, limping a little as if she'd picked up a stone bruise in the thin leather riding boots she wore. Strands of hair were loose across her face. She was drinking from a tin cup as she walked.

309

She looked at him and stopped, clearly anxious, as if he wasn't recognizable at a distance of a hundred feet or more. Jackson humbly removed his hat. Leaves stirred, there was a change of light-play around her head simultaneous with the glow of recognition in her eyes, but Nhora hesitated a few moments longer, teeth on her lower lip as if she were nibbling at some minor traces of restraint.

Then she ran all the way to him and pitched thankfully into his arms.

Midafternoon.

Sun stealth on the glazed oak floor, the fabulous Persian carpets of the Boss-room, sun a hot tickle on the toes of Aunt Clary Gene as she sat softly drowsing, curled in a high-backed chair.

In the bed he stirred; from the first, wakeful change in his breathing he had Aunt Clary Gene's full attention. After several hearty yawns he moved to his right and noticed her.

"What are you doin' here, Aunt Clary Gene?"

He had caught her by surprise after all. She sat up straighter, one hand slowly rising to her heart as if she feared at long last its beat had been lost. She couldn't reply.

"What's the matter with you?" he said crossly. "Swallow your teeth? And what the hell time has it got to be?" He raised himself on one elbow, alert to the angle of the sun through the windows. "Godalmighty!" he yowled. "The whole day shot." He looked disgustedly at the mute old woman. "That's all right, don't bother to be civil to me in my own house. I sure do know how to spoil my niggers, don't I?" She started to rise from the chair, reacting automatically, eyes still full of wonder and fixed on his face. He made a stay-put gesture and said with a big, needling smile, "No, no, don't go to any trouble on my account; I'll just get up from here and pour my *own* coffee."

He sought to get out of bed then, but the shock of weakness drove him down, left him sprawled momentarily

310

breathless and wide-eyed with apprehension. Then he began to laugh, a whiskey rumble.

"Looks like I had a little too much to drink last night. What was the occasion? I don't seem to remember a damn thing."

The door to the bedroom opened and Bull Pete, unnoticed by either of them, looked in.

"Just get me coffee; *coffee*, is that asking too much? I don't need a nursemaid, I'm just hung over. Maybe a little worse than normal." He closed his eyes and breathed heavily. Bull Pete shut the bedroom door. Aunt Clary Gene heard it click into place and swung her head quickly around. When she looked back he was scratching his scalp and yawning again.

"Aunt Clary Gene, after you've fetched the coffee, get the boys up here, will you?"

Her lips trembled. "They all gone now. Every last one. Gone."

That quieted him, and time went by. His eyes were open, looking straight up. The tone of the sun changed, the light of the room was inflamed. Aunt Clary Gene began to fret, as if she felt imperiled by his blankness, by the unfilled space of his remorse.

The bedroom door opened again. Hackaliah came hesitantly in, frowning. Behind him, Bull Pete, breathless, trying not to look scared.

"Asked for the boys," Aunt Clary Gene said to Hackaliah, who stood with his hands clenched behind his back. Bull Pete, no good for this kind of thing, rattled the stem of his corncob pipe against his teeth. Hackaliah gave him a stern look, then shifted his attention back to the thin, ravaged young man on the bed. There was no movement, no sign that they had been observed.

"Boss?" Hackaliah said, bending forward, peering intently at his face.

He was answered by a long and agonizing sob.

There was room after dim room in the hunting lodge and sportsman's club, nothing fancy, just rough plank

311

floors and bunk beds and exposed rafters. There was an odor of cold ashes, mustiness of trophy heads, tiny skittish noises of mice in the walls and kitchen stovepipes. The windows apparently had never been washed. The hard thin blankets they had pulled from cedar-lined closets to nest in were clean, but smelled vaguely of the iron-filled water in which they had been washed. A torn sheet had saved their skins during prolonged lovemaking, one tumultuous orgasm after another. And still they couldn't bear to let each other go.

Sunlight fell in sharp squares on the floor near their feet, vanished, fell bright again, like the pictureless throw of a balky movie projector while, outside, clouds marched across the sun and they heard the sullen trumps of thunder.

Nhora's long body was a match for his as they lay head to head and neatly intertwined, her fingers in his hair; she gazed with curiosity and a trace of regret at the sluglike scars which she'd exposed, then smoothly, tenderly covered them over, a child planting a dead rabbit in clover. Jackson wished there was something he could do about the bruises on her neck. He had an arm around her, the other hand astride a softly cambered buttock. His wearied penis was still half-erect and snugged in tribute against her belly. The heat and balm of repeated couplings had ripened her, and although she'd been far from drab or unvital before, the act of love seemed to have brought Nhora awesomely to life. By contrast he felt overpowered, his resting heartbeat too faint and too cold. Not an uncommon complaint for someone his age, he thought wryly. Yet even as he loved her obsessively he wished for more profit, a shared potency, some of her tremulous, blazoned joy in the aftermath. Anything but this weakness, and nerves, and a low-pitched thrum of dismay.

Thunder again; she stirred, muscling uneasily against him as if preparing to pull away. Jackson smiled, reluctant to give an inch.

"Not yet."

"If there's lightning, Rowdy Boy will be frightened. I

312

need to take him back. And besides—you know." She made a face of necessity. "My kidneys are about to float."

Nhora untangled them with lingering gentleness, stepped out of the bunk bed and crossed to the bathroom gingerly, on her toes, wary of picking up splinters from the floor.

Jackson rose and began to pull on his clothes, feeling the spell of the sensuous afternoon sadly broken. His fingers were stiff and rather cold, his heart pounded lugubriously.

She came back before he put his shirt on and embraced him fiercely, standing eye to eye.

"We haven't said ten words to each other in three hours."

With a pang he noted that her voice wasn't right, a hoarseness from the throttling she'd received, and she was developing the nervous habit of constantly trying to clear her throat.

"Not very civilized," he agreed, kissing her. And again. The truth was they'd consciously, and gratefully, avoided the matters that oppressed them. But their unwillingness to talk seriously now seemed forced, to both of them. The undeniably guilty feeling of time stolen for pleasure, the subtly felt influence of the coming storm, all worked against the mood they were trying to sustain.

Nhora turned away first, looking numb around the mouth, smile barely visible, eyes lonely. She began to dress, standing a little apart from and with her back to him, as if she were shy about the act of covering her nakedness in the bleak, nearly empty space of the long dormitory. Jackson buttoned his own shirt and put on his jacket.

"I'm free, you know," she said, just whispering. "Free to go where I want and with whom I want."

"I hope so."

Thunder; he was feeling light-headed and blamed the sudden drop in air pressure as the storm took shape. He pulled up a wooden chair and sat astride it. "Nhora, about Champ—"

She turned on him with a face he'd seen only once be-

313

fore, when a maid had startled her. "I told you, told you, *told* you something awful would happen, that he just wasn't right! Now this—" She swiftly shielded her throat with an open hand, stood rigidly staring at Jackson with her teeth bared in an unpleasant way. Then the hand dropped hopelessly and a crushing despair changed her face, pulling all the muscles downward in a mask of heroic lament. "I've had nightmares," she said. "And they've all come true. I saw Nancy lying dead in that motel room long before I heard about it."

"Nhora, did Nancy get in touch with you from Kezar County?"

"No. I didn't hear from her at all this time."

"Could she have called, and could you have driven to Kezar County and found her dead, and then driven back to Dasharoons the same night in such a state that by the next morning you didn't remember having made the trip at all?"

Nhora was very still for an improbably long time. The sun that entered the room was no longer geometrically defined; it flooded now like a rising sea, struck highlights in places he hadn't looked before. The head of a razorback hog was mounted on one wall. Bodiless, the tusker seemed not to have surrendered even in death, and something of his transcendental rage and wildness was repeated in Nhora's brilliantly touched eyes.

A small bird, lost in the light, dived against the unshuttered window, startling them. The bird flubbed briefly at the glass, then got its bearings and flew away. Nhora snatched up her stovepipe boots and stormed away to the door, heedless of splinters this time.

"Have you gone *crazy?*" she yelled back at Jackson, and went out to the porch.

He caught up to her as she was sitting on the steps pulling the boots on.

"Nhora, I'm sorry."

"What made you bring that up?" she said, still furious, eyes shut as she stomped her left heel securely into the boot.

"I had breakfast with Everett Wilkes this morning. He

314

claims there are members of the Bradwin family who saw you in Kezar County two nights ago."

"Well, he despises me, and he might say almost anything." The right boot went on; Nhora jumped away from Jackson's hand on her shoulder. The impulse to run from him took her well into the clearing before she stopped. She swayed then as if she might faint, cupping her hands to her face.

"God, how can I tell *anybody* what I'm suffering?"

The heavy noon shade in the clearing had been translated into gloom; the space around them was no longer secluded and inviting, it seemed cavernous and threatened to be uninhabitable. Leaves whipped through the air. The sky was solid brass overhead, purple-dark between the trees. Jackson closed and hooked the shutters, lugged saddle and blanket to the horse and cinched the saddle in place.

When he turned around to call Nhora she was already there, sad taut face again. "Thank you; it's getting bad, I have to get back."

"Nhora, we can tie the horse behind the car, drive slowly."

"I'll make better time across country." She swung up into the saddle, and he handed her the reins. "Are you going to the house?"

"No, I'm out of barbiturates and I need a supply of other pharmaceuticals. I'll take what I want from the clinic and arrange payment later."

"Come as soon as you can!" she urged. She wheeled her horse around and looked up at the sky. "If I get caught in this I'll lay over at the railroad spur, so don't worry." She urged the big horse into a canter, then changed her mind and came back, riding in a big circle around him, horse becoming difficult to hold, side-stepping fractiously with his head thrown back. She leaned over in the saddle, staring at Jackson, face pale with intensity.

"How can I be two people at once?"

"Who's the other one?" he said, fascinated, but feeling dizzy again as if the deepening gloom beneath the trees

315

had invaded his mind. He had to turn to keep Nhora in view.

"A horror! A witch. I can't describe her to you, I don't want to try. But I know she doesn't want me to be free."

The stallion suddenly took control, bolting with her, and Jackson fell back, still within an inch of being knocked down and trampled. Nhora hauled on the reins and looked back, frightened: saw that he was all right. Then she let the horse run, they soon flickered out of sight behind a mass of dogwood trees.

Thunder; the rain coming in huge spaced drops, shattering like silent glassware against the stone barbecue pits.

He walked hurriedly to the car, shuddering, then tingling from the charged air, and something else: an overlay of feeling, the kinesthetically explicit memory of lovemaking, the slow exquisite ways she'd turned in his arms, combing out every nerve until he was half-drunk with sexual longing. He experienced a painful sense of loss, of being somehow physically weaker now that Nhora was no longer there. Recalling the fleet, bitter look on her face as she gave her horse full rein, his pain intensified. Not running from him, but as if she'd deliberately doomed herself to a fated course. *How can I be two people at once?* Did she still feel love for the dead old man, was that what she meant by not being free?

Jackson regretted having let Nhora go until he knew what was on her mind. They could have sheltered the horse inside the lodge, where the accommodations were at stable level anyway. Waited out the storm break there. But he felt it wasn't too late to catch her, persuade her to turn around.

The rain, instead of quickening, had stopped; the air, despite fulminating clouds, was almost windless as the storm mysteriously withheld its power. He reached the car, but a snake was in his way.

Jackson looked absently at it, his mind at a distance. It was a greenish-colored, almost iridescent snake, rather pretty, about two feet long and not poisonous. He sensed that something about the oncoming storm or a recently

316

ingested meal had made it sluggish, unable to head for its nesting place deep beneath the roots of a nearby tree.

Just as he visualized the snake hole and the sinuous passage into dark earth he reached down in a kind of dreaming daze and picked the reptile up, grasping it firmly with the fingers of his right hand just behind the head. The snake yawned wide but didn't hiss at him as it was lifted. Jackson ran his other hand the length of the sleek body.

Deep in the hindbrain there was a residual warning, a dim shriek: *This is terror I'm holding, this is death.* But the old, freezing fear no longer seemed believable. What was the harm in holding it? In fact the snake felt good in his hands, compliant: He let it slip through his fingers and twine around his wrist, feeling the smooth contractions, the running wave of energy, his penis throbbing in response, his breathing husky. The head of the snake arrested in air, eyes absorbing him. He felt pleased with them both, his heart at rest, skin just a little chilly because the temperature had continued to fall. A few, random drops of rain splashed down.

Why had he ever been afraid? He walked across the road in the direction which he knew the revived snake had wanted to go; it glided from his downstretched arm, wriggled a few feet and disappeared into its hole.

Nhora.

Jackson smiled.

He drove back the way he had come, and caught just a glimpse of her, half a mile away in pasture and riding hard, before a wall of gray rain slammed down, cutting off his view.

He intended to intercept her at the railroad spur, where the private car was sitting. In the heavy rain he took wrong turns. After an anxious ten minutes on slick clay he was glad to find the hard road, and a gas station, where he received directions to town.

The worst of the rain had held off until the end of the funeral for Old Lamb, his wife and his granddaughter; the

317

hundred or so mourners were scrambling along the road between the cemetery and the church when Jackson drove by.

He spotted Tyrone walking under an umbrella held by one of the deacons and rolled down his window as he drove abreast of them.

"Tyrone, could I talk to you?"

Tyrone nodded and pointed to the church, a white frame building with a squat bell tower. Jackson parked and ran up the steps. Tyrone joined him half a minute later. They shook hands in the vestibule, rain streaming down Tyrone's face and forming puddles on the worn-out linoleum. Rain was frying loudly on the metal roof.

"Come on to my office, doctor."

Jackson followed him to a narrow book-cluttered room at the back of the church. There was a chamber-pot light fixture, a cracked green shade half drawn over the single end window, a rolltop desk, a wood-burning stove and a scuttle filled with cordwood. A wall clock ticked; it was ten minutes to five.

Tyrone disappeared into a tiny lavatory, emerged shirtless with towels for each of them. He sat down and pulled off his soaked shoes and socks, hung his dark suit coat up to dry. Jackson had a mild case of the shivers and wondered if he was coming down with a summer cold. Tyrone noticed and selected two pieces of wood for the stove. He started a fire. There was a big chipped porcelain coffee pot on top of the black iron stove. Tyrone gave it a shake and set it back down again.

"Just made fresh day before yesterday," he said with a slight smile.

Lightning jerked through the sky as the rain beat against the frail side of the building. The roof had begun to leak. Tyrone put a pan under the steady drip. He gave Jackson his cushioned swivel chair and sat on the window seat.

Don't know which of us looks worse beat up today," he commented. "Guess you didn't get much sleep last night." He finished toweling off, flicked the towel into a

318

corner, put on a T-shirt and socks drawn from a cubby-hole of the desk.

"It was a very bad night."

Tyrone nodded. "For all of us. I was *close* to that old man, he taught me near as much as Boss did." Tyrone paused introspectively, dwelling on his personal loss.

"The funeral happened quickly."

"It's according to our religion, doctor. We're Burning Bushers. The dead got to be buried within twenty-four hours, lest their bodies be defiled by unclean spirits." He paused again. "Understand it's that way with certain of the Jews."

"And some African tribes I know of."

"Well—there are those of us not all that far removed from Africa."

"I was reminded of that again early this morning."

The window glass behind Tyrone's head was misting over. In the stove the wood began to crackle. "How so?"

"There seems to be a full-fledged voodoo cult in the neighborhood."

Tyrone gave him a wide-awake stare. "Voodoo?"

"It's the root religion of the Negro. Long before Christianity was introduced by the—"

"I know, I know all that," Tyrone said impatiently. "I just never heard of it goin' on around here before."

"Nhora and I happened on the oum'phor—the temple—quite by accident. There's an old stove-up steamboat down on the river—"

"I know the one you mean."

"Difficult and also dangerous to get to. A natural sanctuary for those desiring to be anonymous."

"You and *Nhora* saw this?"

"A peristyle with all the ritual paraphernalia—drums, rattles, symbolic serpents."

"You appear to know a little about the subject."

Jackson spent several minutes briefing Tyrone on his background.

"A missionary station? You are *full* of surprises."

"Perhaps you know that Nhora also lived in Equatorial

319

Africa, as a child. Only a hundred miles from where I grew up."

"She mentioned about Africa to me. Maybe that's why we always got along so good. Doctor, I know just about everything that goes on in this community. But I can't tell you a thing about voodoo."

"There's an aspect of this particular cult that has me uneasy, and that's what I wanted to discuss with you."

Tyrone shrugged. " 'Bout all I can do is listen, but go ahead."

"The cult seems to have involved Nhora in their rites."

"If I didn't see you sittin' there cold sober—"

"She's not an initiate. I'd find that bizarre, yes, but not beyond my understanding. She's merely represented, by an effigy. A locket of her mother's, containing a portrait of Nhora, was stolen some time ago. This locket has now turned up as the centerpiece of the effigy. The ritual worship quite obviously is centered on Nhora."

"I don't know enough about it. You mean in voodoo they worship actual living human beings?"

"No," Jackson said, "they don't. They worship a full pantheon of gods and goddesses—the superhuman, the fantastic, the dead. But no living beings."

Tyrone jumped off the window seat. "Doctor, you're sweating real bad. Too hot in here for you?"

It was more of a cold sweat. Jackson swallowed. "I'm—all right. Lack of sleep, the rain, a chill, I suppose."

"Let me pour you a cup of this *strong* coffee. Bet you didn't eat today."

"As a matter of fact, no. But I'm not hungry."

Tyrone hunted up two mugs and poured coffee, which had just begun to boil. Jackson found it surpassingly vile, but he relished the heat of the mug between his hands. A rainy night in August couldn't be this cold, especially after the temperature had hovered around a hundred hours earlier. Freak weather, he thought. But no doubt in his mind anymore, he *was* coming down with something. He yearned for Nhora, her firm hand on his brow.

"Go on," Tyrone said, resettling himself on the window seat. "You were sayin' about Nhora—"

"I don't know just what it is I mean to say," Jackson confessed, and momentarily he felt confused. "Except that—I'm worried. It's an untypical thing for voodoo."

Tyrone said, watching him closely, "*Unnatural,* sounds like."

"Yes. She could be in some kind of danger."

"Ummhmm. See what you mean." Tyrone smiled. "You know, doctor, I'm real glad you dropped by to see me this afternoon."

Confusion again; exactly what *was* he doing here? But he was grateful to have Tyrone's company. He was feeling lonely, curiously isolated. From himself, from the legions of humanity, from the one who meant everything to him.

"We know," Jackson started, and stopped, and made a slow circle in his head to recover his train of thought, "We know that unnatural, freakish things have happened in the Bradwin family. Their lives are circumscribed by nightmare. But why? My own life—for years—the same kind of nightmare—" He shook his head hopelessly.

Tyrone was hanging on his every word. "Just what kind of *power* would you say voodoo has over people?"

"For the initiate, the true believer, the power is immense. Every aspect of his life is ruled by voodoo; the promise of reward, the threat of a terrible vengeance."

"For ordinary people, like you and me?"

"No power at all, I would say." But having spoken, he felt a chill of disapproval in the region of his spine, followed by bewilderment, not knowing just who he had sinned against.

Tyronne leaned forward, making a serious point.

"And Nhora? If she don't believe, then how can it hurt her?"

"I don't know." Jackson found it difficult to draw a steady breath. His extremities were cold, his lips and tongue felt numb. But it wasn't all that unpleasant, more of a sated feeling. He could sleep now, he really could, just close his eyes and drift away. But he didn't want to

321

offend his host. The clock ticked. He stared across at Tyrone, unable to think of anything more to say.

Tyrone rose slowly, not taking his eyes off Jackson. He walked toward him.

"What's the matter, doctor? Are you sick?"

"I don't know—if that's it at all."

"Dyin', maybe," Tyrone said dispassionately.

Jackson felt a small shock. "Why do you say that?"

"It crossed my mind. But you're probably not that close to dyin'. Not yet."

"What do you mean?"

"Can you get up out of the chair, please?" Tyrone said with a frown.

Jackson tried. He couldn't budge. He sweated. Time ticked away. Tyrone shook his head, momentarily stymied by their mutual dilemma.

"Well, now. I just never figured on somebody like you comin' along. Takin' a shine to her." His smile grew ruthless. "Did you get yourself a little today, doctor? That what the matter with you? Did she sure 'nuf fuck the breath of life out of your body? You are some kind of *born* victim, I'd say." He looked down at Jackson, shaking his head in sorrow.

Jackson opened his mouth to speak. But he was just too tired, too worn. Bloodless. The infernal ticking clock had stolen a thousand years from him while he sat there trying to be friendly with Tyrone, unburdening himself. All his fears about the woman he loved.

Tyrone pried the coffee mug from Jackson's hands and set it aside.

"I better attend to a few changes," he mused.

He turned and slapped Jackson hard across the face. But Jackson scarcely felt it, his jaw might have been anesthetized.

"Can you tell me where Beau Bradwin is? Pay attention here to me. Don't go noddin' off now." He smote Jackson again, opening the cut on his chin. Tyrone stepped back with a grimace of displeasure, not liking blood. Jackson's mouth hung open.

322

"Don't know," he said dully. His eyes closed, eyelids twitching.

Tyrone flexed his hand. "Maybe you do, maybe you don't. I can take care of Beau, I reckon. That is, if the Ai-da Wédo don't want him. Meantime, the problem is, what do I do about you?"

He stood there a while longer, pondering this problem. Then he opened the door of his office, looked out into the unlit church. He left the door ajar and returned to Jackson.

A little blood had seeped from under the bandage and was running down his throat. Jackson was no longer conscious.

Tyrone put his arms around Jackson, wincing at the pain in his broken finger. He lifted Jackson from the chair, standing him uncertainly on his feet. Then Tyrone loaded Jackson across his back in a fireman's carry, and lugged him out of the office.

The rain had caught Nhora several hundred yards short of the railroad spur, and by the time she had Rowdy Boy under cover of the large platform roof they were both soaked, isolated, as if on a fragile raft at sea. Nhora stayed close to the stallion to keep him calm as lightning seared the sky almost continuously. She was deafened, mindless, scared to the marrow. But her emotions soon carried her beyond fright, to a state of savage, luminous exhilaration.

And with it, discontent; as if the several sexual episodes with Jackson had failed to take the edge off her prodigious, long-suppressed appetite.

She had nothing to dry the horse with, so she sluiced rain water from his body with her hands, transmitting her own passion, feeling powerful tremors that urged her on until she ached to mount him again, differently, grip him from all sides until his trembling surges gave relief to them both. She fingered the protruding cock, drawing it out to an awesome length, making him dance and leap. She

323

knew the stallion could kill her at any moment; and her excitement was maddening.

Groaning incoherently, she forced him to ejaculate. And as his sperm gushed over her body Nhora turned her face to the stand-out vein in the pulsating belly and bit it.

Rowdy Boy screamed and whirled, slamming her to the floor of the platform; his flashing iron hooves missed her head by an inch. He jumped from the platform into the driving rain, blood flowing from the severed vein. He reared, still screaming, as lightning exploded in his face, and toppled over backward. Nhora groggily raised her head and stared at him. Rowdy Boy thrashed in the mud and regained his feet, but his strength seemed almost gone. He stood there, head down and shaking, then trotted off a little way. He began to wobble, like a newborn colt, then to go in circles. And then he fell down dead.

Nhora rose, rocked by spasms, the blood of the stallion still warm on her lower lip. She began to tear at the buttons of her gingham shirt, shredding the material, freeing her breasts. She turned and went haltingly toward the railroad car, stopped in her tracks every so often by vivid slashes of pain in her belly. As she struggled to breathe her tongue began to flicker between parted teeth. Her eyes were wide and flat and ghostly dull.

As she pulled herself up the steps to the vestibule of the car, lightning struck the cupola of the platform, and the concussion jolted through her. It also brought on the regular, rhythmical contractions she'd been expecting.

Gasping, bare-breasted, Nhora threw open the door to Boss's darkened stateroom and collapsed on the carpet. She had barely enough strength, between periodic cramps, to take off the boots and jodhpurs and throw them aside.

Now naked, she lay back, knees up, clasping her belly, tongue still darting in and out of her mouth, curiously elongated, almost faster than the eye could follow. Rain drummed the roof. She rolled her head from side to side, insensate, groaning, laboring, giving birth again.

Sitting up in the Boss-bed, in the Boss-room, he had worked on the cutting edge of Champ's trophy saber for nearly half an hour, pausing repeatedly to test its keenness, which never satisfied him. Now his hands and wrists were tired. Aunt Clary Gene had turned on a lamp by the bed. She sat praying over her Bible. He was aware of the rain, the artificial dusk, and of other things in the air as night hurried down on them too quickly, things too vague to be named, but portentous.

At last he put the saber aside, knowing it was a good edge, the best he could do given the quality of the steel he had to work with, but an edge not worthy of the task. He needed a magical sharpness, or he would fail.

Hackaliah came into the room empty-handed, smudges of attic dirt on his gray jacket, his forehead beaded with perspiration. Their eyes met. Hackaliah's palsied head trembled restlessly.

"No, suh," he said. "I know it was up there. But there ain't no sign of it now."

"But I *need* it, Hackaliah."

Hackaliah reached for his handkerchief. "Maybe Miss Nhora knows what become of your saber."

"But she wouldn't be any help to us now, would she?"

"No, suh. Not likely." Hackaliah stopped mopping his brow and looked at the gleaming sword in the Boss-bed. He appeared to be sick with apprehension, half-hypnotized. The sword was slowly raised, and rotated in the light. Aunt Clary Gene, struck by a gleam from the blade, lifted her head and joined in their communion.

"We'll make do then, Hackaliah. We'll just have to make do."

Jackson awoke in near-darkness, a taste of ashes in his mouth. Distantly, he heard the rain. His heartbeat was running away, nearly to the point of fibrillation. His arms and legs twitched spasmodically, and he felt oppressed by dread, weighted down as if he had been prematurely thrust into his grave. He cried out in horror and fell strug-

325

gling off a narrow cot, a heavy dark blanket tangled around him like some primordial vine.

In the dark he stood, shedding the blanket, still palpitating but encouraged by his sudden release from the fear of dying. He took a step and bumped his head against a furnace duct. He leaned on the cold furnace. There was a rectangular window off to his left, lit by a gray rain light that barely penetrated the low furnace room. He wondered where he was, and where he'd come from. His chin and jaw hurt. He tried again to concentrate, to draw an inference of location from his seamy surroundings. But he had no useful memory, just disconnected flashes of driving hectically along the back roads of Dasharoons pursuing Nhora, almost catching up to her, then losing her in a lashing rainstorm.

Had he been drinking? It was an odd sort of hung-over feeling, without the sere bad-tasting thrushy mouth and pounding head. His heartbeat had slowed but he felt cold and wan, barely able to take a step. He could use a stimulant of some kind from his medical stores—he knew then, a piece of time falling into place, what he'd been up to, where he was going. Perhaps he was at the clinic already, but why in the cellar?

There had to be a light. He took shuffling steps, hands raised, batting around in the air until he encountered the dangling cord of a fixture. He yanked it and was half-paralyzed by the glare for a few moments.

A better look at his surroundings didn't tell him much. Some sort of meager accommodations for the janitor. A half-empty coal bin. What appeared to be a damaged bench or church pew against one wall. Then steps going up. He crossed the rickety steps and went up them hesitantly, slow dreaming steps. Turned the knob on the door. Opened it and saw Jesus, suffering on the old rugged Cross. A stained clerestory window. Several bowed, gray-textured Negro heads.

But Tyrone wasn't there and he felt mildly embarrassed, looking into the cozy office. Too cozy, he realized he must have fallen asleep while having a cup of coffee. Tyrone had kindly taken the hot coffee from his hands
326

before he spilled it all in his lap. And that was the last thing he could recall. So Tyrone had led him down to the basement, to the janitor's cot, and he had slept it off.

Slept what off? And what time was it now? The cracked crystal of his watch caught the waning light: ten past eight. And still raining very hard.

He got quite wet going out to the car because he still couldn't move very fast. His medical bag was on the seat beside him. He cracked an ampule of smelling salts, which nearly blew the top of his head off. But he felt sufficiently revived to find his way to Flax and Dakin's.

Flax was still there, working in his study. He looked up in surprise when Jackson appeared in the doorway.

"Even', doctor. I called the house a little while ago, but they said they hadn't seen you most of the day."

"What's the matter?"

"I had a very disturbin' report from the state pathology lab." He reached for the pad on which he had made notes, flipped over a page.

"It appears Nancy Bradwin may have been poisoned."

"What type of poison?"

"They ain't said yet. But a little smidge of the deceased's liver injected into a laboratory rabbit killed it in exactly nine seconds."

"My God," Jackson said, and he took a chair. Flax gave him a concerned glance and slid open a desk drawer, producing a bottle of Canadian Club and two glasses.

"Touch of the blended might do us both good right now."

"Thank you. Have you notified Everett Wilkes?"

"Not yet. Hoping to get your reaction first."

"An extremely toxic substance."

"Works faster than strychnine. Maybe you have some idea what it could be. The lab boys don't find it in their books."

Jackson sipped his whiskey, cursing the coldness and lassitude that continued to grip him.

"In Africa, where I grew up, the Negroes are familiar with a variety of poisons we know nothing about. The venom of the mamba is one of the fastest-acting paralytics known; the juice from the leaves of a rather common shrub, in contact with the skin, causes agony and leaves no trace, not even a blister."

"Nancy Baldwin wasn't bit by no snake."

"I know that," Jackson said, but he was uneasy. He downed the remainder of the whiskey, and felt a little better. "I need medicine for Champ. I thought—"

Flax handed over the keys to the clinic. "Help yourself to whatever you want, doctor." He drummed his fingers on the desktop, reached for the telephone. "I better notify the proper authorities. I don't know what Sheriff Gaines will want to do about this. Since Nancy died in Kezar County, he don't have jurisdiction."

"I'm a little worried about Champ, so—"

"Goodbye, doctor. Thanks for droppin' by."

The rain had slackened but seemed to be good for the rest of the night. It was stuffy inside the clinic, he had trouble getting his breath, particularly when he crossed the foyer where Dr. Henry Talmadge had hanged himself. Echoes, shadows, haunting emanations plagued him. Why had Talmadge done it? For a few terrible moments he was absolutely certain that his own life depended on the answer to that question. But no one alive could tell him.

The whiskey had worn off and he was shaking again, so badly that he dropped ampules as he was restocking his medical bag from the clinic's pharmacy. He locked the drug cabinet and paused on his way out, studying the gleam of surgical tools in a glass-front case. On impulse he took several items he had little use for in day-to-day practice, including a small bone saw.

The telephone in the doctor's office was connected. A maid at Dasharoons answered, and told him that Nhora wasn't there.

"She must be there!" Jackson shouted, his heart beating wildly. "I left her hours ago, she must be back by now."

"No, suh. I'm sorry."

"Well, then, for God's sake go and look for her. She was riding—the horse—an accident—*look* for her!"

He hung up, feeling chilled and beginning to sweat

328

again. The flow of blood to his head was so constricted he was afraid of fainting. He sat down heavily and fumbled in his bag. A whiff of amyl nitrite brought relief. But then he began to cry uncontrollably, afraid for Nhora, afraid for them both.

Abruptly his crying stopped; a premonition seized him. He rushed to the filing cabinet and pulled open a drawer, began going through the B files. Baldwin . . . Bates . . . Bradwin, Nhora.

The file on Nhora Bradwin was empty. But Talmadge, shortly before he died, had done a series of tests—*he took strands of my hair and even nail clippings for analysis, can you imagine?*—the results should have been in her file.

"Lookin' for this, doc?"

Jackson turned, involuntarily slamming the heavy wooden drawer shut, just missing a couple of fingers. Early Boy Hodges stood dripping in the doorway, wearing a rain poncho and slouch hat. In one hand he held a revolver. In the other, a sheaf of papers.

"I took these reports out some time ago. Didn't want 'em to disappear. I figured they could be valuable."

"Where did you come from?" Jackson asked.

"Oh, around and about."

"And what's the gun for?"

Early Boy glanced at his revolver, smiled his deformed smile and put the revolver in his belt beneath the poncho.

"Just a chance you might be somebody else." He walked toward Jackson and handed him the papers.

"Maybe you better sit down," he said kindly. "Before you read that."

The four-page typewritten report was headed with the name of a laboratory in Memphis and dated the 24th of March, 1944. Liver biopsy, seroanalysis, urinalysis, the spectrochemical data, it all read like an autopsy report. Extremely high concentrations of an unknown toxic substance had been found in the hair and nail samples, in the liver, in the sputum, sufficient to cause the death of the victim. Of twenty victims.

329

"This is a lie! It's nonsense, someone's idea of a cod! Or, or—there had to be a mixup—"

Early Boy shook his head. "No mixup. Talmadge must have checked it out. He wouldn't have believed it himself. When they told him there wasn't no mistake, that's when he hanged himself. He couldn't face what he had to."

"Don't you realize what you're saying? No human being could survive this level of toxicity!"

"That's exactly the point, doc. Nhora Bradwin ain't human."

"But I—she—"

"No wonder the bugs don't bite her," Early Boy said, scratching his bristly chin, staring implacably at Jackson.

Jackson began to laugh, as if he found Early Boy's attempt at humor irresistible. Then the laughter came in great snorting sobs and he fell out of the chair. Early Boy seized him and hauled him to his feet.

"Don't go off the deep end, doc, I need you!"

Jackson screamed with laughter, his eyes rolling in his head.

Early Boy began slapping him, short, jarring blows.

"Jesus, you're cold. Like a corpse. Snap out of it, you dumb—*cluck!*"

Jackson suddenly stopped in mid-seizure, his eyes wide open, mouth agape. He seemed to be listening. Early Boy hesitated, right hand back for another blow. Jackson's chin was bleeding again. His face was flushed and striped with the marks of Early Boy's hand, the fingers hard and stinging like hickory withes. Jackson's mouth worked, and he spit up a thin bitter liquid.

"Nhora," he gasped. His head jerked up, face animated by joy.

"What?"

"Nhora's upstairs! She called me!" He tried to fight free of Early Boy, who pulled him back by the collar of his jacket.

"You ain't goin' anywhere."

"Nhora needs me. I tell you she's right upstairs!"

Early Boy looked around in dismay, retaining his tight grip on Jackson, who was fighting like an animal in a trap. He sniffed; a broad stench of perfume was drifting over them.

"No, she ain't. What's up there is something called the Ai-da Wédo. Maybe she's just a little like Nhora; I only had one quick look and that'll do me the rest of my life. You ain't goin' anywhere near—"

Jackson went slack and Early Boy lost his concentration for a second, seeking to get a better purchase with his right hand. Jackson ducked his head and bent his knees, then came up full force, the top of his head colliding with Early Boy's chin. Early Boy flew backward and rebounded from a wall, staggered forward with glazed eyes and a tooth protruding through a bloody lower lip, and sprawled across the desk.

Jackson ran to the stairs.

Early Boy clawed at the desk blotter to keep from falling but fell anyway, taking nearly everything on the desk with him. His cheek lay against the hot light bulb of the shadeless lamp. His eyes opened and closed spasmodically.

On the stairs Jackson heard laughter; delicious, buoyant, familiar laughter. Dormant in the mind for nearly twenty-five years, but never quite forgotten.

"Nhora!"

The light flickered along the wall as he reached the top of the stairs; he turned and paused, gripping the railing, enthralled. There was a room at the front end of the hall, the door half closed. In the dark beyond the door she laughed again, pleased by his promptness.

"Jackson! Come in." Her accent distinctively French, where there had just been a lisping suggestion before.

"I—I can't see you."

"Yes, you can. Come closer."

He was momentarily dazzled by a streak of greenish light that played at the level of his eyes, teasing him, leading him closer to the dark doorway, vanishing then, reappearing like a charge of protoplasm. This light form was limpid, luminous, suspended without definition in front of him but wisping at the edges, curling attractively around and around, forming iridescent coils.

He stopped again, arrested by nausea, by a corresponding spasm of sexual excitement that rolled deep and heavy in his loins. His skin had begun to prickle, and to burn, which only increased the sick, sexual rapture he was experiencing.

"Nhora?" For now it had eyes: wise, charming, beastly, grave-sent eyes. He was looked down upon. A final judgment he yearned to embrace.

"Gen. Gen-loa. You remember me, don't you?" The perfume disguised the rot of the indistinct, flitting hag; but her eyes were magnificent, her body alluring as it undulated in rhythm with his pulse. She pretended to pout. "I don't want to believe you could forget me, after Tuleborné."

"It's my—father you want," Jackson said, gulping, feeling shy and ashamed of his boy's body, his lack of experience. "Not me."

"I caught up to your father," she said indifferently. "And he fulfilled his obligation to me. Jackson—"

He blinked. It was almost Nhora, the voice different, the eyes more compassionate. Her body, her love for him. "Remember how it was for us this afternoon? It can be so much better now. I can't describe to you how pleasurable, how ecstatic you'll feel. Love me, Jackson. I need you, I've always needed you. I was reborn for you. I can't live without you."

He pushed the door open wide. He entered the bedroom.

She was reclining naked on the bare mattress of the bed, but naked in a way he'd never seen before. Her gorgeous scales shimmering, cascading with desire. Tongue flickering in and out of her mouth. His erection was unbearable, ejaculation near.

He heard nothing, except for a slight grunt of effort, as Early Boy came charging through the doorway, head lowered, arms reaching out to seize him. The impact of the football tackle lifted Jackson off his feet and in the next instant they smashed through shade and window and went tumbling down the slant roof of the porch to the overflowing gutter, fell without slowing and crashed down hard into drenched shrubbery, the muddy soft turf of the yard.

Jackson got up first, but sagged immediately. Early Boy, the wind knocked out of him, was scrabbling in mud. Jackson turned toward the house.

"Nhora!" he shouted.

Early Boy caught him from behind and yanked him toward the street. Above them, behind the torn dangling shade of the window, there was a pulsating, greenish glow.

"You dumb son of a bitch, don't you know how close you came to looking like Old Lamb? All you had to do was get your dick out of your pants and she would've blown you sky high. Get in the car!" He slapped Jackson hard. "I'm tellin' you, she ain't through yet with you; rain's the only thing keepin' her away. We got to get a move on."

"My medical bag," Jackson said. "Need my bag."

Early Boy groaned, gave him another push in the direction of the car and ran into the house. He was out again in a few seconds, the bag in one hand. He grabbed Jackson on the fly and pulled him to the car.

He opened the car door and shoved Jackson in, ran around to the driver's side. Rain pounded the roof of the coupé.

"Give me the key."

Jackson, shuddering, fumbled in his jacket pocket, unable to take his eyes off the house. Through the heavy rain it looked dark now, and deserted. He came up with the key and Early Boy snatched it, started the car. They lurched down the street, then picked up speed. Jackson turned his head to stare at Early Boy.

"Your face is bleeding."

"Hell, yes, we're both cut. What do you think this is, a cowboy movie? Lucky we didn't cut our throats. But I couldn't think of any other way."

"I don't know—what happened. It was like being in a trance."

"Yeah. That's the Ai-da Wédo; she's Nhora, or part of Nhora—I don't know how that works. Tyrone got to

333

messin' with voodoo a couple years ago, and called her out. Now look."

"Nhora—doesn't know."

"Maybe she doesn't. Maybe she can't help what's happening to her. But she's got to be killed all the same. Both of 'em."

"Killed!" Jackson grabbed Early Boy just as he was making a turn onto a deserted stretch of highway. The car slithered on the wet road, spun around twice before he had it under control.

"Chrissake, I just about cracked up this heap! Get your hands off me, doc."

Jackson slumped back in the other seat, once again finding it hard to breathe. He resorted to the amyl nitrite again. Early Boy caught a whiff of it.

"That's powerful stuff; what else you got in that bag?"

"Why do you want to know?"

"She's chock full of poison. Just one scratch from the lady and you're a goner. So my question is, how do you kill somebody that should be dead already?"

The car was fishtailing again, and Jackson panicked.

"You're driving like a maniac!"

Early Boy grinned sardonically. "You're on borrowed time anyway. And if we don't get to Tyrone before he closes up shop for the night, maybe we don't get him at all."

"Do you know—where he is?"

"At his alternate house of worship, down by the river."

Jackson nodded. "I know the place. The *Stephen Mulrooney*. Nhora and I found it by accident early this morning." He sat shuddering in the wet filthy suit. They passed a single streetlight in a Negro settlement, the thin vein of a neon beer sign in a lonesome window. Then blackness again, rain flooding the unsteady headlights. He had seen blood on Early Boy's tense knuckles as he drove. He heard Early Boy's rasping, painful breath.

"How bad are you hurt?"

"I'll find out later. Maybe a busted rib."

"I can drive."

"Just sit back and enjoy the ride."

334

"Do you still have your revolver?"

"Yeah."

"We don't have to—kill Nhora."

"It ain't just your funeral, it's Champ's too."

"I think I know—what this is about."

"I got a little free time right now, doc. Why don't you fill me in?"

Jackson talked considerably longer, drawing the threads of the past together in a comprehensible pattern, for himself as well as Early Boy. It had begun with his father's encounter with the inhuman Gen Loussaint a quarter of a century ago, and ultimately involved the fortunes of two familes. He explained what little he knew about Nhora's sojourn among the Ajimba, and tried to deduce the rest.

"I never really believed she existed, till now. Gen Loussaint must have lived for a year or two after my father treated her. She was a—a goddess in a decrepit body, badly in need of a successor. I didn't know why a child was chosen. Perhaps she was the image of Gen herself as a child. At any rate they must have planned to raise her as a superbeing, capable of living 150, 200 years, a new leader for a once-great tribe. But by then the Ajimba had been decimated, their tribal identity destroyed. They were wanderers, occasional raiders, confused and desultory in their religion. Whatever plans the aging, reptilian old monster may have had for Nhora, they were forgotten when ultimately the body died. The goddess herself—Gen-loa—didn't die of course, her spirit persevered within Nhora, but dormantly. Gen-loa was helpless to exert her power without the tradition, the force of belief the pathetic tribe no longer had.

"So Nhora was returned to civilization, still a child, but deadly beyond her knowledge. I think they must have fed her on the poison which they fed their hunting dogs, little by little saturating her body so that as she matured she retained the poison. It may even have become more concentrated, with the passage of time."

"What about this fetish thing your daddy made out of your skull bones? Old Lamb talked about that too—he

335

called it 'baka.' Said while you had it, the Ai-da Wédo couldn't touch you."

"That's right. My father died a different sort of violent death, in the war, but he was safe from *her*, as long as he kept his fetish near to hand. So Ai-da Wédo bided her time, as Nhora grew older. Waited for the voodoo adept, the believer who would come along and set her free of the innocent one. Nhora *is* innocent, I swear! And totally helpless."

"Not as long as she's got that poison in her system. If one of those damn killer dogs was runnin' around loose, you'd shoot it, wouldn't you? Use your head, doc!"

They had reached the levee; Early Boy turned off the car's lights.

"No sense givin' him time to scram if he's down there makin' his mumbo-jumbo. See if there's a flashlight aboard, doc."

Jackson found one in the glove compartment.

"Some dinky light," Early Boy complained. "It'll have to do. Come on."

Jackson got out of the car clutching his medical bag. If Nhora was down there with Tyrone then there were drugs he would need immediately. He was afraid again, mortally afraid after his encounter with the seductive serpent-goddess, to descend into the thicket. But it might be true that the power of Ai-da Wédo was diminished by rain, or water of any kind. And his concern for Nhora's safety was stronger than his conviction that it was a fatal mistake to tempt Ai-da Wédo again.

Early Boy wheezed from effort, from the pain in his side as they climbed together down the embankment. He had his revolver in one hand, the small flashlight in the other. The light had only limited effectiveness. Jackson sensed the nearby presence of the hard-flowing, swollen river, recalling its treachery, the sudden whirlpools.

Despite the dark and the rain Early Boy seemed to know where he was going. For Jackson it was a prolonged, slogging, panic-filled nightmare, tangled masses of branches and swirling waters from which there might be no escape if he lost his footing and went under, to be swept beneath submerged dead trees. Every grasping vine that fell across his body reminded him of the fate he'd so recently and narrowly avoided. He sobbed aloud, but the sounds were lost in the downpour. When he faltered Early Boy was quick to lend a hand, to urge and prod, demand that he keep going.

At last they came to more solid ground, approaching the *Stephen Mulrooney* from a different angle. The old steamboat was lit by the wavering glow of a hundred lighted candles in the peristyle of the oum'phor. They surged toward the dryness beneath the roof, curl of smoke from the coals in the pit, candlelight, the illusion of warmth.

Early Boy cocked his revolver, looking slowly around. He approached the buried fire, the forge of the Ogous, and touched the iron bar, the *okou-bha-sah*, half buried in the live coals. He jerked his hand back. It wasn't red hot, but it was hot enough to sear the skin.

"Tyrone!" he called.

"Here."

They both looked up. Tyrone emerged from the pilothouse of the steamboat, walked to the railing around the Texas deck, leaned on it and stared down at them. He was nearly naked, his body decorated with elaborately drawn, beaded white lines. It was an impressive, eerie show by the bar sinister.

"Even', Beau," he said.

"Good even', nigger," Early Boy said with quiet malice.

Tyrone shook his head slowly. "That's the way your brother Clipper would talk. But I did expect better of you." He looked at Jackson. "You still don't look so good, Dr. Holley."

"I've had a rather trying time of it tonight," Jackson said hoarsely. "Where's Nhora?"

"Just won't give up, will you? Don't you know by now she's not good for you?"

"Come down, nigger," Early Boy demanded.

"Might as well," Tyrone said with a slight, elegant, disdainful shrug. He came down a curved broken staircase to the boiler deck, a one-man parade, body glistening,

337

swaying, his nostrils and eyes dilated with excitement. Rain poured down all around them; the air beneath the peristyle was sultry, becoming ominously sweet.

"I'll just have a look on the boat—"

"Stay put," Early Boy said tensely, his revolver trained on the advancing Tyrone. "Don't you smell it?"

"The perfume of Erzulie. My God—"

"I know, I know. Anything comes, you light out and stay low." He shifted his attention to Tyrone. "Nigger," he said, his voice cracking like a whip.

Tyrone stopped, smiling, but he still swayed and throbbed to a spectral rhythm which they didn't yet feel.

"Suh," he said, formal in bearing, cynically deferential. "Let it be known, I have always thought the best of you. I respect you, Beau, for what you tried to do for my people. For having the courage to leave Dasharoons, in shame and rage. You shouldn't have come back, Beau. But I'll allow you to leave again."

"About Clipper. How'd you do it?"

"He was eager to be corrupted. Ai-da Wédo obliged. With a suggestion or two from me."

"Thought so," Early Boy said, and without appearing to aim he fired the revolver. The bandaged little finger on Tyrone's left hand disappeared in a burst of blood. Tyrone whirled around, clasping the shot hand, mouth open in astonishment. Early Boy cocked the double-action revolver again, coolly raising his sights. Tyrone screamed piercingly. In one smooth motion he pulled the *okoubha-sah* from the pit of coals and lunged. Early Boy shot him very near the heart but missed the breastbone and so failed to knock him down. The pointed iron ran through Early Boy's belly and emerged sizzling to strike the ground as Early Boy was slammed backward by Tyrone's weight. For several moments he lay motionless, pinioned, Tyrone leaning over the hot iron that was frying his hands, his eyes nearly bulging out of his head. Then Early Boy raised the revolver under Tyrone's chin and blew most of his face off.

"Doc," he gasped, beginning to writhe. "Doc, Jesus, get it out of me!"

338

Jackson leaped over the splayed ghastly body of Tyrone, seized the hot iron, feeling no pain in his anxiety. He planted a foot on Early Boy's chest and heaved, hurling the *okou-bha-sah* away as it came out of Early Boy with a quick sucking sound. He knelt and clawed the poncho aside and saw the location of the wound, and knew it was bad. Not hopeless, but very bad. He would need expert surgery within the hour in order to survive.

Jackson broke open his medical bag for a syringe and morphine. Early Boy was crying from the agony, clutching at his belly as if he were trying to rip himself open. Jackson got the needle into him and depressed the plunger.

"In a minute you won't feel a thing," he assured the desperate man.

There was faint, suggestive laughter in the air. He thought he heard his name whispered. He looked up in horror, holding Early Boy tightly to keep him from doing violence to himself during the spasms.

"What's—matter, doc?" Early Boy whispered, as soon as the morphine began to work.

"She's coming. I've got to get you out of here, but she's coming!"

"Doc, listen. How am I?"

"You've got a chance."

"How much of a—chance?"

"I don't know, it's beyond my skill. But if I get you to a hospital—"

"What about Champ? Tell me, doc. How much chance has he got, with—the Ai-da Wédo?"

Out of the corner of one eye Jackson saw the surreal, shimmering light.

"Nothing—stops her, right? Except the fetish. Doc, come on, doc, snap out of it or you're a goner for sure!"

"I *hear* her!"

"Can you make one of them things?"

"I—I think so. But it's no use. It wouldn't be powerful enough, without—"

Early Boy's hand was on his arm, fingers digging in as a spasm of pain was partially suppressed by the morphine. "Without the bones. Okay, then. You're—all set." He grinned wearily, and raised a hand to tap his forehead. "Take what you need. Make it powerful, doc. Get rid of her forever."

Laughter, mocking them both. Daring Jackson.

"I can't. Don't you understand, if I get you to a hospital, then you may live. But if I perform crude surgery here and now, then it's the same as murder!"

"I don't feel lucky anymore, doc. I know how bad I am inside. So it's all the same to me. If I go—here, or in a hospital."

The level brilliance of her eyes. The infatuated, flickering tongue.

"Jackson."

"Carry me—out in the rain. Where she can't get at you. And get the job *done,* doc!"

When Jackson didn't respond Early Boy gritted his teeth and made an effort to rise. Jackson caught him as he fainted, stood bewildered with Early Boy in his arms.

Hearing the laughter, seeing the flowing, lightsome coils.

He closed his eyes and staggered, medical bag in hand, with Early Boy, carried him out of the peristyle and into driving rain. Laid him on the ground. Sat hunched over him, blinking, clutching his medical bag against his body.

Then, slowly, he opened the bag and took out an ampule of sodium pentothal.

Her sharp hiss of disapproval sounded louder than the rain. She hovered just below the roof of the sheltering peristyle, posturing seductively.

Trembling, Jackson injected Early Boy with enough sodium pentothal to insure that he would never feel another moment's pain, nor wake again.

Nhora awoke in sweltering darkness on the floor of the railroad car, body numb from the shock of passage, and she began to cry with near-hysterical relief before she was well awake, as if she understood that she had been badly used for the last time.

340

Rain beat on the roof of the car, as it had for hours. She felt a desperate need for the cleansing rain and got to her feet, naked but uncaring, left the car and walked aimlessly along the unlighted platform, arms crossed on her breasts, before venturing into the cold downpour.

In the dark, walking with her head up, mouth open to drink the rain, she stumbled and fell over the body of the dead stallion, striking her head painfully against the slick clay ground.

Lights drilled through her head. She looked up, dazed, rose to her feet, saw a car racing out of the rain toward her. She threw up her hands to ward it off.

The car stopped in time. She stood with her back arched, hands high, blinded. The car just sat there. She edged toward it, timid, then a little afraid, finally conscious of her blazing, wet nakedness.

A car door slammed and he came running toward her. He was as wet as she. His arms went around her. He had a bloody odor, vanishing quickly as the rain washed down.

"Jackson—Jackson!"

He was silent, shuddering, holding her with an almost violent need. She sought to kiss him. Something pricked her in the left buttock, and her eyes widened in surprise. She looked around, and down, and saw the syringe in his hand just as he withdrew it and tossed it aside.

"What—?"

"Don't worry," he said, but something in his eyes frightened her and she struggled instinctively. Too late, as her knees buckled and she slipped slowly down to meet the warm rising tide of the drug, allowed herself to be engulfed without making a sound.

In Nhora's room Jackson went through drawers and closets, making blind selections, throwing whatever came to hand in the large suitcase he had opened on the bed.

Hackaliah, in trousers and undershirt, appeared in the doorway, blinking, nodding, shocked.

"It's three in the mornin', Dr. Holley. What this all

about?" He stared at Jackson's wrecked suit, the mud in his hair.

Jackson slammed the suitcase shut and turned. "Put this in the boot of the car while I bathe and change."

"Miss Nhora goin' someplace?"

"I'm taking her to a hospital. She's very ill. Critical. We must hurry. Do as I say."

"Dr. Holley, you all right?"

"Certainly. Are you referring to the way I look? I had—problems with the car. Had to change a tire. Nhora's sleeping in the seat. Be sure you don't disturb her."

"Yas, suh," Hackaliah said, coming for the suitcase. Jackson brushed by him without further word and ran to his own room.

In the foyer Hackaliah pulled on a slicker and trudged outside with Nhora's case. Something about the slack tilt of her sleeping head made him uneasy. He went around to look in on her. She was naked. He withdrew, and attempted to open the trunk of the car. It was locked. He took the suitcase back up to the veranda to wait for Jackson.

Presently Jackson rushed out of the house with his own luggage. He was clean and presentable again, but the feverish look in his eyes was, if anything, more intense.

"Oh, yes, the key, I'm sorry—here, I'll unlock it for you."

The trunk lid popped up. Jackson gestured for Nhora's case to go in first. Hackaliah was about to oblige, but as he swung the case up he saw the gleam of Boss's saber and hesitated.

"Go on, go on, didn't I tell you we were in a hurry?"

"Dr. Holley, where you be in case we needs you?"

"I don't know yet. I'll call. Don't worry. Everything's under control." He piled his own luggage in on top of Nhora's, slammed the trunk lid down.

"What about—?"

"Champ? You needn't worry there, either: plenty of liquids and bed rest, I'll—I'll see him soon. Tell him that."

He went quickly around to the front and got in, drove off leaving Hackaliah standing in the rain.

At first the *Stephen Mulrooney* had burned slowly, very slowly, but as the candle-fed flames ate into the dry, termite-riddled hull and beams it very nearly exploded, consuming most of the velvet-shrouded body of Early Boy Hodges. Not even the hard rain falling could put out the conflagration. Eventually the old wreck burned to the waterline.

The roof of the peristyle failed to catch fire; Tyrone lay where he had fallen, gaining ripeness, untouched by cleansing flame and ash.

Even before dawn, and despite the rain, the rats had begun to visit.

In the Boss-room, Hackaliah said, "Don't like to wake you when you's sleepin' so good."

"She's slipped through our fingers?"

"I just didn't know how to stop him."

"Gone which way?"

"I don't know, suh." He waited, sipping hot coffee, trying to stay alert, knowing there would be no more sleep, for any of them, until it was finally over.

"Hackaliah, I think we better call the sheriff."

"Yes, Boss," Hackaliah said.

The windows of the tourist court room had lace curtains, half-drawn shades. Through the windows Nhora could see a slice of blue sky, a baseball diamond, boys at play. She had lain awake for nearly five minutes, trying to decide if it was morning or afternoon, too deliciously relaxed to turn on her other side and look at the clock which she heard ticking on a bedside table. She couldn't remember when she'd eaten last, but she felt no hunger pangs. Of course she wouldn't turn down a hot cup of

343

coffee if it was brought through the door this very minute—

Nhora smiled to herself and took a deep breath, then suspended her own breathing to better attune herself to Jackson's sleeping rhythms, slight sibilance of escaping air through his lips, the short taut intake as if he was skirting the edge of a threatening dream. His distress bothered her, intruded on her own very nearly perfect mood, the best sleep she'd had in ages, no morning blues and dreadful unrealized sadness, overhanging terrors.

Should she awaken him? She put a hand lightly on his exposed cheek then withdrew it, frowning: He was very cold. Looking closer she saw that his lips had a bluish tinge. Perhaps his temperature always fell drastically when he slept. It was the first full night she'd spent in bed with him, she had no way of knowing.

Nhora wanted to snuggle close and warm Jackson with her own body, with all the love she felt for him. But he seemed to breathe more easily, the dream averted, and she decided it would be better to let him go on sleeping. She yawned and sat up, looking at the clock. Ten past eleven. Definitely time for coffee, if she could find a place nearby. She had no very clear idea of where they were, or even what day it was. Her memory went back hazily as far as yesterday, then not at all. Things had been very bad at Dasharoons, he had come along, they had fallen in love, it was all she needed or cared to know. She might go back someday, but it really didn't matter.

On the night table there was a used syringe, and Nhora picked it up curiously, remembering what he had told her: It was protection against infection, some sort of thing that was or might go wrong with her unless she had her medicine. He was the doctor. She did what he asked, willingly, unquestioningly. Because she never wanted it to end, this feeling of peace, and freedom, the quiet joy.

She got out of bed and went to the bathroom, pleased to discover that they had made love, a little sad because she didn't remember, as usual. Now she was beginning to feel hungry, really *ravenous* for pancakes, eggs, sausage. A quick shower, and on her way.

As Nhora waited for the water to turn from cold to warm she ran her hands over her legs and decided she'd better shave. What sort of razor did her man use? She looked into his shave kit. Straight razor. Oh-oh, she wasn't too skilled with those, better let it go until she could buy a safety razor of her own. She continued to poke through the kit, curious about all the personal details, the preferences he exhibited in his choice of toothpaste, lotions—

And what was this?

A funny-looking small jar with a cork stopper. The jar fired clay with decorations, porcelain beading. It rattled dryly when she shook it. She pried up the cork and caught a whiff of something faintly decayed. She shook the contents into the palm of her hand.

Some small colored feathers, bits of snakeskin, a tiny bell, claws and animal teeth, and two quarter-size pieces of blood-soaked bone. At least that's what she thought they were. A powerful impulse seized her; she lifted the lid of the toilet and was on the verge of dumping it all, flushing the toilet quickly. What on earth was he keeping it for?

But that was Jackson's business, after all. Maybe there was a medical purpose. She carefully replaced everything in the jar and corked it, then stepped into her shower.

Nhora started to sing, as she always did, but today her mind wandered, and she couldn't seem to remember the words to any of the half dozen songs she began.

Oh, well . . .

In the Boss-room he put on the white Palm Beach suit that was still warm from the pressing iron, and added a string tie. He'd lost a lot of weight and the suit hung on him, but he wouldn't consider wearing anything else. White suit and white shoes and the white Panama hat with the black band . . . he caught sight of Hackaliah in the mirror, and turned.

"How do I look?"

Hackaliah forced a smile. "You looks just fine to me, Boss."

"Far to go?"

"About a hundred miles."

"Been a long time since you drove me anywhere, Hackaliah," he said sternly. "You sure you're up to it?"

"I can still drive, Boss."

"Then we better had get going. Don't you think?"

Jackson knew it was a very hot day, in the nineties, he could tell by the waves of heat visible in the distance as he lay in the bed looking out the windows. But he was in the throes of a deathlike cold, so cold and sluggish he could barely sit up. In a week or two his heart would surely fail, perhaps while he was experiencing the raptures of sexual conjugation.

He had taken every precaution. He kept her mildly sedated, so that in the midst of an orgasm she wouldn't accidentally scratch or bite him. The Ai-da Wédo posed no threat as long as the fetish remained in his possession.

Her very kiss was slowly poisoning him. Yet he couldn't stop wanting her, needing her.

"Nhora?"

His vision was so bad that the pictures on the wall opposite the bed were blurred. His medical bag was on the floor. He reached for it and nearly tumbled out of bed. He was a long time searching for the digitalis he needed, and a clean syringe.

"Nhora," he whimpered. "Where are you?"

He located the vein at his elbow and put the needle in. Stared at the clock while injecting himself. Nearly two in the afternoon. Where was she, how long had she been gone, didn't she know he wanted her with him every minute?

Jackson lay back, exhausted, the glass syringe shattering on the tile floor as his hand fell nervelessly off the bed.

But in just a little while he would have the strength he

needed to rise, and dress, and go out to find her. Bring
her back to the shadowy room. Embrace her. Make love.

Die a little more.

It was a lovely, lazy old town, somewhere in Louisiana,
Nhora thought. At least there were a lot of Louisiana
plates on the cars parked around the square. Spanish
moss was thick in the courthouse oaks. She'd spent a lot
of time, following a leisurely breakfast, just exploring, not
minding the heat. There were brick sidewalks and fine an-
tebellum mansions with full flowering gardens. Scent of
honeysuckle and mimosa everywhere. She would never
grow tired of living here. They probably needed a doctor.
A town couldn't have too many good doctors.

Church bells. She turned a corner near the main part of
town. Narrow white church with a high steeple and a
spacious lawn. Cars pulling up, horses and carriages, Negro attendants in formal cutaways. A bride in billowing
yards of gown, clutch of giggling bridesmaids. They posed
for cameras before going in a side door of the church.
Nhora was charmed. She drifted closer. What a marvelous
thing to actually be married to him, she thought. But that
would come. She mingled with the arriving guests on the
wide walk up to the church, smiling, nodding.

So many guests. They wouldn't mind one more.

A long time since she had been to a wedding.

The Packard touring car sat by the curb a block from
the church, engine softly idling. Hackaliah mopped his
streaming brow, head shaking tiredly. He watched Nhora
disappear into the church.

"What now, Boss?"

"You know where to go."

Jackson walked unsteadily into the Courthouse Café
and leaned against the counter, his lips numb, cold as
ether.

"Good *afternoon*, sir."

"I'm looking for my wife."

"Sir, are you *ill?*"

"What the hell makes you say that?" Jackson snarled.

In the street behind him, a Packard touring car went slowly by.

Hackaliah put the spare key in the trunk lock and raised the lid of the muddy Chevrolet coupé. He reached in and brought out the saber. There was a speck of rust on the bright blade, high up near the hilt. He whisked it away with his handkerchief and a little spit. Turned, and handed it over.

The saber went into its scabbard. They got back into the touring car and drove toward the sound of church bells.

Nhora came out of the church into the bright sun, one of the last to leave because she had been enjoying the tranquility, the gorgeous flowers on the altar. The steps were crowded with wedding guests. The bridal party was lining up on the lawn for photographers. Nhora smiled. The bride couldn't have been more than eighteen, but she was happy, really happy. And Nhora was happy for her.

Hackaliah stopped the Packard touring car behind the church. He turned off the motor. He watched two boys pedaling by on bicycles, tossing a softball one-handedly back and forth, and thought of a young man going berserk on a church altar, the flashing sword. His hands relaxed on the wheel, he bowed his head.

The back door opened, closed. Slow footsteps moving away. Hackaliah didn't look up.

The church bell was tolling again.

Jackson, footsore, palpitating, leaned against an iron fence a block from the church and felt unable to drag himself further. Pretty dresses dotting the green lawn. A tall groom, a petite bride. Milling guests, garden party chatter. Outrageous hats in confectionery colors, parasols in older hands.

A man in a white suit ludicrously too big for him, Panama hat awry on his close-cropped head. Rounding the corner to the front of the church. Something metal in his hands, catching the sun. He stopped short, looking up. Seeing Nhora. Jackson wondered why he hadn't noticed her before, standing so tall in the crowd of ladies on the steps. The boss man in the boss suit had seen her right away. . . .

Jackson started to run, just as the saber came out of its scabbard. Nhora was already walking down the steps, hesitantly, toward the boss man. Heads turned inquiringly, as if attracted by her beauty, or by the suddenness of the sword . . .

Then screams. Terrible, chilling screams.

Nhora sat down hard on the steps, a puzzled look in her eyes as she studied the mass of dripping red on the white pillar next to her. She looked down at her splattered dress and at the arm turned the wrong way in her lap. His shadow fell over her again, and she looked up, catching just a glimpse of the sharp saber point. She tasted rather than felt it enter, though the impact knocked her head back almost against the next step.

His hat had fallen off. He stood there shy and barren-looking in the sun, wincing, mouth twisted in a flimsy, half-apologetic way, sword erect, hands braced on his thigh. He was stiff as a statue, but unbalanced, so the first pair of hands that reached for him tipped him easily, he went rolling down the steps still clutching the saber, rolled face-up and staring into the sun, prone but at attention, not moving a muscle.

Nhora saw Jackson coming and thought to smile, but didn't, and thought to get up, but couldn't; her lap was heavy with lopped arm, there was a lethal congestion in her throat and rising now thickly to her mouth. So she waited for him, wishing he would hurry, seeing him dimmer the closer he came, until at last when he knelt in horror beside her she could barely make him out at all.

Her hand rose and touched his and she tightened her fingers insistently, urging him to come along, but then, shaken by doubt, by the sorrow that had come along to spoil her perfect day, she realized it wasn't fair. And so she released him, reluctantly, withdrawing, seeing faintly the inconsolable look that crossed his face.

She closed her eyes, unaware that Jackson had snatched her hand back, pried open the clenching fingers, set her nails against his cheek. And then, with all his strength, Jackson drew the nails deeply into his flesh.

TITLES AVAILABLE FROM
VGSF

The prices shown below were correct at the time
of going to press (August 1989)

☐	04008 4	HEGIRA	*Greg Bear*	£2.95
☐	04090 4	STRENGTH OF STONES	*Greg Bear*	£2.95
☐	04009 2	ANGEL WITH THE SWORD	*C.J. Cherryh*	£2.95
☐	03988 4	THE OTHER SIDE OF THE SKY		
			Arthur C. Clarke	£2.95
☐	04199 4	BUY JUPITER	*Isaac Asimov*	£2.95
☐	03995 7	WITCH WORLD	*Andre Norton*	£2.50
☐	03996 5	WEB OF THE WITCH WORLD	*Andre Norton*	£2.50
☐	03999 X	YEAR OF THE UNICORN	*Andre Norton*	£2.50
☐	03998 1	THREE AGAINST THE WITCH WORLD		
			Andre Norton	£2.50
☐	03997 3	WARLOCK OF THE WITCH WORLD		
			Andre Norton	£2.50
☐	04000 0	SORCERESS OF THE WITCH WORLD		
			Andre Norton	£2.95
☐	04365 2	SPELL OF THE WITCH WORLD	*Andre Norton*	£2.95
☐	03989 2	TO LIVE AGAIN	*Robert Silverberg*	£2.95
☐	04038 6	UP THE LINE	*Robert Silverberg*	£2.95
☐	04040 X	THE TIME HOPPERS	*Robert Silverberg*	£2.95
☐	04022 X	MISSION OF GRAVITY	*Hal Clement*	£2.50
☐	04096 3	MEDUSA'S CHILDREN	*Bob Shaw*	£2.50
☐	04090 4	WHO GOES HERE?	*Bob Shaw*	£2.50
☐	04011 4	EARTHWIND	*Robert Holdstock*	£2.95
☐	04010 6	EYE AMONG THE BLIND	*Robert Holdstock*	£2.50
☐	04023 8	IN THE VALLEY OF THE STATUES		
			Robert Holdstock	£2.95
☐	04125 0	QUEST OF THE THREE WORLDS		
			Cordwainer Smith	£2.50

Also available: VGSF CLASSICS

☐	03819 5	THE SIRENS OF TITAN	*Kurt Vonnegut*	£3.50
☐	03821 7	MORE THAN HUMAN	*Theodore Sturgeon*	£3.50
☐	03820 9	A TIME OF CHANGES	*Robert Silverberg*	£3.50
☐	03849 7	THE CITY AND THE STARS	*Arthur C. Clarke*	£3.50
☐	03850 0	THE DOOR INTO SUMMER	*Robert Heinlein*	£3.50
☐	03851 9	THE REPRODUCTIVE SYSTEM	*John Sladek*	£3.50
☐	03978 7	A FALL OF MOONDUST	*Arthur C. Clarke*	£3.50

Continued overleaf